Startled, I awoke.

Where am I?

My heart fluttering in my chest, the tightening grip of panic rising up through the trunk of my body, it took several drawn-out seconds for me to remember where I was. We were no longer in the crooked little flat in North London; we were in our new bedroom in our new house in Westlake, Maryland.

Just a dream . . . a bad dream . . .

Beside me, Jodie slept soundly. Her feet and legs, warm to the touch, were pushed against my own legs beneath the sheets. I watched her for a moment, my eyesight acclimating to the lightlessness of our bedroom.

There was someone else in the room with us.

This realization dawned on me not as lucid thought but in the rising of the hairs on the nape of my neck as I sat up. It was a purely instinctual awareness, tethered to some sort of primal foreknowledge, and I had no rational explanation for feeling it. Nonetheless, I was suddenly certain of a strange and unseen presence.

I stared across the room at the open doorway. It was too dark to see anything for sure. If I gazed into space long enough, I could convince myself of anything.

Quietly, I peeled away the covers and climbed out of bed. In the darkness, the house was even more alien to me. I found my way along the upstairs hallway, one hand dragging along the wall, until I came to the winding stairwell. Around me, the house creaked in the wind. I peered over the railing. Ghostly rectangles of moonlight shimmered on the carpet. Somewhere in the belly of the house, a clock loudly counted out the seconds.

My breath caught in my throat as my gaze fell upon a small figure in the farthest corner of the downstairs foyer— a blacker blur among the darkness.

FLOATING STAIRCASE

FLOATING STAIRCASE

RONALD MALFI

MEDALLION
P R E S S

Medallion Press, Inc.

Printed in USA

For Darin,

Jonathan,

and Samantha—

The beauty of this mystery . . .

Published 2011 by Medallion Press, Inc.

The MEDALLION PRESS LOGO
is a registered trademark of Medallion Press, Inc.

Typeset in Adobe Garamond Pro
Printed in the United States of America
Title font by James Tampa

ISBN# 9781605424361

10 9 8 7 6 5 4 3 2 1
First Edition

ACKNOWLEDGMENTS

For their input during the writing of this novel, I bow to Kerry Estevez, Juris Jurjevics, Dave Thomas, Don D'Auria, my wonderful editor Lorie Popp, and James Tampa. Thanks also to Adrienne Jones, Robert Dunbar, Greg F. Gifune, Susan Scofield, the good folks at Horror Drive-In and Horrorworld, Diabolical Radio, Pod of Horror, The Funky Werepig, Susan Rosen, and Wendi Winters. And, of course, my friends and family.

Lastly, thanks to all the fans who have sent me e-mails about this book, hungry for the story it tells. You have all warmly embraced this little tale long before it was ever set free in the world.

Thanks. Truly.

—RM

"Because he is my brother, I will suffer a thousand deaths to vindicate his."

—Alexander Sharpe, *The Ocean Serene*

"All good writing is swimming under water and holding your breath."

—F. Scott Fitzgerald,
in an undated letter to his daughter

PART ONE:

THE PURITY OF THE TERRITORY

CHAPTER ONE

It has been said that nature does not know extinction. In effect, it knows only change: nothing ever truly disappears, for there is always something—some part, some particle, some formidable semblance—left behind. You can boil water into vapor, but it hasn't disappeared. Curiosity killed the cat, but condensation brought it back.

Therefore, such logic should enlighten us to the understanding that if something should happen to develop—should arrive, should become thus, should suddenly appear—then it has always been. Forms evolve and devolve but things always *are*. There exists no creation and, consequently, no destruction—there exists only transformation. It is a collision of electrons and positrons, this life: the transformation of matter to rays of light, of molecular currents, of water to vapor to water again.

When I was twenty-three, I wrote a novel called *The Ocean Serene.* It was about a young boy who, having survived a near drowning, has a door of repressed memories opened in his brain, but in truth it was really about my dead brother, Kyle.

I wrote it in the evenings at a small desk in my depressed one-bedroom apartment in the Washington, D.C. neighborhood of Georgetown (across the street from a smattering of university buildings and just a few blocks from where *The Exorcist* had been filmed many years before). A mug of coffee—black, no sugar—expelled ribbons of steam to one side of my word processor while an ashtray sprouting the flattened, yellowed elbows of cigarette butts sat on the other side. The central air did not always function properly, and I would occasionally crank open the bedroom windows to allow fresh air in. In fact, I remember opening the windows and smoking countless cigarettes and drinking cup after cup after cup of oily coffee more than the actual writing of the manuscript.

I wrote in a fog, in a haze . . . as though a length of gauze had been gently draped over the undulating contours of my brain. After writing the first draft, it took the accumulation of a couple more years and some deep personal reflection before I could once again tackle the manuscript and assemble it into something honest. For whatever reason, I felt this nagging drive to write it as honest as I could. So I wrote the first draft, then tucked it away and busied my mind with other matters until, moons later, I felt I had attained some fraction of personal growth—both in my writing and in the way I interpreted and understood the world—to revisit it. While the story was undeniably an exercise in speculative fiction—a horror novel, in other words—it was as real to me as the memories I carried of my childhood. It was difficult to relive the past. Age brings with it a certain Kryptonite that drains our faith like vampires, and reading the manuscript again almost destroyed me.

But I rewrote and finished it in a fever. It was done, and I couldn't help but feel relieved. It was tantamount to the spiritual and emotional exhaustion felt after my younger brother's death. I did not understand why such a thing had eluded me during the writing of the manuscript, but it struck me like a mallet to a gong after finally completing it. And I found I did not know how to feel about what I had just done.

Without combing through the manuscript for typos and inconsistencies, I sent it to the acquisitions editor of a small specialty press with whom I had maintained a formal yet consistent dialogue over the past several months. While I waited to hear from him, I began to doubt myself—not the book, just myself—and wondered if I'd done the right thing in writing the book. I couldn't tell if I'd commemorated the memory of my younger brother or if I'd cheapened it, ruined it, made it a circus accessible to anyone willing to pay the price of admission.

Weeks later, during an onslaught of rainy weather so violent and unrelenting it seemed the world was preparing to end, the editor informed me that the book had been accepted for publication. He had a few changes, but he said it was a good, strong story written in a good, strong, lucid voice. The book was slated for a hardcover release in the fall.

"One question," said the editor.

"Yes?"

"Alexander Sharpe?" It was the nom de plume I'd used on the cover page of the manuscript. "Since when have you decided to use a pseudonym?"

Over the phone, I tried to sound as casual as possible. "Wanted to see if Mr. Sharpe would have better luck in the publishing department than I've had. I guess he does."

But that wasn't the truth.

I couldn't tell him that I needed to distance myself from it while at the same time I also needed to embrace it. It would make no sense. To me, it seemed a stranger was better prepared to introduce my dead brother's story to the world than I was. A nonexistent stranger at that. Because I was biased. Because I could not detach myself from it, and to not detach myself from it would be to corrupt the story's honesty into loathsome self-pity. And I would not allow that to happen.

Because all good books are honest books.

I celebrated with friends, who bought me shots of gasohol and tried to get me laid despite my recent (though undisclosed) intention to finally propose to my longtime girlfriend, Jodie Morgan, and then I celebrated alone with a full pack of cigarettes, a flask of Wild Turkey, and a stroll around Georgetown. Perhaps out of a need for affirmation, I found myself outside one of the neighborhood bars in D.C., punching numbers on a pay phone. It rang several times before my older brother, Adam, picked up.

"I think I just wrote a book about Kyle," I said, drunk, into the receiver.

"Well, it's about goddamn time, bud," Adam said, and I felt myself grow wings and lift off the pavement.

On occasion I found my mind sliding back to that late autumn when I sat and smoked and wrote about my younger brother's death. I remembered the change of seasons predicated by the changes of the leaves in the trees; the windswept, rain-soaked nights that smelled swampy and full of promise; the retinal fatigue suffered from hours of staring at the throbbing glow of my monitor. It was the only thing I'd ever written that caused me to suffer from sleepless exhaustion. I roved with the flair of a zombie through the streets late at night and subsisted in a state of near catatonia while at my day job as a copy editor for *The Washington Post* (making just enough money to stave off my landlord while maintaining a sufficient stockpile of ramen noodles and National Bohemian).

One evening found me dodging traffic on the corner of 14th and Constitution in downtown D.C., the solitary pedestrian caught in a freezing downpour, until I wound up drunk and with my teeth rattling like maracas in my skull at the foot of the Washington Monument. I proclaimed to the phallic structure, "I will eat you," a phrase that to this day still boggles the mind, whether spoken to a stone monument or otherwise. Then I saluted it and, pivoting on my heels, turned across the lawn toward 14th Street. The series of events that eventually returned me to my apartment that evening remain a question for the ages.

The book was my gift to Kyle, but the writing of it was my punishment; the hours spent curled over that word processor hammering out the story were my penance. Having never been a religious person—having no belief in God or any variation thereof—it was all I had. And in thinking back on that time, I was reminded of the exhaustion that accompanied every moment.

I was thirteen when Kyle died.

And it was my fault.

CHAPTER TWO

We hit flurries coming out of New York, but by the time we crossed into Maryland, the world had vanished beneath a blanket of white. Baltimore was a muddy blur. Industrial ramparts and graffiti-laden billboards seemed overcome by a deathly gray fatigue. Bone-colored smokestacks rose like medieval prison towers, the tops of which were eradicated by the blizzard, and cars began pulling off onto the shoulder in a flare of hesitant red taillights and emergency flashers.

"We should stop, Travis," Jodie said. She was hugging herself in the passenger seat and peering through the icy soup that sluiced across the windshield.

"The shoulder's too narrow. I don't want to risk someone running into us."

"Can you even *see* anything?"

The windshield wipers were clacking to a steady beat, but the temperature had dropped low enough for ice to bloom in stubborn patches on the windshield. I cranked the defroster, and the old Honda coughed and groaned, then belched fetid hot breath up from the dashboard. With it came the vague aroma of burning gym socks, which caused Jodie to rock back in her seat and moan.

"I hope this isn't an omen," she said. "A bad sign."

"I don't believe in omens."

"That's because you have no sense of irony."

"Turn the radio on," I told her.

The snowstorm didn't let up until Charm City was a cold sodium smear in the rearview mirror. Two hours after that, as the car chugged west along an increasingly depopulated highway, the sky opened up and radiated with the clear silver of midday. We motored on through an undulating countryside of snow-covered fields. Houses began to vanish, and telephone poles surrendered to shaggy firs overburdened with fresh snow. The alternative rock station Jodie had found back in Baltimore crackled with the lethargic twang of country music.

Jodie switched off the radio and examined the road map that was splayed out in her lap. "What mountains are those up ahead?"

"Allegheny."

With only the faint colorless summits rising out of the mist, they resembled the arched backs of brontosauruses.

"Lord. Westlake's not even on the map." She glanced out the window. "I'll bet there's not another living soul out there for the next twenty, thirty miles."

Despite the hazardous driving conditions, I stole a glimpse of my wife. Aquiline-featured and mocha-skinned, her springy black hair tucked beneath a jacquard cap, she looked suddenly and alarmingly youthful. Memories of our first winter in North London rushed back to me: how we'd huddled around the wood-burning stove for warmth when we couldn't get the furnace to kick on while watching an atrocious British sitcom on cable. London had been good to us, but we were excited by the prospect of returning to the States—to my home state, in fact—and finally owning our own home.

The past decade of struggling to make ends meet had paid off when my last novel, *Water View*, rocketed in sales and managed to attract a Hollywood option. The film was never made, but the option money put my previous book advances to shame, so we decided to trade in our draughty Kentish Town flat for a single-family home. It hadn't occurred to us to come back to the States until Adam called to say he found us a house in his neighborhood. The previous owners had already moved out and were desperate to sell. At such a bargain, it promised to go quickly. I conferred with Jodie and, blindly putting our trust in my older brother's judgment, we bought the house, sight unseen.

"Are you nervous?" Jodie said.

"About the house?"

"About seeing your brother again." She rested a hand on my right knee.

"Things are okay between us now," I said, though for a moment I couldn't help but remember what had happened the last time we'd been together. Except for the clarity of the memory, it could have been a dream, a nightmare.

"We haven't been around family for Christmas in a long time."

I said nothing, not wanting to be baited into talking about the past.

"I think that you've somehow driven us off the face of the Earth," Jodie said, blessedly changing the subject.

"It's gotta be—"

"There," she said. There was an edge of excitement in her voice. "Down there!"

In the valley below, a miniature town seemed to blossom right out of the snow. I could make out the grid of streets and traffic lights like Christmas balls. Brick-fronted two-story buildings and mom-and-pop shops huddled together as if for warmth. The main road wound straight through the quaint downtown section, then continued toward the mountains where clusters of tiny houses bristled like toadstools in the distant fields. The whole town was embraced by a dense pine forest, through which I thought I could see the occasional glitter of water.

Jodie laughed. "Oh, you're shitting me! It's a god-damn model train set."

"Welcome to Westlake," I said. "Next stop—Jupiter."

I took the next exit and eased the Honda down an icy decline. We came to a T in the road, and Jodie read the directions off a slip of paper I'd stowed in the glove compartment. We hung a left and drove straight through the middle of town, digesting the names of all the businesses we passed—Clee Laundromat, Zippy's Auto Supply, Guru Video, Tony's Music Emporium. The two most creative were a hair salon called For the Hairing Impaired and an Old West–style saloon, complete with swinging doors and a hitching post, called Tequila Mockingbird.

Jodie and I groaned in unison.

We turned down Waterview Court and followed it as it narrowed to a single lane, the trees coming in to hug us on either side.

"Did you notice?" Jodie said.

"Notice what?"

"Waterview. It's the name of your last book."

"Maybe that's another one of your beloved omens," I said. "A good one this time."

Waterview dead-ended in a cul-de-sac. Warm little houses encircled the court, their roofs groaning with snow.

"There he is," I said and hammered two bleats on the car horn.

Adam stood in the center of the cul-de-sac, mummified in a startling red ski jacket, knitted cap, and spaceman boots. He had a rolled-up plastic tube beneath one arm. Behind him, two puffy blots frolicked in the snow—Jacob and Madison, my nephew and niece.

Smiling, I tapped the car horn one last time, then maneuvered the vehicle so I could park alongside the curb. The undercarriage complained as the Honda plowed through a crest of hard snow, and before I had the car in park, Jodie was out the door. She sprinted to Adam, hugged him with one arm around his neck, and administered a swift peck to his left cheek. My brother was very tall, and Jodie came up just past the height of his shoulders.

"Hey, jerk face," I said, climbing out of the car. "Get your mitts off my wife."

"Come here," Adam said, grabbing me into a strong embrace. He smelled of aftershave lotion and firewood, and I was momentarily kicked backward into nostalgic reverie, recalling our father—who had smelled the exact same way—when we were kids growing up in the city. "Man," he said, breathing into the crook of my neck, "it's good to see you again, Bro."

We released each other and I took him in. He was well built, with a studious, sophisticated gaze that was capable of being stern without compromising his charm and his innate approachability. He'd put those traits to work to become the policeman he'd always wanted to be when he was a kid. From seemingly out of the blue, I was overcome by a sense of pride that nearly buckled my knees.

"You look good," I said.

"Kids!" Adam called over his shoulder.

Jacob and Madison, clumsy and bumbling through the snow, bounded to my brother's side, adjusting gloves, knitted caps, earmuffs that had gone askew.

"My God, they've gotten so big," I said.

"You guys remember your uncle Travis?" Adam asked.

I crouched down, bringing myself to their eye level.

Madison took a hesitant step backward. She had been only a baby the last time I saw her so I held out little hope she'd remember me.

Ten-year-old Jacob scrunched up his face and nodded a couple of times. He was the more brazen of the duo. "I remember. You lived in a different country."

"England, yes."

"Do they talk a different language there?"

"They speak the same language as you, old chap," I said in my best cockney accent, "and I rather think they had it first, wot-wot."

Jacob laughed.

Madison was emboldened to take a step toward me, smiling at my ridiculous impression or her brother's willingness to laugh at it.

"Did you bring us anything from England?" Jacob asked.

Madison's eyes lit up.

"Hey, now," Adam scolded. "We don't do that."

Jacob's gaze dropped to his boots. Madison's remained on me, appearing hopeful that she'd reap the rewards of her brother's question.

I exchanged a look with Adam.

He nodded.

"Well, as a matter of fact," I said, dipping one hand into the pocket of my parka. I produced two Snickers bars—uneaten rations from our road trip from New York—and, fanning them like a deck of cards, extended them to the kids.

They snatched them up with the speed of light, and Madison had it in her mouth a mere nanosecond after the wrapper was off.

My sister-in-law, Beth, came out of her house and marched down the shoveled driveway toward us. She was a smart, determined woman whose body bore the rearing of her two children with a mature, domestic sophistication. The last time I'd seen her, which had been just before Jodie and I moved to North London, she'd called me a piece of shit and looked ready to claw my eyes out with her fingernails.

"So good to see you, sweetie," Beth said, gathering Jodie up in a hug. Beth was only slightly older than my wife, but at that very moment she could have passed for Jodie's mother.

They let each other go, and Beth came over to me. "The famous author." She kissed the side of my face.

"Hey, Beth."

"You look good."

She was lying, of course; I'd grown paler and thinner over the past few months, my eyes having recessed into black pockets and my hair having grown a bit too long to keep tidy. It was writer's block, keeping me up at nights.

"All right, enough small talk." Jodie was glowing. "Let's see this house already."

"Yeah," I said, surveying the houses around the cul-de-sac. They all appeared to have cars in the driveways. "Which one is it?"

Adam fished a set of keys from his pocket. "None of these. Come on."

Adam led us toward a copse of pines. A dirt path

cut through the trees and disappeared. We crunched through the snow and headed down the dirt path.

I started laughing, then paused halfway through the woods. "You're kidding me, right?"

Adam's eyes glittered. "You should have seen the movers backing the truck up to the house." He continued walking.

Jodie came up alongside me, brushing her shoulder against mine, and said in a low voice, "If this goddamn place is made out of gingerbread, your brother's in hot water."

Then we stepped into the clearing.

It was a white, two-story Gablefront with a wraparound porch and a gray-shingled roof tucked partway behind a veil of spindly trees. It wasn't a huge house, but it was certainly a world of difference from our claustrophobic North London flat. And even with its obvious cosmetic deficiencies—missing shingles, missing posts in the porch balustrade, wood siding in desperate need of a paint job—it looked like the most perfect house in the known universe.

Adam had sent us pictures over the Internet, but it took being here, standing in front of the house—*our* house—for it to finally sink in and make it real.

"Well?" Adam said, standing akimbo by the front porch. "Did I do good or what, folks?"

"You did perfect." Jodie laughed, then threw her arms around me, kissed me. I kissed her back.

Jacob and Madison giggled.

"You did perfect, too, baby," she said into my ear. I hugged her tighter.

The house sat on three full acres, with a sloping backyard that graduated toward the cusp of a dense pine forest. It was immense, the type of forest in which careless hikers were always getting lost, covering what could have been several hundred acres.

On closer inspection, the house appeared almost human and melancholy in its neglect. The shutters hung at awkward angles from the windows, and the windowpanes were practically opaque with grime. Frozen plants in wire mesh baskets hung from the porch awning, each one so egregiously overgrown that their roots spilled from the bottom of the basket and hung splayed in the air like the tentacles of some prehistoric undersea creature. Veins of leafless ivy, as stiff as pencils in the cold, trailed up the peeling, flaking wood siding, which was mottled and faded, hinting at shapes hidden within the deteriorating wood.

Adam tossed me the house keys. "So, are we gonna stand around here freezing our butts off, or are we gonna check out the new digs?"

I handed the keys to Jodie. "Go ahead. Do the honors."

Jodie mounted the two steps to the porch, hesitating as they creaked beneath her. There was a porch swing affixed to the underside of the awning by rusted chains, the left chain several inches longer than the right. The wicker seat had been busted out presumably a long time ago, leaving behind a gaping, serrated maw. The electric porch lights on either side of the front door were bristling with birds' nests, and there was bird shit speckled in constellation fashion on the floorboards below. Yet if Jodie noticed any of this, she did not let on.

Jodie slipped the key into the lock as the rest of us gathered on the porch behind her. We waited patiently for her to open the door. Instead, she burst into laughter.

"What?" I said. "What is it?"

"It's insane," she said. "This is our first *home*."

The house had a very 1970s feel to it, with ridiculous shag carpeting and wood paneling on the first floor. At any moment I expected a disco ball to drop from the ceiling. There were floor tiles missing in the kitchen, and it looked like the walls were in the process of vomiting up the electrical outlets, for many of them dangled by their guts from the Sheetrock.

The Trans-Atlantic movers had deposited our belongings pretty much wherever they found space, and we maneuvered around them like rats in a maze as we went from room to room.

Jodie gripped my hand and squeezed it. "This is great."

"It needs some work."

Upstairs, there were two bedrooms—a master and a spare—as well as a third room that would make a perfect office for my writing and Jodie's work on her doctoral dissertation. A second full bathroom was up here as well. With some disdain, I scrutinized the chipped shower tiles and the sink that could have been dripping since Eisenhower was in office.

"Travis," Jodie called from down the hall. "Come look. You won't believe this."

She was in the master bedroom at the end of the hall. The movers had propped our mattress at an angle against one wall and left our dresser in the middle of the room. Boxes of clothes crept up another wall.

"Look," Jodie said. She was gazing out of the wall of windows that faced the backyard.

I came up behind her and peered over her shoulder. Beyond the white smoothness of the lawn and seen through a network of barren tree limbs, a frozen lake glittered in the midday sun. On the far side of the lake, tremendous lodgepole pines studded the landscape, their needles powdered in a dusting of white. It was a breathtaking, picturesque view, marred only by the curious item toward the center of the lake—a large, dark, indescribable structure rising straight up from the ice.

"Did you know there was a lake back here?"

"No," I said. "Adam never said anything."

"Jesus, this is gorgeous. I can't believe it's ours."

"It's ours." I kissed her neck and wrapped my arms around her. "What do you suppose that thing is out there? Sitting on the ice?"

"I have no idea," Jodie said, "but I don't think it's sitting on the ice."

"No?"

"Look at the base. The ice is chipped away, and you can see the water."

"Strange," I said.

Suddenly, we were both startled by a high-pitched wail, followed by the quick patter of small feet on the hardwood floor. It wasn't the type of frustrated cry typical of agitated young children; there was fear in this shriek, possibly pain.

I rushed out onto the upstairs landing and glanced down in time to see Madison running into her mother's arms in the foyer. Beth scooped up the little girl and hugged her tight.

"What happened?" I said, coming partway down the stairs.

Beth shook her head: she didn't know. She smoothed back Madison's hair while the girl clung to her like a monkey.

Adam appeared beside them and asked Madison what was wrong, but she did not answer. Her crying quickly subsiding, she seemed content to bury her face in Beth's shoulder.

Adam looked at me. "What happened?" The amount of accusation in his tone rendered me speechless. "What'd you do?"

It wasn't until Jacob came up behind me on the stairs that I realized to whom Adam had been directing his questions.

"What happened?" Adam repeated.

Jacob shrugged. The kid looked miserable. "Maddy got scared."

"Scared of what?"

Again: the slight roll of tiny shoulders. "Something scared her. Wasn't me. I promise."

Adam sighed and ran his fingers through his tight, curly hair. "Get down here, Jacob."

Expressionlessly, the boy bounded down the stairs.

I followed, stuffing my hands into my pockets. I paused beside Beth and rubbed Madison's head.

She squirmed and swung her legs, causing Beth to grunt when she struck her in the belly. "Cut it out now," Beth muttered into her daughter's hair.

"You never said anything about a lake out back," I said to Adam.

"Didn't I?"

"And the basement? Where is it?"

"In the attic. Where else?"

"Ha. Don't quit your day job." I strolled past him down the hallway toward the one door I hadn't yet opened.

Adam called after me: "The movers put all your boxes marked *storage* down there."

"Thanks." I opened the door on a set of rickety wooden stairs that sank deep into a concrete cellar. Somewhere down there a light burned, casting a tallow illumination on the exposed cinder block walls. I descended the stairs halfway until I saw an exposed bulb in the center of the low ceiling, hanging from several inches of wire. Its pull cord swayed like a hypnotist's pocket watch.

A number of boxes were stacked at the foot of the stairs. I stepped over them and tugged on the pull cord, which broke off in my hand and sent the bulb swinging, casting alternating shadows around the room.

"Goddamn it."

Standing on my toes, I reached up and steadied the light but couldn't slip the cord back into place to shut it off. In the end, I padded my fingers on my tongue, then gave the bulb a half turn. The light went out.

We spent the rest of the daylight hours moving boxes from room to room, putting pieces of furniture together, scrubbing the bathrooms and the kitchen, and overall warming up to our new surroundings.

By the time night had fallen, we were all hungry

and exhausted. The kids began to fuss, and Beth herded them home, insisting that we join them for dinner.

Their house had a closed-in porch, heated in the winter, where we charged through a meal of roast pork, some string bean and bread crumb concoction, mashed potatoes, and corn bread. For dessert, Beth set out an apple pie and ice cream, eliciting cheers from the children, and Jodie poured the coffee while Adam hunted around his basement for a bottle of port that was bent on remaining elusive. My brother finally returned from the basement empty-handed and defeated, then cut himself a giant slice of pie to make up for his efforts.

Beth talked about my last novel, *Water View*, and how she'd introduced my work to the neighborhood book club. "You'll meet most of them next week. We're having some people from the community over for a little Christmas party. It'll be a great opportunity for you two to meet your new neighbors."

"Please, Beth," I said. "Don't go wearing yourself out on our account."

"My book club was going to meet anyway. I'll just invite a few more people over, have them bring some desserts. It'll be fun."

"It's a nice town," Adam said. "Quiet, friendly."

"Did you know the people who used to live in our house?" Jodie asked.

"The Dentmans," Adam said. "We knew them a little, I guess."

"We didn't know them at all," Beth corrected. "They were weird. Kept to themselves."

Adam shrugged. "Desiring privacy doesn't make you weird, hon."

Beth flapped a hand at her husband, then turned to Jodie. "Don't listen to him. They were *weird*."

"Well, the house was a steal," I said.

"Property isn't very expensive out here," Adam said, his mouth full of pie. "It's like a well-kept secret from the rest of the state. Those mooks in Baltimore don't know what they're missing."

"Mooks," Madison parroted, giggling.

"And," he went on, "it's the perfect place to raise a family."

"Yes, Adam," Jodie piped up. "Please explain that to my husband. He seems to be ignorant of the whole biological clock phenomenon."

I groaned and leaned back in my chair. "A week ago we were stuffed in a two-room flat with no central heating. We had to chase homeless people off our front steps every morning. You wanted to introduce kids to that?"

"Look around. We're not there anymore."

"Hey," Beth said, lifting her glass of wine. "I want to make a toast. I'm so happy you guys moved out here."

She glanced at me, too obvious not to notice. Anyway, I think she wanted me to notice. "To new beginnings."

"New beginnings," Adam repeated.

We drank.

CHAPTER THREE

It was closing on ten thirty when Jodie and I walked down the snow-covered dirt road that led to our new home. The air smelled of winter and of grist from the distant mill on the outskirts of town. Immense and overarching, the dark trees leaned down toward us like living things hungry to pick us off the Earth. Our commingled breath puffed out in clouds.

I gave Jodie a squeeze. "You happy?"

"Of course." She'd been quiet and introspective for the rest of the evening following dessert.

"What is it?" I said.

"I wish you'd be more open to discussing things."

This was about the comment Adam had made at the table—this was about getting pregnant and having babies.

"We just moved in the house today. Can't we do

one thing at a time?"

"We're adults. We're capable of doing more than one thing at a time. We're capable of making adult decisions." We paused at the foot of the porch. The house, dark and brooding and contemplative, looked down on us. "Don't you want kids?"

"Eventually."

"Well," Jodie said, "my eventually will eventually run out."

"Can we not have this discussion now? Can we at least enjoy our first night in our new home?" I reached for her hands, but she quickly tucked them inside her coat.

"It's cold out here," she said. "I'm going in."

Jodie went immediately upstairs. A minute later, I heard the water pipes clank and start to hum and the sound of water filling the bathtub.

Standing in the darkness of our new living room, an assortment of cardboard boxes crowded around me like tourists gazing at a street performer, I exhaled a deep, pent-up breath. From nowhere, a defeating weight clung to my shoulders, pulling me down, down, down. I was still picturing Jodie from moments ago, standing like a ghost outside in the snow, her face hollowed by futility.

Fuck it, I thought and went outside, a cigarette already between my lips.

The front porch creaked and grew restless under

my weight. I sucked down a lungful of smoke and felt my eyes grow wet in the bitter cold. Across the front yard, the naked trees seemed to undulate almost imperceptibly like living things. Beyond the trees, the moon was a luminescent skull behind black wisps of clouds.

I heard the snapping of twigs and the crunch of frost and dead leaves before I saw a figure emerge from the woods several yards down the winding dirt path that emptied out onto Waterview Court. The figure was carrying something as he—for the figure was undeniably male—made his way in my direction.

It was Adam.

"Freeze," I called out.

He stopped and peered through the darkness before spotting me mixed in with the late night shadows on the porch. A cloud of vapor trailed up from his silhouette. "Jesus. The hell are you doing out here?"

"Hiding."

"Want company?" He held up what must have been the bottle of port he'd been hunting for earlier.

"Depends. Who you got in mind?"

Adam took a swig from the bottle and wedged his free hand into the hip pocket of his dungarees. He leaned against the porch railing. It groaned but held him. "I hope you guys like the place."

"What's not to like?"

"I hope I didn't start anything with that talk of

raising a family," he said.

"It's fine."

"Is it a sore subject?"

"It is what it is."

Adam took another swig of wine. He refused to join me on the porch and did not look at me as he wiped his lips with the back of his hand.

"What's on your mind? I know you didn't just come over here to make sure I got home safe."

He lowered and shook his head. He was smiling but there was nothing humorous about it.

Again, I was temporarily taken aback by Adam's resemblance to our father. This ignited a memory of our old man's Chrysler pulling into the driveway of our tiny duplex in Eastport, a Christmas tree strapped to the car's roof. This had been when Kyle was still alive and we still decorated a real tree. The memory was sudden and fierce and nearly brought tears to my eyes.

"I guess I'm just hoping this was a good idea," Adam said, calling me out of my reverie. "You guys moving out here and everything. You and me living across the street from each other, I mean." He tapped his wedding ring against the wine bottle. "Do we need to talk about things? You and me?"

"I don't think so."

"Because last time we saw each other, things didn't end well."

I looked out over the yard. Beneath the moonlight the snow radiated like something not of this world. "Forget about it. We were both drunk."

"It bothered me for a long time."

"It's in the past."

"You really feel that way? Don't shut me down if you don't really feel that way."

For an instant I searched deep within myself only to discover I didn't know *how* to feel. Yet fearing that my silence would condemn me, I quickly said, "Of course."

"We've already missed out on too much time. And for no good reason."

"Now we can make up for it," I told him.

He nodded once perfunctorily. "Good. I'd like that. I really would."

"So it's settled. No hard feelings. The past is history. Water under the bridge. Whatever other cliché I can't think of at the moment."

Adam chuckled and took another drink from the bottle. "I should probably get back. Unless you want to get shitfaced on the rest of this port with me?"

"No, thanks."

"Wanna get shitfaced by yourself, then? I'll leave you the bottle."

I smiled. "Maybe tomorrow."

Adam heaved himself off the railing. "Fair enough." He raked a set of long fingers down the side of his unshaven neck. The sound was like sandpaper. It occurred to me that some of his courage to speak his mind was in that bottle. "You know where I live. Don't be a stranger."

"It's good to see you again," I said, watching him plod through the snow toward the trees.

Without looking back at me, he raised a hand in response.

I watched him go for as long as the dark allowed it.

CHAPTER FOUR

Startled, I awoke.

Where am I?

My heart fluttering in my chest, the tightening grip of panic rising up through the trunk of my body, it took several drawn-out seconds for me to remember where I was. We were no longer in the crooked little flat in North London; we were in our new bedroom in our new house in Westlake, Maryland.

Just a dream . . . a bad dream . . .

Beside me, Jodie slept soundly. Her feet and legs, warm to the touch, were pushed against my own legs beneath the sheets. I watched her for a moment, my eyesight acclimating to the lightlessness of our bedroom.

There was someone else in the room with us.

This realization dawned on me not as lucid thought but in the rising of the hairs on the nape of my neck as I sat up. It was a purely instinctual awareness, tethered to some sort of primal foreknowledge, and I had no rational explanation for feeling it. Nonetheless, I was suddenly certain of a strange and unseen presence.

I stared across the room at the open doorway. It was too dark to see anything for sure. If I gazed into space long enough, I could convince myself of anything.

Quietly, I peeled away the covers and climbed out of bed. In the darkness, the house was even more alien to me. I found my way along the upstairs hallway, one hand dragging along the wall, until I came to the winding stairwell. Around me, the house creaked in the wind. I peered over the railing. Ghostly rectangles of moonlight shimmered on the carpet. Somewhere in the belly of the house, a clock loudly counted out the seconds.

My breath caught in my throat as my gaze fell upon a small figure in the farthest corner of the downstairs foyer—a blacker blur among the darkness. I studied the contours of a head, a cheek, the slope of a neck. Yet the longer I stared at the figure, the less discernible it became, like when you look directly at a distant star as opposed to catching it peripherally. After another dozen or so heartbeats, the shape was one of many among unpacked boxes and displaced furniture.

Downstairs, I pulled my parka on over my undershirt

and pajama pants, then climbed into the sneakers I'd left by the front door. One hand was already digging around inside the parka to locate my cigarettes and a lighter.

When I stepped out into the night, I was accosted without mercy by the cold, making me suddenly and completely aware of every single molecule that fabricated my body. Even from within my parka, my arms broke out in gooseflesh. Shivering, I could feel my testicles retreat up into my abdomen. I lit the cigarette with shaking hands and sucked hard, savoring it.

I studied Adam's footprints in the pearl-colored snow while my mind slipped back to our conversation from earlier. It was something I didn't feel like revisiting now. I meandered around the side of the house and came to stand beside an outcrop of trees, the bitter wind temporarily blocked by the angle of the house. The yard looked expansive, surreal, untouched. Before me, spread out like a stain on the snow, my shadow loomed enormous. The purity of the territory.

I thought I saw a figure move in the darkness a few yards ahead of me: it passed briefly from the sanctuary of the trees and across the lawn, its form silhouetted for a moment against the backdrop of the moonlit lake. I froze, watching for several seconds, anticipating the figure's return. But when it refused to reappear, I began doubting my own eyes, just as I had back in the house.

I headed to the backyard. Most of the trees here were firs, doing their best to blot out the moon with their heavy winter cloaks, but farther back and in studded rows stood tall oaks, now leafless and skeletal. From my vantage, I could make out a glitter of moonlight on the frozen surface of the lake.

I continued on through the stand of trees toward the water. The wind was relentless, biting into every available square inch of flesh, and I hugged myself to keep warm. Tears froze against the sides of my face and burned down the swells of my cheeks. Closer to the edge of the lake, as the embankment sloped gradually down toward the water, the snow thinned out. Stepping on it, I broke through a frozen layer of crust, and my sneaker sank several inches. A moment after that, ice water permeated my sneaker and shocked my foot.

"Shit."

My sneaker made a squelching, sucking sound as I liberated it from the freezing slush. I leaned against a tree for support while doing my best to wring out the leg of my pajama pants. My toes were already growing numb. Directly ahead of me, the lake opened up like a tabletop, the frozen surface nearly reflective. That odd structure rose straight through the ice, the color of milk in the moonlight. From this new perspective I could see just how large it was. And it was certainly not a rock nor a crest of stone. It was man-made.

The structure was only twenty yards from the shore, and I needed a better look at it. Against my better judgment, I advanced through the thinning snow and stepped onto the frozen lake. Cautious, I treaded lightly, testing the strength of the ice beneath my feet. For a split second I was plagued by images of drowning in black water, trapped beneath the ice and struggling for breath as my lungs cramped up. I imagined thrusting upward through the water, seconds away from unconsciousness, slamming my head against the underside of the frozen lake, desperate to break through and liberate myself from inevitable death.

But the ice felt sturdy beneath my weight. I inched forward, sliding more than walking, too guarded to actually lift my feet from the ice.

As I closed the distance, the monstrosity took shape: perhaps ten feet high, four feet wide, immense, structurally sound, constructed of faded boards of wood. It was layered—beveled—on one side.

It was a staircase.

Confounded, I paused just a few feet from it.

A staircase rising straight out of the lake.

Made of planks of wood, weather soured and spotty with frost-whitened mildew, it looked like the same type of wood used to build the deck of a house. It was not resting *on* the ice but rising up *through* it, just as Jodie had observed from the bedroom window earlier that day. The ice around its base had melted, leaving an open moat of sludgy dark water perhaps four or five inches wide surrounding the entire structure.

I took a step forward, and that was when my foot broke through the ice.

My breath seized, and I heard my foot splash into the water. Instantly, my leg, straight up to mid-thigh, went numb. And I went forward and down, unable to prevent the fall. My heart lurched. Instinct thrust my hands out, and I managed to catch the side of the protruding staircase, preventing myself from falling farther through the ice. Holding on to the side of the staircase, I caught my breath before extricating my soaked, anesthetized leg from the lake and hoisted myself up and on my feet.

The cold night air immediately froze the water on my leg, the flimsy material of my pajama pants clinging to me like a second skin. A freezing burn traced up my thigh toward my groin, and once again my testicles performed their disappearing act. My whole body trembled.

Stupidly, I lost my balance and fell in an arc down onto my left side. I hit hard, rattling the teeth in my head. I heard something crack; I couldn't tell if it was the ice beneath my weight or the bones within my flesh. The nub of my cigarette went flying, and I watched the ember cartwheel through the air in slow motion. I felt ice water seep against my ribs, my arm. Like a dream, the ground shifted beneath me: the ice had cracked and was breaking apart.

I uttered a train wreck of curses and quickly rolled onto my back, retreating from the widening fault in the ice. Even as I rolled, I heard the ice splitting; the sound was like the crackling of a fire.

I continued to roll away from the breaking ice until some internal sense told me I could stop. So I stopped. My eyes were closed, though I couldn't remember closing them. My breath whistled through the narrow stovepipe of my throat.

Then, for whatever reason, I burst out laughing.

I'm a goddamn moron.

Rolling onto my side, I crawled, still trembling with a case of the giggles, toward the embankment. Once I was close enough, I grabbed a tree branch that extended over the lake. Finally secure in my footing, I hauled myself up and crossed from the frozen lake onto solid ground. Despite being the only living soul in the vicinity, I felt like an imbecile.

A tree limb snapped behind a veil of trees in front of me.

I froze. Again, I thought I saw something move beyond the intertwining branches, but I couldn't be sure. "Hello?" I called. My voice shook. "Someone there? I could use some help if there is."

No one answered. No one moved.

I kept my gaze trained on the spot between the trees, but I could see nothing. A deer, perhaps? Some forest critter creeping through the underbrush? Whatever it was, I was freezing my ass off out here trying to figure it out.

Shivering, my entire body slowly being consumed by the numbness originating from my deadened left leg, I took a deep breath and made my way up the snowy embankment toward the house.

CHAPTER FIVE

It has been said that nature does not know extinction—that once you've existed, all parts of you, whether they've dispersed or remained together, will always *be*. Thick dust may hide the relics of human history, but it cannot erase the memory.

Picture a large, square conference room, with teal carpeting and alabaster acoustical tiles in the ceiling. Look around. You will notice that the mahogany benches are dull beneath the heated spotlights and crowded with suburban onlookers. At one end of the room are two large double doors with tapered brass levers, newly shined.

A cluster of people, solemn and reposed in what they so ignorantly consider their most formal attire, stands against the back wall, shuffling uncomfortably from right foot to left foot. The men with their hair awkwardly parted and grease matted to their scalps, the women with half-moon impressions on their palms where their nails have been digging in. Their hairstyles are outdated, and their inability to recognize this fact only reaffirms their small-town-ness. These are my mother's people from small towns across America, unified in the big city, my father's city, at last for this occasion.

At the other end of the room subsists a large podium-like assembly, modular and archipelagic in construct, cordovan-stained, teak, and recently shellacked. There are many people seated on the benches and standing at the back of the room, wedged together as if for warmth, but for the sake of this retelling, there exist only four individuals that we should concern ourselves with: the middle-aged father with the vacuous stare and wrinkles in his suit like the creases in a worry; the mother who cannot seem to focus on anything, anything at all, despite her constant stare. Then there are this duo's two remaining adolescent sons, particularly the thirteen-year-old mope with the sticking-out-too-far ears and the restless hands.

The boy, this thirteen-year-old, stares at his father's eyes. The boy's mouth goes dry, and he is only vaguely aware that he has unraveled the thread binding the little black plastic button on his blazer and that he is now squeezing the button hard between his right thumb and forefinger. Just before he brings this button to his mouth, his hand spasms and the button drops to the carpeted floor.

It occurs to him that he is the only one at the entire funeral service who knows he has dropped this button. Something in that knowledge comforts the boy, as if he has found some safe and hidden haven far away from everyone else—even his father, his mother, his older brother, the cold body of his younger brother, the baby of the family, in the casket at the front of the room. And when he looks over the sea of stoic, hardened, country faces, he feels only slightly less afraid.

Sometimes we go in; sometimes we go out.

In the months following Kyle's death, I grew sullen and withdrawn. At first there wasn't anything special about my grief to separate me from Adam or my parents, and even if there had been, no one else in my family was in any frame of mind to notice. It wasn't that my mother and father became more and more despondent or unavailable since Kyle's death; it was simply that the both of them, always well-meaning and kind, could not regain the sense of energy and dedication that had defined them as parents prior to this horrible tragedy. There was something lost to them, and they knew not how to get it back.

The little duplex in Eastport closed in on itself like something dark and hibernating or like a corpse withdrawing into a grave. A troubled canyon had formed between the remaining members of the Glasgow family, the distance too great to fill by the time we became aware of its presence.

My mother, who'd been a generous and soulful woman with no further understanding of a life beyond matrimonial domestication than the generations before her, took up religion. She'd drag me to St. Nonnatus every Sunday where we'd sit in a pew that smelled of Pine-Sol and listen to the priest expatiate from the pulpit on the glory of God. This churchgoing lasted just over a year. If it did my mother any good, I couldn't say. I know it didn't do *me* any good, although I'm not quite sure if it was ever meant to. I took this to be some sort of penance for my role in Kyle's death, but I never said anything about it to my mother.

My father, who'd always been an intimidating physical presence, seemed to grow smaller day by day, some vital bone or organ now broken within him. He reminded me more and more of those rusted old cars on concrete blocks, colorless weeds growing all around him. He became an alcoholic after Kyle's death and maintained that ungodly and self-deprecating profession until prostate cancer punched his card many years later.

In those final years my memories of the man who had once been athletic, even-tempered, stern but compassionate, an overall good father and husband was even worse than the image of the old car on blocks. He was an indistinct and shapeless imitation of a man slouched in a recliner before the television set, a bottle of Dewar's on the end table beside his chair, the medicated look of an asylum inmate on his face.

Adam became no more than a stranger to me—another neighborhood kid whom I did not know except to glance at with a sense of vague recognition on the school playground. A stranger whose bedroom was across the hall from mine.

For a short time, my dark, angry secrets were the baby birds I squeezed to death in the nest behind the shed and the ants I stuck to bits of Scotch tape, watching them squirm until they eventually stopped.

There was a small brown frog, too, which hopped out of a mud puddle in the street after a brutally unforgiving rainstorm brought down a number of trees, as well as a telephone line in our neighborhood. I caught the frog and carried him in cupped hands behind the shed in our backyard. I sat on a cord of firewood while the little thing trampolined inside my hands for what must have been hours.

By the time I opened my hands and released the frog, which bounded away through the underbrush, tears streaked my face. My reign of terror over the tiny creatures of my neighborhood was over . . . but left behind in its wake was the hollow ringing of culpability.

Ultimately I became a jumpy, twitchy mess who not only made myself nervous but troubled those around me. Everyone expected me to eventually fall on some jail time, which at different points in my life I probably deserved, but it never came to that. I was in what one therapist termed "the indefinite present," some sort of constant flux. Ever changing, ever evolving. I thought of silkworms metamorphosing into moths and those fat, greasy pods that burped up phosphorescent green ooze in the movie *Gremlins*.

I feared Kyle's vengeful return from the grave. On the eve of his first birthday following his death, I convinced myself he would come for me. Sleep was not to be found that night; I was too wired, sitting up in bed listening for the sounds of bare feet in the hallway and water dripping from his clothes. He would walk into my bedroom, his head smashed and broken, his skin a blasphemous blue green like the mold that grows on bread, and stare at me not with eyes but with black, soulless divots that leaked muddy water down his rotting face.

He'd point one accusatory finger at me as he stood in my doorway in a spreading puddle of dark water. *You did this to me*, he'd say. *You did this to me, Travis. You were my older brother, and it was your job to protect me, but you killed me instead. And now I'm here to take you back with me, take you back beneath the water where you'll sink into the ground and break apart like broken glass.*

I thought, *You did this to me.* Because when you kill your brother, part of you dies with him.

I began to lock my bedroom door at night. No one cared and no one said anything. On the occasion when my old man would lumber out of bed and stagger drunkenly to the bathroom, my heart would catch in my throat, and a fine film of perspiration would break out across my flesh. I was certain it was Kyle coming for me. Then I would hear the toilet flush, and I'd know I was safe for the time being. But soon . . . soon . . .

My dreams came in a whooshing funnel of kaleidoscopic imagery—of ice-cold water as dark as infinite space; of being suspended indefinitely in the air, unable to fall yet afraid of falling; the dull whack of bone on some solid, invisible surface.

One recurring nightmare had me chased through a maze of slatted wood boards, my freedom glimpsed occasionally through the slats and knotholes in the wood but unreachable just the same. Finally, overcome by fatigue, I would collapse to the ground only to learn that the ground was not solid beneath my feet but instead a miasma of cloud-like steam and quicksand. I struggled but knew it was futile: I was slowly pulled down to my suffocating death, though not by the quicksand but by what felt like tiny hands around my ankles.

That deadness in the house was growing, too—suffocating, nerve-wracking, black as the basement of hell, and about as subtle as an avalanche.

When I hit eighteen, knowing my parents had no legal authority to come after me, I split. What followed was a jigsaw assemblage of snapshot indiscretions better left in the dark. The acquaintances I made during this period of my life looked like something out of central casting for degenerates—leather jackets, vintage seventies shirts with wide collars, tattoos, partially shaved heads beaded with piercings, an overall distrust of anyone even slightly removed from their clique—and I got into a lot of bullshit no one should be proud of. Street fights resulted in black eyes, boxed ears, and a semiserious laceration along my left bicep from a hypersensitive stranger's reflexive swipe of a butterfly knife.

I spent nights sleeping on benches in metro stations, certain that every midnight footfall was my dead brother coming to claim me. *You did this to me.* But in the end none of that mattered because I was in the infinite present, a silkworm undergoing permanent transformation, a stream snaking down a mountain in search of a river. Find a river. Find an ocean.

As it turned out, the ocean happened to be my

childhood home, for I returned there visibly defeated after only a few months living in the streets on my own. My mother cried and hugged me, then hurried off to the kitchen to prepare me a warm meal. My father, his presence forever an imposing one even in the face of the weakness that had claimed him since Kyle's death, examined me in thunderous silence, his expression one of complete and utter resignation. Adam, who'd been away at college when I took off, was there when I returned.

It was over Christmas break, and my mother had strung up a few decorations in the front hall. Adam and I were both old enough and proud enough to maintain mutual distaste for each other. I kept telling myself he would say something to me—how disappointed he was in me for running away like a coward, how much he hated me for worrying our mother sick, anything—but he said nothing the entire break. He left with my father in the family Chrysler very early one morning to return to college.

Through the front windows I watched him go, my face burning and red, my eyes welling with tears. Adam played football, got good grades, and wanted to be a police officer. I had murdered our younger brother, then saddled what remained of our crumbling family with my emotional baggage. What could we possibly say to each other?

Sometimes we go in, the therapist once told me. *Sometimes we go out. You're in a state of constant flux, Travis. You need to cast an anchor and hold on to something before you can change direction. What is it you're always writing in those notebooks?*

Sometimes we go in; sometimes we go out.

Because homelessness was not something I desired, I completed two years at the community college where I wended through my classes with the enthusiasm of a zombie. Surprisingly, I got good grades. This earned me nonspecific commendation from my father, a zombie in his own right, and he paid my way through my two remaining years at Towson. My heart wasn't in it, yet my grades were always good, and I graduated with honors.

(My only memories of Towson are the nights of excessive drinking with my roommate, a flagrant homosexual with spiky blue hair and horrendous breath; vomiting in the bathroom for hours on end until I thought my esophagus was probably swirling around in the sewer pipes somewhere; and attending classes in bedroom slippers and the same stinking sweatshirt for much of the week—a stunt that earned me tortured-artist status among the liberals, making it possible for me to bed a few fairly attractive if not meticulously groomed girls from the liberal arts college. One of whom, I believe, eventually became a lesbian.)

Somewhere down the line I'd settled into a state of semicomplacence. It turned out those notebooks were filled with dozens of stories I'd written, and once I'd left college and moved out of the Eastport duplex for good, I rewrote a number of them and began to get them published.

What was it Fitzgerald had once written in a letter? Something about all good writing is swimming underwater and holding your breath? Well, this was true. I'd written *The Ocean Serene*, the novel about Kyle, and it was published as well. That was when I was living in Georgetown and dating Jodie and, for the first time in a long time, felt a glimmer of hope for my future. My writing was not only therapeutic; it was *absolution*. I was finally putting old ghosts to rest. (Sleep, old spirit, though I know you still hunger!)

My relationship with Adam became tolerable, even civil, and we spoke regularly on the telephone. Kyle was an unspoken presence standing in the room with us each time we were together, which was not very often. When Adam married Beth, I was his best man. I visited when both his children were born. Together we laid our father to rest after a brief battle with prostate cancer, and Adam was my best man at my own wedding the following year. Yet all the while that damnable therapist's voice resonated in my head— *You need to cast an anchor and hold on to something before you can change direction*—and because I'd never cast that proverbial anchor, I eventually struck an iceberg on the night of my mother's funeral.

Due to the amount of alcohol I'd consumed that evening, coupled with my own personal desire to wipe as much of the memory of the event out of my head, I am only able to recall bits and pieces of what transpired between Adam and me. What I *do* remember, I only wish I could forget.

It happened at Adam's house. We'd both been drinking, though I was the only one drunk. I opened my mouth and made a foolish comment about three-fifths of our family being dead and buried, then turned on Adam without provocation and accused him of blaming me for Kyle's death. Speechless, Adam could only shake his head. I motored on, bawling while shouting at him. I'd killed our brother after all. I just wanted to hear Adam say he blamed me, *needed* to hear it. Instead, he reached out to embrace me. Yet my addled mind transposed his attempt to hug me as a threat, and I swung a clumsy fist at him, striking him in the eye.

Jodie and Beth shouted simultaneously. Somewhere in another dimension, a dish fell to the floor and shattered. I swung again, much steadier this time, and even through my drunken stupor felt the solidity of my older brother's jaw against my knuckles. Then I felt his fist against *my* face, the force of it knocking me to the floor, his hulking shape—our father's?—looming before me, blurred by my tears.

Jodie peeled me off the floor while Beth called me a piece of shit and told me to get the hell out of her house. I threw a drinking glass across the room and heard the children in their bedrooms start crying.

Jodie ushered me out into the cold night, a firm hand against the small of my back. I staggered as if in a fever. She said things into my ear as we headed to the car, although I can recall none of them and I probably wasn't even listening to her. Similarly, I remember nothing of the drive back to our apartment.

I spent the next two weeks at the bottom of the world. Overcome by obsession, I thought about Kyle and trembled under the weight of my own guilt. With the dedication of someone newly possessed, I scribbled furious entries in my notebooks and smoked cigarettes like a longshoreman. I quit changing my clothes, which was no longer considered artistic as it had been in college.

My guilt was a pool in which I was drowning . . . though to suggest I was drowning elicits visuals of flailing arms and shouts of help. That was not me. I drowned in my grief with grotesque acceptance, like the captain of a ship who sinks with obligation to the ocean floor, tethered through sacrifice and commitment to the ship that drags him down. Something suggestive of fever claimed me—I let it claim me—and I spent several days in bed, muddy-eyed and swaying back and forth, at least spiritually, like a cattail in the wind. I feared Jodie would leave me. She didn't, but my depression seemed to weaken her, too. Two weeks later, by the time I returned to some semblance of normalcy, there was an unspoken fatigue that had run its course through both of us like some strain of illness undiagnosed.

I would not speak with Adam again until much, much later, well after Jodie and I had moved across the Atlantic to North London.

Sometimes we go in; sometimes we go out.

CHAPTER SIX

I was vaguely aware of a sudden sweeping sound followed by the sharp knife of bright daylight stabbing me through the eyelids. I groaned and rolled over onto Jodie's side of the bed, which was cold in her absence.

"Explain to me," came Jodie's voice from some ethereal vortex, "how this happened . . ."

Some stupid, delinquent part of me was not in the bed in our new house but instead suspended in midair over a glistening lake, night having fallen all around me, the moonlight sparking like bursts of electric current on the black waters. Trapped in a freeze-frame, I held my breath while waiting for the icy plunge that would never come. Jodie's voice was the disembodied voice of God, shocking me into consciousness.

Weakly, I opened one eye and winced at the

daylight pouring in through the part in the curtains. Jodie stood at the foot of the bed holding my pajama pants.

"Morning," I growled.

"You must have some brilliant explanation for this, I'm sure." She shook the pajama pants in both hands. "They're soaking wet. The hallway carpet is wet, too. What gives?"

"Must have been a wet dream." I dropped my bare feet onto the floor, my naked flesh prickling at the chill in the air.

"Hysterical. Your sneakers are half frozen by the front door, too," she said, balling the pajama pants up and stuffing them into the laundry hamper. "If I didn't know better, I'd say you raced the Iditarod before coming to bed last night."

All at once I remembered creeping out of the house and going down to the frozen lake. Had it not been for the soaking wet pajama bottoms, I would have written it off as a vivid dream. Now, in the sobriety of daylight, I realized just how careless I'd been last night. "What time is it?" I said, rubbing my eyes.

"Noon."

"Why'd you let me sleep so late?"

"I tried waking you about an hour ago, but you wouldn't have any of it." She disappeared into the bedroom closet only to return a moment later, her arms laden in clothes that had yet to find a home. She dumped them on the edge of the bed. "I'd like you to move that desk into the spare room." Unsure where to put the desk, the movers had left it in the hallway upstairs. "Also, go through some of the boxes in the basement, if you have time. I feel completely unsettled."

I sighed. "That's because we are unsettled."

"Help me out here, will you?" She selected a blouse from the pile and carried it over to the bevel glass beside the bedroom door. I watched her peel away her shirt and slip into the blouse. Her dark hair was pulled back with a barrette, and she was wearing makeup.

"Where are you going?"

"To the college to see about transferring those outstanding credits."

This had been Jodie's only hesitation about moving from North London back to the States. She'd been on course to receive her doctorate in psychology by the end of the upcoming spring semester and was on the verge of completing her doctoral thesis; the last thing she wanted to do was lose credits in the move.

"There shouldn't be a problem, but I wanted to make sure, just in case. I don't think I have the patience to make up any course work. I'll sooner quit the program." She tucked her blouse into a pair of nice black slacks, then examined her reflection in the glass.

"You're not going to quit."

"Maybe I'll take up bartending. Or stripping."

"Cut it out. You'll be fine."

Adjusting the top button of her blouse, Jodie came over and planted a kiss squarely on my forehead. "Don't forget those boxes. And the desk."

"I won't."

"See you later, alligator," she said and left.

Somewhat awkwardly, I negotiated Jodie's desk down the hall and into the spare room we'd decided to turn into an office. There were more boxes hoarded against the walls here, too, and the closet was already overflowing with Jodie's clothes. I moved a few of the boxes out of the way, then dragged the desk along the carpet where I finally set it beneath the single window that looked out upon the side yard. Through the window I spotted the appliqué of black tamarack pines running down the slope of the property to the lake.

Then I noticed a small, rectangular perforation in the Sheetrock at the base of one wall, only slightly bigger than a doggy door. I would have missed it completely had I not moved boxes out of the way to make room for the desk. I knelt down and realized it was actually a little door, no different than the cubbyholes we'd had in our North London flat, which we'd utilized for storage. The cubbyholes had been hinged on one side and stayed closed by a magnetic latch on the inside of the door.

I pushed against the door and felt the magnetic latch give. A second later, a bracket of darkness appeared in the wall as the door opened. A breath of freezing air issued out of the opening, causing shivers to cascade down the length of my spine. Poor insulation.

I opened the door all the way and looked inside. The squared-off compartment was no bigger than the inside of a washing machine, the flooring unfinished wood boards, the struts in the walls covered by opaque plastic through which tufts of pink insulation burst like stuffing in an old couch.

I managed to make out a few items on the floor. One was undeniably a baseball. A tattered Scrooge McDuck comic book. Several Matchbox cars (and just seeing these jabbed me with a cold spear, for I was suddenly thinking of the Matchbox cars I'd found under Kyle's bed after his funeral and how my father, in his grief, had beat me with his belt before going off to sob in his study). There was a cardboard shoe box back there, too, covered in a fine coat of dust.

This had been some little kid's secret hideout, I thought, reaching in and sliding the shoe box toward me. I picked it up, leaving a distinct handprint in the dust on the lid, and set it in my lap. The box felt very light, though not empty. I opened the lid and, with lightning quick reflexes, shoved the box off my lap while simultaneously scooting backward on the carpet.

The box tumbled over on its side, and two of the things inside bounced out.

The shoe box was full of dead birds, their eyes the color of marble and twisted, skeletal claws frozen in the air. Catching my breath, I leaned forward and studied the birds that had rolled out of the box. They were frozen stiff, their brown-gray feathers glistening with pixels of frost. Some of their beaks were partially opened.

I reached for a wad of packing paper and scooped the dead birds up with it, setting them back in the box among the others. Each one was as weightless as a Christmas ball. The shoe box was like a mass grave. There were about nine birds squeezed in there. What kind of child—

Of course, I was accosted by a vision from my own youth, hiding out behind the shed with a frog trapped in my hands and the nest of baby birds I'd swatted out of the shrub behind the garage. How I squeezed each one until sticky yellow fluid bubbled out of their rectums and their tiny beaks opened wide. I felt sick to my stomach.

"Fuck this." I replaced the lid on the shoe box, closed the cubbyhole door, and took the shoe box to the kitchen where I slid it into a garbage bag. Then I took the bag out to the yard and dumped it in one of the trash cans.

The basement was a schizophrenic jumble of chairs, boxes, and randomly discarded objects that no longer fulfilled their purpose. It appeared that the previous owners, the Dentmans, had hastily erected Sheetrock walls to section the basement off into various rooms, transforming what had once been a wide, yawning expanse of low-ceilinged open space into a honeycomb of secret pockets, mazelike walls, and right angles.

I located a flashlight in my toolbox and took it around with me, casting the beam into each little room—one of which was no bigger than a tiny closet—as I went around. My original notion was that the Dentmans, or whoever had put up these walls, had intended to finish the basement. But on closer inspection it became obvious that the layout was atypical. There were six of the makeshift rooms in all, the Sheetrock old and gouged in places, nailed directly against the studding of the house. None of the rooms had their own electrical outlets, which suggested very poor planning, and two of them had a panel of Sheetrock as the ceiling instead of the open beams and tufts of pink insulation like the rest of the basement. In one of these rooms I bent down and focused the flashlight on a wall where chunks of the drywall had fallen away. The cement floor was coated in a powdery white film. I felt the gouges in the wall.

"Bizarre," I mumbled, moving back into the open area to address the boxes stacked in the center of the room. Yet I paused just outside the doorway to the tiny makeshift room, my flashlight beam reflecting off a series of small puddles on the concrete floor. I hadn't noticed them before, but they were quite evident now. I flicked the flashlight's beam toward the ceiling where a network of copper pipes ran in every direction. It occurred to me that if there was a leaky pipe somewhere, I didn't even know where to find the goddamn water shutoff.

But the pipes looked dry. To make sure, I ran one hand along them, my palm coming away caked in bluish-gray dust but dry as bone. I dipped my fingers into one of the puddles. Ice-cold water. Casting the beam farther along the concrete floor, the puddles seemed to suggest a vague alternating pattern.

Footprints. Wet footprints.

The puddles negotiated the length of the basement, then ended directly in front of one of the slabs of Sheetrock nailed to the wall. Vanished into nothingness.

I was tweaked temporarily as the world around slipped a notch. Too easily I could recall my childhood fear of Kyle slinking back from the grave to claim my soul, dripping foul black water in the hallway of the little duplex we had all happily lived in together. In my head, the sounds of his feet on the hardwood floor were the empty soulless beats of a vampire's heart.

I shocked myself by uttering, "Kyle?" The instant

the word left my mouth, I felt my blood run cold and my body begin to quake. Surely I was scaring myself for no good reason. Surely I was creating something out of nothing.

Just water . . . just puddles of water . . .

I grabbed a towel from the laundry room and mopped up the wet footprints, all the while trying to convince myself they weren't footprints at all. One was even crescent shaped and bore the suggestion of five splayed toes . . . yet I still managed to talk myself out of it.

I spent the better part of the afternoon unpacking countless boxes and transporting the items to various locales throughout the house, as well as dumping a good number of things by the curb for bulk pickup, until sometime later I heard the front door slam upstairs. Jodie entered the house and tramped across the floorboards above my head. Aiming the flashlight at my wristwatch, I saw it was ten after two. I was suddenly hungry for lunch and wondered if Jodie might be interested in accompanying me into town to check out the local scenery and grab a bite. Anyway, I was exhausted and didn't want to spend any more time in this lousy dungeon mausoleum.

I clumped up the narrow staircase and crossed the kitchen where a pot of coffee was overpercolating on the stove, coughing steam into the air and spitting gouts of black sludge onto the stove top.

"Goddamn it."

Grabbing a dish towel from the kitchen counter and wrapping it around my hand, I yanked the coffeepot from the stove and shut off the burner. The pot still burped and bucked in my grasp. I set the pot in the sink and wiped the stove top with the dish towel.

Upstairs, Jodie thumped her foot down twice to get my attention.

"I know. I know. The coffee's burning. I got it." I cleaned up the remaining residue with the dish towel, then wrung it out over the sink.

Two minutes later, searching the second-floor landing, I could not find Jodie. I checked the bedrooms, the bathroom. They were empty. Yet I knew I had heard her. Back downstairs I went to the front door and found it locked. I called her name but she didn't answer. Momentarily, I stood at the foot of the stairs, staring up into the well of risers climbing to the second floor, until I realized I was alone.

Later, in the lazily falling snow, I wandered outside and trekked down the snowy slope of the backyard to retrace my steps from last night's bizarre little escapade. Despite the evidence of the wet pajama bottoms and a pair of frozen Nikes left by the front door, I could almost convince myself all that had happened by the lake had been a dream. Yet the footprints in the snow leading around the side of the house, down the sloping embankment, and through the trees toward the water was proof beyond refute. Hugging myself in my parka, I hiked to the foot of the lake where the frozen surface was accumulating a dusting of fresh snow.

I paused here and fished a pack of Marlboros from my jacket pocket while looking out at the floating staircase protruding through the ice. Though still enormous, the daylight betrayed its mystery, exposing it for the joined bits of rotting wood, nails, and splintered planks that it was. More careful of my footing than I had been last night, I got as close to it as I could—close enough to examine the graying skin of the staircase, the weathered and warped planks, the bone-like suggestion of the thing. I didn't realize it right away, but the preliminary stirrings of a story were yawning and stretching in the far recesses of my brain as I stood there, my hands stuffed into my pockets, a Marlboro smoldering between my lips.

I turned north along the lake and followed its perimeter until the slope of the land became too treacherous. I stared down at the lake from a plateau perhaps fifteen yards above the frozen water, the ground below covered with twiggy undergrowth and sharp, biting rocks that rose out of the snow. The trees were all barren, their branches providing sturdy handholds that

I held on to before I lost my footing and spilled over the edge. Those sharp rocks below would tear me to pieces like crocodiles awaiting a careless gazelle.

From this vantage I could make out the entire circumference of the lake. It was larger than I'd originally thought, the view from my house impeded peripherally by tall pines bookending the perimeter of my property. From here, the view opened up and was even more spectacular; I could only imagine what it looked like in the summer, with all the trees in full bloom, the sun burning a brownish-red smear on the horizon, the sky crowded with scudding cumuli and heavy with birds. The odd wooden staircase looked like the tower of a submarine breaking up through the ice.

There was only one other house here along the lake, directly at my back and seen through the spindly, interwoven arms of the naked tree branches. It was a cabin-style home with a stone chimney, like something you'd see on the bottle of maple syrup. It had an elaborate wraparound porch, which overlooked the lake: a view, I was certain, that was probably better than ours. A flag of smoke twisted lazily up from the stone chimney, stark against the faded gray of the afternoon sky. A fence of pines ran from one side of the house to the highest point of the incline, the trees resembling people standing shoulder to shoulder, their limbs twitching in the wind.

When Jodie came home later that evening, she found me on the living room sofa writing in a string-bound notebook.

"How'd it go at the college?"

"Compared to the professorate in North London, these guys are like extras from *The Andy Griffith Show*."

"It can't be that bad."

"I'm exaggerating but not much. The head of the department wore a goddamn bolo tie."

"What about the credits?"

She leaned over the arm of the sofa and pressed her cold nose against my temple. "I'm happy to report that they all transferred over. I'm a happy girl tonight, Mr. Glasgow. You better take advantage of me while you can."

I closed the notebook and kissed her. "Sounds like a plan."

"You working on something?"

"Just jotting down some notes."

"Finally beat the writer's block?"

I shrugged, noncommittal. "Don't jinx me."

She straightened up and tugged off her coat. "Did you get to those boxes in the basement?"

"Of course." I thought of the watery footprints again. A chill raced down my spine.

Jodie leaned her head on my shoulder and ran one hand up the length of my neck and into my hair. "You smell good."

I turned and kissed her. She eased onto the sofa and pulled me down on top of her. Out of nowhere I was overcome by an animal lust I hadn't felt since the days before our wedding. I was certain Jodie felt it, too, and a moment later, we were making love on the couch, my jeans dangling from one ankle as I wrestled Jodie's blouse, which was only partially unbuttoned, over her head. The whole thing lasted only three or four minutes, but the ferocity and passion made up for the duration.

When we were done, I rolled onto my side as Jodie sat up. She put her blouse on, then leaned down and rested her head against my chest. Our labored respiration was in perfect syncopation.

"That was something," I said after a few moments of silence.

"Hmmm." She sounded far away and close to sleep.

"Hey," I said, squeezing one of her shoulders, "falling asleep afterwards is my job."

"Sorry. I'm just exhausted. I didn't get much sleep last night."

I thought about my midnight jaunt to the lake and grinned. "Oh yeah?"

"I kept having a strange dream."

"What dream was that?"

"There was someone in our room. Someone just standing there at the foot of the bed watching us sleep.

It was so real I kept waking up. I must have dreamt it four or five times."

I felt a cold sweat break out along my body. While I remembered going to the lake last night, I'd forgotten—until now—the reason I'd woken up in the first place: the sensation that someone else was in the bedroom with us. I'd even gotten out of bed and stood in the upstairs hallway looking down over the landing, momentarily certain I could see a crouching visitor lurking in one darkened corner of the foyer.

"Hey." Jodie rubbed my chest. She craned her neck so she could look at me. "You're sweating like a champ."

I squeezed her shoulder again and kissed the top of her head. "You wore me out, lady."

CHAPTER SEVEN

The party at Adam and Beth's came as a much-needed reprieve from all the work Jodie and I had been doing on the new house throughout the first week. Most of the fixes had been cosmetic—painting walls, repairing broken tiling, fixing the electrical outlets that dangled like loose teeth from the walls—and we ended our first week at 111 Waterview Court dappled in dried paint and with blisters on our fingers.

Jodie fell back into the swing of her graduate program and picked up a teaching internship at the college during winter semester three days a week. Ideally, her absence should have afforded me the perfect opportunity to get some writing done . . . yet truth be told, the writing had stopped coming to me months ago. Admittedly, my writing notebooks were currently overflowing with drawings of cartoon animals humping each other in a vast assortment of acrobatic positions.

Holly Dreher, my editor at Rooms of Glass Books, had started leaving exasperated messages on my cell phone asking about the rest of the chapters I'd promised her. Though I hadn't checked my e-mail in several days, I was pretty sure my in-box would be filled with her pushy, overanxious messages as well. I still had two months before the official deadline, but at the rate I was going, I was beginning to consider photocopying pages from the latest Stephen King novel and FedExing them to her.

People started to filter into Adam's house around a quarter to six. The Goldings were the first to arrive. A furtive little couple, they came bundled in woolen earth tones and proffering a small Crock-Pot covered with a tinfoil tent, then spent an unusual amount of time hovering over the small Vinotemp carriage that, this early in the evening, was equipped only with a stack of leftover Christmas napkins and a small plastic vial of toothpicks.

Ten minutes later, a few more couples filed in. Adam selected an Elvis Presley Christmas CD for the stereo, and with the addition of each newcomer, something akin to a party took shape.

"For the most part, everyone here in the neighborhood is tolerable," Adam said, preparing drinks for his guests. We were alone for the time being in the kitchen. "Of course, as with any town, there are a few individuals that'll make your skin crawl." He cut a lime into half-moon wedges and added, "Gary Sanduski, for example. He gets talking about his car dealership, you'll want to drive a cocktail fork through your brain."

"Okay. So I'll need a cocktail fork handy. Check."

"And the Sandersons. They're an odd duo. I'd bet a hundred bucks the husband's gay. He runs an interior decorating company from the house, and his wife's a mortgage broker or something. Point is, we're not really friends with everyone here, but Beth wanted to invite the whole goddamn neighborhood. She said it makes for good karma, and, anyway, you should know all your immediate neighbors." Adam clucked his tongue. "Ever the strategist, my wife."

The Escobars; the Sturgills; the Copelands; the Denaults; Poans; Lundgards; de Mortases; Father Gregory, the cherubic Catholic priest from Beth's congregation; barrel-chested Douglas Cordova, my brother's partner on the police force; Tooey Jones, the owner of Tequila Mockingbird, the tavern Jodie and I had passed while driving through town—my brother's house magically unfolded into a veritable cornucopia of chambray work shirts and foresters' boots, of Allegheny colloquialisms packaged in alpine-scented skin.

Many of my new neighbors insisted on having a

drink with me. Not wanting to be rude, I was half in the tank by the time most of the men cornered me in Adam's kitchen. They were all good-natured, overly friendly in a small-town way, and the excessive alcohol made it so I didn't mind the bombardment. Jodie was occupied in the den with the women, their voices loud and screechy as they filtered down the hallway and into the kitchen nook.

Tooey poured shots into half-pint glasses from a dark-colored, label-less bottle. At first I thought it was liquor—bourbon, maybe—but as it poured I could see a foamy head forming at the surface. A few of the men laughed in unison at something Tooey said, and one even clapped him on the back. Someone tried to pinch one of the glasses, but Tooey playfully slapped him away.

"Wait, wait, wait," Tooey said, shoving a half-pint glass in my free hand. "Make sure everyone's got a glass first."

"How come you didn't play bartender at my Christmas party, Jones?" one of the men wanted to know.

"Maybe I should have. It certainly would have livened things up."

Some bullish laughter.

"Come on. Come on," said another man.

I turned to Adam, who had also been burdened with a glass of the dark, foamy liquid, and whispered,

"What is this stuff?"

"Tooey's Tonic," he said.

"But what *is* it?"

"Beer."

"For real?" I held it up to the light. It was greenish in color, and I could see pebbly particles swimming around near the bottom of the glass. I thought of witches cackling about toil and trouble while stirring a cauldron.

"He changes the recipe almost weekly," Adam said close to my ear. "Been trying to get a distributor for the stuff for years. His bar's the only place you can actually buy it."

"It looks like it should be outlawed," I said and perhaps a bit too loud, as a few of the men chuckled.

"Green," Tooey responded, "is the cure for cancer. Green is what makes the world go round-round-round. Green is gold."

"It's not easy being green," I added.

Tooey's mouth burst open, and a fireball of laughter burst out. It looked forced but wasn't. He had a wide mouth, with narrow, sunken cheeks, and I could see the landmarks of his fillings from across the kitchen. His clothes—a flannel shirt, suede vest, faded blue jeans—hung off him like clothes draped over a fence post. The only remotely handsome feature was his eyes—small, faded blue, genuine, somber, humane.

"Good one, Shakespeare," Tooey said. Anyone else calling me Shakespeare would have irritated the hell out of me, but there was an easiness to Tooey Jones—in his eyes, perhaps—that made it sound comfortable and almost endearing, the way old army buddies had nicknames for one another. "But—*but*—but *taste* it. Taste it."

I brought the glass to my lips and took a small swallow. Fought back a wince. "Uh . . ."

Tooey laughed again. "Well?"

"It's delicious," I said.

"Come on. Be honest."

"I'm new here," I reminded him. "I don't know if I can. I'm trying to win friends tonight—"

"Come out with it!"

Still grimacing, I said, "It's horrible. It tastes like motor oil mixed with cough syrup."

"Ahhhh! So you're saying I used too much cough syrup?"

"Or too much motor oil," I suggested.

Following my lead, a few of the braver men tasted Tooey's Tonic. Mutual grimaces abounded.

"Drink it all, man," Adam said at my side. He was looking forlornly at his own beverage. "It's tradition."

I imagined crazy little Tooey Jones mad-scientist-ing away in the supplies cellar beneath Tequila Mockingbird, bubbly test tubes and smoking vials suspended by a network of clamps, pulleys, and hooks over his head, concocting his latest brew.

A handful of men who had previously been in the den with the women appeared in the kitchen doorway, strategically after the last of Tooey's Tonic had been choked down.

Mitchell Denault nodded at me and took a step in my direction. "I don't want to embarrass you," he said, a few hometown minions at his back, "but I wanted to get your John Hancock on this." Like a Vegas mogul displaying a royal flush, he slapped a paperback copy of my latest novel, *Water View*, on the kitchen counter.

A fellow behind him—Dick Copeland, an attorney—patted the breast pocket of his Oxford shirt for what I assumed was a pen.

"I see Adam's still trying to weasel his fifteen percent by promoting my work," I said, gathering up the copy of *Water View* and opening it to the title page. The pages were pristine and the spine had no creases; I could tell the book had been recently purchased and not read. Dick's pen finally materialized, and he handed it over to me with the excited impatience of a ten-year-old displaying an honor roll report card. I signed the book and thrust it in the general vicinity of Mitchell, Dick, and their horde of cronies.

By ten o'clock, most of the guests had left. I shook

hands and grinned while committing to dinners at houses hosted by people I did not know. Only a few stragglers remained. The women still occupied the den, now talking quietly and in that secretive, whispering way only women have. The few remaining men lingered in the kitchen, picking at the leftover dip and finishing off the hard liquor.

I had drunk way too much; sometime during the night I'd become overwhelmed by the threat of senselessness that accompanied excessive drinking. But it made the more intrusive of the remaining guests more tolerable, and conversation flowed freely toward the end of the night.

I went over to the buffet table to scrounge around at the last of the food, balancing a plate in one hand and a Fordham beer in the other.

A man hovered over the buffet table beside me. He had small, angular features and dark oil-spot eyes swimming behind the lenses of thick, rimless glasses. His eyebrows were like nests of steel wire, and his face was networked with vibrant red blood vessels that betrayed the man's affinity for drink. I pegged him to be in his midfifties.

"I don't think we've met," I said, setting my beer down on the buffet table and extending my hand. Even in my simmering state of inebriation, I felt sobriety rush up to greet me. "I'm Travis Glasgow."

He shook my hand—a slight, effeminate grasp followed by a quick release. A man who did not like to shake hands. "I'm Ira Stein. You and your wife are the newcomers—is that right?"

"Yes. We've been here a full week. We were living over in London before Adam told us about the Dentmans' house coming on the market."

"Nancy and I are your next-door neighbors. You can just barely see our house without the leaves on the trees."

"So you guys are the log cabin overlooking the lake," I said. I recalled the way the smoke from the chimney climbed into the gray sky that day I'd walked north along the edge of the lake. "It's an amazing view."

Ira nodded once almost robotically. "It's very nice, yes."

"I'm still shocked we got our place so cheap."

"Well, we're glad you and your wife . . . ?"

"Jodie."

"We're glad you and Jodie moved in. The Dentmans were a peculiar family, as I'm sure you've heard. Not to speak ill of those poor people and what happened to them, of course. Nonetheless, they were peculiar."

"What do you mean? What happened to them?"

"I'm talking about the tragedy. What happened to the boy."

I shook my head. Fueled by an overconsumption of alcohol, I felt a wry grin break out across my face. "I'm sorry. I have no idea what you're talking about."

"The Dentman boy?" He raised a peppery eyebrow.

"What about him?"

"Oh." Ira stared at his plate, which was empty except for a few olive pits and a plastic toothpick in the shape of a fencing sword. Then he looked across the room at a frail, amphetamine-thin woman I assumed was his wife, Nancy. She was leaning against the wall and peering into the sunken den where the other women were talking. Ostracized from the group, she could have been a lamp, a decorative statue on an end table.

Nancy turned her head and returned our stare. I thought she would smile but she didn't.

"What happened to the Dentmans?" I said again.

"I'm sorry," he muttered, waving one hand. "Really. I shouldn't have said anything."

"No," I said. "What—"

"Really, really," Ira said and actually stuck out his hand for me to shake.

Perplexed, I didn't take it right away.

"It was careless. Never mind. It wasn't my place and I apologize. Travis, it's good—it's good to meet you."

I watched him join his wife against the wall. They talked with their faces very close together, the uniform arcs of their backs and bends of their necks forming, as is occasionally depicted between lovers in cartoons, a crude heart between them.

Jodie bustled by me, burdened with a tray of desserts. "Some shindig," she crooned without stopping.

I hardly heard her; I was still staring at Ira Stein from across the room.

After everyone had left, Adam and I smoked cigars on the back porch. Surrounded by darkness and the deep sigh of wind through the pines, I never felt farther away from London, from D.C., from all the places I'd always pictured myself living and growing old.

"What happened to the Dentmans?" I asked.

Adam looked sidelong at me, and for a moment I couldn't tell if he was going to smile or scowl. In the end, he did neither. Adam had always been tough. Somehow, perhaps through some cosmic interference, he had always known what to do, what to say. Now I felt I was getting a firsthand view of a different side of my older brother—the Adam who was just as lost and vulnerable as every other human being who had ever walked the Earth.

"Hey," I went on, "what's the big neighborhood secret?"

"I'm assuming someone said something at the party," he said, turning away from me.

"Ira Stein mentioned it, but he didn't go into any

detail. He seemed embarrassed about bringing it up. What happened?"

"Ira Stein," my brother muttered under his breath. His tone suggested he did not completely approve of him.

"Come on, man."

"An old hermit owned your house for like a billion years, long before Beth and I ever moved here. Bernard Dentman. I can't say anyone in the neighborhood even really knew the guy, although I guess Ira Stein and his wife may have known him better before he'd gotten ill. The Steins have been here for pretty much their whole lives, so they know what goes on behind every door." Again, that nonspecific tone of disgust.

"When we first moved here, the neighborhood kids used to scare Jacob by saying the old man was really a ghost over two hundred years old and he haunted that house. I finally convinced him that Bernard Dentman was just an old man and nothing more.

"Last year Dentman got sick, and his two grown children moved in with him. David and Veronica." Adam shrugged. "They were equally as weird. Veronica had a son about Jacob's age, but none of the kids around here played with him or even saw him except when he'd play in the yard. Elijah was slow and home-schooled. I don't think he was, you know, retarded or anything like that. Autistic, maybe. Anyway, Veronica and David stayed on at the house and took care of their father until he died."

Adam sucked on his cigar, then pulled it from his mouth to watch the ember glow red. "Elijah drowned in the lake behind your house last summer. That's why Veronica and David moved out in such a hurry and why the place was such a steal. I guess it was too hard on them. They needed to get the hell out of there."

I felt my palms go clammy. I couldn't speak.

"You probably noticed the floating staircase, the one coming up through the lake."

I nodded. "What is it?"

"An old fishing pier. A storm came through a few years ago and uprooted it, tossed it on its side. No one ever knew whose pier it was, so no one ever had it removed. Neighborhood kids congregate around it in the summer, dive off it, whatever. Last summer Elijah was out there playing on it." Again, Adam shrugged. We could have been talking about the weather or the worsening economy. "We worked the investigation and concluded he fell off the staircase, injured his head, and drowned." His voice had taken on an eerie monotone, as if he were trying hard to sound disinterested in the whole story. "Someone should have been watching him."

"Christ. Why didn't you tell me about this?"

"Because I didn't want to ruin this move for you guys. The last thing I wanted to do was burden you with this morbid fucking thing. It's a nice house, a nice neighborhood. What happened to that little boy is not your cross to carry. And anyway, I know how your mind works." He sighed and sounded like he could have been one hundred years old.

Again, I thought of our father. I thought of the way he'd beat me with his belt after Kyle's funeral service, then disappeared into his study where I could hear his great heaving sobs through the closed door.

"What do you mean you know how my mind works?"

"Fuck me." Adam pulled the cigar from his mouth and examined it as if he'd never seen a cigar before. "Are you really going to make me say it?"

I didn't need him to say it. I knew the reason he hadn't told me about Elijah Dentman was because of what had happened to Kyle. It didn't take a brain surgeon. Nonetheless, I was a irritated at his overprotection. I wasn't a little goddamn kid anymore. "Do you think I wouldn't have bought the house if I'd known?"

He looked at me. His eyes were hard and piercing. Sober. "Would you have?"

I shook my head in disappointment and gazed out at the black woods. "Sometimes I think you don't know me at all."

"I'm worried about you."

"Don't."

"I'm your older brother. It's my job."

"Stop doing it." A thickening silence simmered between us for the length of many heartbeats. "Smells like Christmas," I said finally, eager to shatter the silence and change the subject. "The air. It's smoky here."

"It's the pines."

"We used to have a real tree every year in the house at Christmas when we were kids. Remember?"

"Of course."

"Jodie and I, we started putting up a fake tree every year in London. It became its own tradition. Or some bastardization of tradition, I guess. A fake tree . . ."

Adam chuckled. "We got one now, too."

"They don't smell the same."

"Not like Christmas," Adam said.

"Not at all," I said. "Don't tell Jodie about it, okay? The drowned boy?"

"I wouldn't."

"You're right. It's not our baggage to carry."

"I'm glad you think so," he said and put a hand on my shoulder.

Ahead of us, the blackness of night seemed to make up the entire world. For all we knew, at that moment we could have been the only two people on the cold, dark face of the planet.

PART TWO:

THE BEAUTY OF THE MYSTERY

CHAPTER EIGHT

Christmas came and went. We celebrated the New Year with Adam's family at Tequila Mockingbird, Tooey Jones's pub off Main Street. A heavy snowfall blanketed the town of Westlake that first week of January, and old-timers propped up on stools at Tooey's bar or at the local barbershop proclaimed this to be the coldest winter they'd seen since they'd been young boys which, by the look of the lot of them, must have been approximately three hundred years ago.

With the exception of a less than reliable heating unit in the basement, the new house gave us little worry. The day after New Year's, someone from the gas company examined our heating system. After toiling around with the heating unit, the technician said there appeared to be nothing wrong with it. He then examined the thermostat upstairs, which registered at an even sixty-eight degrees. "Could be the thermostat's busted," he suggested. "You'll have to make an appointment to have someone else come out."

Sales for *Water View* were good, as were the scatter of reviews my publisher managed to secure on websites and in a variety of print magazines. Yet despite this good news, I tried to avoid contact with my editor, Holly Dreher, because I hadn't written a single damned thing on the new book since leaving North London. For whatever reason, there was a giant brick wall seated in the epicenter of my brain. However, I knew I couldn't keep up the chase forever.

During one slate-gray afternoon, with the bare tree limbs shaking with the threat of a storm, my cell phone began to chirp in the kitchen. Its persistent call echoed throughout the empty house. (Beth had whisked Jodie away for an afternoon of shopping in town.) At that very moment I had been staring at a blank notebook page, tapping a ballpoint pen against my wrist. And because God enjoys irony as much as anyone, I knew the call would be from Holly.

Sure enough, snagging my cell phone off the kitchen counter, I recognized the 212 area code: New York. "Hey, Holly."

"I was beginning to think you died out there, Travis." The tone of her voice suggested she knew I'd been avoiding her like some virulent disease.

"Nope. I'm still alive and well."

"I was just making an assumption based on the number of phone messages I've left for you that have yet to be returned." She sighed. I could hear her lighting a cigarette. "How's the new house?"

"Needs some work."

"Christ. You're not tearing down walls or putting up walls or anything like that, are you?"

"No, it's not that bad."

"You haven't answered my last couple e-mails, either."

"Our Internet connection is spotty at best." Which wasn't a lie; we'd had some difficulty. We'd complained to our provider, but they assured us the problem wasn't on their end. Nevertheless, even if I'd been able to access my e-mail for more than a few fleeting seconds at a time before our connection went dead, I wouldn't have had the fortitude to check Holly's messages in the wake of the severe writer's block I'd been suffering.

"Well, you should get your ass down to the local library, buddy, and let a gal know you're okay at least. *Capisce?*"

"Haven't had much time to explore the town. I don't even know if there *is* a library. You know how it is out here in the sticks."

"God. Don't remind me. I grew up in Incest,

Pennsylvania, remember?"

Outside, the wind grew stronger and rattled the kitchen windowpanes. The house creaked and groaned all around me. It was like being in the belly of a giant fish.

"Had you read those e-mails," Holly motored on, "you would have found high praise from me on those first few chapters." Dramatic pause. "I'm anxious to read the rest."

"Sure," I said . . . then froze. Movement from the hallway caught my attention. I saw—or thought I saw—a shadow receding down the length of the wall. My bowels clenched, and my heart was suddenly a solid chunk of granite. Covering the phone's mouthpiece with my hand, I called out Jodie's name and waited for a response. None came. Anyway, I would have heard the front door open had it been Jodie . . .

"We're doubling the print run on this one, too," Holly droned. "At least, that's what I'm shooting for. But I need you to deliver."

I crept down the hallway in time to see the basement door at the end of the hall slowly close. The latch catching sounded like someone charging a handgun. I swallowed a hard lump of spit.

"You're frighteningly contemplative. You're not going to ask for an extension on this, are you? Because the book is already slated—"

Somehow I found my voice. "No. That's good news." The words all but stuck to my throat. I heard the basement steps squeaking as someone descended. Heart pounding like a jackhammer, I approached the basement door.

"What the hell's the matter with you?" Holly barked. "You sound completely out of it, man."

"I'm gonna have to call you back," I said.

"What is it?"

"I think someone just broke into my house."

"Travis? Broke into your *house*?"

"I gotta go."

"Do you want me to call—"

"I'll call you back," I said and hung up. The cell phone was a sweaty block in my hand. I slipped it into my pocket, then opened the basement door. There was a light on down there, one I was positive I hadn't turned on. And Jodie had not been in the basement at all as far as I could tell. "Hey," I called, trying my damnedest to sound threatening and failing miserably. "I know you're there. Come on up and we'll talk. No need to call the police."

I stood at the top of the stairs, sweating like a hostage, for what seemed like an eternity. Just as my heartbeat began to regain its normal syncopation, a muted thump followed by a peppering of distant, hollow clacks—pencils falling to the concrete floor?—issued from the basement, causing the sweat to immediately freeze to my flesh. I was about to convince myself that some animal had gotten into the house and was down there scrounging around and raising hell until I saw that the carpeted runner on the stairs held the distinct and undeniable impression of wet footprints.

Invisible hands closed around my neck. All of a sudden, the simple act of breathing became a monumental task. I dug my cell phone out of my pocket and prepared to dial 911 . . . although there was a horrible clenching feeling in the core of my soul that suggested whatever was down here could not be shot by bullets or restrained in handcuffs.

No, a voice countered in the back of my head. *That's stupid. Quit trying to frighten yourself.*

I descended the steps with excruciating slowness, the risers groaning beneath my weight. At the bottom of the stairwell, I took a deep breath while counting silently to five, then swung around the wall, exposing myself to whatever might be waiting for me.

The basement was empty. The main room was packed with our orphaned belongings—things we had not yet decided where to put—and the single bulb in the ceiling, which was on, cast shadows in every direction. I stood there holding my breath, waiting to hear another sound in order to pinpoint the exact location of the intruder—a raccoon or possum, surely—but other than the slamming of my own heart, the basement was silent.

Then something caught my eye: something that should not have been there because I'd thrown it away after we'd moved to England. In fact, my memory of throwing it into the trash behind our flat was so crystal clear I could almost feel the fading warmth of the sun on my shoulders and smell the trees off the back lot.

Because it's not here, I thought. *Because I threw it away and it no longer exists.*

Nonetheless, I crept over to it, my shadow stretching long and distorted on the far wall. I knelt, still gripping my cell phone, and stared at it.

You need to cast an anchor and hold on to something before you can change direction, the therapist used to say. Then: *What is it you're always writing in those notebooks?*

What was splayed out before me on the basement floor, like a bullet fired straight out of the past and into the future, was one of those notebooks. It was opened in the middle, and I recognized my childish handwriting on the pages, the ink smeared in places. These were my words about what happened to Kyle, a subconscious coping mechanism from my disheartened youth (something else the therapist had termed).

I placed one hand on the notebook, as if touching it would shatter the reality of it and send it back in a scatter of fluttering confetti and dazzling disco lights to whatever secondary universe from which it had come. The pages were cold, cold.

Holding my breath, I turned one page and knew what I would find before I was actually staring at it: a faded Polaroid picture of Adam, Kyle, and me standing at the river's edge in Eastport, our arms slung around each other, Kyle's short blondish hair contradictory to Adam's and my own dark furry mops, all of us squinting at the cameraman—our father—whose shadow darkened Kyle's image in some hideous rendition of prophecy. I'd taped the photo into the notebook on the afternoon my father had driven Adam back to college while an unmentionable and foreboding silence ran like ice water through our house.

I closed the notebook but did not immediately stand. Truth was, my legs had surrendered to the strength of my horror; I could no more trust them to hold me up than I could trust the legs of a scarecrow. Instead, I swiped at my eyes with the heel of one hand, the moisture in them temporarily blurring my vision. And when my vision cleared, I happened to be looking across the room at one of the walls of hammered Sheetrock.

During the first week in the new house and at Jodie's recommendation, we'd bought a few gallons of semigloss paint and painted the foyer and living room a cool sage color. The whole thing took us the better part of two days, and when we finished, we had about half a gallon left over. I'd hammered the lid back into place, then stashed the paint can in the basement underneath the stairs. The paint can was no longer there; it was on the floor between two pairs of winter skis and an old end table. The lid was on the floor next to the can, the paint-splattered underside facing the ceiling. On the wall, smack in the center of that barren landscape of white Sheetrock, was a tiny, sage-green handprint.

Later and for the rest of the week, as my mind returned to this very moment over and over again, I would come to understand that I knelt on the floor staring at that handprint for no more than ten or fifteen seconds . . . but at the time it seemed like a full hour ticked by with the hypnotizing lethargy of planetary evolution. I was aware of the fibers in my clothes, the heat suddenly radiating off my flesh, the goose bumps that prickled along the base of my neck. Capering before my eyes were the ghostly vinegar amoebas of broken blood vessels. I felt every crease in the musculature of my beating heart, every strand of fiber and sinew that networked throughout my body.

I rose and, on unsteady legs, made my way over to the handprint. I brought two fingers up and touched it: the paint was still tacky, not yet completely dry.

Small: a child's handprint.

"Who's down here?" Somehow I managed these words, though they came out shaky and unimpressive. Then, frightening myself further, I muttered, "Kyle?"

There came another faint clacking sound from across the room, startling me straight out of my skin, and I whipped around and practically dropped my ass straight into the open paint can. I rolled onto my side as the paint can skidded out from under me. In slow motion I watched it tip on its side and spin in a semicircle across the floor, leaving behind an arc of sage-green paint on the concrete.

"Christ!" I picked myself off the floor.

The clacking sound continued until it finally concluded in a deep-belly *whump*: the furnace kicking on.

"Jesus Christ." I forced a nervous laugh, then went to the sink basin against the wall and turned it on. The pipes clanged and rattled before a gush of freezing water the color of copper came spurting out of the faucet. I thrust my hands beneath the icy water, which made me all the more conscious of the sweat that had broke out on my body. Then I grabbed a roll of paper towels and proceeded to clean up the spilled paint on the floor as best I could. I went through pretty much the entire roll of paper towels and only managed to smear the paint in great magnolia blossoms on the concrete.

Holding the last paper towel, I contemplated wiping

the tiny handprint off the wall . . . but in the end, I decided against it. I knew why right away, although it would take me until later that evening to finally admit it: I wanted Jodie to see it and to prove to myself I wasn't going crazy.

The shrill of my cell phone startled me so badly I nearly had a heart attack. When I answered it and before I could even say hello, Holly's high-pitched voice erupted over the line: "Travis, are you okay? Should I call the police?"

CHAPTER NINE

"Yeah," Jodie said, crouching down. "It's a handprint."

"But *whose* handprint?" I said. I was standing behind her, hands folded across my chest as if obstinate about the whole situation. She'd come home only two minutes before, her arms laden with shopping bags from Macy's and smelling of various perfumes from the department store's perfume counter, when I'd grabbed her wrist and dragged her down the basement stairs while the headlights of Beth's car were still retreating from our driveway.

Now, staring at the handprint, Jodie reached out to touch it.

"Don't," I said a bit too loudly.

Jodie jerked her hand away as if some animal had just snapped at her, then shot me a quizzical stare from over her shoulder.

"Don't mess it up. I want it preserved."

"Why? Do you think this is Bigfoot's handprint?"

I hurried to her side and crouched down next to her. "You don't find this strange? Impossibly fucking strange?"

"That there's a handprint on our wall?"

"That it's a *child's* handprint that just happened to *appear* here," I specified, drumming a finger against the drywall a safe distance away from the print.

"So? The Dentmans had a kid. Is it that hard to believe some—"

"No, you're not getting it." Again, I tapped the wall. "This is our paint, the paint we used upstairs. Don't you recognize the color? You picked it out, for Christ's sake."

"The same paint you spilled all over the floor," she added with mild condemnation, glancing around the room. "Nice."

"Forget about the floor. What about the handprint?"

"A coincidence?"

I couldn't help but laugh. "Are you serious?"

"Why not? It's a common color."

"There wasn't a single room in the house painted sage when we moved in, and anyway, I would have noticed this before."

"Yeah?" Jodie said, and there was a disquieting tone of condescension in her voice. "Would you?"

"What do you mean?"

She stood, brushing her hands on the thighs of her jeans. "My bags are all over the hallway upstairs. Want to give me a hand?"

"Are you kidding? What about *this*?"

Jodie sighed. Her gaze went from me to the handprint, then back to me again. Finally, she said, "So do you have a theory about it you'd like to share?"

This caught me off guard. "A theory?"

"Yes. Where do *you* think it came from?"

"I-I don't know," I stammered.

"Then come upstairs and help me with the bags. I'll get dinner started, and we'll open a bottle of wine." She turned to leave.

"Wait," I said, grabbing the notebook off the floor where I'd left it. I held it out to her and shook it like a prosecutor proffering evidence to a jury. "Then there's this."

Jodie didn't say anything; she looked merely resigned as she leaned against the wall and studied the notebook.

"I threw this out in London when we were trying to make room for all our stuff in the flat. Do you remember?"

"Travis . . ."

I ran my thumb through the pages, making a zipping sound. "I told you about my notebooks, the ones I wrote in when I was a kid after Kyle's death. I threw them all out in London, but now it's here."

"I did that."

I gaped at her.

"I did that," she repeated. "I found the notebooks in the trash and brought them back to the house. I stuck them all in a box and never told you."

"Why?"

"Because I thought you were being careless." Jodie rubbed her face, leaving red streaks on her cheek. "I thought someday you might regret getting rid of them. I didn't want you to regret it."

I could say nothing; I could only stare at the notebook cover, the black and white jungle cat print.

"Travis, he was your *brother*. I didn't want you to make a mistake and hate yourself for it later." Gently, she touched my shoulder. "Is that what this is all about? Kyle?"

Hearing her say his name caused a keening steam engine sound to resonate in the center of my head. I tossed the notebook atop a stack of books, though I continued to stare at my hands as if I still held it.

Jodie came up behind me, wrapped her arms around me. She kissed the crook of my neck, and I could feel her heartbeat against my back. Again, I could smell the department store perfume on her. "You're not angry with me, are you? For doing that?"

I squeezed her hands, which were joined at my waist. "No."

"I love you, you know. I want to take care of you, look after you."

"That's my job," I said.

"We'll do it for each other. Okay?"

I squeezed her hands tighter. "Okay."

"Come on." She withdrew her arms and moved toward the stairs, her shadow trailing behind her on the wall like the tail of a comet. "Let's have some dinner. It's freezing down here, anyhow."

Jodie knew about Kyle; of course she did. What she knew was that I'd had a younger brother who'd died, simple as that. What she didn't know was how his death had been my fault. (As far as I was aware, aside from me, the only people alive who knew the truth were Adam and Michael Wren, a Maryland State Police detective . . . provided Detective Wren was still among the living.)

The night I told Jodie about Kyle, we were in bed in my Georgetown apartment, having been engaged for less than a week. We were naked and sweaty and breathing heavy in the afterglow of making love, both of us staring noncommittally at the ceiling that suddenly seemed too close to our faces. *The Ocean Serene* was going to be published, and I—or rather Alexander Sharpe—had simply and succinctly dedicated it to Kyle. Jodie had read the galleys earlier that evening while I had been at work at the newspaper and asked me who Kyle was.

"My brother," I told her.

"Is Adam—"

"My younger brother. His name was Kyle. He died when I was thirteen."

"Oh. Oh, Travis."

"It's all right."

"No," she said, "it's not. I didn't know . . ."

"I didn't tell you," I responded.

"Sweetie, I'm sorry."

"It's okay. It was a long time ago."

"Do you want to talk about it?"

No, I didn't want to talk about it. But I was also committing the rest of my life to this woman, and I understood that such a commitment carried with it certain rights, and Jodie deserved to know about Kyle.

"He was ten," I heard myself say, and it could have been someone else's voice issuing through the end of a long, corrugated pipe buried deep beneath the earth. "We were living in Eastport, small boating suburb outside Annapolis and just off the Chesapeake Bay, with lighthouses and a quaint little drawbridge and everything. In hindsight, I guess it looked like a Jean Guichard photo. But it was a good place to grow up."

Outside, traffic shushed back and forth in the streets like the ebb and flow of the tide. The sparkle of sodium lights twinkled in the raindrops on the windowpanes.

"There was a river behind our house that led into the bay. We used to swim there in the summer."

I paused, lost in melancholic reflection, and Jodie hugged me tighter. There was a pack of Marlboros on my desk. I got out of bed and snatched them up, along with a book of matches, and went to the window. The stubborn thing was stuck, but I finally pushed it open; a cool midsummer breeze filtered into the stuffy apartment. Half hanging out the window, I lit a cigarette and inhaled deeply. Jodie had been trying desperately to get me to quit smoking and chastised me about it every chance she got. That night, however, she said nothing.

"Kyle drowned in the river that summer," I said flatly. Somewhere between climbing out of bed for the cigarettes and lighting that first smoke, I had made up my mind not to tell Jodie the specific details of what had happened—what I did and what I didn't do on the night Kyle died. There was no need, and I didn't think I could actually tell it, anyway. (I'd told it just once in my lifetime to Detective Wren, and that had been more than enough; I'd never had to speak it aloud since I was thirteen.)

In a small voice, Jodie said, "No."

I tossed the cigarette butt out the window, then shut it. My body was cold but my face was numb. I realized that I had been crying and my freezing tears were stinging my cheeks. I wiped them away, then padded back to bed and slipped underneath the covers. "That's all," I said, as if it had been so simple, so pat.

"Are you okay?"

"Yes."

"How come you never told me?"

"I don't know."

"You could have told me."

"Yeah," I said, but I was hardly listening to her.

"I'm here, if you ever want to talk about it again."

"Thank you," I said. "But I'm okay."

"Just keep that in mind, baby."

"I will."

"My baby."

"Yes."

And that was all I ever said about it to Jodie, who later became my wife.

Jodie made tacos and Mexican rice for dinner while I set the table, put an Eric Alexander CD on the stereo, and opened a bottle of Chateau Ste. Michelle. Even though the handprint on the basement wall still hung over my head like a black aura, I didn't want my wife to think I was completely out of my mind, so I even lit a couple candles and put on my best face at the dinner table. To my surprise, by the time Jodie was halfway through telling me about her afternoon, the handprint diminished to only a vague and distant throbbing toward the back of my cranium. Another hour and a few more glasses of wine and I convinced myself I could forget all about it.

"You know, we've got that perfectly good office upstairs that we're currently utilizing as a storage locker," Jodie said, setting her fork down on her plate and pouring herself another glass of wine. "We could put my laptop up there instead of leaving it on the coffee table in the living room, and you can organize your writing stuff. I'm going to need a quiet place to finish my dissertation, and I'm sure you don't want to continue writing on the sofa for the rest of your life, anyway."

Of course, I hadn't been getting much writing done on the sofa, either. "Give me the next couple days, and I'll set it up real nice. Are you teaching tomorrow?"

"Yes. You should come out to the campus, take a look around. They've got a nice library." She smiled sweetly and innocently, and for one mesmerizing second, I saw her as she had been as a young girl. "You could have lunch with me."

"How long is the winter course?"

"Just a few weeks. But listen," Jodie said, setting her wineglass on the table, "I've been meaning to talk to you about something."

I raised my eyebrows and said, "Shoot."

"They've got a full-time slot opening up this spring, and I was thinking about applying for it."

"Teaching?"

"I know it sounds crazy, and I know I didn't just sit through six years of graduate school to end up back in the classroom . . ."

"But what about your post doc? What about the clinical work you wanted to do?"

"I know. I know," she said, laughing, and rested her chin on her hand. "I've really enjoyed teaching. I like the kids. I like the students."

I sensed the conversation sway dangerously close to our one area of incongruity—Jodie's desire to have children. I felt a momentary flare of contempt for her, as if this were some passive-aggressive attempt at bringing up that old subject—*I like the kids.* But that feeling was just a spark quickly eclipsed by the look of genuine contentment on my wife's face. Her eyes gleamed like jewels in the candlelight.

"Well," I said, "if that's what you want to do . . ."

"You mean you wouldn't have a problem with it?"

"Why would I have a problem with it?"

"Well, I mean, after all the schooling . . ."

"You should do what you want. If you change your mind down the road, you can always go back to clinical work. Do you think you have a shot at getting the position?"

"I do," she said nearly breathless. "I really do."

"Hell," I said. "Then go for it."

We made love again that night and it was very nice, although it lacked the unconstrained sense of lust displayed by our previous coupling on the living room sofa the first week in the house.

"What is it?" Jodie asked me immediately afterward.

"What do you mean?"

"You seemed distracted."

"It sounded like you enjoyed yourself," I said.

"Is it the notebooks? That I took them out of the trash in London?"

"No." To my own ears, my voice sounded very far away.

"Then what is it? There's something." She rubbed my chest. "I can tell."

Kissing her forehead, I folded her up in my arms and hugged her.

"You're not going to say anything, are you?" she asked after a while.

I said nothing more and eventually fell into a dreamless half sleep while Jodie got up and showered before coming back to bed.

Sometime during predawn, I was awoken by what felt like a cold hand touching my chest. I jerked upright in bed, a shriek caught midway up my throat.

Jodie slept soundly beside me; I was surprised my start hadn't woken her. Across the room and through the part in the curtains, I could see the three-quarter moon cleaving through the inky darkness of space and the pearl-colored luminescence of the frozen lake below.

I pawed sleepily at my face while my eyes adjusted to the darkness. There was a needling sense of urgency directing me to get up, get up, get up. I peeled back the blankets and stepped onto the ice-cold hardwood floor. A shiver shot like a bolt of lightning through my body, and I felt my testicles, those two wrinkled cowards, shrivel to the size of dried figs. I pulled on my pajama bottoms and crept out into the hallway, still unaccustomed to the placement of the squeaky floorboards; I winced inwardly each time one creaked, afraid I'd wake up Jodie. But she was snoring steadily and lost in her own dreamland, and I made it to the carpeted section of the landing without incident.

As I'd done on that first night in the house, I peered over the railing to the foyer below. The boxes were no longer there, and moonlight poured in through the front windows unimpeded. I stood without moving, my hands balled into sweaty fists, and listened to the silence of the house all around me. Listened, listened. What was I waiting for? I had no clue. What had awoken me? I did not know.

In the basement, I fumbled for the cord of the

ceiling light, and after floundering around in the dark like a mime semaphoring to a fleet of jetliners, I finally felt it wisp against my face. I pulled the light on and my retinas burned. Wincing, I stood in the center of the basement until my eyes adjusted to the light. Then I glanced around for any pools of water on the floor. There were none.

My gaze fell on the handprint across the room. Some fearful, overly sensitized part of my soul was convinced it would be gone—or worse that I'd find more of them now, dozens more, covering every section of the wall—but it was there. That lone child's handprint.

Of course, I was still troubled by its presence . . . but something else from earlier that evening was needling at me now, too. Something important that I'd missed, though just barely. I couldn't quite put my finger on it.

I returned to bed accompanied by the uneasy feeling that I had overlooked something, then spent much of the following morning in a similar state. With Jodie at school, I attempted to get some writing done but found, not surprisingly, that my mind refused to focus. Soon I was drinking too much coffee while wandering around the house, watching a light snowfall through the upstairs dormer windows.

By noon, I'd checked on the handprint three times. Nothing had changed except that in the daytime it seemed less ominous. In fact, by one thirty I was beginning to convince myself that maybe Jodie was right—that perhaps this handprint had been here all along. The open paint can? I'd probably just left it there when I'd finished using it and hadn't placed it under the stairs as I thought I had. It was a child's handprint after all. And we had no children.

I decided to clean up the room that would become our office. There were still stacks of boxes in here, some of them nearly to the ceiling. I grabbed one and almost fell backward at the weightlessness of it: the thing was empty. I drummed my fingers along the side as I carried it and a number of other empty boxes out to the trash.

Some latch finally caught in the recesses of my lizard brain, and I suddenly realized what I'd been struggling to decipher about the handprint on the wall downstairs. Strangely, it had nothing to do with the handprint and everything to do with the wall. Because the drumming on the empty boxes made the same sound as my finger tapping against the drywall last night.

Hollow.

I rapped a set of knuckles along the drywall in the basement. Sure enough, it sounded hollow, as if there was nothing on the other side of the wall. I moved down the length of the wall, still knocking, until I heard the difference in the sound where the drywall had been hung directly over beams or cinder block.

Fueled by curiosity and an unanchored surge of emotion, I cleared junk from the hollow wall until the whole section was exposed. I traced the seams of the drywall, which hadn't been taped up, while I calculated approximate square footage in my head: the basement was smaller than the ground floor, though I found no reason why this should be. By all accounts, the basement should have approximated the perimeter of the ground floor. Of course, that didn't mean—

Sliding down the seam between two sheets of drywall, I discovered a tiny hiccup. I looked closely at it, practically pressing my nose against the wall. It was a hinge. Farther down the seam was a second hinge . . . and toward the bottom I located a third.

It wasn't a wall at all.

It was a door.

But there was no doorknob, no handle, no way of opening it. I went to the opposite seam and attempted to cram my fingers between the two sections of drywall in order to pry it open, but it was impossible. Perhaps the door had been sealed shut long ago?

A door to where? Another room?

I hadn't a clue.

Then I heard my old therapist's voice saying, *Sometimes we go in; sometimes we go out,* while I thought of the storage cubbyholes we'd had in our

North London flat: little hinged doors in the walls that were held closed by magnets.

Sometimes we go in; sometimes we go out.

I pressed a palm flat against the "wall" and pushed slightly. I felt it give perhaps half an inch . . . then unlatch itself from the wall as it eased open on squealing hinges. The door opened only three or four inches, revealing a vertical crack of darkness.

I didn't realize just how excited I was until I reached out to pull the door open farther and saw how badly my hand was shaking. In the back of my throat, a weak little laugh escaped.

I opened the door.

CHAPTER TEN

By the time Jodie and I moved into the house on Waterview Court, I had already authored four novels in the supernatural or horror genre, dealing with spooks and specters and villainous entities with villainous designs. As I stood before the open doorway in the basement wall, it occurred to me that I had written countless scenes like this one. In my writing, I have always attributed an indistinct merging of trepidation and fear to my characters as they stood on the cusp of uncertain discovery.

But I was not afraid, as so many of my characters had been in the past; instead, I felt a cool, almost menthol satisfaction wash through me, as if I'd just figured out the final clue in an unusually taxing crossword puzzle.

Therefore, my first thought upon opening the

door was, *Fuck, I've been doing it all wrong.*

It was a cramped little room with no windows. Dark humping shapes loomed in a suggestion of pattern, although I couldn't figure out just what I was seeing. I opened the door wider to allow for more light, but the single bulb in the center of the basement ceiling wasn't cutting it. On a whim, I reached into the room and fumbled along the inside wall and, to my astonishment, located a light switch. I flipped it on and waited several seconds for my mind to catch up with what I was seeing.

It was a child's bedroom . . . or at least the *suggestion* of one: a tiny bed was squeezed into one corner, its mattress overloaded with piles of small, colorful clothes. Against one wall was a little writing desk on which sat a lamp with a cowboys and Indians lamp shade, and a bookshelf burdened with countless toys and children's books climbed another wall. There were a plastic chair in the shape of a giant cupped hand by the desk and a toy chest overflowing with stuffed animals at the foot of the bed. Glow-in-the-dark stars and crescent moons stuck to the ceiling and against the back wall, which was bare, unpainted cinder block. Several cardboard boxes were stacked in the center of the room, no different than the boxes we'd used in our move; they had been the looming dark shapes I'd first seen.

It looked like a museum display, a re-creation of

a child's bedroom circa 1958, something you might see behind glass in Epcot with a brass plate reading Replica Bedroom of American Boy.

I entered the room, bracing myself for violating some sacred space, but I felt only a faint light-headedness. Except for a filthy throw rug tucked halfway beneath the bed, the floor wasn't carpeted, and my footfalls on the concrete echoed in the tiny chamber. I examined the shelves of toys and the stacks of folded clothes on the bed. With the toe of my sneaker, I lifted the lid of the toy chest the rest of the way and looked into a well of drowning stuffed bears, pigs, monkeys, and other less definable creatures.

Then I walked two complete circles around the stacks of boxes at the center of the room. The cardboard appeared old, covered in places in a black slick of mildew. I opened the top box: more colorful and small clothes, just like the ones piled on the bed. I took out a striped polo shirt that looked practically new, then dropped it back into the box. I set this box on the floor so I could access the one beneath it. This one contained more clothes. A third was burdened with toys: a stuffed bear, a baseball hat, a worn baseball with frayed stitching. Sneakers here, too, their laces tied together, their soles caked with petrified mud. An electric pencil sharpener. What looked like the axle off a toy car with a plastic black wheel still attached to each end. A children's illustrated edition of *Treasure Island*.

I went through all the boxes in this fashion— with a mix of utter disbelief and mounting light-headedness—until I reached the one at the bottom of the stack. Yet it wasn't a box at all but a bright blue plastic container with a red rope handle. I felt a twinge of something crucially significant lock into place, like a dead bolt sliding home, but I wasn't sure what it was at first.

I crouched down before the blue container, which was no bigger than a can of paint, and popped off the lid without the slightest difficulty. They say olfactory sense is the one linked most directly to memory, and I had no doubt this was true. The scents that struck me were of cedar chips and the bedding of hamster cages, of cured wood, and, just faintly, of polyurethane. Inhaling that intermingling aroma ushered me back to an early childhood, much earlier than those horrible days following my brother's death.

Inside the blue container were wooden building blocks of varying colors, shapes, and sizes, a replica of the set I'd had as a child myself. By the time my mother had sold my blocks at a yard sale, they were riddled with gouges and nicks, and most of the colored paint had peeled away. These blocks, however, looked brand-new and practically unused. I picked one up, brought it to my nose, smelled it. The bittersweet scent of childhood.

I recalled Adam's story about Elijah Dentman, and I knew that I was standing in Elijah's bedroom. This was all Elijah's stuff. As horrible as this little dungeon was, he'd slept here, played here, said his bedtime prayers here.

A cold sweat broke out along my neck. My mouth went dry. What kind of parent keeps their kid in a hidden bedroom behind the basement wall? A bedroom with no windows, no natural light?

Without warning, I recalled the Christmas party at Adam's house and my conversation at the buffet table with Ira Stein. Clear as day, I could hear Ira saying, *The Dentmans were a peculiar family, as I'm sure you've heard. Not to speak ill of those poor people and what happened to them, of course.*

"You've got to come downstairs and see this," I said when Jodie got home. It was five thirty, the sky had grown prematurely dark, and I'd spent the entire day going through Elijah Dentman's stuff.

Looking exhausted, Jodie set her books and purse down on the kitchen table. She eyeballed me as if I'd just approached her in a dark alley as she went to the refrigerator and took out a beer. "Don't tell me you found more handprints on the walls." There was a none-too-subtle condemnation in her voice.

"Better," I said.

"Did you even shower today? You look brutal."

"Come on," I said, already heading down the hallway toward the basement. "Come see."

She followed me.

"There was a little boy who lived in the house before us," I said at the foot of the stairs as Jodie plodded tiredly down the risers. "Elijah came here with his mother and uncle when the grandfather got sick." I deliberately left out the fact that the kid had drowned in the lake behind our house. When she reached the bottom step, I took her wrist and rushed her over to the opening in the basement wall. "You're not going to believe this, but I think I just found the kid's bedroom."

Together we stood shoulder to shoulder, like a couple waiting to get on the subway, in the doorway to Elijah Dentman's bedroom. I laughed, still amazed by my archeological find, and stepped into the room while negotiating around the boxes I'd placed randomly on the floor after going through them.

Jodie remained in the doorway. There was a look of perfect incomprehension on her face. No, not just incomprehension—*apprehension*. Fleetingly, I conceded that maybe I wrote those scenes in my books right after all.

"Look at this place," I said. "They kept the poor kid down here like a prisoner."

Slowly, Jodie brought a hand to her mouth. Her face had gone the color of soured milk.

"It was like unearthing a bomb shelter or a time capsule or something after a nuclear holocaust."

"How . . . how did you find this?"

"It was right here behind the wall. I pushed on the wall, and it opened like some pharaoh's secret fucking passageway." I waved her in. "Come here and look at this stuff."

"No." She didn't move.

"What?"

"Get out of there. I don't like it."

"What are you talking about? Isn't this totally fucking bizarre?"

"Yes. It is."

I tapped my sneaker against the plastic container of wooden blocks. "I even had these same blocks when I was a kid."

"How nice for you. Please come out."

I watched her on the other side of the doorway—really, on the other side of the wall—and for all the distance I suddenly felt between us she could have been in an alternate universe. It was just a temporary feeling, though, and once it passed I went to her and rubbed her arms.

Jodie looked at me, but at the same time her eyes were distant and unfocused, as if I were made of smoke and she could see straight through me.

"Hey," I said, "what's the matter with you?" Then

the answer dawned on me, and my goofy grin faded. "You know about Elijah. You're creeped out because you know he died here. That's it, isn't it?"

My words surprised her—she'd known, but she hadn't expected *me* to know. Before I could fully read her face, she turned away. It wasn't forceful enough to betray any sense of emotion, but it caused my hands to drop from her arms just the same.

"Tell me," I said. "You knew, didn't you?"

"A woman at Adam and Beth's Christmas party told me." Jodie wandered over to the washer and dryer where she feigned casual interest in the big orange box of detergent on one of the slatted shelves beneath the basement stairs. I wondered if the woman in question had been Nancy Stein. "I asked Beth about it later, and she said it was true."

"Why did you keep it a secret from me?"

"Didn't *you* keep it a secret from *me*?"

"I was trying to protect you. There was no need to tell you about it."

"And I was trying to protect you, too." When she faced me I could tell she was fighting tears. "I won't have you chastise me for this. I won't allow it. I remember that night at your brother's house after your mom's funeral. And I've been there for your low points when Kyle's memory haunts you. I hear you talk in your sleep about him. But mostly I know how you are and how you dwell on things, how you torture yourself." She clenched her beer bottle so tight I feared she would shatter it. "So, yes, I didn't think you knew, and I had no plans to ever tell you. If I had to keep that secret for your own mental health, then I would have taken it to my grave."

"Christ. I'm hurt you think I'm so weak."

"Grow the hell up. Don't try and make me feel guilty. I won't."

Jodie was right. Notwithstanding the sting of betrayal I felt, I understood why she'd kept it from me. Too clearly I could summon the memory of that night after my mother's funeral, the words that were said in anger and the punches that were thrown.

"Okay," I said at last, closing the distance between us. I hugged her and felt the beer bottle press into my abdomen. "Okay."

Jodie sighed against my shoulder, and I let her go. I expected her eyes to be moist but they weren't. She just looked incredibly tired.

"I want you to call someone, have them come out and get rid of all that stuff," she said, nodding in the direction of Elijah's bedroom. "And I don't want to talk about what happened to that boy anymore. It's unsettling but it has nothing to do with us."

"Right," I said, massaging her shoulder with one hand. "It has nothing at all to do with us."

CHAPTER ELEVEN

The following morning I telephoned a company called Allegheny Pickup and Removal and spoke to a fellow with the unfortunate name of Harry Peters about getting rid of Elijah Dentman's things. It would take ten days for them to fit me into their rotation: a duration Jodie wasn't too thrilled about. Yet if Jodie gave the hidden bedroom and its cache of childlike artifacts more than a passing thought each day, she did a spectacular job not letting it show.

I, on the other hand, found myself creeping down into the basement bedroom any chance I could get—and against the promise to my wife that I would do just the opposite—because I felt an inexplicable longing to sift through all Elijah's things.

The story Adam had told me about Elijah's accidental death coupled with the discovery of the boy's tomblike bedroom had caused a previously diminishing spark to reignite in the center of my creative soul. My writer's block evaporated like clouds of heavy fog retreating out to sea; once again I was able to see the bright lights of that grand city.

I lost all interest in the manuscript I'd been trying to write—the first few chapters of which Holly had already read and loved—and began fleshing out descriptions of a make-believe family (that maybe wasn't so make-believe) rooted in some disturbing and interpersonal dysfunction. A single mother and her young son come to live with the boy's uncle and ailing grandfather in the final days before the grandfather passes on. What sort of life did these characters live? What happens to a young boy who's forced to live in a ten-by-ten room that resembled something out of "The Cask of Amontillado"?

Of course, the similarities between Elijah's death and my own brother's were not lost on me. Both had drowned at roughly the same age. Both of their bedrooms had been left eerily undisturbed following their deaths—Elijah's in the basement of 111 Waterview Court and Kyle's in our house in Eastport. Since Adam was the eldest, Kyle and I had shared the bedroom. After Kyle's death, my father moved my stuff out, and I bunked in Adam's room until that cold December day when my parents, silent and moving as if manipulated by strings, finally packed up all Kyle's belongings and transferred them to the garage.

(Whatever happened to Kyle's stuff after that remains a mystery to me; after our father died and our mother went to live with her sister in Ellicott City, Adam and I returned to our childhood home to take care of our father's estate. I'd expected to find Kyle's stuff still in the garage—expected to be mercilessly confronted by it like a murderer facing Judgment Day—but was surprised to find it gone. And somehow that was worse than having to see that stuff all over again, because it meant that there had been at least one specific moment in time when my parents had to go through everything in order to get rid of it, and it hurt me to think of the grief it must have caused them.)

Because of these similarities and because I had no idea what Elijah Dentman had looked like, I gave my fictional little boy characteristics very similar to Kyle's—slight of frame, bright hair, handsome eyes with great fans of lashes, gingery spray of freckles across the saddle of his nose. The only towheaded male in our family: the odd man out. The writing came in a fury and left me drained but excited by the end of each session.

One afternoon while Jodie was out with Beth, I phoned Adam and told him to come over as soon as he could. He showed up on the front porch in his dark blue police uniform, his hat in his hands. The uniform made him look twice as big, the body armor he wore under his shirt giving him the overall rounded appearance of a whiskey barrel.

"What in the world is so important? You were practically out of breath on the telephone."

I took him downstairs and showed him the room.

"Holy shit." Adam stared in awe at what I'd uncovered. "Are you *kidding*?" Like Jodie, he remained in the doorway, as if an invisible barrier were preventing him from crossing the threshold.

Later that evening, I was overcome by another strong impulse to put words to paper. But I was tired of sitting on the sofa with a notebook on my lap. I located a rolling chair stashed away with various other forgotten relics in the basement and wheeled it into Elijah's bedroom and right up to the kid's desk. I adjusted the chair so that it came to an agreeable height, then flipped open my writing notebook and scribbled furiously.

I sketched out caricatures of Tooey Jones, Ira and Nancy Stein, the Christmas party at Adam's house, and the basement bedroom secreted behind the wall. I wrote detailed passages describing the floating staircase on the lake. And of course I wrote of Elijah Dentman, my central character, my tragic figure, the poor boy held captive in an underground bedroom dungeon. What kind of child was Elijah? What does being trapped in a basement do to a ten-year-old boy? (I thought of the shoe box of dead birds and felt a numbness creep through me like a fever.)

For now, I had overpowered the writer's block and was sailing into port on a soaring, lightning-colored dirigible, high above the blinking lights and the network of distant industrial causeways. Soaring, soaring.

When I finally put down my pen, my hand was throbbing and there was a sizeable blister on my index finger. What I had in the notebook were wonderful passages and detailed descriptions. What I was missing, though, was a *story*. I knew too little about the Dentmans to accurately riff off their lives. I kept putting my little boy in a basement dungeon but couldn't understand how he got there. Who was Elijah? Who were the entire Dentman family?

I needed to find out.

CHAPTER TWELVE

It was only 11:15 in the morning by the time I arrived at the Westlake Public Library, and already there were iron-colored clouds crowded along the horizon promising snow.

The library was a squat, brick structure set at the intersection of Main and Glasshouse Streets and fortified by a fence of spindly, leafless maples. Inside, all was deathly quiet. As had become my custom whenever I found myself in a library, I crossed to the *G* aisle and located only a single, tattered copy of my novel *Silent River* among the stacks. It appeared to have been someone's preowned copy that had been donated to the library, as I found the name G. Kellow printed on the inside of the front cover.

At the information desk an elderly woman with a kind, grandmotherly face smiled at me from behind a pair of bifocals. She was massaging a dollop of Purell into her hands.

"Hi," I said, "I was hoping to search through some back issues of the local newspaper."

"That would be the Westlake city paper? *The Muledeer*?"

"The city paper, yes." Thinking: *What a perfectly backwoods name for this town's rag.*

"How far back do you want to search? If it's roughly within two years, we'll have the newsprint copies in the storage room. Beyond two years, you'll find it on microfiche." She adopted an apologetic tone and added, "I know the microfiche is a tad outdated, even for out here on the tip of the devil's backbone, but the library hasn't gotten around to transferring all those files onto the computer yet."

"It's no problem," I assured her.

Though there was no one else around to overhear, she leaned across the desk and whispered conspiratorially, "Truth is, I don't like computers. Don't trust them. Too many buttons, too many things to go wrong. Anyway, I'm an old woman, and I'm not about to learn the tango and the two-step, if you know what I mean." She smiled, her powdered cheeks flushing red. "Lord, I must sound like the perfect paranoid fool."

"Not at all," I said. "I prefer to do all my writing

by hand. And I don't think I'll need the microfiche. I need to go back to last summer or thereabout."

"Well," she said, "you'll need the unicorn."

I blinked. "The what?"

The librarian sifted around in a shoe box she'd produced from beneath the counter and came up with a set of keys. Dangling from the key chain was a rubber unicorn figurine. Its paint worn away and its hindquarters decorated with what appeared to be teeth marks, the little rubber figurine could have been a hundred years old.

"This way," said the librarian, and I followed her around the front desk and through a maze of book-shelves. "Lord knows why Vicky insists on locking the door. It's not like someone's going to break in and rob us of all our old newspapers."

"What was that comment you said before? The one about the devil's backbone?"

"The tip of the devil's backbone," she repeated. "Something my mother used to say. It means the middle of nowhere. Like out here in Westlake."

"I like it."

"Oh, don't get me wrong," she said. "It's a wonderful little town."

I'd meant I liked her mother's saying but didn't see the need to explain myself.

We arrived at a nondescript door at the rear of

the library. There was a poster on the door depicting a fuzzy orange kitten dangling from a tree branch. The caption, strangely misspelled, read, Hang in Their!

The librarian selected the appropriate key and opened the door. She leaned inside and flipped on the light, bringing into view a room no bigger than a water closet. A rack of shelves stood against one wall, sagging with stacked newspapers. There was a table and a chair in there, too, and a yellow legal pad hung from a peg in the drywall.

"That notepad on the wall is the index," she said and handed me the keys. "There's a key to the bathroom on there as well. Guess Vicky thinks someone's going to come in and steal our toilets, too. Would you like some coffee?"

"No, thanks."

"Well, give me a shout if you need anything. I'm Sheila."

"Thanks, Sheila."

When she'd gone, I stepped into the room and shut the door behind me. The air was stale and—of course—heady with the moldy, woodchip scent of old newspapers. I unhinged the legal pad from the peg and scanned the pages. It took a good minute or two to decode the index, but once I figured out the system, I located specific dates without much difficulty.

The Muledeer was a weekly newspaper, each issue

not much thicker than a menu from a roadside diner. I had no specific date for the drowning of Elijah Dentman other than the fact that it had happened last summer, so I started with the first week of June and walked myself through the pages. Because the papers weren't very wordy I didn't think it would take me much time to search, and, anyway, something as profound as a neighborhood child's death would, I surmised, surely command a front-page presence.

Overall, there wasn't much going on in Westlake, Maryland. For the most part, the newspapers were chock-full of human interest stories, reviews of local talent shows, publicity write-ups for local businesses, and the occasional memorial for an elderly resident who had passed on to that great assisted living facility in the sky. While the articles offered very little newsworthy information, they provided a resourceful peek into the heart and soul of the small town I now called home.

Then there it was, the headline staring straight at me—

LOCAL BOY DROWNS IN LAKE

I felt an icy wave rush through my body. I was rendered paralyzed by the reality of it. I wasn't breathing: I was aware of this but couldn't do anything about it.

Just beneath the headline and to the left of the

article was a school photograph of Elijah Dentman. He was fair skinned and towheaded, with a round face and squinty little eyes, but there the similarities between him and Kyle stopped. There was something slow, something underdeveloped about his appearance. It was one of those Kmart portraits with the fake wooded background, so simple and commonplace, yet something in the boy's eyes made me want to break down and sob.

According to David Dentman, the boy's uncle, Elijah had been swimming in the lake that afternoon and playing on the floating staircase while David watched him from the living room window and Elijah's mother slept upstairs. When it began to get dark, David looked up to find Elijah gone. He rushed down to the lake and called for Elijah, but the boy did not answer. He waded out into the lake, still shouting the boy's name, but to no avail. Panic apparently set in when David noticed what appeared to be blood on one of the wooden stairs of the floating staircase. He hurried back to the house and phoned the police.

The cops executed a cursory search of the lakeside and the surrounding woods. They also interviewed neighbors, and there was a quote from Nancy Stein in the article that corroborated David Dentman's story: she'd been out walking her dog and saw Elijah playing on the floating staircase. Then later that afternoon she heard what she thought to be a sharp scream by the water. Nancy Stein hadn't thought anything of it at the time, of course, but now . . .

By the time I read to the end of the article, I felt as though I'd been punched in the stomach, for there was one bit of crucial information Adam had neglected to tell me after the Christmas party at his house: Elijah's body had never been found. The Westlake Police Department had sent a scuba unit into the lake but did not find Elijah. According to the chief of police, the lake was deep during the summer months, and with all the rain they had been having, the sediment at the bottom was churned up, making visibility difficult. They continued to dredge the lake all evening and well into the following morning, but they never found the boy. *They never found the boy.*

The final determination was located on the front page of the following week's paper. Police deduced that the boy had fallen off the staircase and struck his head on one of the stairs, knocking himself unconscious and ultimately drowning. DNA proved the blood on the stair was, in fact, his. The scream Nancy Stein allegedly heard had most likely been Elijah as he fell off the staircase before he struck his head on the step. And just like that the case was closed.

I read and reread the article, unable to comprehend it. The lake was large, sure, but it was a self-contained body of water. How had they been unable to find a body? Had the kid fallen in and been swept away that quickly? It made no sense.

"Brought you some coffee, anyway," Sheila said, causing me to launch out of my skin. Deep in concentration, I hadn't even heard the door open. Sheila set down a Styrofoam cup on the table beside the newspapers. Peering over my shoulder, she examined the headline, then shook her head as if gravely disappointed. "I remember that. A horrible tragedy."

"They never found the body," I said, my voice paper-thin and incredulous.

"Always such a tragedy when something like that happens to a person so young." Then she frowned, her face collapsing in a cavalcade of wrinkles. "Why would you want to read about such a terrible thing?"

"My wife and I just moved to town, and I heard about what had happened." I offered her a wan smile. "I guess I was just curious."

"A young man like you shouldn't be curious about such morbidity. You should be thinking about football and fishing and spending time with your wife."

"I'm a horror writer. Morbid curiosity is my bread and butter, Sheila," I confessed, picking up the cup of coffee and taking a sip.

She beamed like a proud mother at my use of her name. "So, what do you write? Short stories?"

"Novels."

"Really? That's fantastic! Have any of them been published?"

"All of them." I've always hated this question.

"Well! Would we have any here at the library, then?"

"In fact, you've got one of my books right out there on the shelf. Filed under *G* for Glasgow." I suddenly wanted to get rid of her and figured this might be the way to do it.

"Now isn't that something? Glasgow, did you say? Like the city in Scotland?"

"The very same."

Sheila's smile grew so wide I thought it might just cleave her face in half. "Do you know what I'm going to do? I'm going to find the book and have you autograph it. I hope you don't mind. I'll put up a nice little local author carousel by the front doors." She clasped her hands against her bosom. "It's like having a celebrity in the neighborhood."

As Sheila scuttled off, I replaced the yellow legal pad on the wall peg. Before leaving, however, I surrendered to a sudden compulsion and flipped back to the newspaper articles about Elijah Dentman. Casting a cursory glance over one shoulder, I tore the pages out of the newspapers and hastily folded them into the back pocket of my jeans.

CHAPTER THIRTEEN

"Why the hell didn't you tell me they never found Elijah Dentman's body?"

It was Adam's day off, and we were sitting at the bar at Tequila Mockingbird, plowing through beers. The 'Bird, as it was known to the regulars, was a gloomy, rustic pub, with smoked brick walls and floorboards as warped as the nightmares of a madman. A splintered bar clung to one wall and faced an arrangement of circular tables. An old jukebox collected dust beside the restroom door, and exposed ceiling joists, all blackened and unreliable, spoke of past grease fires gone horribly out of control. With all its ghosts and vapors, it was no different than every other small-town bar throughout America.

The only exception was the one wall comprised not of smoked bricks but of a giant assembly of mahogany shelving on which sat hundreds—perhaps thousands—of leather-bound books. Spines cracking and flaking, many of the embossed titles worn illegible, the books occupied every possible slat and crevice of the wall-length shelves. Some were wedged horizontally while others were driven vertically between neighboring volumes and evidently pounded into place with a forcefulness that made retrieving them about as difficult as extracting nails bare-handed from a length of wood. Framed reproductions of various panels from William Blake's *Songs of Innocence and Experience* hung on the walls, the colors behind the glass sharp and brilliant and completely out of place in the midst of this dreary rural pub.

"What are you talking about?" Adam said. "I told you the whole story."

"No. You told me he drowned. You never said his body was never found."

He flicked at the foamy head of his beer with one finger and looked suddenly bored. "Okay, yeah. We never found him."

"How is that possible? It's a self-contained lake."

"A very big, very deep lake." Adam sighed and rubbed his face. "No one actually saw the kid fall in, so we had no real time of death. The only thing we had to go by was Nancy Stein's statement about hearing what sounded like a scream. By the time we showed up on scene, that scream took place over two hours ago. Do you know what happens to a body that's gone underwater for two hours?"

"Hey," I said, holding up both hands in mock surrender, "I'm not criticizing."

My brother's eyes narrowed. "What have you been doing, anyway? Asking around about this stuff?"

"I went to the library and looked at some old newspaper articles."

"For what reason?"

I tried to appear cavalier. I didn't want him to know I was writing a book. "Curiosity, I guess."

"Yeah, right." The tone of his voice said he didn't believe me.

"Were you there that day? Part of the search?"

"Yes."

"What was it like?"

"It was horrible. It made me sick." Adam placed both his palms down flat on the bar top. "Out here, the biggest things we got going on are the occasional vandals on Main Street and the rowdy bunch of teenagers who decide it'll be funny to take a dump on the steps of the post office."

"So you guys weren't prepared for an investigation into what happened to Elijah?"

"We're good cops, if that's what you're insinuating. We know how to do our jobs, and we do them well."

He looked hard at his beer. "We lost a guy over in Iraq. Left the force on a whim, said it was some calling and he had to answer. Fuck." He stared off into the dimness of the bar. "We're a good police force is what I'm getting at."

"I have no doubt."

"Fuck," he said again and finished half his beer in one swallow, then ordered another round.

"Who interviewed Nancy Stein?"

"My partner," Adam said. "Douglas Cordova. You met him at the Christmas party, remember?"

I did vaguely: giant barrel-chested guy with a pleasant, almost childlike face. "Sure," I said. "Were the Dentmans ever suspects?"

"Not officially."

"But you guys had some question about them?"

"No. But when a kid disappears . . ."

"You look to the parents first," I finished for him. "Or in this case, the mother and the uncle."

"It's not unusual to search and search and never find a body," Adam said.

I thought, *Yeah, if they happen to drown in the Atlantic fucking Ocean*. I got the distinct impression that he was trying to convince himself, not me. "And what about the kid's bedroom I found hidden in the basement? It's the single creepiest thing I've ever seen."

"Sure is." Noncommittal. I'd lost him somewhere along the way.

"But let's forget about the room for a second. Veronica Dentman left all that stuff behind on purpose, packed away back there and hidden like a dirty secret."

"That's not unusual," Adam said.

"Children's books, baseball hats, woolen knit gloves, sneakers, clothes, toys . . ."

"Everybody deals with death in their own way. For Veronica Dentman, maybe that was the only way she could deal with it—to get out quick and leave everything behind."

"Just seems a bit callous and insensitive. Strange."

Adam groaned. "What about Mom and Dad?"

I sipped some beer and said, "What about them? They had their little period after Kyle died, but they didn't erase his memory. There were still pictures in the house, still some of his things around. It took them almost a full year before they cleared out his bedroom, for Christ's sake." And thinking of this caused the vivid memory to rise through the murk again: finding Matchbox cars under Kyle's bed after his death. I blinked repeatedly and had to clear my throat with another sip of beer.

"That's exactly my point," said Adam. "Everyone deals with it in their own way. Mom and Dad dealt with it in their own solitary ways. Fuck, I became a cop because maybe I felt some subconscious drive to help those who can't help themselves."

I felt him staring at me, but I wouldn't look at him. I was still thinking of those Matchbox cars, and the safest place to look was my beer.

"You went and wrote a bunch of books about him," he said finally.

"One book," I said. "Just one book. And anyway, Alexander Sharpe wrote that one, not me."

I could see Adam's reflection smirking in the mirror behind the bar. He squeezed my shoulder. As if I were an accordion, I felt the wind wheeze out of me. "Little brother, I hate to break it to you, but you've written four novels, each one about someone who drowns or almost drowns or an apparition rising out of a lake. You mean to tell me you've been blind to what you've been doing this whole time?"

His words shook me to my core. This had never occurred to me in the slightest. But just hearing him say it enforced the truth of it, and suddenly, like a great explosion just over the horizon, I could see it. Even the goddamn *titles* professed a similar theme that had eluded me until this very moment: *The Ocean Serene*, *Silent River*, *Drowning Pool*, and *Water View*. Not to mention the title I'd scrawled on the cover sheet of the manuscript pages I'd sent to Holly before leaving London—*Blood Lake*.

Fuck, had it been so obvious to everyone else? Was I truly that blind? I bit my lower lip and refrained from admitting to Adam that the tentative title I'd given my most recent work—the outline for the story about Elijah Dentman and the dysfunctional family who'd lived in my house before me—was *Floating Staircase*.

"So you're saying you became a cop because of what happened to Kyle?" I said, anxious to change the subject. My voice shook the slightest bit, but I didn't think my brother, who'd had twice as many beers as I had, noticed.

Adam rolled one big shoulder. "Maybe. I don't know. I mean, I'd be surprised to think Kyle's death had nothing to do with it. That's like saying we're unaffected by all that goes on around us, all that happens to us. Our kid brother died; of course it had a significant impact on both our lives."

I wanted to ask him if he ever woke up in a pool of sweat, gasping for air and feeling like invisible ghost hands were dragging him down to a watery grave. I wanted to ask him if he'd ever sat up in bed in the middle of the night because he thought he heard footsteps in the hallway—footsteps that conveniently fell silent the moment you held your breath and waited for them, waited for them, waited for them. These were all the things that had tormented me as a child . . . but lately they'd resurfaced, coming back to haunt me like an old ghost, and I wondered what powers my new house held. What ghosts haunted those hallways?

The thought sent chills down my spine.

"Anyway," Adam went on, "from a professional investigator's point of view—that would be me, by the way—I'd say you jumped to some conclusions pretty quickly with that room you found in your basement."

"Yeah? What conclusions would those be?"

"For starters, you assume that room you found had been Elijah's bedroom just because you found his bed and all his stuff in it."

"And that's a poor assumption?"

"It's a fair assessment, but that doesn't make it fact. You've got to eliminate all other avenues before coming to one solid conclusion. One other avenue being that Veronica and the kid's uncle, David Dentman, moved all that stuff down there *after* the kid died. Just like Mom and Dad moved Kyle's stuff out into the garage." He rubbed his thumb around the rim of his pint glass. "And you guys don't have a garage."

"Shit," I said. For the second time in less than five minutes, Adam was easily poking holes in my sense of reality. And the bastard was drunker than I was. "I guess you got a point. I hadn't thought of that." There was a rapidly deflating balloon in my stomach. The excitement I'd felt in writing about the make-believe Dentman family seemed to blacken and shrivel, and I feared the fog of writer's block would roll back in and cover up the city.

"Still . . ." Adam's voice trailed off.

"What?"

"Well," he said and proceeded with what I perceived to be, even in his inebriated state, careful steps, "it's just that even if that wasn't the kid's bedroom, one question still remains."

"What's that?"

"What was that room used for in the first place?"

I let this sink in. Maybe we both did, because Adam didn't say anything for several drawn-out seconds.

"Fellas," Tooey said, sweeping past the bar and winking at us like a conspirator. "We doin' okay?"

I raised a hand at him. "Doing fine, thanks."

Behind us, someone brought up a Johnny Cash tune on the jukebox.

"I want to confess something," I said after too much silence had passed between us. I told Adam about how I'd thrown away my old notebooks, the ones with my early writings about Kyle, after we moved to London. "I didn't fully understand why at the time, but I think I do now." I waited for Adam to say something, to at least ask why I had finally come to this realization, but he didn't say a word. Instead, I cleared my throat and said, "It was because I felt horrible about what happened between us after Mom's funeral. I acted poorly, and it wasn't fair to you or Beth. Or even Jodie."

He was looking intently at his beer. "Or yourself, I'd imagine."

"I threw those notebooks away because I thought it would finally put the past to rest."

"And did it?"

My face felt red and hot, like a glowing ember. I glanced at my reflection in the mirror behind the bar just to make sure waves of heat weren't rising off my scalp.

"Did it?" Adam repeated.

"I hate saying it."

"Why?"

"Because it did. I'm almost disgusted to say it, but I hardly thought about Kyle at all in London. It was like none of it ever happened. I even remember reading in the papers about a little girl who'd drowned in Highgate Ponds, and as I'm reading it I thought, *Oh yeah, that happened to Kyle. I forgot.*" I rubbed beer-sticky fingers over my eyes. "God, I sound horrendous."

"You're just trying to find a middle ground," Adam said, finishing his beer. "The answer's not to condemn yourself and live with the grief, but it's not to totally erase it from your memory, either." He checked his watch. "We should get going. It's late."

I almost grabbed his wrist and asked him the one remaining question that was on my mind—that had been on my mind for many days now: *Do you believe in ghosts?* But before I could react, the absurdity of it struck me like a hammer, and I decided to keep my inquiry to myself.

After all, everyone knows where dead people go: in the ground.

When I got home that evening, Jodie was already asleep in our bed. The house was freezing, so I covered her up with an extra blanket and kissed the side of her face. She stirred and hummed. One of her hands slipped out from beneath the covers and found my arm. She squeezed it.

"Didn't mean to wake you," I whispered, sitting on the edge of the bed.

"Hmmm," she breathed sleepily. "It's all right. Are you coming to bed?"

"Not yet."

"Do you want to hear something funny?"

"Sure," I said, still whispering.

"Just before you came home I got up to go to the bathroom."

"You're right," I said, rubbing the topside of her hand. "That's a riot."

"No," Jodie said. "Listen."

"I'm listening."

"I went to the bathroom and turned on the light and had to, you know, squint because the light was so bright and I'd just been asleep. You know what I mean?"

"Yes," I said.

"So I was squinting in the light and looking at the mirror, and I saw my reflection. And you know what? I wasn't me." Her face, floating on the white mound of her pillow, looked ghostly and pale like the moon. "Do you know who I was?"

"Who?"

"You," Jodie said. "I was you. Only for a split second. But I was you."

I bent and kissed her forehead. She felt very warm. "You were dreaming," I told her.

"No," she said, "I wasn't. I was awake. What do you think it means?"

"I don't know," I said, tucking the blankets in all around her.

Jodie rolled on her side, and I caught the hint of a smile on her lips. "Neither do I," she said, her eyes fluttering closed. "I guess that's the beauty of the mystery."

I kissed her a third time, then slipped into the hallway to examine the thermostat. It still registered sixty-eight degrees, although it felt more like forty-five in the bedroom. I could even see my breath.

"This is fucking ridiculous."

A glow caught my attention in the office across the hall from the bedroom. I poked my head in and flipped on the light switch. Jodie had assembled her desk against one wall, on which sat a computer monitor radiating waves of amethystine light, a prehistoric printer, and a collection of jazz CDs. The entire wall behind the desk was covered in framed awards, diplomas, a Who's Who Among Students in America, an Outstanding Woman of the Year plaque from her undergraduate alma mater. On the floor, like a tiny city in the process of existing, stood towers of psychology textbooks and reams of photocopied papers, charts, and graphs networked with multicolored lightning bolts. I felt like a heel, having neglected cleaning this room out so Jodie had done it herself.

Shivering, I went downstairs. Because of our struggle with the temperamental and unreliable furnace, I'd taken to chopping firewood in the backyard, which we used almost around the clock in the living room fireplace. I grabbed a couple of fresh logs from the front porch and tossed them into the fireplace.

In about five minutes I had a pretty healthy fire going. I retrieved a bottle of Chivas from our sad little liquor cabinet in the main hallway and poured myself a finger into a rocks glass. I sat on the floor with my back against the couch and watched the fire dance in the hearth. The whiskey burned going down and blossomed into comfortable warmth in my toes.

I spent over an hour in front of the hearth watching the fire dwindle and finally die while I revisited my conversation with Adam at Tooey's bar. I'd freely told him how I'd forgotten about Kyle after the move to London and how miserable I now felt about having been able to do it. That was true. But returning to the States and moving to Westlake—moving into this old house with all its whispers and secrets and cold hands on my chest in the night—had brought everything right back to me. If the little London flat had been a sanctum, I was now in the well, struggling to keep my head above the surface. And what frightened me was that I wasn't completely sure I was being haunted by my memories of Kyle. What frightened me was the possibility that maybe something else was working at me, chipping away like a stonecutter, breaking me down.

I thought of Elijah Dentman and how they'd never recovered his body from that silent, dark water. Which meant he was still down there somewhere: a whitish, bloated corpse whose skin had been picked over by fish and whose eyes had sunken into the recesses of his skull. In my mind's eye I saw blackened fingertips from which the bones poked through and greenish hair waving like kelp off the dome of a gleaming skull in the silt.

Fuck, I thought.

I got up and headed to the liquor cabinet where I replaced the bottle of Chivas, then turned for the stairs.

Something metallic clanked and reverberated in the belly of the house, like someone deliberately striking a wrench to a frozen metal pipe.

I stopped halfway up the stairs, my pulse suddenly picking up tempo.

There issued a second clanking noise, this one startlingly crisp and issuing straight up one of the heat vents. A distant whistle followed, and it reminded me of how a fire engine sounds when it's still just a bit too far away. Then the sound slowly scaled louder and louder until it became a steady, resonant hum.

I crept down the stairs and got on my hands and knees in the foyer, putting my face very close to the floor vent. I could feel no heat coming up, although it certainly sounded like the furnace had just kicked on. That peculiar, continual humming . . .

It sounded like a voice.

Some fundamental part of my soul responsible for animal insight fired a flare up and over the bow. I pushed one ear against the vent and listened more closely—an indefinite *rheeee* sound behind which I could just barely make out faint whispering—then the furnace shuddered and died. The winding down of its mechanics was like the fading laughter in a crowded auditorium. My ear still pressed to the metal grate, I hadn't realized I'd been holding my breath until now. I exhaled in a trembling wheeze, and a moment later, I thought I heard someone on the other side of the heating vent breathe back.

I bolted upright, my heart crashing like a wild animal against the constraint of my ribs.

In less than ten seconds I was standing at the top of the basement stairs, peering down into that infinite, inky darkness, my hand sweating on the doorknob. "Enough now," I said, my voice hardly as demonstrative as I would have liked. "This has to stop."

I waited for a moment, too afraid to admit to myself that I was waiting—and fearing—some sort of response to rise out of the darkness: a furtive shuffling noise or even a pair of glowing eyes to open at the bottom of the stairwell. But nothing happened.

Cold, I went to bed.

CHAPTER FOURTEEN

"I want to take some of Elijah's stuff back to his mother," I said.

It was a bright January morning, the smell of mesquite in the air. Adam and I were walking the perimeter of the lake, steaming Styrofoam cups of coffee in our hands. Up ahead, Jacob and Madison darted in and out of trees, flinging clumps of muddy snow at each other. Their laughter was like church bells. It was warmer than it had been over the past few weeks, but the ice on the lake still looked thick and permanent. The newly cleared sky brought into sharp relief the chain of mountains at the horizon.

Adam sipped his coffee, then wiped his mouth with the back of his hand. "Why?" He looked at the frozen lake and the fence of black pines at the opposite end. His eyes were the color of steel and looked very sober. A contrail of vapor wafted out from between his chapped lips.

"It's hard to explain," I said. "I just feel like it's something I'm supposed to do. For me and maybe for the kid's mother, too."

He hit me with a sharp look.

I quickly added, "It's about finding that middle ground, remember? The happy medium that we talked about at Tooey's bar?"

"Why are you even telling me this?"

"Because I'm assuming you know where Veronica Dentman lives now. Or, being a cop, you could at least find out for me."

His laughter burst like a firecracker.

"What? So now I'm an asshole for wanting to do something I feel is right?"

"We've been over this. Veronica Dentman left that stuff behind for a reason. Whether you approve of her decision or not, that quite frankly doesn't matter. I thought you said you called a junk service to come get that stuff, anyway."

"They won't be around for another week yet," I said, but that was a lie. This morning I'd called Allegheny Pickup and Removal and cancelled my order. I hadn't told Jodie, and I certainly wasn't going to tell Adam . . . but after last night and upon reflection of everything else that had been going on since we'd moved to Westlake, I felt having random strangers come to collect and quite possibly destroy all of Elijah's belongings wasn't supposed to happen.

"I think this is a bad idea."

"You're wrong."

"I'm not. I think you're crossing a line, messing with other people's lives. That woman lost her son last summer. She knew damn well what she was doing when she left those boxes behind."

"Well, see, that's just it," I countered. "I don't think she did. I mean, maybe at the time it was the best way for her to cope, but I think now, after some time has passed, she'd be happy to get her son's stuff back."

"Who are you, Dr. Phil?"

"I'm being serious. What if she regrets leaving that stuff behind? What if it was all totally reactionary, and now she hates herself for it?"

"Even if that's the case, why do you care?"

Because something in the house wanted me to find that room, I almost said. *Something in the house wanted me to find that stuff for a reason.*

We reached a clearing in the woods beside the cusp of the lake. I could see the Steins' house opposite us beyond the rocky crags and up through the naked gray trees. We sat down on a tree stump that was large enough to accommodate the two of us while Jacob and Madison bounded farther through the field, snow crumbling off their boots and arcing off their heels as they struggled to run.

Adam offered me a cigarette, which I accepted. He popped one into his mouth, then balled up the empty packet and tossed it into a tin trash can that was conveniently nailed to the bole of a nearby tree.

I hadn't answered Adam's question, and it hung in the air between us like some mutual embarrassment.

"Listen," Adam said eventually. "What do you do if you show up to that poor woman's house, your car loaded with her dead son's toys, and she breaks down on you? What if she just collapses at your feet, sobbing her eyes out? You think that will make you feel better? You think it'll be for *her* benefit?"

"You don't understand."

"I understand perfectly. This isn't about the fucking Dentman kid at all."

"Then what is it?"

Adam turned away. "Forget it."

"No," I said. "I want you to tell me."

"Goddamn it, man. Don't you see? You've come to another classic impasse in your life, and in typical Travis Glasgow fashion you're willing to do or say whatever you want as long as it makes you feel better for the time being, regardless of anyone else's feelings."

He would have hurt me less if he'd cracked me across the jaw. I think he realized this, too, because his gaze lingered on me a millisecond too long, and before he looked away, I saw his expression begin to soften.

I tossed the cigarette on the ground and stood.

"Fuck," Adam groaned. "I'm sorry. That came out harsher than I'd intended."

"It came out, all right." For some reason my hands started shaking. I stuffed them into my pockets to hide them.

"Hate me if you want, but I can't keep my mouth shut if I see you heading for harm."

"Fuck all, man. You think you're this great fucking fortification against all the horrors of this world, that you're burdened with being some goddamn martyr because you're my older brother. In case you hadn't noticed, I'm not thirteen anymore. I can take care of myself."

"Cut it out, will you?" Adam sounded so goddamn calm I wanted to belt him across the cheek. "The world's not against you. Neither am I. This whole woe-is-me thing ran its course years ago."

Something vital snapped inside me. I whirled around. "You're a piece of shit—you know that? You shut me out when we were younger because of what happened with Kyle, and every time you disagree with me you throw those same stones right back at me. You're a prick, Adam."

He jumped off the tree stump with a fierceness that I would have thought beyond him. I hated myself for flinching and taking an involuntary step back.

"I never shut you out, and I never blamed you for Kyle's death," he said. "I blamed you for the asshole you became after his death."

"You had no idea what I went through—"

"I was a fucking kid, too. You had no idea what *I* went through." Those steely eyes were locked on mine, and I hated that I couldn't look away. I hated that he was the stronger one in that instant and probably for the bulk of our lives. "I lost a brother, too, you dumb fuck."

The shaking in my hands had negotiated up my arms. I opened my mouth to say something—anything—but I was only able to offer a weak and uncontrolled grunt. An instant later, Adam doubled, then trebled in my vision.

"Christ," Adam said and slung an arm around my neck. He kissed the side of my head.

"Get off me," I muttered, but I didn't mean it.

"You're my brother. You're all I've got."

"You've got Beth," I countered. Then I nodded toward his kids who were slugging it out in a snowbank, their voices rising to ear-piercing cries. "And you've got those two sweethearts."

Adam chuckled as Madison fell backward on her ass in the drift. "Hell," he said, arm still around my neck. "I guess there's a chance you might even be right."

He stopped by the house later that evening with an address scrawled on a sheet of lined notebook paper.

CHAPTER FIFTEEN

Sometime during the night I was awakened by the sound of bare feet padding along the upstairs hallway. Dazed, I shook myself out of bed, just partially conscious of Jodie's slumbering body beside mine, and stepped into the hallway, my eyes still fuzzy with sleep. I groped for the light switch, but it had apparently disappeared. Listening, I could hear the sound of the bare feet moving swiftly down the stairs.

For a long-drawn-out moment, I did not move. I couldn't tell if I was fully awake, still dreaming, or caught in some abstract stasis of half sleep. My skin felt frozen while my insides were burning up as if with the onset of fever. Like a ghost, I crossed to the second-floor balcony and peered down into the foyer. At first I saw nothing. The longer I stared, I saw what appeared to be a small child standing motionless at the bottom of the staircase against one wall. Without pause, I turned and began moving down the stairs, one hand snaking along the banister in the darkness for support.

But when I reached the bottom of the stairs, the child had vanished. Moonlight pooled in through the large foyer windows and painted glowing blue panels on the carpet. I stood there, my body shivering yet covered in a tacky film of sweat, unable to decide what I should do next.

"Elijah . . . ?" It was only a whisper—not even a whisper, as my constricted throat was incapable of creating such a sound as forceful as a whisper at the moment—and the ghost boy did not acknowledge me.

I thought I heard something behind me. I turned. For a split second I forgot where I was. Oddly serene, I continued down the hallway searching for a boy I knew was not there. Everything appeared dramatically overemphasized—my own breathing, the creaks and pops in the floorboards, the sound of my bare feet transitioning from the sticky hardwood to the carpeted front hall. Beneath my feet the carpet felt overly fibrous, almost sharp. My footsteps shushed along.

There is clarity here, I thought, not certain as to what it actually meant.

The hallway emptied out into the living room.

I thought, *Reality is a state of mind, just like dreaming, just like fiction. Everything is fiction. The trick is to grab on to something—to hold on to it for all you're worth—until you're able to regain some semblance of normalcy again.*

I thought, *Find an anchor.*

This was where I stopped, right there in the center of the living room, cold and alone and not quite sure what the hell I was doing. I could see the bulbous piercing eye of the moon through one of the windows; I could feel the light from the streetlamps needling against my retinas. I thought I heard the basement door open at the other end of the house . . . thought I heard those same small, bare feet taking the steps quickly, two at a time, descending into that freezing, forgotten darkness . . .

But I did not move.

I was done chasing ghosts.

PART THREE:

THE OCEAN SERENE

CHAPTER SIXTEEN

Veronica Dentman lived in a nondescript Maryland hamlet that straddled some ambiguous demarcation between Cumberland and the Potomac Highlands of West Virginia, where the nightly television news filtered in from a station in Pittsburgh.

For much of my journey I followed a nameless and undisciplined ribbon of roadway that wound through dense, white-powdered forests and an undulating countryside. I'd spent the morning fueling my body with black coffee and smoked cigarette after cigarette in assembly-line fashion: paltry attempts to calm my jitterbugging nerves. Also, I'd awoken with a throbbing headache and weakness throughout my muscles, which was a sure sign I was coming down with something. Getting out into the wilderness and away from the confines of the house did me some good, but I could feel nervousness roiling around at the center of my guts like a parasite.

Beside me on the passenger seat was a single cardboard box of items I'd carefully selected from Elijah's room to return to his mother. Tucked between both seats were several different road maps of western Maryland, a number of which did not even have Veronica's small town of West Cumberland listed.

I anticipated the drive to take roughly an hour—not just from what Adam told me, but from the estimated distance between West Cumberland and Westlake on one of the maps—but near the end of my journey, I goofed up on some of the narrower, wooded back roads, confusing and twisting myself around like the dial on a compass, clocking unnecessary time to my travels. I'd heard stories of people even in this day and age getting lost in the woods, never to be seen alive again. Or seen at all, for that matter. Suffice it to say, I was more accustomed to traffic lights and road signs than long tracks of snow-packed dirt roads and evergreens for as far as it was possible to see.

After about twenty minutes of backtracking, I maneuvered the Honda through the empty, unkempt streets of a forgotten mountain community. It was not at all what I'd expected. While Westlake was tidy and warm and clean and, above all, a little too Norman

Rockwell, this place looked like Westlake's degenerate brother. The houses here—little more than double-wide trailers—were packed together like boxcars at a depot. They were small and pitiful, mismatched in color, with missing shutters and peeling siding. Some had old automobile tires nailed to the roof. Aluminum laundry carousels sprung up out of yards like miniature electrical towers and shone dully in the sun.

All the houses were fenced in, though not with the white picket style so common in Westlake: these yards were encased in rusted, chain-link prisons, vaguely reminiscent of the wire meshwork found in the windowpanes of mental institutions. Beside one front door stood the remnants of an immense television antenna, like some rib cage picked clean by vultures. Even the snow looked dirty.

After a few more minutes of hapless navigation, I located Veronica's street (which was not an easy task since the street sign had been knocked at a right angle and jutted out into the roadway like the arm of a tollbooth). I hooked a right (giving the tollbooth arm a wide berth) and peered through the windshield to catch the first house number I could. This, too, was not an easy task: some of the homes had those wrought iron numbers tacked beside the front door and half shaded beneath a crumbling portico while others had numbers nailed to the wooden mailbox post, the only evidence of their existence in the numeral-shaped discoloration on the wood itself.

The street dead-ended at the base of a forested foothill. I hadn't caught sight of Veronica's address and wondered if perhaps Adam had gotten the wrong number. I dropped the car in reverse and retraced my route just to make sure, all too conscious of the kinks in the blinds and the sets of eyes watching me from darkened windows. Once again I came to the forested dead end and stopped the car. Either Adam had given me the wrong address, or a tornado had relocated Veronica's house.

But wait. I leaned over the steering wheel and gazed out the windshield. The glass had fogged up in my exasperation, so I hit the defogger and waited a couple of seconds as the breath blossoms dematerialized on the glass. I'd missed it the first time around but could see it now: a rutted dirt path cleared of snow, running straight up the hillside through the pines.

I eased off the brake and coasted forward, the low-hanging branches of the pines thwapping against the hood of the car. The forestry was so impenetrable there was hardly any snow on the ground. I followed the road to the top of the hill where a shallow clearing opened up all around me.

At its center was a modular home, significantly larger than the double-wide trailers that preceded it along the avenue, but it did not look to be in much better shape. Like the rest of the residences of West Cumberland, Veronica's home looked as if it had been dropped from some great height only to crash firmly down in this yard of dead and frozen weeds, hideously large novelty sunflowers, and dilapidated lawn furniture. There was an old tractor tire near the front of the house posing as a planter for a skeletal, flowerless shrub. A pyramid of wire mesh cages—crab pots or rabbit traps—stood against the left side of the house, stiffened hunks of colorless bait still harnessed within.

I was breathing heavy, fogging up the windows again.

I shut the car off, grabbed the box from the passenger seat, and got out. Movement off to my right caught my attention, and I jerked my head toward the side of the house where I was somewhat relieved to find an umbrella-shaped clothes wheel shaking in the wind. In the distance, an unfriendly dog was anxious to be heard.

I mounted the front porch, the boards brittle and gaping with splintered holes hungry to bite at my ankles, and knocked on the frame of the outer screen door.

Waited. Waited for an eternity. I couldn't hear any movement inside. Also, there weren't any cars parked anywhere.

The front door opened, leaving only the dirty screen door between us. It was Veronica Dentman—I was certain of it—although she looked nothing like

I thought she would. She was small, disconcertingly thin, with large dark eyes and choppy black hair. She was maybe thirty-eight, forty at best, but the sallow features and emptiness in her gaze made her look much, much older.

Those large roving eyes took me in.

I waited for her to say something, but she only stared at me. "Miss, uh . . . Veronica Dentman?"

Her eyebrows came together. "Who're you?" The words came out sharp and quick, almost mashed together. I caught a glimpse of bad teeth.

"I'm real sorry to disturb you, ma'am. My name's Travis Glasgow. My wife and I moved into your old house in Westlake."

"Was my father's house." Her gaze shifted toward the box in my arms. I could see in the slight softening of her features that she knew what was inside. Then she stared at me, her piercing black orbs boring into me through the moss-discolored screen.

"I'm sorry," I said again. I could think of nothing else to say. "I didn't mean to intrude."

Veronica pushed the screen door open several inches; the squeal of its hinges sounded like a cat being boiled alive. "Those my boy's things in that box?"

"Yes, ma'am."

Those searchlight eyes addressed me again, taking in every nuance of me as if to catalogue it for later reference. Just when I became certain she'd tell me to get the hell off her property, she pushed the screen door open farther and motioned me inside.

The place was small and cramped, furnished in a tawny shag carpet straight from 1975 and mismatched furniture that hung around like strangers forced together in a waiting room. The walls were almost completely barren, and the windows had their curtains drawn. I could faintly smell coffee brewing from the kitchen nook. The whole interior was dimly lit with wood-paneled walls, and something about it reminded me of a church confessional.

"I didn't think I was going to find the place," I commented, trying to sound conversational.

"Who sent you here?"

The question caught me off guard. I stammered, "Uh, no one."

"Why are you here?"

"To bring this to you." The box was growing heavier and heavier in my arms. I shifted it uncomfortably.

"Set it on the table," she said, motioning in the general vicinity of a circular card table by the front door.

I set the box down on top of several envelopes addressed to David Dentman. Until just then, it hadn't occurred to me that she might still live with her brother.

Stuffing my hands into the too-tight pockets of

my jeans, I faced Veronica. She was unhealthily thin to the point where it looked like her drab little housedress (which looked homemade) was still on its hanger. Her arms were long and emaciated; fat blue veins were all too visible beneath her skin. She'd tucked her ratty hair behind her ears when I wasn't looking, and I could see now the railroad scar that began high up in her hairline, dipped along her left temple, and hooked around underneath her left ear.

It was all I could do to find my voice. "I didn't know what to do with them. The boxes, I mean. There were so many, and I couldn't just get rid of them. And anyway, I thought you might . . . maybe . . . I'm sorry for your loss."

"David put them down in the room, didn't he? Behind the wall?"

"Yes," I said. "In the basement. What . . . what *is* that room?"

In the kitchen something sizzled, and I could smell the coffee overpercolating.

Veronica didn't say a word. She just pivoted, barefooted, and practically floated like a ghost out of the room and into the kitchen.

I held my breath and heard the coffeepot rattle and cupboards opening and closing, their hinges just as vocal as the screen door's. In her absence I scanned the rest of the room. The whole place had the smell, the feeling, of someone who'd lost a child: that closed-off-from-the-world stagnancy, like uncharged batteries. But there was something else, too . . . something that took me more than just a few seconds to work out. And then I suddenly knew what it was. There was a complete lack of any personal effects. No photos, no magazines, no books, no bric-a-brac. The only thing in the entire room that didn't serve a strictly functional purpose was the television, which was muted and tuned to QVC.

Veronica returned, cupping a mug of steaming black coffee between her hands like a nun carrying the Holy Eucharist. Wordlessly, she extended it to me.

"Thank you," I said, aware that I was talking just a hair above a whisper. As if to speak any louder would send this fragile creature scurrying for cover.

"Do you want something from me?" she said. "Is that why you're here?"

"No. I told you, I just wanted to bring back some of Elijah's things."

She cringed at the sound of his name.

"I haven't gotten rid of anything," I went on. "All that stuff is still in the basement. My wife wants me to get rid of it, but I came to make sure you didn't want it back."

"I don't want to talk about that stuff."

"Okay."

Somewhere out in the front yard I could hear a vehicle approaching. Veronica whipped her head toward the door. The engine died and I heard a car door slam. When she turned to me, she looked like someone who'd just witnessed a horrible car accident.

"Is that David?" I said. "Your brother?"

"You shouldn't have come here."

"I didn't mean to upset you."

"It's not good that you're here." She grabbed the coffee cup from me, sloshing thick brown sludge onto my hand and scorching the skin. "You shouldn't be here."

The front door opened. I hadn't realized just how gloomy the house was until the sun broke in like the finger of God. I winced. The figure that paused in the doorframe was hulking and broad-shouldered, the silhouette of a lumberjack or a walking cement truck.

I nodded once compendiously in the man's immediate direction.

David Dentman entered the house, allowing the screen door to slam against the frame behind him. He was light skinned and broad featured, with sandy-colored hair and very clear, somber eyes, the color of which I'd never seen. He wore a chambray work shirt cuffed to the elbows, exposing a pair of sunburned arms that could have been pythons sliding into his sleeves. "What's this?" he asked no one in particular.

"My name's Travis Glasgow," I said, stumbling

over my words. I was sweating profusely, only partially
due to the fever I knew was working its way through me.
"My wife and I moved into your old house in Westlake."

"Glasgow," he repeated, tasting the name. One
of his big catcher's mitt hands disappeared behind his
back to dig around in the rear pocket of his dungarees.

For one heart-stopping second I was sure he was
going to produce a knife and take a swing at my face.
Instead, he fished out a worn leather wallet nearly as
thick as a paperback novel and tossed it on the table
beside the cardboard box.

"House belonged to my father," he said matter-of-
factly. Same as his sister had. "There something I can
help you with, Mr. Glasgow? You come all this way
from Westlake?"

"I was just bringing by some things."

Dentman swiveled around to the cardboard box.
He seemed to recognize it immediately.

Perhaps he had been the one to pack up the boy's
belongings after his death. Too easily I could picture
those immense, steel-banded arms cramming those
boxes full of stuffed animals. The image should have
been comical, but thinking of it now while standing
in this house, I found it utterly terrifying.

"You a cop?"

"Do I look like a cop?"

"Strohman send you here?"

"Who's Strohman?"

Dentman advanced toward the box, popped open the lid, and peered inside. He chewed on his lower lip as he did so. The dim light in the house struck him then in just the right fashion, causing the sheen of beard stubble at his chin and neck to glitter briefly. Disinterestedly, he faced me. "The cops send you out here?"

"Of course not. I found that stuff in the basement and thought I'd bring it by. I guess that was a mistake," I added after swallowing what felt like a chunk of granite.

"You bought the house as is."

"I beg your pardon?"

"The house. Bank should have told you. Anything in there's yours now, not ours."

"You misunderstand. I'm not here to complain. I just wanted to—"

"Glasgow's a cop," he said. "I know that name."

"I'm not a cop. You're thinking of Adam Glasgow who lived across the street from you. He's a cop and he's my brother."

"He send you out here?"

"No," I insisted. My apprehension was quickly being replaced by anger. "Listen, David, I just wanted—"

"I think *you* better listen," David said, taking a step toward me. Instantly, I felt my bowels clench. "My sister and me moved here to get away from what happened in Westlake. We sure as hell don't need nobody coming around reminding us about it. You understand?"

"I understand that you've got me pegged completely wrong."

He jabbed a finger at me, so close to my face I could almost count the hairs on his knuckles. "You're standing in my house right now, friend. Uninvited, far as I'm concerned. You best consider that next time you want to crack wise." He toed the screen door open with his boot. "Think it's time for you to go. What do you say?"

As I headed for the door, I cast a look over my shoulder at Veronica. She'd been silent the whole time, and I hoped I could read her expression to help explain this bizarre confrontation. But Veronica was no longer there, most likely having retreated into another room while I wondered whether or not her brother was going to box my eyes shut.

"Look," I said to David, pausing on the other side of the door. "I'm sorry. I didn't mean anything by it. I swear."

Except for slamming the door in my face, David Dentman offered no response.

CHAPTER SEVENTEEN

The fever came, shuddering and without mercy, and I spent the next two days in a web of mind gauze. My dreams—what dreams I could remember—were erratic and paranoid, shot by a director on a bad acid trip.

In one, I was running down a dark, narrow corridor, the walls and floor and ceiling tightening up the farther I ran, until I had to drop to my hands and knees and crawl like an infant. I crawled until I came to a tiny door, like something out of *Alice in Wonderland*. The door appeared to be comprised of many small wooden blocks of varying colors, woven together like bamboo stalks in a raft.

I pushed the door open and squeezed through the opening. As if the doorway were a living thing, I felt it constrict around my rib cage. Ahead of me, the darkness shifted. Shapes—or the idea of shapes—moved closer to me, then farther away, tauntingly alternating their distance. A light illuminated a little antechamber. Directly in front of me, nestled in a web of tree branches, dead leaves, and old sodden newspapers, were four hairless, sightless critters, grayish in color like a waterlogged corpse, moving only slightly.

I was trapped between walls, between realities, like the hidden bedroom in the basement. *There is clarity here.* I smelled something sickeningly sweet and thought of chamomile tea. Then, from behind me, I heard a great rushing, rumbling sound and felt the walls all around me beginning to quake. In that blind, frantic instant, the corridor in which I was trapped filled with cold water, so cold it burned my skin. And I drowned.

In another dream I was shivering and wet, a towel draped around my shoulders like a cape, with Detective Wren asking me what happened that night by the river. Behind him in the creeping dawn, uniformed police officers patrolled the wooded paths and blocked the area off with yellow tape. I heard the boats moaning in their moorings and smelled the diesel exhaust breathing in off the bay.

Suddenly, Detective Wren's arms were burdened with paperback novels. He dumped them on a table that instantly materialized between us, and we were in an interrogation room, with greenish fluorescent lights fizzing and colorless cinder block walls.

—These your books? he asked. You write these books?

I nodded.

—How'd you come up with this stuff?

I said I didn't know.

—Everything you wrote in these books happened last night at the river, said the detective. He was a big guy with oily skin and sharp, soul-searching eyes. Everything you wrote down in these books happened just like it did by the river, boy, Detective Wren went on, which makes me think this thing, see, maybe this thing was planned.

I sobbed and said I didn't do it on purpose.

Detective Wren looked at me with disgust. Then his face slackened and purpled, and his eyes peeled away and readjusted themselves at either side of his rapidly narrowing head. His arms retreated up the sleeves of his rumpled suit, and his trousers loosened around his waist until they dropped straight to the floor. What lay exposed were not legs but the tapered, intestinal body of an eel. I watched in horror as Detective Wren slithered out of his suit, an enormous man-sized eel that snaked its way down the muddy embankment before splashing into the dark river. It raised a dorsal fin like a shark and zigzagged through the inky tide.

Then David Dentman was glaring at me, one hand palming the side of my head as he repeatedly slammed my skull down on the steps of the floating staircase.

I awoke, my throat rusty and my flesh sticky with sweat, with Jodie's cool hand on my forehead smoothing back my sodden hair. There was a sunset burning on the horizon, and through the bedroom windows, the trees looked like they were on fire. I stared at the side of the street where Jodie stood talking with Beth in the snow. Something cramped up inside me. Before I could scream, the cool hand withdrew from my forehead.

Dreams . . .

Then something about a castle of cardboard boxes, of boating piers stacked one on top of the other until they formed a ladder straight into the heavens. At one point I dreamt I was married to a woman with a monster growing in her belly, and my name was Alan, and we lived by our own special lake in a different part of the country. Even in this dream, I could feel the heat of imaginary summer on my back and shoulders, pasting the shirt to my body and causing my skin to practically char and sizzle. Confused fever dreams.

There was one moment in my dream when I crept from my bed and floated down the hallway. Downstairs I could hear the faint phantom sound of someone talking in a low voice. I glided across the landing and gripped the banister with both hands. I peeked over the side. I could make out only a fleeing shadow against one wall. So I turned and floated down the stairs to the foyer. There, the voice became slightly more audible, and I knew with intuitive certainty that it was Jodie.

I floated into the living room. Even in the dream I had the detached feeling associated with feverish hallucinations. My feet hardly touched the carpet; my head was a helium balloon. A brutal wind whipped about the living room and bullied the curtains over the front windows, and I wondered only vaguely where it was coming from. From my vantage I could see the back of Jodie's head as she sat on the sofa. I went to her, listening to her words . . . and realized she wasn't actually talking; she was singing softly and tenderly and lovingly and handsomely. It was the way my mother used to sing to me when I was a child:

> *A, you're adorable*
> *B, you're so beautiful*
> *C, you're a child so full of charms*
> *D, you're delightful*
> *E, you're exciting*
> *F, you're a feather in my arms . . .*

I placed a hand on her shoulder. Her voice stopped cold. I looked down at her lap . . . where the undeniable image of a young boy cradled in my wife's arms quickly blinked out of existence.

—Where'd he go? I asked.

—He'll be back, Jodie said quietly . . . and began humming.

—Was he . . . ? I began.

—Yes, she said. It's him.

—I thought it might be.

Her humming was soothing.

—You sound so beautiful, I told her.

This made her smile: I could feel it radiate from her and did not need to see it.

—Thank you, she said.

—Too bad I'm dreaming, I said.

—No, Jodie said. You're not.

CHAPTER EIGHTEEN

When you withdraw from the world, you find that the world withdraws from you, too. Then all that's left is the Grayness, the Void, and this is where you remain. Like a cancerous cell. Like a cut of tissue, diseased, in a Petri dish. You glance down and there it is: this gaping gray hole in the center of your being. And as you stand there and stare into it, all you see is yourself staring back.

I was you, Jodie said. *Isn't that funny?*

You have been set aside, replaced by air, by molecules, by particles of electric light. You have been erased, removed. There is almost a popping sound on the heels of your disappearance as these molecules filter into the space you occupied only one millisecond beforehand, covering up both space and time and eradicating the whole memory of your human existence. You are no longer.

Isn't that funny?

When you withdraw from the world, you find that you were never really there—that you were never really in the world—because nature does not know extinction, and if you no longer exist, that must mean you never existed in the first place.

I returned to the land of the living on a Wednesday. The house was quiet and Jodie was at the college. Another snowstorm had come and buried the town, and the distant pines looked like pointy white witches' hats.

The house was freezing. The thermostat promised it was a steady sixty-eight degrees, but I knew better than to trust it. My illness had left me drained and cotton headed, and my mouth tasted like an ashtray, so I went to the kitchen and put a pot of coffee on the stove.

By the time I'd finished my second cup, I was feeling better and decided that I would head over to the Steins' to ask them about the Dentmans. After my visit to Veronica and David's house in West Cumberland on Sunday, it was obvious that something was terribly, terribly wrong with that family. The bizarre descriptions I'd given the make-believe Dentman family in my notebooks had not even lived up to the real thing. Adam had told me all he knew about them, but that wasn't enough. The Steins had been their next-door neighbors; surely they must have some insight into the family. I was hungry to find out as much about them as I could, not just for the sake of my own writing but to satisfy my increasing curiosity.

The story I was laying out in my notebooks depicted a troubled young boy held captive in a basement dungeon by his mentally disturbed mother and an uncle who found a sick pleasure in physically hurting the child. When the child becomes old enough to speak his mind, the uncle—my David Dentman character who, for the sake of continuity, retained his real-life counterpart's name—knows something must be done, so he murders the boy and makes it look like an accident. That was about as far as I'd gotten, having already filled up three notebooks with my frantic scribbling, but I wondered just how on the mark I'd been about them . . .

The telephone rang. The voice on the other end was as old and rough as an ancient potato sack. "Is this Travis Glasgow?"

"It is. Who's this?"

"Well, Mr. Glasgow, my name's Earl Parsons, and I suppose I'm Westlake's answer to Woodward and Bernstein. I got a phone call from Sheila Brookner—what she called a tip, so to speak—and she said we had ourselves a celebrity in our midst."

"Sheila Brookner?" I intoned. Then it occurred to me. "Oh." She was the librarian who'd let me into the archived newspaper room. For one crazy moment I thought this guy was calling about the articles I tore out of the papers.

"She said you came by the library doing some research for a new book or something like that."

"Hmmm. Something like that." I considered his Woodward and Bernstein comment, then said, "You're a reporter."

Earl Parsons laughed—the sound of a stubborn old tractor trying to start up in cold weather. "Well, now, you say it like that and you'll give me a swelled head. I'm actually a retired mill worker, but I do much of the freelance writing for *The Muledeer*, seeing how the town's so small. I'm a bit embarrassed to admit that my contemporaries on the paper are made up mostly of journalism students from the college."

"What can I do for you?"

"It's not often we get someone famous like yourself coming to live in Westlake." Another rumbling chuckle. "Never, actually."

"I think you use the word *famous* too generously. I've written a few horror novels."

"One of which I'm reading right now," Earl said, perhaps trying to impress me, although I didn't think he was lying. "Creepy stuff, for sure."

"They're certainly creepy," I said.

"I'd like to write up a nice human interest piece

on you, if you'd let me. You moving out here's probably the biggest news since Dolly Murphy won the pie eating contest last fall."

I thought of Elijah Dentman drowning in the lake behind my house and how that had surely been bigger news but didn't say anything.

"Understand I don't mean to be a nuisance," Earl motored on. "If you had the time—and weather permitting—I'd like to meet with you for an interview."

I was about to say that wouldn't be a problem when movement in the living room caught my attention. Seeing that it was the dead of winter, there were no windows open in the house . . . yet the curtain covering the front windows appeared to be billowing out as if manipulated by a breeze. I felt something solid click toward the back of my throat, and for a couple of seconds I could formulate no words.

"Of course," Earl said, no doubt interpreting my silence as disapproval, "if it would be too much of an inconvenience . . ."

"No," I finally managed. The word came out in a squeak, but I didn't think Earl noticed. "No, that's fine. I'm flattered."

"How's tomorrow sound?"

"That'll be fine."

"I work out of the house so you'd have to come—"

"Just stop by here," I told him. My gaze was locked

on the curtains. They were made of a semitranspar-
ent material that dulled the daylight on the other
side to a melancholic nimbus. Through the fabric I
could make out the undeniable shape of a small child,
an ethereal silhouette against the front windows but
behind the curtain, the curtain covering him up like
a death shroud.

Him, I thought. *Elijah Dentman.*

"How's noon strike you?" It was as if Earl's voice
were coming from the moon.

"Fine."

"Hey! Terrific! I'll see you then, Mr. Glasgow."

"Good-bye," I mumbled and hung up.

My palms were tacky with sweat, and that awful
taste was back in my mouth. Slowly, I closed the distance between the kitchen and the living room. With
each step I took, the shape of the child behind the
curtains—the child I knew to be Elijah Dentman
or whatever remained of him in this world—took
on the shape of the holly bushes outside, pressed up
against the windowpanes and shaking in the wind.
Once I reached the curtains, I did not have to sweep
them aside to see that I had mistaken these bushes for
the ghost of a lost child. Their horned leaves scraped
against the glass like grinding teeth.

I bent down and put my hand over the floor vent
that was beneath the curtains, covering the expulsion

of cold air that was streaming through the vent. The curtains stopped moving. I held my breath. A second later, a stiff, crinkling sound emanated from somewhere behind me. I turned my head and saw one of my notebook pages flutter and ripple. The page didn't actually turn, but it looked like it wanted to.

I called out Elijah's name and waited.

There was no response.

Something else turned over inside me, and I called out Kyle's name. Louder this time. I was confused. For a moment, I thought I was a child again, thirteen or fourteen, back in my parents' house in Eastport, lost and confused in the middle of the night. But no—I was here, an adult in his home. There were no ghosts. There were no dead boys, no dead brothers.

Five minutes later, after putting on a pair of work boots and an overcoat, I grabbed an unopened bottle of pinot noir, then trudged out into the snow. The wind was biting, and the snow was still coming down as I hiked up the hill toward the Steins' house. Beyond the trees I could see a banner of charcoal smoke rising from the stone chimney, listing like a thin tree in the northerly winds. I climbed the porch and thumped frozen knuckles against the solid oak door. I thought I heard lilting orchestral music from inside the house.

To my left, a sweep of velvet curtains parted in the window, then fell back into place. A moment later,

Ira Stein answered the door. "Mr. Glasgow," he said, no doubt surprised to find me standing on his porch. He was dressed in a pair of pressed slacks and a zipper-fronted sweater the color of sawdust. He smiled somewhat disarmingly behind the too-thick lenses of his spectacles. "A bit nasty to be out for a walk, isn't it?"

"I felt a bit awkward when we met at my brother's Christmas party. I wanted to bring you this." I gave him the bottle of wine.

"Well, thank you. I hope I didn't stir up anything that evening."

Whoa, boy, you've got no idea, I thought and had to fight back a maniacal laugh. "Not at all. I mean, I didn't know what happened to the Dentman kid, but Adam told me. It's okay. No harm done."

"Please come in." Ira stood aside, holding the door open for me.

I stomped the snow from my boots, stepped inside, and Ira shut the door behind me.

The place was a museum. There were enormous lithographs of old Roman buildings, Mediterranean grottoes, seagoing vessels, and countless European landscapes housed in expensive brass frames on the walls. All the furniture looked pristine and undisturbed, like photos from a catalogue. The Oriental carpet was as thick as a mattress, resistant to the impression of shoes when walked across. I took in the stone hearth where a fire burned and the display of glass-fronted bookshelves where numerous leather-bound volumes, their spines perfectly intact and absent of creases, were filed. Everything smelled of mahogany and pencil shavings and the memory of old cigars, like the meeting room of an ancient fraternity.

It's because they don't have children, said a voice in the back of my head that sounded very much like Jodie's.

"Wow," I said. "This is a beautiful place."

A white Maltese sitting in front of the fireplace on a satin-covered ottoman raised its head and scrutinized me with leaky black eyes. In the background, an old Victor Victrola phonograph popped and crackled as one orchestral number ended and another took its place.

Ira went immediately to an elaborate bar beside a set of sliding glass doors that led out onto the back deck. He opened the bottle of pinot noir and poured some of the bloodred wine into two glasses. He handed me one, then offered me a seat in a wingback chair piped with brass tacks. I sat as he sat opposite me in an identical chair before the fire.

The Maltese was still eyeballing me, a fluffy white pharaoh with its eyebrows triggering quizzically back and forth.

Nancy's voice filtered down the hallway, calling her husband's name.

"In here."

She appeared in the doorway, just about as frail as I remembered her from the Christmas party. She wore brown corduroys and a sweater that looked disconcertingly identical to her husband's. The Maltese began its high-pitched yapping, to which she told it to hush, be a good little Fauntleroy and hush now, hush.

"You remember Mr. Glasgow from next door, don't you, hon?"

Nancy nodded in my direction, her face chilly and unsmiling. I noticed Audubon prints on the wall behind her. "Mr. Glasgow."

"Please," I said. "It's Travis."

"I met your wife at the Christmas party. Lovely woman."

"Yeah, she's all right. I'll keep her around." I was joking, of course, but Nancy didn't seem to have much of a sense of humor.

"He brought wine," Ira informed her, an uncharacteristic garrulousness in his voice that hinted at possible alcoholism. "I could pour you a glass."

"Not before dinner," she said firmly. "Well, I'll leave you men to it." She turned and disappeared down the hallway.

"Ahhh," Ira said, leaning his head back against the chair as the record changed songs. I wasn't sure, but it sounded like a Duke Ellington number. "Listen to that, will you?"

I looked out the glass patio doors where, through the naked arms of the winter trees, I could make out the frosted sheen of the lake. There was a large Canada goose on the wall beside the doors, poised so that it appeared to be flying straight out of the lacquered wooden shield that held it to the wall.

Ira must have thought it was the goose I was admiring, because he said, "Do you do any hunting?"

"Not really." Crazily, I thought of the dead birds I'd found in the shoe box last month.

"Shot that one over on the Eastern Shore two summers ago," Ira commented, peering at the bird from over his shoulder. The goose stared back at us with dead eyes. "I used to hunt all the time with my father when I was a boy. I hardly ever get out anymore—I've got the gout something terrible these days—but I try to do it at least once a season." He examined his wineglass. "This is good wine."

It was cheap table wine, much cheaper than the stuff he was probably used to drinking, but his comment had cemented my original assessment: Ira Stein was an alcoholic.

"I'll confess to an ulterior motive for coming here today," I said after Ira had refilled both our glasses and changed the record on the phonograph.

"How's that?"

"I'm writing a book about the history of small

towns. Westlake in particular." I didn't feel comfortable jumping straight into an interrogation about the Dentmans, so I chose this avenue as a way to possibly sneak up on the subject without appearing too obvious or overzealous. "It's my understanding you and Nancy have lived here for many years."

"For almost twenty-five years now. We were one of the first couples to move into town. We'd come up from Pennsylvania after I accepted a position at the university. English lit." Ira gestured to the fireplace with one hand, indicating the neighborhood beyond. "I remember when there were only two houses on Waterview, and with the exception of Main Street, everything else was forest."

"I'm assuming the two houses would have been yours and the Dentmans'?" It was a logical deduction: all the other houses were on the opposite side of the street, each one a cookie-cutter replica of the next. Our house and the Steins' were the only ones with any individuality.

"That's back when they built good, solid houses. Not like this clapboard stuff they put up today." He lowered his voice and addressed me like someone with whom he'd been planning a bank robbery. "You and I have got more acreage between our two properties than the rest of the folks on this street combined. Just look at them. They're wedged in there, for Christ's sake! You can't take a shit in any of those houses without your neighbor balking at the stink."

"Ira," Nancy said, having once again materialized behind us. "Lord." She shook her head and moved into what I assumed, based on the sounds of pot and pans clanking, was the kitchen.

"It's the truth, anyway," he concluded, more conscious now of the volume of his voice. Then it shot up again: "Nan, get the album! Nan!"

"You don't have to shout," she shouted back. "What is it?"

"The boy wants to know about the history of the town. Where's the album?"

"Really," I began. "It's not necessary."

"It's inside the ottoman," Nancy said.

"There we go." Ira pulled himself out of his chair and went over to the ottoman where good little Fauntleroy was catching up on his beauty rest. "Up!" Ira shouted at the dog, clapping.

"Don't yell at the dog."

"Up!"

Disgusted, the Maltese looked at Ira Stein with more emotion in his muddy little eyes than I would have thought capable of a dog and hopped down onto the carpet. He wasted no time curling up into a ball directly in front of the fire.

Ira opened the ottoman, shifted around inside,

and produced a vinyl photo album that he dropped unceremoniously onto my lap before sitting back down.

"What's this?" I said, opening the cover. The plastic on the pages stuck together.

"Old photos from when we first moved in."

I turned the pages and desperately feigned interest, as many of them weren't of Westlake at all but Ira and Nancy in their younger years, as well as a slew of complete strangers who must have been friends or relatives.

"We've been lucky, though, even with the new developments," Ira said. "We're still pretty underdeveloped, which is fine by me." Then he made a sour face. "Why in the world would you want to write a book about Westlake?"

"I guess I'm fascinated by its secrets."

"What secrets are those?"

"Whatever secrets it has." I leaned forward in my chair, balancing the photo album on one thigh while cradling the wineglass between my knees. "How well did you know the Dentmans?"

"Not very well."

"When did they move into town?"

"Lord knows." He finished his wine, pushed himself out of his chair, and strode over to the bar. "They were here long before us."

"So the Dentmans were the first family to move into the neighborhood?"

"Depends on your definition of family. It was just the old man and his daughter. Bernard, his name was. The son—he was a bit older than the girl, maybe sixteen or seventeen back then—came and went. The girl couldn't have been older than thirteen when Nan and I first moved here."

"What happened to the kids' mother?"

Ira returned to his chair. He sat down while simultaneously expelling a great burst of air, as if the whole process had exhausted him. "Never knew of any mother."

"What kind of man was Bernard Dentman?"

"He was a hermit. Lived in that house until he died last year, and I don't think he'd been outside more than a dozen times in all those years. Isn't that right, Nan?"

I turned around to find Ira's wife standing in the doorway again, cradling a mug of something hot and steaming in her hands. She looked infinitely bored. "What my mother would have called a haunted soul," she said, and the phrase triggered a shiver of queasiness through me.

"What about the children?" I asked. "David and Veronica?"

If Ira was surprised by my knowledge of their names, he did not let it show. "Like I said, the boy came and went. Maybe he was going to school somewhere."

"Or off getting into trouble," Nancy added.

Ira executed a hesitant shrug, which conveyed he didn't completely disagree with his wife's assessment.

"And the girl?"

"An odd duck," opined Nancy. She had a voice like an out-of-tune violin, and each time she spoke I felt my skin prickle. "Pale as a ghost, too. Hardly ever came out of the house, except to go to school, but even that stopped after a while. She was teased horribly from what I understand."

"So the kids grew up and moved out," I said, trying to keep them on track.

"Well," Nancy said, holding a hand to her throat. "The boy came back for a while, remember, Ira? Stayed at the house. I assumed he returned to help his father raise the sister."

"And after that?" I prompted.

"They left," Ira stated. Again, he got up to refill his glass, which wasn't even empty. Behind me, I heard Nancy sigh disapprovingly. "Hadn't even thought of those kids till they came back here last year when the old man got sick."

"It's January," Nancy corrected. "That would have been two years ago."

Ira waved a hand at her without looking up. He poured himself another glass, then carried both his glass and the bottle over to the fireplace. He refilled my glass and set the near-empty bottle down between the two wingback chairs on an antique end table.

"Hardly recognized them," Ira continued. "Of course, the girl had her own little one in tow by that time."

"Elijah Dentman," I heard myself say, and it was like reciting a prayer. Self-consciously, I set my wineglass down on the antique end table before I broke it in my hand.

The Maltese lifted his fuzzy head off the carpet and whined.

"Bitsy-bitsy-bitsy," Nancy cuckooed, adopting a ridiculous baritone that made her sound mentally unstable. "Poop-a-doop bitsy!"

Ira, who was undoubtedly accustomed to such nonsensical outbursts, hardly seemed to notice. "When the old man died, I figured those kids would move out soon after. Sell the house, make some money. But they didn't. They stayed. Probably would have stayed forever had that kid not—"

"Be kind," Nancy said, and I wasn't quite sure if she was talking to Ira or the dog anymore.

"There was something wrong with that boy," Ira said. "They never sent him to school. Had a woman come by and try to homeschool him but that didn't last too long."

"Althea Coulter," said Nancy. "She lived over in Frostburg. I remember her. We spoke sometimes when we ran into each other in the court."

"Did she ever say anything about the Dentmans?"

Ira frowned and answered for his wife. "What would she have to say?"

"I don't know. If they were as strange as everyone seemed to think, I'm sure she would have had some stories from being over at the house. Some little anecdotes, maybe?"

"Well," Ira said, "I would never have asked, and I'm sure Nancy never did, either."

"She was a good woman," Nancy said, addressing her steaming mug. The way she said it made me think Althea Coulter was dead.

"Would have been unprofessional," Ira went on, as if his wife hadn't spoken. Then he leaned closer to me, and I could see the bleariness of his eyes as they swam behind his glasses. "Someone should have been watching him that day by the lake."

The conversation was closing in on the details of Elijah's death. I felt a giddy sense of elation at that— an emotion for which I would hate myself later, once I had ample time to replay the entire conversation in my head.

"What exactly happened that day?" I asked, and it was like firing a flare into the night sky.

"No one was watching him," said Ira simply. "He was out there playing on that damnable staircase when he fell and cracked his head and drowned."

"Did either of you hear or see anything?" Of course, having read the newspaper articles, I already knew the answer to this question. But it seemed the next logical jump, and I wanted to keep them going.

"Nancy heard him cry out."

"I heard *someone* cry out," Nancy corrected.

I asked her what she meant.

"It was late afternoon. It was a cool day so we had the windows open. I'd just started dinner when I heard a high-pitched . . . I don't know . . . a high-pitched wail."

"About what time was this?"

"Around five thirty. If I eat dinner too late, I get horrible indigestion."

"And you're not sure it was the boy?"

"Honestly, I didn't think anything of it at the time. As you'll soon learn, there're plenty of noises around the lake in the summer—birds, animals, children playing. You can even hear traffic on the other side of town echo out over the water on cool summer nights, and God help us when the loons come back to roost. The thing about the lake is it plays with the sound, twists everything like a riddle, and bends it out of proportion. You think you hear something off to the left, but it's really a quarter of a mile out on the other side of the lake past the pines."

"So when did you realize it had been Elijah?"

"I guess after the police came by and asked if we'd heard anything unusual," Nancy said. "I thought about it long and hard and said I'd heard someone cry out—or *thought* I did. But I never said with any certainty that it had been that little boy," she added quickly and in such a fashion that I suddenly knew this poor woman had lost sleep over this many nights. "It's important to understand that."

"I understand," I said. "Did either of you see Elijah out there that afternoon?"

"I saw him," Nancy said, and it was as if she were confessing to some heinous crime. She looked miserable. Her skin had grown so pale I thought that if she pricked herself with a needle, she wouldn't bleed. "I'd been out walking Fauntleroy earlier that day by the lake. Elijah was standing on the staircase and jumping off into the water like a diving board. I remember shaking my head and thinking how dangerous it was."

"There's the rest of the boating pier just under the surface of the water," Ira interjected. "You dive too deep and strike your head." He made a face to show that his premonition about the dangers of the floating staircase had obviously come true. "We're always chasing the neighborhood kids away in the summer."

"Did you see or hear anything that day, too, Ira?"

"It was a weekday. I was teaching a late class at

the college."

"What time was that?"

"Class ended at six fifteen. I would have went to my office to gather my things before heading home." Considering, he said, "I suppose it was around seven o'clock when I finally got home."

I considered this, then turned back to Nancy. "Was he alone when you saw him? Down by the water?"

"Yes." She dropped her voice like someone about to spread a rumor and said, "None of the other children ever played with him."

"How come?"

For the first time since we'd started this conversation, the Steins both went silent. Nancy stared at her mug, which was no longer giving off steam. For a split second I feared she might return to the kitchen.

Eventually Ira said, "Go on. Tell him about the dog."

"Chamberlain wasn't just a *dog*," Nancy scolded, sounding genuinely hurt.

"We used to have two of these moppets," Ira said, motioning with one loafered foot at Fauntleroy. (The dog must have recognized the condescension in Ira's voice because he growled way back in his throat.) "Chamberlain got cancer two summers ago and died last spring."

"The treatments wouldn't take," Nancy said miserably.

"Doc gave us some pills to put in his food when

the time came. It was nice and easy."

"And painless," added Nancy.

"The next morning I found him dead right over there," Ira said and pointed to the rectangle of sunlight that spilled in through the glass patio doors. "Probably been sunning himself when he finally passed."

Nancy sniffled. I couldn't bring myself to look at her.

"I took him out into the woods and buried him halfway down the slope, just before the land gets too rocky. Whole thing must have taken a good hour—you really underestimate the size of a lapdog when you got to dig a hole in the ground for it—and when I looked up, exhausted and sweating, I saw the little Dentman boy staring at me through the trees. He was maybe twenty yards away. I didn't think anything of it until I happened back that way a couple of days later on my way to the water for some fishing and found the grave dug up and the dog's body missing."

"Lord, have mercy," Nancy whispered and actually genuflected.

Across the room the record ended, filling the silence with the pop-sizzle-hiss of the needle.

"Wait a minute," I said. "Are you saying Elijah Dentman dug up your dead dog and made off with it?"

"I'm *saying*," Ira intoned, emphasizing the word, "that he'd been the only living soul who'd known where I buried the dog. And a few days later, that hole was dug up and Chamberlain was missing. You do the math."

"But . . . why?" I had no idea what else to say. This tidbit had blindsided me, even in spite of those dead birds I'd found in the cubbyhole last month.

"Who knows?" Ira said. "You tell me."

"This is such morbid talk," Nancy said, turning away and hurrying into the kitchen. I thought I heard her begin to sob once she was out of sight.

"What's all this got to do with the history of Westlake, anyhow?" Apparently Ira hadn't drunk enough wine for the peculiarity of our conversation to elude him.

As if to bolster my undercover role, I turned back to the photo album and riffled through a number of pages. "I guess we just got a little fixated. Veered off topic."

Ira got up to replace the record.

I continued turning the pages of the album without really looking at the photographs while I struggled to digest all that had just been relayed to me. Could it be true? Had Elijah actually dug up the Steins' dead dog? And if so, for what purpose?

What type of motive can you really expect from a troubled young boy? said the therapist's voice in the back of my head. Again, I thought of the baby birds I'd squeezed to death in a fit of anger and confusion following Kyle's death. The world could be an angry, hurtful place.

Ira put on a Billie Holiday record and remained standing in front of the phonograph, swaying drunkenly to the music.

My hand froze in the middle of turning one page. I hadn't been paying attention but happened to glance down at just the right moment to catch it. The right photo. The impossibly *right* photo. I started sweating so profoundly I thought I might leave stains on the wingback chair.

"What's this?" I managed, hearing all too clearly the way the words stuck to the roof of my mouth.

Ira came over and looked over my shoulder. "That's the staircase before the big storm came and uprooted it, throwing it into the middle of the lake. It was an old fishing pier—didn't I tell you? See how all of that is now submerged underwater? It's very dangerous for kids to dive off."

My heart was slamming so loudly I waited for Ira to ask what the sound was. A single pearl of sweat plummeted off my brow and dropped onto the photograph, so loud I swore I could hear it: *lop!*

It was a photo of the double dock, a replica of the one from my childhood. The one that had assisted me in murdering my brother over twenty years earlier.

CHAPTER NINETEEN

The summer of my thirteenth year found me at my most rebellious. Much of it was due to my own restlessness, which had started the previous school year when my classes became tediously boring and my mind began to wander. I drew obscene and quasi-pornographic doodles in the margins of my textbooks and penned grotesque little fables about zombies and werewolves in my composition pads. I earned a week's detention for bouncing a few smart-ass retorts at a substitute teacher, and once, at the urging of some friends, I flooded the second-floor boys' restroom by stuffing balls of paper towels into the urinals, then securing the flush levers in the down position with industrial rubber bands.

It was my last year in middle school before joining Adam in high school, and much of my rebellion was an act to garner unspoken acceptance among my older brother and his friends.

That summer brought with it a previously prohibited wealth of freedom, where my curfew was extended and I was finally permitted to ride my bike across the Eastport drawbridge and into downtown without an adult. These new freedoms afforded me the luxury of tagging along with Adam when he'd traipse off to one friend's house or another, and although he would sometimes grumble and tell me to get lost, most of the time he didn't say anything.

We'd play baseball at Quiet Waters Park and sometimes drop crab lines tied with chicken necks into the oily waters by the marina. We would swim, too, though we could do this easily in the river behind our house where our mother would be able to call us in when dinner was ready and the sky burned fine threads of fuchsia at the horizon. Sometimes Kyle would wander out onto the back porch and peer down at us from over the roof of the shed.

That summer Kyle turned ten and was allowed to follow us to the river, provided Adam kept an eye on him. Kyle could swim—growing up on the river in the little Eastport duplex, we could all swim at a very early age—but the current would sometimes turn on you without notice. Although we'd never known anyone to whom this had actually happened, the local folklore wasn't without its stories of careless boys and girls getting snared in a riptide and dragged straight out to the bay.

(Gil Gorman, a chunky redheaded bully in Miss McKenzie's social studies class, claimed to have had a cousin who'd been carried away by the tide and out into the Chesapeake. Many months later, the poor kid's body had washed up, mostly picked apart by fish—Gil always emphasized this part of the story—on the shores of England, clear across the Atlantic. Though I'd always suspected much of Gil's tale was bullshit, even at my young and impressionable age, sometimes while lying awake in bed at night I would think about Gil's ill-fated cousin swept out to sea and bobbing like a cork in the pitch-black waters of the Atlantic Ocean, screaming to a blanket of stars for help while some overlarge and unseen sea creature nibbled off his toes one by one.)

Summer nights, when our father's workload lightened and he could spend more time with us, we would sometimes camp out on the back porch with him after my mother had gone to bed, listening to the whip-poor-wills in the trees and watching the silver orb of the moon through spindly branches.

My father would smoke short brown cigarillos that smelled like bourbon, and if we pestered him long enough, he would eventually succumb to the telling of the most frightening ghost stories I have ever heard, even to this day. Ghosts, he said, populated the woods and waterways of this region, and many of the homes and inns and taverns in the historic district were haunted. He told us of Ellicott City, an old mill town in Howard County, and of its seven rolling black hills and the fire-scarred institute, long since defunct, that sat on a wooded hillside high above the railroad tracks. He told us of the Wendigo, and we would listen for its breathing. He told us, too, of a small boy formed straight from some young girl's imagination, like a fairy tale, living in the woods somewhere up north, subsisting on small animals and sometimes on small children.

Kyle would always become scared, and Adam would always grow bored, but I could have listened to those stories, as make-believe as I knew them to be, until the sun broke free over the river. After we'd all gone to bed, I would attempt to frighten Kyle with stories of my own until our father's head appeared as a dark outline in the doorway and told us to go to sleep.

Those are all good memories. If I could, I would wrap them in plastic and store them in some lead-lined safe in the back of my mind, protect them from the world. And while I suppose I will always have those memories to take with me, the darkness of what happened later that summer has overshadowed all else, corrupting their beauty and curling up the edges of those memories like pictures burned in a fire.

Even now, some twenty years later, I cannot recall how it all started that summer or who had discovered the double dock to begin with. Could it have been Adam or one of his longhaired, pimply faced cohorts? Or maybe they'd heard about it from someone else at school. Either way, the double dock was finally discovered, and you would have thought we'd unearthed a treasure chest in the sand.

As I've already described, the double dock was just that: one fishing pier stacked atop another, providing a roof of slatted, mossy boards for the pier below it. The upper pier was equipped with a winch and pulley. It was later explained to us by one of Adam's friends whose father was a waterman on the shore that the purpose of the double dock was to hoist boats out of the water after they'd been winterized so the ice wouldn't cut through the fiberglass hulls. It was a fair enough explanation, but no one cared what practical purpose the double dock served. What we cared about was what we used it for: a raised platform from which to spring out into the midnight sky, soaring blindly through the black, not knowing which way was up and which way was down, unable to believe the water was still there until you actually broke through its surface. Exhilarating.

We did not know who owned the dock until after Kyle's death when the owner—a grizzled old fisherman with rubber waders and overalls, his skin like that of a football, his eyes narrowed in a chronic wince—approached my father in the street while I looked on through the living room windows. To offer his condolences and (I assume now in hindsight) feel our old man out about the possibilities of a lawsuit. (There was never a suit.)

Prior to that, my only other encounter with the owner had been one night Adam, his friends, and I had gotten a little too loud—loud enough to alert the old bird from what was probably a half-drunk, midnight snooze on his sofa. He stormed out of the house with what looked like a broomstick disguised as a rifle. A few of Adam's friends took off through the bushes along the shore, and one kid made it clear across the river to the other side, no small feat. Adam and I swam directly beneath the dock and held our breath.

I remember the man's waders clacking on the boards above our heads as he shouted, *You kids, whoever you are, I'll shoot you, you come round here again!*

Our heads bobbing like seals under the dock, Adam and I stifled our laughter.

A second later, a sharp explosion directly above our heads echoed across the river like thunder. Then the old man returned to his house, no doubt to sit watch in the shadows of the willow trees, the broom-stick that was not actually a broomstick after all propped up on one shoulder.

After that, it seemed none of Adam's friends wanted to risk life and limb for the three seconds of excitement they got from double docking.

"Cowards," Adam told me after I'd pestered him about why we hadn't snuck out of the house in over a week. "Bunch of chickens. You still want to go?"

I'd been just as frightened from that experience as Adam's friends, but I wasn't going to have my older brother consider me a coward and a chicken. So I said I wanted to go back. Sure I did. Sure.

"Me, too," Kyle said, spying on us from the hallway.

Adam and I were in Adam's room, and we both turned to stare at our younger brother.

"Go away," Adam told him.

"I want to sneak out at night, too."

"You can't," Adam said. "You're too young."

"I'll tell." This was his ace in the hole, and we'd been expecting it for some time now. "I'll tell Dad."

"No," Adam said, "you won't. Otherwise we won't take you swimming in the river after lunch."

"Travis?" Kyle said.

"He's right," I said. "If you tell, we won't take you swimming anymore. And I won't let you keep the night-light on in the bedroom when you get scared, either."

"You just turned ten," Adam told him, sounding uncannily like our father whether he meant to or not. "You shouldn't have a night-light anymore."

"I don't hardly use it," Kyle protested.

"You won't use it at all if you tattle," I promised him.

And that was the end of it. That night, after our parents were asleep, Adam came to our bedroom and roused me from sleep. I sat up and dressed soundlessly while across the room Kyle rolled over in bed to let me know he was awake. I told him to go back to sleep, and he made a slight whimper, like a dog who'd just been reprimanded.

Sneakers and bathing suit on, I crept out of the bedroom and followed Adam down the hall to the living room. We exited through the patio door at the back, since it was the farthest point from our parents' bedroom and would elicit the least amount of noise. Before following him out, I glanced over my shoulder to see Kyle standing at the far end of the hall, a milky and indistinct blur in the darkness, watching me. Like a ghost.

It went on this way for much of the summer until Adam came down with the chicken pox. He got them pretty bad and was laid up in bed for two weeks, looking depleted and miserable, his skin practically indistinguishable, expect for the knobby red splotches, from the white sheets on which he rested.

Kyle and I had gotten the chicken pox when we were both very young (and despite my mother's deliberate exposure of Adam to us in our mutually reddened and itchy state, he hadn't caught them from us), so there was no concern that we, too, would become ill. I remember Kyle and I eating grilled cheese sandwiches for lunch at the foot of Adam's bed while the three of us watched the portable television our dad had transported to the top of Adam's dresser. This vision, however mundane and uneventful, is one of the most vivid I have carried with me into adulthood.

Of course, we'd stopped going down to the river and to the double dock at night. Yet summer was coming to an end, and I'd gradually become addicted to the thrill of springing off those boards and soaring like a blind bat out into the night, interrupted only at the end by the icy, bone-rattling crash through the black, salt-tasting water. I feared he might be sick straight until winter when it would be too cold to resume our nightly jaunts.

Then one night after I was certain our parents were asleep, I sat up in bed and whipped the light sheet off my legs.

I heard Kyle's bedsprings creak as he rolled over and propped his head up on one hand. He watched me dress silently in the dark. "Are you going alone?"

"Quiet. Yes."

"Mom and Dad say never to swim alone."

"Mom and Dad also don't want us sneaking out of the house in the middle of the night, do they?"

Kyle was silent; he looked like he was unsure if I'd asked him a legitimate question that required an answer or if I was teasing him.

I sat on the floor and pulled my sneakers on over bare feet. I'd grown accustomed to sneaking out of the house with Adam and had done so on numerous occasions without much concern—I believe some part of me understood that had we ever been caught by our father, Adam, the older of the two, would have sustained the brunt of our father's wrath: for me, a buffer of sorts—but on this night I was cutting out alone and with no buffer. With some hesitancy, I questioned my loyalty as a brother: if caught, would I try to lessen my punishment by throwing Adam under the bus, claiming this had been his plan from early in the summer and I was only continuing the trend?

"Let me come," Kyle said from his bed. The moonlight was filtering in through the partially shaded windows, making his blond hair shimmer a ghostly white.

"No."

"I could be a good lookout."

"I don't need a lookout."

"What if the man with the gun comes back?"

I paused, lacing up my sneaker. "How'd you know

about that?" We'd never said anything to Kyle—or anyone—about the old goat who'd fired his rifle into the air.

"I heard Adam talking to Jimmy Dutch in the yard before he got sick."

"Did you say anything to Mom or Dad?" I knew that he hadn't, otherwise it would have been our hides. Still, I had to ask.

"No."

"And you better not."

"I won't. But let me come. I'll be quiet. I'll be good."

(This is the moment I relive every time I shut my eyes, every time I think back to the events of that summer. There is no escaping any of it. There is no denying.)

"Okay," I said after a time. "But you have to be quiet, and you have to do everything I tell you. No question. Got it?"

"Yeah." He sprung upright in bed; even in the darkness I could make out the ear-to-ear grin on his round face.

"Now get your stuff."

It is fair to say both those boys died that night. I will; I will say it. I am a testament to that. The walking dead.

—and these two brothers sneak out of the house, quiet as mice treading the floorboards of a vicarage. They enter the woods, wearing nothing but their swimming trunks

and sneakers, each with a towel draped around his neck. The dark shapes of the trees crowd in all around them. They are convinced the trees are moving around them like living creatures; yet when they turn and look at them head-on, they are as still as statues . . . as trees. They walk swiftly beneath the cast of the moon through the wooded path, then finally down to the bank of the river. This is summer; this is grand; this is what it is all about.

Up ahead, the river opens wide as it approaches the mouth of the bay. Both boys feel the immensity of it in their guts. The older boy, the thirteen-year-old, continues quickly down the riverbank toward the looming double helix structure.

"Are the stories real?" the younger boy wants to know.

"What stories?"

"The stories Dad tells."

The older boy, who has dark curly hair and a body like a lizard or a bird, with long arms and long legs, says, "Yes. Of course they are, stupid." Trying to frighten his little brother. "Why would Dad lie to us?"

"I don't know."

"They're real, all of them."

"Even the Wendigo?"

"Especially the Wendigo. It's probably out there right now, watching us."

"No," says the younger boy. "Stop it."

"Stop what?" Chuckling.

"You're just trying to scare me."

"Will you be scared when it comes time to jump?"

"Jump where?"

The thirteen-year-old points at the threatening dinosaur shape of the double dock. "Off there. Off the top pier."

Suddenly, the younger boy looks very frightened. All their father's stories are real to him, the monsters and the imaginary boys who live in the woods and eat children. It is a warm night, but the little boy stands there shivering, his pale chest pimply with gooseflesh and his teeth chattering like a rattlesnake's warning. He looks white, too white. Almost transparent. The older brother thinks, Ghost.

"Climb the stairs to the top," instructs the older brother, "then take a deep breath, run, and jump off."

"Jump," parrots the younger brother, the uncertain tone of his small voice bending the word somewhere between a statement and a question.

"You're not scared, are you?"

The younger brother shakes his head.

"Then climb up and jump. I'll hold your towel."

"First?"

"First what?"

"You want me to go first?"

"Unless you're too scared. Unless you're a chickenshit."

"Don't say that," reprimands the little brother, though his voice is too weak and trembling to sound imposing. "Don't say that word."

"Shit," repeats his brother. "Shit, shit, shit."

"Stop it."

"And fuck, too," says the older brother, lowering his voice. This is the forbidden word, the word of all words. Biblical in its mystery and strength. "Are you a fucking chicken?"

The little boy looks like he wants to cry.

"You wanted to come out here," says the older brother. "If you're not scared to do it, then do it."

There is much hesitation. Paradoxically, just as the older brother is about to club him on the shoulder and tell him to sit in the weeds and be quiet, the little brother hands him his towel and takes off his sneakers.

The brazenness surprises the older brother—had the situation been reversed, he's unsure whether or not he'd be able to summon an equal amount of courage.

The younger boy steps around the shrubs in bare feet, leaving little prints in the mud, and proceeds to climb the staircase leading to the upper pier. His climb slows midway, where he glances down at the ground, and then he continues until he reaches the top. He is just a black blur, an outline in the darkness. The moon is distant and covered by trees and clouds; the night is as dark as the basement of lost dreams, and the older brother can hardly see him.

He whispers to him, "Be careful."

The little boy's small, frightened voice comes back to him: "I will." There is the sound of a deeply inhaled breath.

He's really going to do it, *the older boy thinks.*

Small, hurried footfalls race along the planks of the upper dock, the sound like a distant train rattling a wooden bridge.

Wow, he's really going to do it. I don't believe it.

Then silence as the little boy reaches the end of the pier and leaps into space. Somewhere out there, suspended in the black.

One Mississippi, two Mississippi . . .

The older boy anticipates the splash—he can hear it and feel it before it even happens.

But it doesn't happen.

There is no splash.

There is a sound, though—a harsh, sickening thud from the water. It reminds the older boy of baseballs slapping the hide of a catcher's mitt. No splash. He calls his brother's name, and there is no answer, either.

No splash. No answer. Just that sickening thud that froze his marrow and paralyzed his feet to the ground . . .

"All right, son," said Detective Wren, placing a doughy hand on my thin, quaking shoulder.

Tears blurred my vision, and my chest hitched with each sob.

"It's all right. Calm down for a minute, and we'll keep going when you're ready."

A small floating dock—no bigger than a twin mattress and covered with a panel of slate two inches thick—had broken free of its moorings earlier that evening. It floated unanchored and unobserved for several hours, making its way up the river and toward the bay. By the time Kyle leaped off the upper pier of the double dock, the floating barge was directly below him, invisible in the darkness.

The sickening thud I heard was the sound of Kyle's head opening up on the slate before he rolled, unconscious, into the river where he sank like a stone and drowned.

CHAPTER TWENTY

At seventy-seven, Earl Parsons had a face like an old bloodhound who'd been scolded one too many times for rooting around in the trash. His body was of the long-limbed variety, like an orangutan or a tree sloth, and he came packaged in pale blue polyester slacks, a checkered flannel work shirt, American flag suspenders, and a bulky nylon ski jacket with a faux fur collar that looked like something a sheriff might wear in the mountains of Colorado. His graphite-colored hair was unevenly parted and plastered to his scalp with what must have been several handfuls of camphor-scented liniment. It was my assessment he didn't often comb his hair. Yet he arrived with such an air of genuine appreciation and country pleasantness that I couldn't help but like him immediately.

"This is great," he said. "I mean, I really appreciate your time, Mr. Glasgow. If I had to write one more article about Mora Chauncey's cocker spaniels, I think my head would cave in."

We were sitting in the living room, Earl leaning forward in a cushioned armchair while I sat across from him on the sofa. Jodie was perched on the sofa's arm beside me, beaming. Sheila the librarian had probably mentioned to him that I was married—I remember saying something about my wife to her that day at the library—so he arrived not only with his spiral-bound notebook and a camera slung around his neck but hoisting a bouquet of wildflowers, which Jodie graciously accepted and put into a vase.

"I'm just flattered you think I'm newsworthy," I told him.

"Not to downplay your accomplishments as an artist, but anything louder than a fart around here's newsworthy to me," he said, then glanced at Jodie and looked horrified. "Oh, ma'am, I'm sorry. I'm just a tactless old fool who spends too much time alone. My apologies."

Jodie waved him off. "Please. Do I look like some debutant who's never heard a fart before?"

He smiled, his teeth nicotine stained and choppy, and growled laughter at the back of his throat. "I guess you're a woman of the world, all right."

"Well said." To me, she said, "I like this old man. Can we keep him?"

This sent Earl into a fit of laughter that reminded me of gravel crunching beneath car tires, his eyes tearing up and his big, rough hands slapping his knees so hard I feared his legs would crumble to powder. The laughing jag lasted several seconds and was contagious; by the end of it, we all felt like old friends.

"Before we begin," he said, removing a paperback from his coat pocket, "I was hoping you'd scribble your John Hancock in this for me. If, of course, it's not too much of an imposition."

He passed me the book. When he said on the phone he was reading one of my novels, I just assumed it was the copy of *Silent River* from the public library. But this was a copy of *Water View*, newly purchased and, as evidenced by the creases in the spine and a few dog-eared pages, already read.

"It was great," Earl said, handing me a pen. "Those last thirty pages flew by. I've already started *The Ocean Serene*, too. I know I'm reading them out of order, but to be honest, I hadn't planned on reading any beyond this one here. It sucked me in and I had to read more."

"That's very nice of you. I'm glad you enjoyed it."

On the title page, I wrote:

To Earl Parsons, my wife's new pet—
May all your farts be silent but deadly.

Travis Glasgow

I gave him back the book and expected him to read what I wrote, but he didn't. He stuffed it into his pocket and, grinning like a child, said, "I really appreciate that. I never got a book signed by anyone before."

The interview lasted for almost half an hour, with Earl asking the usual questions about how I got started in the business, where I got my ideas, and which one of my novels was my favorite. He segued into our reasons for coming to Westlake and our impressions of the town so far. I supplied him with the requisite answers. The old guy seemed pleased.

During a break in our conversation, Jodie convinced him to stay for lunch. Although he seemed fretful about imposing, Jodie's pestering broke him down and he agreed. Jodie slipped into the kitchen to make coffee and sandwiches.

"She's lovely," Earl said after she'd gone.

"Are you married?"

"You're looking at a bachelor of the first order right here in your living room." He winked at me, a glitter in his eye. "Doesn't mean I ain't ever been in love before, though. Went through my fair share of broken hearts."

"How long have you been working for the newspaper?"

"Lord," Earl said, sitting back in the chair. He looked too big for it, his legs like oversized pistons jutting at awkward angles. "Must be about a decade or so. Just after I retired from the mill."

"Do you know about what happened to the little boy who lived in this house? The one who drowned in the lake?"

He pressed two fingers to his forehead and, almost as if reciting poetry from memory, said, "Elijah Dentman, ten years old. Mother's name was Veronica. Didn't have no father."

"That's a good memory. Do you know who covered the story for the paper when he drowned?"

"Sure do," he said. "Was me."

I blinked. "No kidding?"

"Like I said, I'm the resident Woodward and Bernstein around here." He drummed his fingers against the camera that hung across his chest. "Resident Annie Leibovitz, too, I suppose."

"I read your articles about what happened," I confessed and leaned forward in my seat.

"You know, I joke about nothing ever happening here worth writing about, but the truth is, I'd prefer writing about pie eating contests and cocker spaniels than to ever have to report on something like that again."

"Were you on the scene while they were searching for the body?"

"All evening and well into the night. I left when the divers gave up the next morning."

"Without the body," I said. This wasn't a question. I was testing the air between us.

"Without the body," he repeated, and we looked at each other for a beat longer than necessary.

"Don't you find that odd? That this is a self-enclosed lake and the body was never recovered?"

Earl didn't answer me right away, and I thought maybe I'd insulted him somehow. Then he cleared his throat and glanced over my shoulder, possibly to make sure Jodie was out of earshot. "There's plenty strange about what happened to that boy, the least of which is the fact they never found his body. I assume, based on your timing asking these questions, that your wife doesn't know about what happened?"

"She knows a boy drowned in the lake. That's about it. She hasn't pursued the details."

"You mind me asking why you're interested in the matter? If it's none of my business, please say so and I'll shut my yap."

"I think things were overlooked," I said. "I think the cops didn't know how to handle an investigation of that magnitude and didn't turn over every stone. I think a boy doesn't just drown in a lake and completely disappear, even if the police didn't start searching for him until a couple hours later after he went missing."

"What are you saying?"

"I think Elijah Dentman was murdered." It had been on my mind for some time now, not only in the writing I'd been doing but in real life, too. The pieces didn't add up to make a complete whole. What cinched it for me was the visit to West Cumberland where I stood face-to-face with David Dentman.

To my surprise, Earl did not scoff at the notion. Just the opposite: he seemed to embrace it. "You got a suspect in mind?"

"Could be anyone, I guess. Could be some vagrant that ran into the kid down by the water. Could be someone the kid knew from town."

The old man shook his head. "No, that ain't what you think. Tell me what you think."

"I believe David Dentman did it," I said, and it was almost like confessing my sins to a priest. "I believe the boy's uncle killed him."

Almost too casually, Earl said, "He got a motive?"

"Maybe. I don't know what it might be, if that's what you're asking." But of course I knew that in real life, motives were not as indispensable as they were in books and movies. In real life, sometimes people did horrible things for no discernible reason.

Jodie returned with coffee and ham and cheese sandwiches.

Earl's face lit up as if his girlfriend had walked

into the room. "Thank you kindly, dear. You're too good to this old fool, and we've only just met."

"I have a soft spot in my heart for fools," she said, smiling. Then she twirled a finger in my hair. "Just ask my husband."

After Earl snapped a couple of photos of me to go along with the article, he gave Jodie a one-armed fatherly hug, and I walked him to the front door.

"I'll let you know when the article comes out," Earl said, tugging on his sheriff's jacket and stepping onto the porch. Beyond the tamaracks, the sky was a mottled cheesecloth color that made me feel instantly sad for no perceivable reason. "And again, I appreciate your time."

"No sweat."

"Here." Earl thrust one of his hands into mine, his callous fingers like barbed fruit against my palm. When he withdrew his hand, there was a folded piece of notebook paper in mine. "If you don't mind a messy bachelor pad and stale beer, you come on by, and I'll show you some stuff you might be interested in." He zipped his jacket and shoved his hands into the pockets. "I know what it's like to sit awake at night thinking the thoughts of a haunted man."

This struck me as oddly profound.

"You take care, Travis."

I watched him leave and didn't look at what he'd written on the slip of paper until after his pickup had pulled out of the driveway. In an old man's spidery, hieroglyphic handwriting: his address.

CHAPTER TWENTY-ONE

E arl's bachelor pad was a double-wide that looked suspiciously like an old boxcar, with multiple TV antennas and drooping Christmas lights (even though it was mid-January) on the roof and a few old junkers rusting away in random places on the lawn. It sat atop a wooded hill at the end of Old County Road, which wasn't exactly part of Westlake, although the lights of Main Street were clearly visible from his front door. It was late afternoon, two days since the interview at my house, and the sky was bruising to a cool, steady purple along the horizon.

As I pulled in beside the trailer, a sharp-faced black dog barked at me from the far side of the yard. It was tied to the bumper of a vintage Chevrolet, though the bumper didn't look secure enough to prevent the critter from breaking free and charging for my jugular. Up in the mountains, wind rolled like a thousand drums.

Earl walked out the front door just as I got out of the car. He wore faded jeans, an open-throated flannel shirt, and brown forester's boots, all of which seemed two sizes too large for his frame. He raised one hand in welcome, then shouted something at the dog, which quieted the mongrel as effectively as if he'd whipped it with a birch branch.

I slammed the car door and crunched through the snow, a backpack over my shoulders. I held two of my writing notebooks under one arm, the third one having vanished, one might surmise, into thin air.

For the past two days I'd searched the entire house from top to bottom for the missing notebook but couldn't find it. I'd pestered Jodie about possibly misplacing it, but she swore she hadn't seen it. I dug through all the boxes in Elijah's bedroom, which had become my writing office as well, on the off chance that I'd accidentally packed it away with some of the boy's stuff. While bent over one particular box, I thought I heard footsteps . . . then someone breathing down my neck. I spun around, expecting to see Elijah, blue-skinned and bloated, muddy water pooling on the cement floor about his feet, standing an arm's length from me in the half dark. But there was no one there; I was alone.

Earl nodded at me as I approached. "Snow's thinned out some. How's the driving?"

"They've got much of downtown cleared up, but it's still a bit treacherous here in the hills."

We shook hands. Across the yard, the large black dog started barking again.

"Come on inside," Earl said, turning and pushing the door open. "It's cold as a witch's tit out here."

Inside, I was treated to wood paneling and startling neon carpeting, a sofa that looked as if it had been salvaged from the set of *Sanford and Son*, and garish prints of hunting dogs, cattails, and bulging-eyed bass leaping out of rivers. Mounds of clothes seemed to rise from the floor and move when you weren't looking directly at them, and empty beer bottles and pizza boxes were placed almost strategically throughout the cramped interior. Despite the amassment of television antennas on his roof, Earl's tiny, prehistoric Zenith worked off a pair of rabbit ears capped in aluminum foil. It was the den of a career bachelor, that wily and elusive animal who has never been scolded to pick up his socks, iron a shirt, or wash the dishes.

"I warned you the place was a mess."

I followed him onto an elevated section of the floor, where the shag carpeting gave way to crude linoleum, and stood shifting from one foot to the other while Earl cleared half-eaten Chinese food containers and stacks of newspaper off what I construed to be the kitchen table. With some humility, I noticed a stack of my paperback novels on one of the countertops, the top one splayed open and upside down to save his page.

His arms laden in refuse, Earl nodded toward two lawn chairs folded against one wall. I put my notebooks on the circular table, then set up both chairs around it. A single paper lantern hanging from a cord above the table was the only immediate source of light. I sat in one of the chairs as Earl returned with an accordion folder and two bottles of beer, caps off.

He handed me one of the beers, proclaimed, "Cheers," and clinked the neck of his bottle against mine. Then he sat down heavily in his chair and placed the accordion folder neatly at the center of the table. "Before we begin, I want your word that much of what I show you tonight stays between us."

"I'm not even sure what this is all about, but okay. You've got my word."

Earl motioned to my notebooks. "What are those?"

"Notes for a new book." After a pause, I said, "But I think they're more than that, too."

He said nothing but watched me as he chugged his beer.

"It sounds stupid, but I've been plotting out this story based on what I already know about the Dentmans," I said, sensing I needed to explain myself. "I'd been suffering this lousy writer's block, and it wasn't until I learned about Elijah's drowning that my creative spark returned. I've been writing like a madman for the past couple weeks." Almost apologetically, I added, "There's a third notebook but I must have misplaced it."

"I'm a wannabe reporter for a small-town community newspaper, so I won't pretend to comprehend the inner workings of a genuine creative mind," Earl said. "But do you mean to tell me you're actually writing a book about the Dentmans?"

"Not exactly. It's difficult to explain." For a moment I felt myself on the verge of telling him about Kyle—a realization that shook me to my foundation, because not even Jodie knew the truth, and I'd just met this man two days ago—but chickened out. "It started that way, but then the story turned into something else. The characters took on lives of their own based on the parameters I'd set. But now . . ." My voice trailed off. I didn't know how to finish the thought.

"The following is based on a true story," he said, chuckling. "Names have been changed to protect the innocent and all that jazz . . ."

"Exactly," I said, but oh, did I feel like a heel lying to this old man: I hadn't changed a single name; my notebooks were rife, were polluted, with the good citizens of Westlake, Maryland. Even down to Tooey Jones and his gut-wrenching tonic.

Earl exhaled heavily out of flared nostrils. "Before we get into this, I want to show you something." He shuffled over to a credenza overburdened with stacks of papers and unopened mail. Humming beneath his breath, he sorted through one of the piles, his back toward me.

I was startled to spot an Irish wolfhound lounging silently beside the credenza, shaggier than the carpet itself and roughly the size of a grown man. From beneath its fringed bangs, it eyed me with soulful black eyes. Somewhere in the shadows, a space heater whirred to life.

"Ah, here it is," Earl said and returned to the table. The sound he made when he dropped into the chair was like an old bicycle horn.

He handed me a grainy photograph of a man in cutoff jean shorts and a tank top, dragging a washrag across the windshield of a yellow Firebird. The man was perhaps in his midforties, although the picture was somewhat out of focus, making it impossible to tell for sure.

"Who's this?" I said.

"My son."

I had no idea where this was going, so I slid the picture back to him without saying anything.

"A careless affair in the days of my youth," Earl said, taking the photo from me and looking at the photo with what I assessed to be a mixture of longing and regret. "It's not necessary to go into that. I just wanted to show it to you because, for whatever reason, you sort of remind me of him. Not that you look anything like him, and to tell the God's honest truth, I've never spent any time with the boy to know if you two share any of the same mannerisms. I guess maybe you're how I sometimes think he might be." He set the photo on the stack of papers atop the credenza. "I'm sorry."

"It's okay," I told him, though I still had no idea why he'd showed me the picture.

"That was my roundabout way of explaining why I'm about to show you this stuff. Because I feel a bit of a kinship to you, I guess, which means I trust you not to exploit me. You say you're writing a book, and that's just dandy, but I can't have what I'm going to show you go beyond these walls." He rattled a cough into one fisted hand before resuming. "I know you're a stranger to me, and I may just be an old fool, but something is telling me I can trust you to keep that promise. That internal voice ain't never steered me wrong in all my years. I hope you won't be the one to prove it wrong."

"I swear it," I said. "What you tell me stays between us."

Earl slid the accordion folder in front of him. "It

ain't so much as what I'm gonna tell you as it is how I came across what I'm going to tell you." He undid the string and opened the folder. A ream of multicolored papers bristled from inside. He took out a slender stack of white paper held together with an industrial-sized paper clip and gave it to me.

I scanned the front page, seeing David Dentman's name right off the bat, as well as his West Cumberland address and other personal information—social security number, telephone number, date of birth. "What am I looking at?"

"David Dentman's criminal history."

I peeled back the pages, skimming them as I went. "How did you get this?"

"I'm not going to say. It's probably illegal, me just having that stuff, and I ain't about to rat anyone out."

"Then I won't ask again." I paused to read one of the pages more closely. "He's had three arrests. If I'm reading this correctly, I mean . . ."

"Oh," said Earl, "you're reading it just fine."

"Two for aggravated assault, another for—what's 'A and B'?"

"Assault and battery."

"Jesus Christ." I read closer. "What does 'nol pros' mean?"

"Latin for *nolle prosequi*. Means he was arrested but wasn't prosecuted."

"So he got off on all three charges?"

"So it says."

"How come?"

Earl shrugged and rubbed his stubbly chin with one of his big grizzly bear hands. "Could be for a number of reasons. Not enough evidence against him. Or maybe the victims dropped the charges."

"Who're the victims?"

"I have no idea."

I reread the pages. "The most recent arrest was only three years ago. That was the assault and battery. Are we talking bar fights here or . . . ?"

"No way to tell."

"Is there a way to decipher . . . I mean, who were the arresting officers on these?"

"Can't tell by reading that gobbledygook," said Earl.

"So David Dentman has a criminal record," I said. "Surely the cops looked into this after Elijah disappeared?"

"I'll bet they knew about it. Sure."

"So the guy's nephew allegedly drowns, the body's never recovered, and his statement's the only thing they have to go on? Sounds awfully slipshod, doesn't it?"

"There's the woman, too," Earl suggested. "She saw the boy down by the water and later heard a scream. Don't forget."

"Right. Nancy Stein. I spoke with her and her husband a few days ago. It was only after being interviewed by the police that she said she'd heard a scream. A wail, she called it." I frowned, shook my head. "But she had reservations when I spoke with her, as if she'd been thinking about that wail and her subsequent statement to the cops for many nights since that day. I think *she* thinks that maybe they talked her into saying she heard Elijah scream."

Earl was dragging a set of fingernails down the bristly side of his neck; he froze upon hearing my words and glared at me from across the dimly lit table. "Are you talking about a police cover-up?"

"No, no, nothing like that. I just think that maybe whoever questioned Nancy might have accidentally put words in her mouth and thoughts in her head. Think about it. You hear a noise like someone crying out but think nothing of it. Later a bunch of cops show up at your doorstep and tell you the neighbor's kid is missing and that he probably drowned in the lake. They ask you if you heard anything, maybe a shout or a struggle or a scream. And of course your mind returns to that one lone cry you heard—or thought you heard—earlier that day. Then all of a sudden you're certain you heard it, and that's what the police write down in their little notepads."

"Sure," Earl said. "I'll buy it."

"Did you interview David or Veronica for the newspaper articles you wrote?"

"No. Police wouldn't allow it."

"So who gave you all the details?"

"The officers at the scene. Later on, Paul Strohman's office issued an official release that I used to check my facts."

"Paul Strohman?" I had heard the name but couldn't remember where.

"He's the chief of police. Wait . . ." Earl dove back into his folder and thumbed through several more papers before he produced a newspaper clipping.

It was a brief write-up about the Westlake Police Department closing the investigation into Elijah's disappearance, satisfied that it was an accidental drowning. Alongside the article was a granular black-and-white photo of Chief of Police Strohman. Even in the lousy picture, I could tell Strohman was good-looking and well put together. He was wearing a handsomely cut dark suit as opposed to the police uniform one would have expected him to be wearing, and he sported the Cheshire cat grin of a Washington lobbyist. By all accounts, Paul Strohman looked nothing like the police chief of some backwater mountain village.

David's face loomed up into my memory like a ship breaching fog, firing questions at me as I stood in his living room: *You a cop? Strohman send you here?*

"Understand that what we got here is nothing definitive. This is just another door, another avenue."

Another bit of evidence, I thought.

"In fact," Earl added, returning once again to his accordion folder, "the entire Dentman family has an equally sordid past. The cheese, in this case, does not stand alone." He brought out more papers—lined notebook pages cramped with handwriting I recognized to be his—and held them nearly against his nose so he could read them. "David's sister . . ."

"Veronica," I said.

"She's spent her life in and out of mental health facilities. Most recently she spent some time in Crownsville back east before they closed the place down a number of years ago."

"How much time?"

"Six months, though my sources may not be completely accurate."

I didn't bother asking who his sources were.

"And I've got no record of who was watching her kid all those times," Earl continued before I could ask that very question, "though my guess is it had been David."

"Not the kid's father?"

"Don't know who the father was. But I had my source run a background on Veronica. Her record came up clean." He tapped the printout of David's criminal record, which I'd laid on the table, and said,

"That place in West Cumberland listed as his address? Same as hers. And before that, they were both apparently living together in Dundalk. A brief residency in Pennsylvania—"

"Let me guess," I said. "Same address."

He set both his hands down flat on the vinyl tabletop and leaned close enough to me so that I could smell the beer on his breath. "Those two have been living together their whole lives. She must have been one unbalanced nutcase in order for her brother to have to take care of her is my guess."

"Taking care of her *and* her kid," I said. "What does David do for a living, anyway?"

"He's in construction. I found his information with the state carpenters' union."

I thought of the makeshift little rooms throughout my basement and the prison-like bedroom hidden behind a wall of Sheetrock. I let this all sink in while Earl got up and retrieved two fresh beers from the refrigerator.

"So you can see why I don't want some of this stuff getting out beyond these walls," he said, sitting down and handing me another beer. "I've been playing reporter for just over a decade now, and I may not be Woodward and Bernstein as I sometimes like to joke, but I do know how to be a journalist. I've cultivated my sources over that time. The last thing

I'd want to see is someone close to me lose their job simply for appeasing the whimsy of a nutty old man."

I took a long, hard pull on the fresh beer. The chill of it raced down my throat and triggered a pleasant tingling sensation just above my buttocks. Something suddenly occurred to me.

"You knew something was fishy from the very beginning," I said. It was not a question. "Otherwise, why would you have had your sources run background checks on David and Veronica?" It was my turn to lean toward him across the table. "I believe you're a good journalist. I do. Something about this case didn't sit well with you from the start, either. Am I right?"

Earl set his beer on the table and, holding one finger up like a schoolmarm, rose once again with some difficulty. He returned to the credenza and riffled through more paperwork. From over his shoulder, he said, "Keep talking. I think you and I are on to something, all right."

I told him about the basement bedroom and how all of Elijah's things had been left there, sealed up behind the wall. I told him of the unsettling supposition made by Ira Stein about Elijah digging up his wife's dead dog and slinking away with it like some grave robber in an old Universal monster movie. Lastly, I told him of my visit to the Dentman house in West Cumberland (at which time Earl suspended his search through the paperwork, turned halfway around, and offered me an astonished yet envious grin) and of my unsettling confrontation with David following a brief and utterly uneventful discourse with Veronica.

"The fact that she's been institutionalized half her life doesn't surprise me in the least," I said. "Talking to that woman was like talking to one of Jack Finney's pod people."

"You sure she wasn't just in mourning over her son?"

"I thought she was at first, but then I could tell something was . . . well, *off*. She seemed terrified of her brother."

"Here," Earl said, finally locating what he'd been searching for. He hobbled over and gave me a stack of eight-by-ten color glossies.

As I looked through them, I was aware of the old man's hand coming to rest on my shoulder. I felt a pang of sadness for him and couldn't help but wonder about the backstory between him and his estranged son.

I flipped through several photos before I recognized the location. "This is my backyard. I've never seen it in summer, the leaves on the trees and all the bushes and flowers in bloom. You took these?"

"Annie Leibovitz, remember?"

One shot was of the lake behind my house, the foliage around the lake as heavy as a shroud. There were police officers gathered around the cusp of the lake, and two divers were rising out of the water in scuba gear. Another photo had the front grille of a police cruiser in the foreground, parked down in the grass of the sloping hillside. There were a couple of shots of David speaking with police, but his face was mostly blocked by police hats. Lastly was a photo of Veronica standing by herself and halfway concealed by trees. Her face had that same vacuous, haunted expression she'd had when I'd knocked on her front door.

"That's the shot," Earl said from behind me, looking over my shoulder. "That's the one that gave me chills for nights afterward. Just like you said—that goes beyond a mother in shock, beyond a mother in mourning. In fact, how would you say she looks to you? You're the writer. How would you describe her?"

I thought long and hard before admitting she looked absolutely terrified.

"Right," Earl agreed without hesitation. "Scared to death."

There was something else that bothered me about the photos. I flipped through them a second and third time, trying to figure out what it was, but it eluded me.

"There were enough people milling about by the lake that afternoon, as you can imagine," Earl said. "I blended right in, and after a while no one paid me any mind. I got close enough to eavesdrop when the cops were questioning David. The guy was calm and specific, unruffled by the cops' questions. When it came time to ask Veronica some questions, she just sounded like a record skipping on a groove—'I was asleep. I was asleep. I was asleep.' Finally, David told the cops to leave her alone, that she was delicate and they were upsetting her." He shook his head, his eyes distant and glassy. "I can still hear her clear as day—'I was asleep. I was asleep.'"

"You think she was coached?"

"By David?"

"Who else?"

"It's possible. But it's hard to tell with that woman. I don't think a single word that ever came from her mouth has sounded natural. That'd be my bet."

"Hmmm," I said, still flipping through the photographs. "You're probably right."

"None of them ever made it to print," Earl said, still hunkering over my shoulder. "Fat Figgis said they were too gruesome for *The Muledeer*."

"Fat Figgis?"

"Jan Figgis," he said. "My editor. The woman's four hundred pounds if she's an ounce."

"Can I hold on to these?"

"The photos? Shoot, you can keep 'em."

"Thanks," I said, slipping the glossies inside the cover of one of my notebooks. "And can I bother you with a favor?"

"Bring it on, son," he said, returning to his seat

across from me at the table. (The epithet did not slip by me unnoticed.)

"I want to put your investigative skills to the test. I need you to locate a woman named Althea Coulter for me. All I know is she used to live in Frostburg and she's most likely licensed as a grade school teacher." I thought about how Nancy had referred to the woman, then added, "There's a good chance she might already be dead, though."

"Can I ask who this Althea Coulter is?"

"For a brief time, Elijah Dentman was homeschooled when he lived in my house. According to the Steins, Althea Coulter was his teacher. I want to talk to her."

"Alive or dead," Earl promised, "I'll find her."

CHAPTER TWENTY-TWO

Honest writing, much like honest people, comes without wanting anything in return. I found myself on an exploration of characters—characters that begot story; story that begot emotion—traversing through Edenic pastures and Elysian fields where dead boys frolicked in barefooted bliss on the dew-showered plains, and terminal skies reflected the roiling slate seas instead of the other way around.

I was out back chopping firewood when Adam came over. I heard his boots crunching through the crust of snow before I actually saw him emerge from the trees.

"Hey," he said.

"Hey." I went on chopping. The goddamn furnace was still uncooperative, so Jodie and I were going through several logs a day in the fireplace. It hadn't snowed for days, but it was still deathly cold.

"Haven't seen you in a couple days. I popped in yesterday, but Jodie said you'd gone out somewhere. Some book research or something."

"Yeah."

"You ever take any of that stuff to Veronica Dentman? I never heard how it went."

"I did," I said, splitting another log.

"And . . . ?"

I rested the axe head in the snow and leaned on the handle. I was out of breath and sweating despite the cold. "I brought her a box. She was . . . standoffish."

"Understandable. You probably gave her one hell of a shock showing up like that."

"Then David came home, and he gave *me* one hell of a shock. He thought I was a cop."

Adam chewed his lower lip. "Nothing happened, did it?"

"What would happen?"

"Never mind."

"Did you guys know he has a criminal record?"

Adam looked away from me. His nose was red and one nostril glistened. "Don't tell me that just came up in conversation with him."

"No. I found that out on my own."

"How?"

"That's not important," I said, not wanting to get

Earl and his elusive sources mixed up in all this. "Did you know?"

"About David's past? If you're questioning the PD's investigative techniques, that's really none of your business."

"It's just a simple question."

"Of course we knew. We ran a background on him. What do you think, we're a bunch of Barney Fifes out here, tripping over our shoelaces and shooting ourselves in the foot?"

"Okay," I said. "That's all I wanted to know."

"To know for what?"

"Forget it." I hefted the axe over my shoulder.

"I happened to talk with Ira Stein yesterday. It's the reason I came over yesterday looking for you."

Fuck, I thought, dropping the axe in the snow. I glared at him. "What are you doing, trying to set me up or something? Catch me in a lie? Yeah, I spoke with Ira."

"He said you're writing a book about what happened to the Dentmans."

"That's not what I told him. He was drunk by the time I left and he'd misunderstood."

"He said you asked a lot of questions about them. You upset his wife at one point, too."

"Jesus Christ, she got upset when her husband started talking about her dead dog. I told them I was interested in the history of Westlake. We got side-tracked and started talking about the Dentmans. It was completely incidental."

"So then it's not true? You're not writing a book about the Dentmans?"

I stared at him and counted my heartbeats. When I spoke, I surprised myself with how even and steady my voice sounded. "I don't have to answer any of your questions. We're not in one of your fucking interrogation rooms."

"Fine. You don't have to answer shit. But let me give you a little brotherly advice. This is a small town and gossip travels fast. You want to keep yourself out of trouble, you'll stop poking around."

"Fucking unbelievable," I howled. "Now you're threatening me—"

"I'm not threatening you, asshole. I'm warning you. You've got a nice setup out here, and your wife deserves it. Don't muck it up for her and embarrass her by acting like a fool."

I blurted out, "I think David Dentman killed his nephew."

"Is that so?"

"The pieces don't fit. Things don't make sense."

"Really? And what evidence do you have? Aside from some assault charges for which he'd never been prosecuted?"

What *was* my evidence? The overall weirdness of the whole thing? The fact that David had looked like he wanted to punch me in the throat when he'd come and found me in his home with his mentally disturbed sister? I knew what my gut was telling me, but those gut feelings didn't translate well into actual facts.

My silence at this point was condemning.

"We deal in facts," said my brother. "Murderers have motives, innocent people have alibis, and you can't lock someone up behind bars because pieces don't fit. Sometimes in real life, things don't fit. This is real life, not one of your books."

But what if it is? I thought.

"There was no body," Adam said. "Those people never got any closure. Leave them alone."

Still fuming, I kicked my boots off on the front porch and tossed my jacket over the sofa as I entered the house. On the coffee table in front of the sofa, Elijah's colorful wooden blocks were stacked into a pyramid.

Upstairs, I stood in the doorway to the office. Jodie was hunched over her desk before a display of psychology textbooks and reams of photocopied journal articles. She had one finger looped through the handle of a steaming mug of what smelled like chamomile tea.

"Working hard?" I said.

"Thy feelest the crunch upon thee."

"Did you set up those blocks on the coffee table downstairs?"

"What blocks?" Her nose was buried in one of her books; she didn't turn around to look at me.

I chortled. "Come on. The blocks on the coffee table."

She turned around in her chair. Her face looked plain without makeup, almost puritanical. "I'm trying to work here. What are you getting at?"

"Someone stacked a bunch of toy blocks on the coffee table downstairs."

"You look different," Jodie said, her gaze lingering on me a bit too long. She was reading me. I felt nude standing there in the hallway. "Are you okay?"

"What do you mean?"

"I don't know. You haven't seemed like yourself for the past few days."

"Who have I seemed like?" I said, and I couldn't help but recall the night Jodie had said she'd gone into the bathroom in the middle of the night and it was my reflection staring back at her from the mirror. *I was you.*

"You know what I mean," she insisted.

"No, I don't. Tell me."

Jodie sighed. "Why don't you go shower and shave, clean yourself up a little bit? You'll feel better."

"I feel fine."

"You look haunted." Her words chilled me.

"Maybe you're working yourself too hard on this new book. Take a few days off."

"All right," I said, not wanting to prolong this conversation any further.

"You're stressed out. That's why you've been having those nightmares."

"What nightmares?"

"I don't know." She drew her eyebrows together. "You sort of whimper like a puppy in your sleep."

"Do I?"

"It's stress," Jodie said, returning to her schoolwork.

"What about those blocks?" I questioned the small of her back again.

"I don't know what the hell you're talking about. I don't play with blocks."

I went downstairs and gathered the blocks, carried them into the basement, and returned them to their plastic blue pail. With a huff I sat at Elijah's tiny writing desk, my knees crammed beneath it at awkward angles, and opened one of my writing notebooks.

Staring up at me were Earl's eight-by-tens, the top one the shot of Veronica partially hidden behind a stand of junipers. Once again I felt that needling insistence that something was trying to jump out at me from the photos, waving its arms like a drowning man to come to my attention. Yet just like before I couldn't figure out what it was.

Let the writing hunt for it, I thought, grabbing a pen and setting the photos down beside one of my open notebooks on the desk.

In college I'd had a creative writing instructor who'd once said, "Quite often fiction is the best reality; cruelties are so much easier to swallow when they're dressed up and capering about like circus clowns."

So I let the writing hunt for the missing puzzle piece, printing lengthy descriptions of what I saw in each of Earl's photographs, describing the leathery gray water, the crenellated staircase rising from its glassy surface, the police cars and the fullness of the summer trees, and the scudding cumuli on the horizon. I described the vacuous look in Veronica's eyes and the blurry, almost nonexistent face of David behind a wedge of policemen's hats.

(Although I couldn't be certain, I swore—throughout the entirety of the writing—that someone had come up behind me, slight and hesitant, and began stacking the wooden blocks on the floor. I was aware of this only distantly and through a mental fog, the way drunks remember bits and pieces of their escapades after waking up the next morning with a hangover.)

I was writing and studying the photographs with such intensity that I hadn't heard Jodie come down the basement stairs. She nearly sent me through the roof when she cleared her throat in deliberate irritation.

"Jesus," I croaked, my heart pumping like a piston.

"What's going on here?" She leaned against the cutout in the wall, her arms folded across her chest. Whether it was subconscious or not, she hadn't taken a step into the room.

"What do you mean?" I quickly set one of my notebooks down over the photos.

"This room," Jodie said. "This stuff. I thought you called someone."

"I did."

"And what happened?"

I thought about lying to her.

But before I could think of what to say, she interrupted my train of thought. "You're scaring me. Something's not right with you."

"Hon . . ."

"Don't shut me down. Have you looked in a mirror lately? You look like shit."

"I know. I know. But I'm right on the verge of something here."

"The verge of something," she echoed. "It's more like you're obsessed."

"I'm just trying to figure something out."

She touched a pair of fingers to her chin. She looked on the brink of tears, and when she spoke again, her voice trembled. "Adam said you've been going around the neighborhood asking people about that boy who died."

"Adam doesn't get it," I said, and it was a chore keeping my voice calm. What I wanted to do was call him a son of a bitch who couldn't keep his nose out of my business. "What happened to that boy wasn't an accident. He was killed."

I didn't like the way Jodie was looking at me— like I was a stranger and she was trying to understand how I got here.

"Adam's worried about you," she continued as if I hadn't spoken. "So am I."

"There's nothing to be worried about. I swear it."

"I'm just afraid you're doing it again . . ."

"Doing what again?"

"What you did after your mom's funeral. The depression that followed, the days you wouldn't get out of bed. Your obsessive behavior. You're becoming that same person again." Her voice cracked. "You've been sitting in this depressing goddamn coffin of a room down here scribbling stories about dead boys in your notebooks. It's scaring me."

Somehow I managed to offer her a meager, harmless little smile. "You said it yourself just ten minutes ago—it's the stress. I guess I'm stressed out. You're right."

She shook her head, her eyes blurry with tears.

"Upstairs, remember? You said I should take a couple days off from writing. Maybe we should get out and do something together—"

Jodie continued to shake her head with mounting vigor. "No," she whispered. "No, Travis. We had that discussion last night, not ten minutes ago. You've been down here almost a full day."

The absurdity of this caused me to laugh. In hindsight, that laugh probably frightened her more than it helped to ease any tension, but admittedly I wasn't in the best frame of mind at the time. "What are you talking about?"

"You've been down here since yesterday evening."

"That's not—" I cut myself off. My mind was spinning like a wheel. Frantically I tried to put the pieces together, to assemble the time and date, but I couldn't. Was it actually possible? "Jodie . . ." I took a step toward her.

She held up both hands and took a step back. "No. Stop."

"Babe—"

"Stop it. I want you to stop it. I want you to snap out of it."

"I'm not—"

"Because you're scaring me."

I stopped walking, one foot over the threshold of the hidden basement bedchamber. Jodie had backed into the washer and dryer, her hands still up in a heartbreaking defensive posture. She was genuinely,

visibly frightened. Her fear of me was unwarranted—
I'd never struck her or any other woman in my life—
and made me tremble.

"Don't be afraid of me."

"I'm not afraid *of* you. I'm afraid *for* you."

"Listen—"

"No. Just stop." She took a shuddery breath. "Listen
to me and don't get angry. I'm going to stay the night
with Beth and Adam. I want you to know that I won't
come back to this house until this room is cleared out,
all that stuff is carried away, and the wall is sealed
shut. Am I understood?"

"You're overreacting."

"Am I under-fucking-stood?"

A chill rippled through me. "Yes," I rasped.

"Okay." Jodie went for the stairs and was halfway
up when she paused and said, "I love you. But I'm not
doing you any good pretending nothing's wrong."

I listened to her heavy shoes clump up the stairs
and tread across the floorboards above my head. There
was some rustling around, and then I heard the front
door slam. If she was taking any bags with her, they
were probably already across the street.

*A whole fucking day? I've been down here over-
night?* The sheer implausibility of it caused me to
laugh again, the sound of which instantly chilled me
to the roots of my soul.

Something was moving around behind me in Elijah's

room. I turned and saw nothing out of the ordinary at first . . . yet on closer inspection I noticed that two of the colored blocks—a yellow one and a green one—now stood on the writing desk, one standing vertically while the other balanced horizontally atop the first. Together they formed a capital *T*.

When the phone rang upstairs, I literally cried out. I pounded up the stairs and snatched the receiver off the kitchen wall, anticipating Adam's stern and overbearing voice to shout at me. I answered with a steely determination already seeded in my voice.

"Travis? It's Earl Parsons."

I cleared my throat and apologized for my initial abruptness. "I thought you were someone else. Is everything all right?"

"Right as rain," he said. He sounded like he was eating something. "I found Althea Coulter."

I felt a measure of triumph rise up through me. "Fantastic. Please tell me she's still alive."

"I guess that's a matter of opinion. She's got a permanent room in the Frostburg Medical Center's oncology ward. According to her son, who I spoke with earlier after telling him I was an old friend of his mom's, she's coming down to the wire."

"Cancer," I said flatly. "Jesus." Momentary clarity dawned on me. "I can't go harass a woman dying in a hospital bed."

"Then don't harass her," Earl said peaceably

enough. "Go visit her, bring her some flowers, make her feel good. Her son says she's pretty lonely, even though he tries to see her as much as possible. It might be good for her."

I took a deep breath and saw Jodie trembling against the washer and dryer again. "I'm being selfish about this, aren't I?"

"That depends," said Earl. "Are you doing this for you, or are you doing this for Elijah Dentman?"

"Both," I said after a very long time.

I jotted down Althea's room number at the Frostburg Med Center on the palm of my hand then thanked Earl for his help. He asked me to keep him in the loop on any further developments, and I promised I would apprise him of all that I'd learn.

"You really think we may have something here, don't you?" he said, and even though he inflected the end of the sentence into a question, I knew he felt just as strongly as I did.

Just as I hung up the phone I noticed something on the kitchen table. I went over to it and stared at two sections torn from a newspaper. I did not have to look closely to know the folded bits of newsprint were the articles about Elijah's alleged drowning that I'd stolen from the public library; they still held the creases where I'd folded them and stuffed them into my pocket. I must have forgotten to take them out of my pants, leaving them there for Jodie to discover when she went through the pockets before dumping my pants in the wash.

Splayed out on the table like evidence in a murder trial, those fragments of newsprint caused something heavy and indescribable to roll over deep down inside me.

CHAPTER TWENTY-THREE

Fortified against the cold in a heavy, fur-lined parka and a pair of wool gloves, I parked in one of the visitor spaces outside the Frostburg Medical Center's broad brick façade. Beside me on the passenger seat, a small leafy plant vibrated to the tune of the car's engine.

From the outside, the building looked like an ancient cathedral, all winding spires and Gothic architecture, the wing safeguarded behind a black cyclone fence crowned with spearheads. There was a long gravel driveway that trickled like an estuary up to the automatic doors beneath a reinforced portico. Its windows were small and barred, insulated with mesh wiring. The brick face was sterile and white, like bone heated in a kiln. A stand of pine trees loomed behind the building, immense and towering and dusted with snow. From where I parked, I could see a large weighted birds' nest nestled above the mezzanine, all sticks and bony branches. Two large falcons stood guard at either end of the mezzanine.

I climbed out of the car. The air was sharp and scented with winter. Craving a smoke, I produced a pack of Marlboros and popped one into my mouth, then chased the tip of it with my lighter, my hand cupped around it to keep out the wind.

The main thoroughfare of the hospital was shaped like a uterus. The carpeting was an institutional shade of brown orange (that specific brown orange only hospitals seem capable of duplicating), and large sodium lights fizzed above my head.

Following the numbered plaques on the walls, I turned down a long, claustrophobic hallway. There was surprisingly little lighting, and the staff was practically nonexistent. There was no receptionist at the bank of desks at the end of the hall, either. This wasn't the section of the hospital someone came to for a routine checkup or for any type of surgical procedure. This was where people came for good when they knew they were never going to leave again. There were no checkout procedures here.

Before locating the room number Earl had given me yesterday evening over the phone, I ditched into a men's restroom and saddled up to the sinks. That morning I'd showered hastily but hadn't shaved or washed my hair. My face was pallid and sunken at the cheeks, where bristling black hairs like spider's legs corkscrewed out from the flesh. Purplish crescents hung beneath my eyes, and my eyes themselves appeared bloodshot and shellacked. In brown corduroys, a thermal knit shirt with a flannel vest, and my ski parka, I looked like a vagrant who had shuffled in off the street.

"I could have at least shaved," I muttered to my reflection. I turned on the water at one of the sinks, washed my face, and matted down my too-long hair as best I could, pulling the knots out with my fingers.

I was startled when someone exited a stall behind me. The man nodded in quiet recognition, then left without washing his hands. He must have heard me talking to myself and figured it was safer risking potential bathroom-borne disease.

Taking a deep breath, I reexamined myself in the mirror. I thought of Jodie saying, *I was you*, and a burning ember briefly winked into existence at the small of my back.

I was you.

Room 218 was the closed door at the end of the farthest hallway. Carrying the potted plant in both arms, I approached the door, expecting all the while to feel a hand clap me on one shoulder and ask me who I was and what I was doing here. But that never happened.

I summoned a mental picture of Althea Coulter, and what I projected was a weak, elderly woman, her charcoal eyes blazoned with milky cataracts, her lips perpetually twisted into a bitter snarl. Her hands would be like claws—the serrated hooks of a carnivorous bird—and her head would be thick and unmoving and simply there. The room was going to smell of sour breath and medication and the ghostly traces of urine. She would be asleep. And I wouldn't be able to wake her, to ask her even a single question, and even if she was awake, she would be so far gone into a land of her own that the answers she provided (given that she provided any at all) would be of the fuzzy, make-believe, nonsensical variety. I pictured Althea Coulter as an ancient, mummified manikin, whose skin was scorched cloth and whose brain was a ball of string.

What the hell am I doing here?

Pausing outside the door, uncertain if I should knock or simply allow myself entry, I swallowed a hard lump that seemed to stick in the back of my esophagus.

I am standing on the line between fiction and reality.

I opened the door and stepped inside.

The woman in the bed was perhaps sixty, though with her sunken features, cobwebby wisps of hair, and blighted countenance, she looked like she could have been a hundred-year-old mummy rolled out on display.

I entered the room as silently as I could, careful not to let the door catch the latch too loudly as it shut. The room was dark and musty. There was an amalgam of odors clinging hotly to the air, each of them distinct and clinical: the reek of ammonia; the acrid underlying stench of urine; the insipid redolence of Althea Coulter's stale, immobile body beneath the paper-thin hospital bedsheets. There was another smell, too—though more like the hint of a smell rather than a smell itself—and I knew without a doubt that it was the smell of impending death.

She was awake, her frail body propped up on a cushion of pillows. As I moved farther into the room, she turned absently away from the single window beside her bed (it was covered by venetian blinds, impeding any actual view of the outdoors) and acknowledged me with only the subtlest of glances. Then she returned her gaze to the sheathed window.

"Ms. Coulter?" I said. My voice was amplified in the empty room.

She didn't say anything. In the silence, I could hear the labors of her breathing. The cogs were winding down, slowing with time.

I tried again: "How are you feeling?"

"Not hungry," she practically croaked, her voice

strained and tired. The sound was like guitar strings wound too tight.

"Oh," I said, "I'm not with the hospital."

Like a wooden puppet, her head slowly rotated on her thin neck until her attention settled back on me, this time with greater scrutiny. She was black, but her skin was as pale as ash, her lips white and blistered. I imagined one of the nurses attempting to draw blood from this living scarecrow only to be awarded with a puff of ancient dust as the needle broke through the dying woman's flesh.

She didn't need to speak; the question was in her eyes.

"My name's Travis Glasgow. My wife and I just moved to Westlake last month. We're in the old Dentman house." I didn't know where to go from here, and the woman's urgent stare was unrelenting. I grasped at a straw. "The Steins send their regards. They wanted me to give you this, actually." I made a gesture as if to extend the flowered plant to her, although I knew she would be unable to physically accept it.

Something in her face alerted me to the fact that she no longer remembered who the Steins were. At this, I felt a sinking loss drop through my body. This trip, it appeared, was going to be a bust.

Althea grimaced, scrunching her lips together to start up the motor of speech. When she spoke, her voice was the creaking sound of a coffin lid. "Set it down over here, son, where I can smell the flowers."

I walked around the side of the bed and placed the potted plant atop a small nightstand piped with industrial steel. The only other thing on the night-stand was a picture of a handsome young boy in a dark blue cap and gown. I wondered if it was her son Earl had spoken to on the phone.

"What'd you say your name was again?"

"Travis Glasgow. I hope I'm not disturbing you, ma'am."

With fossilized hands, she smoothed out the blankets on her lap. There was an IV attached to one broomstick arm. "I look busy to you?"

I offered her a crooked smile. "No, ma'am."

Her lower lip quivered as her face folded into a frown. "You say you live where, now?"

"The old Dentman house in Westlake. The one on the lake."

"The old Dentman house," she said. In her condition, it was impossible to gauge the tone of her voice.

"You used to tutor the Dentman boy, didn't you? Elijah Dentman?"

Despite her illness, Althea was no less perceptive; she picked out something unsettling in my question and hung on to it in temporary silence, perhaps going over my question and the reasons for why I'd be here asking such a thing. I listened to her wheezing respiration and did not hurry her. Eventually, she said, "You a friend of the Dentmans?"

"Not really, ma'am. I didn't even know anything about them until I moved into their house."

"So why'd you come here? I appreciate the company, Lord knows, but I don't understand it. All this way to bring me someone else's plant?"

This made me smile a nervous smile. It made Althea smile, too. She had the yellowed, plastic-looking teeth of a skeleton, a corpse.

My hands, the traitors that they were, had been unraveling a thread from my parka. Suddenly aware of this, I started to unzip my coat but paused halfway. "Would you mind if we talked for just a bit?"

"Only person comes to see me is Michael," she said wanly, "and he certainly don't bring me plants. So you're welcome to stay . . . provided I don't get too tired on you."

I took my parka off and draped it over the back of a metal folding chair that stood next to the nightstand. I sat down in the chair, my gaze returning to the framed picture of the handsome young man in the cap and gown. "This is Michael?"

"My son, yes," Althea said, and this time there was no mistaking the emotion in her voice. "My only baby. He's a good boy, this one. Got his demons like everyone, sure, but he's a good one."

"He's a handsome kid. Athletic."

"This here's his college graduation picture. See that? First in my family to graduate college. On a scholarship. How you gonna like that?"

"Good for him."

"He just needs to find himself a better job. It's tough today, kids out of school trying to find jobs."

"Does he come to see you much?"

"Used to. It gets hard for him. I don't blame him."

"My mom died of cancer several years ago. Breast cancer. She hung on for a while. It was rough on her. On my brother and me, too." This, of course, made me think of her funeral and how Jodie had dragged me out of Adam's house in a fit.

"Mine's the stomach," said Althea. "They been cutting little pieces of me away, a bit here and a bit there, snip-snip, but it really ain't the pain that's so bad. It's the sick. I get really sick in the mornings. Hard to eat food. Sometimes, too, I can't even sleep at night."

"There's nothing more they can do for you?"

"What's to do? What's left? Look at these things," she said, extending her arms with great care. They were as thin and as shapely as the cardboard tubing inside rolls of toilet paper. A network of veins, fat and blue-black, was visible beneath her nearly translucent skin. "Scrawny things. Jab me full of needles, drain me like a sieve." But her tone wasn't bitter. In fact, there was almost a sense of humor in it. Then she sighed. "We can put people on the moon and send radio pulses and whatnot into outer space, but we've yet to completely explore the mysteries right here on Earth, the mysteries right here inside our own bodies."

"I'm sorry," I told her. "If I'm disturbing you, I'll go."

Althea looked like she wanted to wave a hand at me. "Death is the disturbance. People are just passing road signs along the way. But listen to us, sharing cancer stories, trading them like baseball cards. Who wants to talk about cancer?"

"Not me."

"Me, either." She looked at me, then the picture of Michael. It was like she was desperate to find some sort of similarity between us, although she would be hard-pressed to find it. "You said you were married, I b'lieve. You got any children?"

"No, ma'am."

"You wanna stay and chat, you best quit being so damned polite, boy. I ain't your mamma. It's insulting."

"Sorry. I'll try to be ruder."

Althea cleared her throat, and it was a rather involved process. Aside from the scratchy, phlegm-filled rattle in her chest, her eyes also watered up, tracing tears down the contours of her face. It was disturbingly easy to make out her skull beneath that thin veil of stretched skin. Finally, after her throat was cleared and she'd wiped away the errant tears with the heels of her hands, she said, "So how come you're visiting some strange lady you ain't never met before?"

I'd had a whole song and dance routine prepared, no different than the one I'd performed for Ira and Nancy, as a way of greasing the wheels . . . but looking at this woman, I was suddenly certain she would easily see through such a lie. *She can see straight down to the pit of my soul*, I thought without a doubt.

"Do you believe in ghosts?" I hadn't known what I was going to say until the words were already out of my mouth. It had been a question I'd been dying to ask someone since moving to Westlake, but until now, I did not think I'd found the person who'd be able to answer it.

"Ghosts?" Althea said, as if she'd misheard me.

"Yeah," I said. "I know it sounds crazy."

"You're not a police officer, are you?"

"No," I said, thinking, *You a cop? Strohman send you here?* "I'm a writer."

"A writer who wants to ask an old woman about ghosts?"

I smiled warmly and rubbed my hands together between my knees. "Do you know about what happened to Elijah Dentman? That he drowned in the lake behind their house last summer?"

"Read about it in the papers." She stared at her

twisted fingers atop the bedclothes. Her knuckles were like knots in a hangman's noose.

"I'm bothered by that," I told her. "I'm bothered by the fact that he died and they never found his body. I'm bothered by what I think was a slipshod investigation by Westlake's finest. I think something happened to that little boy, and it was not an accident. But I've got no way of proving that, so I've come here to talk to you."

"And what is it you think I can tell you?"

"Honestly, I don't know. Maybe nothing. But maybe you know something that you don't realize is important, something that when added to everything else I've uncovered will help complete the puzzle."

Althea merely looked at me without a change of emotion. If she felt anything—anything at all—on the heels of what I'd just said her face did not betray such emotion. "Be a dear and open those blinds, please," she said finally, her voice still sedate.

I stood and crossed to the window. There was a plastic length of tubing the width of a pencil hanging vertically from one side. I turned it until the blinds separated, then pushed them all to one side. Outside, there was no bright sunshine, no dazzling blue sky, only a lazy drift of cumulous clouds. Everything looked hollowed out and the color of old monochromatic filmstrips. I could see my car in the parking lot.

Above it, the two falcons I'd witnessed nesting in the mezzanine earlier were circling in the air, waiting like buzzards for my Honda to die.

When I turned back around, Althea was looking once again at her son's photograph on the nightstand. "What do you write?"

"Novels."

"What sort of novels?"

"Dark ones. Horror novels. Mysteries. People chasing old ghosts, both figurative and literal."

Disinterestedly, she managed to lean to one side and adjust herself on her pillows. I could tell the act was not without pain. "Personally," she said, "I've always preferred romances. Do you ever write anything romantic? A love story?"

"They all start out that way," I answered, meaning it.

Althea glanced out the window. I could not tell if she was disappointed at the weather or if it was exactly what she'd expected. With Althea Coulter, I found I could assess very little.

"I don't know what it is you're hoping I can tell you," she said after a time.

"How long did you tutor Elijah?"

"For just over a month. I was sent there through a service with the county. I guess someone found out there was a little boy there who'd not been going to school. The county got after his mother."

"Veronica."

"Yes. Veronica."

"Did you know Veronica's father, Bernard Dent-man? It's my understanding Veronica and her brother, David, came back to Westlake to take care of him before he died."

"That's my understanding as well, though I didn't know the elder Dentman. He had passed before I got there."

"Why'd you stay only a month?"

"Because my illness was beginning to get the better of me."

"I'm sorry."

"Also, there was very little I could do for that child."

"How's that?"

"He was different."

My mind returned to Adam's description of the boy on the night of the Christmas party: *Veronica had a son about Jacob's age. Elijah was slow and homeschooled . . .*

"I doubt he was ever officially diagnosed," Althea continued, "but my guess is he was autistic."

"Why do you say that?"

"I could just tell. He had trouble communicating, trouble expressing himself, and his overall skills were way below the average ten-year-old. He spoke in fits and starts, like a tractor engine trying to turn over in cold weather. We'd go over simple math problems, and he'd become frustrated and hide under the kitchen table. Sometimes he could be lured out with cookies, but other times he would stay under there until after I'd left for the day. In fact, that's sort of how we got our relationship going, the boy and me, and I would bring him candies and dole them out to him at the beginning of each session."

"How was his relationship with his mother?"

"She loved him very much. But she was a shattered person herself—I'd always thought something traumatic had happened to her at some point, perhaps when she was a child—and she had difficulty rearing Elijah."

"What about David Dentman, Elijah's uncle? How was his relationship with the boy?"

"I hardly saw the man," she said. "I came by weekday afternoons, mostly when Mr. Dentman was out at work."

"But you'd met him before?" I said.

"Yes." There was a timorous hitch in Althea's voice. "Two days in a row, toward the end of my month at the Dentmans' house, David Dentman answered the door after I'd knocked. I knew who he was of course—little Elijah had spoken of his uncle to me on a number of occasions—but this was the first time I'd seen the man."

She expelled a bout of air, the sound like someone squeezing an old accordion. Then she frowned, wrinkles like estuaries running from every direction down her face. "He was very cold to me. He just opened the door and said, 'Elijah's not feeling well today.' I had my mouth half-opened to ask whether or not the boy's illness was a serious one that required his uncle to stay home from work, but he shut the door in my face before I had a chance to ask the question."

"That sounds about right," I agreed. "You said it happened twice?"

"The next day I returned to the house and knocked on the door. Once again, Mr. Dentman answered and spoke the same exact words to me through the crack in the door—that Elijah was not feeling well. He said it like he was reciting dictation from memory. But this time I was ready for him, and I was able to speak before he closed the door on me. 'I'm sure you're aware the county only allows for a minimal number of days for a child to be ill if he's going to receive a home tutor,' I said. This was only half true—the kid could have his sick days just like anyone else—but something in that man's presence alarmed me. After that first day, I'd spent the whole night thinking about the boy. When Mr. Dentman said the same thing on that second day, I knew something was wrong, and I wasn't going to let him off the hook that easy."

"What'd he say?"

"He looked me over from that crack in the door.

And not until he opened the door wider did I realize just how big he was. Broad shoulders and thick arms. I realized, too, that he had almost a baby's face, tender and soft in places, which didn't seem to fit with the rest of his body. Something about his face made me feel sorry for him, I remember."

"Yes," I said. "I've met him." Although unlike Althea, I'd recognized nothing in David's face that had made me feel sorry for him.

"He told me to come back tomorrow, that Elijah would be feeling well tomorrow. 'I'll certainly be back,' I told him. 'Elijah and I have a lot of catching up to do.' See, I'd intended for those words to hold more meaning, and maybe they would have for someone brighter than Mr. Dentman, but I don't think he understood the message I was tryin' to send."

"That's probably a good thing. My impression is he wouldn't take well to veiled threats."

"Needless to say, I came back the next day, and it was like the previous two days had never happened. David was gone, and Veronica answered the door when I knocked. Elijah was there, and we went through his lessons with the same practiced replication we'd done every day beforehand."

"How did he act?"

"Quiet and introverted as he always did but not the least bit under the weather." She knew where I was headed and said before I could ask my next question, "Looked him over quickly for bruises, too, of course. We're taught to do that if we feel something may be unusual. Even if it's just supposition."

"Did you notice anything?"

"Not a thing," she said, and I felt a sinking sensation at the core of my being.

"But I was still curious," Althea went on. "Before the day was over, I said to Elijah, 'Well, it seems like you're feeling better. Were you sick the past two days?' He just stared at me with those big eyes of his and didn't answer, which wasn't unusual if you knew the boy. He would sometimes ignore you deliberately. It wasn't his fault; as I've said, he was beyond my ability to help. He should have been seeing a specialist."

"Did you ever suggest that to anyone?"

"I did," she said quickly—so quickly, in fact, that she had to gasp for breath before continuing. "I went straight to the supervisor of the board. But before any next step could be taken, the cancer had different plans for me, and I had to withdraw my tenure. By that time, summer was already here. That's a bad time to get things passed through the board, seeing how they enjoy their summer vacations as much as—if not more than—the students. And before the next school year—"

"He had died," I finished, already familiar with the timeline.

"Yes. I remember reading about it in the newspapers, like I said. I felt so horrible for the little boy, of course, but also for his mother. She was such a lost soul herself, I often felt like she and her son were equal halves of the same whole. Almost like incomplete people holding on to one another for fear that if they let go, they'd both blink out of existence."

I nodded, shaken by the power of her insight. "Did you ask anything more of Elijah that afternoon?"

"I certainly did. You see, I had already started down the path, and my curiosity had bested me." Althea raised one hand and gripped my wrist, and I imagined I could feel the cancer boiling her blood beneath her flesh. "Sometimes when you follow something, you eventually end up chasing it."

I thought, *Sometimes we go in; sometimes we go out.*

"I asked him again if he'd been sick," she continued, "and once again he only stared at me without answering. So I approached it from a different avenue, asking him if he'd gotten in trouble in the last couple of days." She lowered her voice, as if the Dentmans were actually in the next room and she didn't want them to overhear our conversation. "If you coach children and tell them how to answer certain questions, they will typically answer those questions exactly in the way they'd been coached. But if you address them from different angles—angles they hadn't been prepared for—you'll find the answers you're looking for."

"What answers did you find?" I said, my voice as equally hushed.

"He said his uncle had yelled at him about the animals. He'd gotten in trouble about the animals."

"What animals?"

"The dead ones," Althea said. Her voice caused a muscle to jump in my right eyelid. "He told me about his pets—how he collected them when he found them in the woods and brought them back to the house. He told me about the rabbit and the squirrel—he'd found them both out in the yard that spring—but he said he'd gotten yelled at for the dog. 'Because it was too big and I couldn't hide it,' he said."

"The dog . . . ," I said, my voice trailing off.

"I had no idea what the poor child was talking about, and I told him so. That was when he got up from the table and very calmly asked me if I wanted to see some of his pets. Elijah said he'd kept some hidden, and his uncle hadn't been able to find them. I said okay, and he left and went upstairs for a time. I sat by myself at the kitchen table, and I could feel the cancer moving around in my stomach like something alive. The boy's mother never sat in on any of our sessions, but she was always hovering somewhere close by, like a ghost, and I could sometimes hear her through the walls.

"When Elijah came back, he was clutching an old shoe box to his chest. I asked him if his pets were inside, and he nodded and set the box on the table. I asked him if I could open it, and he nodded again. Are you beginning to understand what it was like talking to that child?"

"Yes," I said. I thought of Discovery Channel specials I'd seen on feral children growing up in condemned buildings in Europe and in the forests of South America, raised by wild dogs.

"So I opened the shoe box—"

"And saw birds," I finished. There was almost an audible snap as one of the puzzle pieces fell into place. "Dead birds."

Althea stared at me as if I'd just professed some secret of the universe. Then her chalky eyes narrowed, and her thin, bloodless lips pressed tightly together. For one hideous, depressing moment, I could actually hear her heart thudding behind the shallow wall of her chest.

"You know about the birds," she said, and she was not asking me a question but merely stating fact. If she was curious as to how I knew, she never asked. "In the end, he replaced the lid of the shoe box and climbed back up in the kitchen chair. I asked him if he knew the birds were dead, and he didn't say anything. I asked him how I found them, and he told me he would sometimes go off into the woods and find them at the foot of the trees, hidden under the brush and half buried in the dirt."

"In other words, you wanted to know if he was killing them," I suggested. I couldn't stop thinking of that time I'd squeezed the baby birds and the frog that popped in my hand like some windup toy. In all my therapy sessions after Kyle's death, I'd never spoken of that incident to the therapist. Distantly, I wondered what she would have said.

"Yes," Althea said, "but he wasn't killing them. He only found them that way, same as he'd found a rabbit one time and the squirrel."

"You mentioned a dog, too."

"Elijah said he found it buried in the woods by the lake. When he brought it to the house, he said his uncle yelled at him and told him to drag it back down to the woods and leave it there. 'Is that when you got in trouble?' I asked him. Elijah didn't nod or shake his head—didn't say anything, either, of course—so I asked him one last time if he'd really been sick the past two days. The child finally said, 'I went away.' Course, I asked him what he meant, but he only repeated the phrase—he'd gone away."

"Gone where?" I said.

"That's exactly what I asked him. 'Where'd you go?' Elijah didn't say, just kept repeatin' it—'I went away.' I asked him who took him away. Again, he didn't answer. He was scared—that much was evident—and I knew that if I continued down this path I might lose him and that he'd shut whatever door I'd managed to temporarily pry open. But as I've said, sometimes when you start out following something, you end up chasing it. So now I was chasing it. I leaned over the table and rested my hand on top of his. Even this simple gesture was risky; he never liked no one to touch him, not even his mamma, and I knew there was a good chance I'd send him running off into the next room. But I was desperate to reach out to him."

"Did Elijah run away?"

"No." Spittle had dried to white globs at the corners of Althea's mouth. "I asked him flatly if anyone had hurt him—his mamma or uncle or anyone. Elijah just looked at me for a long time. I remember I could hear the wall clock in the silence, the minutes climbing and multiplying. Then the boy slid his hand out from beneath mine and held it against his chest, rubbing it with his other hand, as if I'd burned him. 'Uncle David was mad,' he said. 'I went away.'

"I opened my mouth to speak just as a shadow loomed over us—the boy's mother stood in the kitchen doorway, looking like the ghost of a woman who'd been thrown off an old pirate ship. There were black circles around her eyes and that scar along the side of her face." Althea raised one thin arm, the elbow like a knot in the trunk of a tree, and mimed where Veronica's scar had been down the side of her own face. "It looked bright red against her pale skin. She'd damn near given me a stroke sneaking up on me like that."

"What did she say?"

"She told me she thought her boy might still be feeling a bit under the weather and it was probably best for me to finish up with the lessons before I caught whatever illness he had. 'Ma'am,' I told her, 'I don't think there's a thing in the known world this little boy can give me be worse than what I already got.' But she said, 'Go on now,' and floated out of the room.

"By that point, I'd already made up my mind to go to the board and tell them what had happened. And that look the boy's mamma had given me . . . well, it just chilled me straight to the bone and made me sicker than any chemotherapy I'd ever had. So I packed up my things and left the house.

"The following week, my stomach had gotten so bad that I called *myself* out sick. When it didn't look like I was going to feel any better, I called out for good. I never went back to that house again."

Without a doubt, Althea Coulter was a tough old woman who wasn't easily spooked, yet I wondered just how much of a role her stomach cancer actually played in her reluctance to return to the Dentman house, or if it had served as a convenient excuse.

"As far as you know," I asked her, "did anyone ever report any suspected child abuse?"

"Other than my suggestion to the board that something strange was going on in that house," Althea said, "I don't believe so. And understand *I* never suggested any type of child abuse to the board." Again, her small eyes narrowed. They were the color of candle wax threaded with reddened blood vessels. "These are strange things you've come to ask me, son. You've already said you don't think what happened to that little boy was an accident. Care to tell me what you do think happened?"

"I think he was killed." The words came assuredly and without reservation. Any doubt I'd been holding on to regarding this scenario was gradually sloughing away. "I don't know how to prove it, but I think the boy's uncle did it."

The old woman raised her eyebrows, and it was almost comical. "Have you gone to the police with your theory?"

"Sort of," I said, thinking, *What theory? All I've got are a bunch of innuendoes, hunches, and an unfinished, handwritten manuscript. There is no motive, no hard evidence.* "My brother's a cop. I spoke to him about it."

"What did he say?"

I smirked. "That I should let things go. That I'm digging around and wasting all this time—chasing what I started out following, as you say—for no reason."

A wry smile caused Althea's cadaverous face to look somehow more sinister. Death was breathing down her neck; all of a sudden I caught a whiff of it—the stale, decaying, almost sweet smell of a mummy. Then she shifted in her bed. "You've asked me all your questions?"

"Yes, ma'am."

"Good. Because I have one of my own," she said. "But if I'm gonna ask it, I'm gonna need some water to wet my throat. They've got cups at the nurses' station out in the hallway. Would you mind?"

I went into the hallway. There was now a young nurse, attractive and middle-aged with very brown skin and nice teeth, behind the circular Formica desk. I requested a glass of water for Althea, and she said it would be no problem. Then she asked if I had already signed the visitors' log. I assured her I had not. To this, she only smiled wider and slid a clipboard in front of me. There was a pen attached to it by a length of string. For reasons that still remain a mystery to me, I printed the name Alexander Sharpe in the appropriate box, then handed the clipboard back to her.

"Even trade," said the nurse, accepting the clipboard and handing me a Tupperware pitcher half-filled with water and a small plastic cup with the hospital's initials printed on the side in permanent marker.

Back in the room, I filled the cup with water and handed it to Althea. She accepted it, holding it with two hands like a child, and I watched her with some trepidation, certain that she would either spill the water all over herself or begin choking on it at any moment. But she did neither.

"Ahhh." She sighed, emptying the cup. She seemed much weaker than she had just moments ago—the death clock, clicking one more minute closer to demise. "Good, good."

I took the empty cup from her. "More?"

"Not unless you want to buzz someone in here to change these sheets in about three minutes." Althea waved a brittle hand at me, and I set the cup down beside the photograph of her son. "Stuff goes through me like lightning nowadays." She blamed the medication she was on for thinning her blood.

Sitting down in the chair, I folded my hands between my legs and leaned closer to her. "What is it you wanted to ask me?"

"Earlier you mentioned ghosts."

"Yes. I asked if you believed in them."

"Did I give you an answer?"

"No."

"Would you like to hear one?"

Feeling that she was toying with me, I couldn't help but grin. I said, "If it suits you."

Jangling like a newborn colt, the old woman raised her arms and flattened out her wrinkled bed-sheets. She sucked in a shallow breath as her eyes began to tighten with what I believed to be deeper scrutiny of my character. But as she began to speak again, I realized she was going back to her youth, retracing those fading footprints down the path of her own childhood.

"In the summer of my sixth year," she began, "my mother took odd jobs throughout the county. You see, my father had run off the previous summer with some woman he'd met down at Orville's drugstore—this was in Louisiana, where I grew up—and my mother wasn't going to let her only child starve because of him. He left her with nothing but the clothes on our backs and the ramshackle little tar paper hovel over in Cameron. We'd needed a car soon after he'd left, and I remember going with my mother to the used auto dealer off Best Street where, for one hundred and seventy-five dollars, she bought an old Chrysler the color of a house fire and about as reliable as the man my mother cursed the whole drive back to Cameron.

"The jobs my mother took consisted of housekeep-ing services for a rotation of regulars in the upper-class section of the city—great big gabled mansions with white columns and gardens so rich and thick you could actually get lost in 'em. She hit each house on her rotation once a week, and since I was too young to be left on my own and because there was no sense in payin' a babysitter more than my mamma was probably making cleaning those big houses, she dragged me along with her.

"Mostly, I would sit in the living room on some expensive couch, my hands firmly in my lap while I watched the television for hours. My mamma wouldn't even let me have a drink or a snack or anything like that, for fear I'd spill it on the couch. Other times I would sit and draw pictures at the kitchen table and leave them for the homeowners. You might think these home owners saw us as help and nothing more, and for the most part you'd be right, but it would be a lie to say I didn't go into some of those homes to find my artwork on their refrigerators, just as if I was their own child."

Her eyes twinkled with the memory, and I could tell it was a very important one to her.

"My favorite house belonged to the Mayhews, a handsome couple who had three older children away at college. The house was a beautiful bit of architecture—it certainly took my mamma all day to clean—but the best part was the sloping green lawn and surrounding gardens that dipped toward a lush palmetto grove that separated the Mayhews' backyard from the house directly behind them.

"One afternoon I was out playing in the palmetto grove when I saw a little girl, perhaps just slightly older than me, through the trees in the other yard. She was a skinny, pale-faced little thing with eyes like hen's eggs and very delicate features. Even at my young age, I recognized an intimate fragility in her. She wore a head scarf of floral design over what appeared to have been a bald scalp. When she waved at me, I giggled and waved back. Then she took off across the yard and into the grove where she hid behind the palmetto stalks. We played hide-and-seek all afternoon until my mamma called me from the back porch that it was time to go home.

"During one of our drives to the Mayhew home one morning, my mamma asked me what I did playing in that grove all day, and I told her about the little girl. I told her about the head scarf, too, and how she looked like she might be bald under there. My mother said the little girl was probably ill and I should be careful not to get her too wound up when we played together. 'What's her name?' my mamma wanted to know, and it occurred to me that I'd never asked her name. In fact, we hardly ever spoke with each other—we'd only hide in the narrow boles of the trees or behind large fans of palmetto leaves, and we would certainly laugh, but we'd never exchanged names.

"So mamma planted a seed. That afternoon, when the little girl came running through the trees to find me hiding beneath a moss-covered log, I said, very prim and proper, 'Hello. My name is Allie Coulter. What's your name?' That's how my mamma always told me to speak to folks for whom she worked. And even though my mamma didn't work for this girl's family, they were neighbors to the Mayhews, so I figured that was good enough.

"The girl did not answer me. Her smile faded, and then she just turned and ran back through the trees. I watched her go, I suppose, or maybe I called out to her—as vivid as this whole memory is for me, I've lost many of the details over the years—but she just kept going.

"That night when I told my mamma what happened, she said maybe the little girl was scared of me because I was new to her—which I later came to learn was my mother's way of saying I was black and the other girl was white and maybe our differences were becoming apparent to one another. But back then I had no concept of that.

"The following week, I was playing in the palmettos again. The girl with the head scarf appeared through the trees, watching me with those big, sad-looking eyes. I waved to her and she turned and ran—not away from me this time, but just as she always ran when we played, with a big smile on her thin face, her knotted knees pumping like pistons. We played our games all afternoon, and I never once asked her name again."

Something behind Althea's eyes grew cloudy, like splotches of ink spilling into a glass of water. "One night on the drive home after leaving the Mayhew place, my mamma said she asked about the little girl. 'Mr. Mayhew said the family who lives there used to have a little girl, but she died of leukemia several years ago,' she told me. This was so many years ago—decades and decades—but my memory is that my mamma was scared something terrible on that drive home. I remember her knuckles as white as pearls on the steering wheel and her skin was darker than mine. 'You're to stay in the house from now on when we go out there,' my mamma said. 'If that little girl wants to play with you, let her come find you and knock on the door.'

"I cried about it that night—not because I understood what my mother had told me but merely out of sorrow that I would no longer be allowed to run with the little girl through the palmetto grove. And next week when we went back, I stayed inside and sat by the windows that looked out into the yard, waiting—and hoping—for the little girl to knock on the door and set me free. But she never came. And I never saw her again."

There was an unease not unlike seasickness that trembled through me in tiny waves.

"As I've said," Althea said, her voice hoarse now from too much talk, "my memory is faulty, going back so far into my childhood, but I can recall with certainty that the little girl always wore the same clothes. And there were times during our play, when she would hide and I would seek her out, that I was never able to find her. I recall one time in particular when I gave up and went to the porch, feeling small and miserable. I caught a glimpse of that floral head scarf—I know I did!—and chased it down through the trees . . . but again, when I'd reached the spot, the girl was gone."

"Is it possible you were playing with a different girl? That the girl with leukemia had simply been someone else?"

"Of course," Althea rasped. I poured her another glass of water, but she didn't drink it immediately. "Anything's possible. But that's not what I believe."

"If she was a ghost," I said, "why were you able to see her?"

"Perhaps that is the bigger mystery." Two skeletal hands wrapped around the plastic cup, she sipped noisily before setting it down on the nightstand. "I like to think that maybe she realized how lonely I was that summer. How much I needed a friend." She smiled weakly. Horrifically, hers was the face of a jack-o'-lantern gone to rot. "Ghosts are no different than anything else in this grand universe. Why shouldn't they exist? Are they not the spirit, the part that gives the body life? So that spirit must reside somewhere after the person has died. Every schoolchild is taught the old scientific adage—that matter cannot be created or destroyed, correct?"

"Okay, sure." It was something I'd been taught as early as sixth grade, and I remembered our frumpy old science teacher, with the electrical tape on his loafers and his comical toupee, boiling water in a glass beaker over a Bunsen burner.

"It's true. Matter cannot be created or destroyed. So why should the soul be exempt from such laws of the universe?" Then Althea said something that I would carry with me for many, many years—something so profoundly simplistic that its clarity resonated through me like the clang of a bell. She said, "Nature does not know extinction. It knows only change. Metamorphosis. It knows that when life is snuffed out and the soul vacates the body, it must, by definition, go somewhere. And if you don't believe in God or a god or in heaven and hell, then where do souls go?"

"Here," I said, and it was like she had drawn the word right out of me. I hadn't even paused to think. "They stay right here with us."

"As ghosts," she said.

"As ghosts," I repeated, smiling in spite of myself.

Returning the smile, Althea shut her eyes and let her head ease all the way into her pillow. I could tell she was in pain, but I could also tell she was trying to hide her discomfort from me. Finally, just when I thought she had fallen asleep, her eyes opened and she sought me out, as if she'd forgotten where I'd been sitting.

"I'm going to leave now," I told her, getting up and grabbing my parka. "You're tired."

Her watery eyes fluttered shut.

"Are you in pain?" I whispered.

"Always in pain . . ."

"Do you want me to get a nurse?"

"To do what? Tell me I'm dying? I already know that."

Pulling on my coat, I headed to the door. "I appreciate your time, Althea. I wish we could have met under different circumstances."

"Make me a promise," she said from the bed, her voice no stronger than the rustling of tissue paper.

"Anything," I told her and waited for her to speak again. But the next thing I heard was the labored grinding of her respiration as she faded off into unconsciousness.

CHAPTER TWENTY-FOUR

Several miles outside of Frostburg, the setting sun torched the land below, casting trails of golden light across the frozen hillsides. Small black birds sat on power lines like semicolons. In the fading afterglow of my meeting with Althea, my mind returned to the events of the past two months at 111 Waterview Court—the mystery I had begun to unravel, which revolved around my gradual understanding that David had murdered his nephew, as well as the more inexplicable events that had plagued me since that first night in the house when I'd heard bare feet padding down the hallway.

Althea's story of the ghost girl did not so much frighten me as it caused a hot serpent of misunderstanding to coil at the base of my guts. Was I misinterpreting those nightly sounds, the handprint on the basement wall, the strange splotches of water on the concrete floor that too closely resembled a child's footprint? We have been taught by popular culture that ghosts are restless beasts, hungry for vindication and revenge on those who have wronged them. But was this all just nonsense? I couldn't help but replay Althea's words over and over in my head—*I like to think that maybe she realized how lonely I was that summer. How much I needed a friend.* If that was true, was I missing something with this whole Elijah-David scenario?

Inevitably, my mind returned to Jodie. *I was you.* My interest in the Dentmans had frightened her badly enough to send her across the street to my brother's house. I hated myself for it.

Can't I just forget the whole thing? Can't I throw in the towel on this murder-mystery fiasco? Call the haulers to come get Elijah's stuff out of the basement and burn my goddamn writing notebooks? Can't I just shake this thing and let Jodie and me move on with our lives?

But I didn't think I could do it. Moreover, I didn't think I was supposed to do it.

When I reached the outskirts of Westlake, I eased behind a small queue of cars at a traffic light. Leaning over, I popped open the glove compartment and rooted around until I found a pen and a curl of paper, which was actually an old Office Depot receipt. On the back of the receipt I wrote, *It has been said that nature does not know extinction*, knowing that it would make the perfect opening line for my *Floating Staircase* novel if I ever actually finished it.

The light changed, and the driver behind me laid on the horn.

Nervous and jittery, I felt like a bullet shot from a gun. I was on the verge of revealing some great and hidden truth—I knew this without question, though I had no concept of how I knew—and I floored the accelerator the rest of the way home.

The house was a dark shell. Warmer temperatures had caused the snow to start its retreat, and I could see the grayish lawn at the edge of our property. I drove up the gravel driveway as evergreens rushed in on either side of the car. Some small part of me was holding out hope that Jodie would be home, but the realistic part of me knew that wouldn't be the case. She was hardheaded; she would stick to her guns.

Climbing out of the car, I stood staring at the house as if it had just appeared in front of me out of thin air. The front porch slouched under the weight of melting snow. The windows looked pebbly with grit.

I am not willing to lose my marriage over this bullshit, I thought. I'd already decided that I would call the junk haulers tomorrow to get Elijah's stuff out of our basement. Then I would go over to Adam's house and see Jodie.

I walked to the rear of the house and wended through the naked trees on my way to the lake. The neighboring pines whispered their conspiracies all around me. I paused as the lake came into clear view. Much of it was now unfrozen, save for a Texas-shaped panel at the lake's center. It was the first time I'd actually seen the water. The lake trembled in the moonlight.

Find an anchor, the therapist piped up.

"Shut the fuck up," I told the voice, turning and walking back to the house.

Inside, it was cold as hell. Darkness pressed against the windows. I turned on very few lights. From the basement I retrieved Earl's crime scene photos. I stuck them to the refrigerator with magnets, sat on the floor, and studied them, my back against one kitchen wall and a plate of cold chicken in my lap. I was missing something in those photos, something important, but it remained elusive.

Find an anchor.

There was one last thing I could do; oddly enough, it had been something my brother had said to me the other day while I was chopping firewood in the backyard. *Murderers have motives, innocent people have alibis, and you can't lock someone up behind bars because pieces don't fit.* I grabbed the telephone and punched in Earl's number. It rang a number of times before his sleep-heavy voice growled a rough hello into the receiver.

"Sorry to wake you," I said. "It's Travis."

"Shoot," he garbled, "I was awake. What's the news on Althea?"

"She's a sweet old woman who's dying a painful death. I felt horrible for her."

"What did she say about the Dentmans?"

I relayed to him the story of Elijah's mysterious two-day illness and the boy's response that he "went away" for those two days. I told him, too, of the dead animals the boy had been collecting and how Uncle David did not approve of such behavior. "Just how much he didn't approve," I appended, "is the million-dollar question."

"Did you tell her your theory? About David having murdered the boy?" There was a youthful exuberance that ran through the old man's voice.

"The only solid thing I was able to get from her was that they were a bizarre family. She knew nothing definitive."

"Well, have we reached an impasse?"

I was still studying those photographs on the refrigerator. "Not quite. I guess there's one more thing you could do for me, but I'll be honest—I feel like a heel asking you to do this."

"Nonsense."

"I just don't want you getting into any trouble."

"I'm a big boy. Why don't you tell me your little plan, and I'll decide for m'self just how much trouble I'm lookin' at."

So I told him my plan. "Don't use your real name," I warned him. "If you can't think of one on the spot, give them my name. I don't want you getting jammed up in all this."

"Hell," he cooed, then whistled. "You've got one hell of a sneaky streak in you, son, don't you?"

"I'm not holding out much hope on this. In fact, I'm not quite sure what you'll find or even what it'll prove until I see it in front of me."

"I'll get on it first thing tomorrow," Earl promised. In the background I could hear one of his dogs whining. I thought of the monstrous wolfhound guarding the credenza in Earl's tiny double-wide.

"Just be careful," I said and hung up the phone.

Around eight o'clock I fixed myself a peanut butter and jelly sandwich and a pot of coffee. Carrying the stack of crime scene photos, I sank back into the basement.

I am missing something.

Something important.

The basement was charred, sooty darkness, blank as tar paper. The bulb in the ceiling was dead, and I couldn't find any replacements. Instead, I located a flashlight and cast its beam into Elijah's hidden room behind the wall. On the desk, someone had constructed a staircase out of the colored wooden blocks. Holding a coffee mug in one hand and with the eight-by-tens tucked under my arm, I just stared at those blocks, spotlighted in the beam of my flashlight. The coffee burned all the way down to my toes with each sip. *Thing about coffee*, I thought, *is that it forgives you no matter what.*

I sat down at Elijah's writing desk, clicking on the small lamp in one corner. For a while I studied the photographs in my lap. Drank coffee. I ignored the blocks until I could ignore them no longer. One block at a time, I picked them apart Jenga-style, until the structure lost all semblance of form and function. It turned into nonsense. *There.*

I slid one of my notebooks in front of me, turned to a clean page, and began to write. I wrote as my mouth started to bleed onto the page and then onto my shirt. Bringing a hand up to my lips, my fingers came away smeared with blood. It occurred to me that I'd been chewing on the back of my pencil and hadn't even felt one of the splinters jab my lower lip. Had I swallowed any without knowing? I imagined a thousand shavings of wood sizzling in the feverish acid of my stomach.

Then I looked at the photograph of the lake. Then

down at the page where my spidery handwriting leaned and spiked like waves. Then back down at the photo. I thought, *Sometimes we go in; sometimes we go out.* And I thought, *Something doesn't add up here.*

I focused on the photo of haunted Veronica Dentman standing among the trees. Empty. Blinded. Terrorized. Already dead. *Already dead*, I thought. I flipped to another photo, this one of a group of police officers trudging through the trees toward the house. A number of them had turned to catch the photographer just as he snapped the picture, their faces blurred from the movement and as indistinct as the faces of passengers glimpsed in the windows of a passing train.

I looked at what remained of the wooden staircase. All the blocks were red. I could have sworn they were multicolored when last I left it. Looking closer, I noticed the newspaper clippings I'd ripped from the papers at the library underneath the blocks. The photo of Elijah Dentman glared up at me, nearly accusatory. His vacant eyes professed a sinister malevolence tonight.

My back creaking as I rose, I gathered my notebooks and the crime scene photos and staggered up the stairs. *Bath*, I thought, *then bed.* Before heading to the second floor, I paused by the telephone. Stared at it like it owed me money. Behind me, the clock on the microwave read 88:88. Finally, I picked up the phone and punched in Adam's number.

On the other end, the phone trilled and trilled and trilled, and no one answered.

Do they have caller ID? Is it possible they're actually avoiding my calls now?

I stopped at the liquor cabinet and made off like a thief with a bottle of Wolfschmidt.

Upstairs, the hallway was a mine shaft. Slatted blue light pulsed in from windows at the end of the hallway. Up here, Jodie's perfumed scent still lingered. Absently, I wondered if she'd come back in my absence to retrieve more of her things.

I went directly into the bathroom, punched the light on, and closed the door with one foot. After taking a preliminary swig, I set the plastic bottle of vodka on the counter and stared at my reflection in the mirror. Scraggly, matted beard, sunken eyes, unkempt hair curling down into the fans of my eyelashes. Disgusted, I looked away . . . but the sight of Jodie's bobby pins beside the sink caused my eyes to burn.

Turning on the bathtub, I watched it fill with water as steam clouded the mirror, eradicating that hideous monster. I took another chug from the bottle, peeled off my reeking clothes, and left them in a smoldering heap on the floor.

That's right, friends and neighbors. Getting fuck-drunk tonight.

Still clutching the bottle of vodka, I climbed

into the tub and winced at the scalding water. With one foot, I adjusted the temperature before settling into the water. The faucet bucked and gurgled and steamed. The hot water felt good; my knotted muscles started coming undone.

The crime scene photos were spread out on the bathroom floor. Their glossy surfaces were hazy with moisture from the steam. Again—crazily—I thought of my old science teacher boiling water in a beaker over a Bunsen burner. Jefferson? Johnson? For the life of me, I couldn't remember the son of a bitch's name.

Out in the hallway on the other side of the closed bathroom door, I heard the creaking of floorboards. I thought I caught movement at the crack beneath the door. Laughing, I choked back more of the horrible-tasting vodka and rested my head against the shower tiles. And—

And I was standing outside in the darkness of night. The wind was slamming against me, prickling my skin and freezing the marrow in my bones. The force of the wind caused me to realize I was balancing precipitously on some structure, high above the world. Looking down, I found my bare feet planted on the top riser of the floating staircase—only this staircase was a skyscraper, a monolithic finger jutting straight up toward the blackened, star-littered heavens, not wooden and pyramidal but golden and tubular, spiraling like a corkscrew. A million miles off in the silvery distance, I could see the blinking diodes of light that comprised Westlake.

Directly below me, someone floundered in the black water. I jumped. Hurling through the blackness of space . . . but it wasn't space at all; it was water. I heard the roaring in my ears as I speared into the freezing, lightless depths. Holding my breath, I swam through the murk toward a shimmer of spectral light. Things impeded my passage: pines. Underwater pines. The whole forest was submerged, and I swam through it toward that swirling light. Evergreens sprung up like fence posts, their boughs impossibly thick and weighted, like waterlogged pillows. Tentacular vines snaked up from brown murk, twining themselves around my ankles. My face scraped against scabrous bark, and clouds of red stained the water.

I swam through a part in the pines, the light now like the glow of searchlights on a sunken battleship, only eerily green. I pushed on, my lungs burning and about to burst, just as my fingers grazed a doughy, pliable object. A body floated by me, its eyes swelling like jellyfish from their sockets, hair a fan of colorless seaweed waving in the current, the corrugated ridges of a purpling brow—

Screaming, I sat up, awake. My heart was like a blender on purée. The bathtub was filled nearly to capacity. The bottle of vodka floated between my up-raised knees.

Leaning over the side of the tub, my breath coming in great whooping gasps, I gathered the photos from the floor, wiping away the condensation. I looked at the picture of the policemen trudging up the lawn toward the house, then flipped to the one of Veronica standing between the trees.

The trees.

A laugh tickled my throat.

And then it all came clear as the missing piece of the puzzle finally snapped loudly into place.

The sound was nearly deafening.

CHAPTER TWENTY-FIVE

Adam answered the door in his bathrobe and slippers. His hair was a jumble of tight curls, matted at the back, and I guessed I'd just woken him from a nap. He muttered something—I caught my wife's name in his garbled intonation—but before he could finish, I stormed past him into the house, my boots leaving wet banana shapes on the hardwood.

"What are you doing?" he said more forcefully, letting the front door slam behind him.

I motored straight into the kitchen. My hair was still wet from the bathtub—I was aware of ice crystals already starting to form in clumps—and I'd simply thrown on my old clothes in an obsessive rush to get across the street as fast as I could.

"Where is everyone?" I said, noting the quietness of the house.

"Jodie and Beth took the kids to a movie. What are you doing here?"

Pulling out a chair, I dumped the stack of eight-by-tens on the kitchen table, then sat down.

Adam glared at me from across the room.

"Sit down," I told him. "I want to show you something."

"You're drunk. I can smell the alcohol coming off you in waves. Do you really think that's such a good idea?"

"Please. Just sit."

With obvious reluctance, he pulled out the chair opposite me and eased into it like someone eases into a hot tub. His eyes never left mine.

With both hands, I pushed the photographs in front of him. "Tell me what you see."

Still staring at me, he picked up the photos, dwarfing them in his big hands. Finally, he averted his gaze and examined the first couple of photographs. There was no expression on his face. "You came here to bring me pictures of your backyard?"

"Keep looking."

He flipped through a few more, pausing when he understood what he was seeing: crime scene photos from the search for Elijah Dentman. "Where'd you get these?" His voice was practically a snarl.

"Does it matter?" I reached across the table and plucked the photos from my brother's hands. I set them down between us so we could both see them. "I don't need to tell you when these were taken. You're even in one of them." I drummed a finger on one of the photos. "These are some of the cops walking up from the lake toward the house. All the faces are blurry but this one is you." I pressed one finger on the second cop from the left. "You can tell it's taken much later in the day than some of the others because of the positioning of the sun."

Adam would not look at the picture.

"Then there's this one," I went on anyway, turning to the shot of Veronica and her blank stare. "She's looking toward the lake in this shot, probably just catching the photographer as he snaps the picture. It's evident the photographer's down by the water shooting up at her. You can tell by the angle, and if you'd walked the perimeter of the lake and glanced toward my house—"

"Travis . . ."

"Just look at them." I turned both photographs around so that he could view them right side up. But he didn't look down.

Eerily calm, my brother said, "I don't believe this. I swear to God I don't believe this." He regarded me with such abject disappointment, it was all I could do not to get up and flee from his house like a crazy person. "When I opened the door a minute ago, I guess

I had some hope that you'd come to your senses and were here to see your wife."

"You're missing the point. Look at the photos. Look at the trees."

"I don't—"

"Just look at them, damn it!"

Tiny beads of perspiration had popped out along Adam's upper lip. Finally, he looked at the photos on his kitchen table. He said nothing, waiting for me to continue.

I said, "What do you notice?"

"About the trees?"

"Yes. What do you notice?"

"I see . . . I see trees."

"Yes," I said. "That's right. Trees. A ton of them. A goddamn shitload. It's the middle of summer, and the whole goddamn yard is infused with trees."

"Your point being?"

"My point being David Dentman's statement to the police is bullshit. He said he was watching the boy swim in the lake that day from the house. It's his eyewitness testimony that claims when he could no longer see the boy, he ran down to the lake to find him. That's when he noticed he was gone." Again, I tapped both pictures. "But that's bullshit. You can't see the back of the fucking house through the trees, which means you can't see the goddamn staircase from the house. You can hardly even tell there's a lake back there in the summer, I'll bet."

Adam scowled. "What are you talking about? I've seen it from your house. You and Jodie marveled about the lake the day you moved in. You can see it out your bedroom window."

"Sure," I said, nodding. "In the winter. And even then you have to look through a meshwork of tree branches. When spring comes and those branches fill up with leaves, you probably can't see a single drop of water from my bedroom window. Or any other window of the house."

Adam sighed and leaned back in his chair. I couldn't tell if he was working over what I'd just told him or if he was about to tell me to get the hell out of his house. His expression was unreadable.

"You were there that day." I pushed the photo of the cops closer to him across the table. "You couldn't see the house through those trees, could you?"

"You're asking me to remember *trees*?"

"Christ, why are you being so obstinate about this? It's not just about the fucking trees; it's about what Dentman said."

"So this makes David Dentman a liar," he stated.

"It does."

"Irrefutably?"

"W-well, sure," I stammered, trying to think of

any holes in the story before Adam could point them out. "He lied to cover up what really happened."

Adam folded his arms across his chest. "So what really happened?"

I slumped against the chair. "I'm not exactly sure. I mean, I haven't worked everything out in my head . . . just a . . . a . . ."

"Just what?" That classic Adam Glasgow condescension was in his voice, an uneasy serenity in the face of all I'd just showed him. At that moment I realized that I would never stop feeling like his younger brother—his subordinate, his weak and guilty little brother.

"You're refusing to put the pieces together." I slammed one hand down on the table. The photographs fluttered.

"Don't do that," he said, glancing at my hand.

"David Dentman has a criminal record," I trucked on, ignoring him. "David Dentman lied in his statement to the police. Elijah Dentman's body was never recovered from a goddamn self-enclosed lake!"

Adam breathed heavily through flared nostrils. I found myself temporarily mesmerized by the pores in his nose and the dark sheen of beard that looked painted along his jawline. I couldn't pull my gaze from him.

"So David Dentman killed his nephew," said my brother.

"Yes."

"And these pictures are your proof of that? These"—he gestured at the photographs—"trees? A confused and heartbroken man's statement taken in the midst of searching for his nephew's corpse?"

"I know what it sounds like," I admonished. "But it doesn't change the fact that—"

"Man, there *are* no facts." Adam shocked me by reaching across the table and covering one of my hands with his own. Tenderly.

I fought the electric urge to buck backward as if injured.

"Listen to me, okay? We've investigated the matter. It's not unusual for divers to come up empty, even in what you call a self-enclosed body of water. Do you have any idea how big that lake is? Do you know how many boles or submerged deadfalls or rock formations are on the floor of the lake? How many rocky caves and underground tributaries going out to a hundred rivers? All those places where a body can get lost, get trapped. Forever." He shrugged. It was a hopeless gesture. "As for these photos, David Dentman says he saw the kid by the lake. Who's to say he didn't? And Nancy Stein saw him. Is she a liar, too?"

I pulled my hand out from under his. "Nancy Stein saw him because she was walking her dog by the water. You can't see the staircase from their house, either. The Steins both said so."

"Christ, maybe the goddamn wind was blowing, or maybe the trees weren't as thick—"

"That's bullshit. Come on."

"Then where's the body, huh? If David Dentman killed the kid, you tell me where to find the body."

The kitchen fell silent. All I could hear was the ticking of the wall clock behind my brother's head. It sounded like industrial machinery.

"I want you to really listen to me good, Bro, all right?" Adam leaned farther over the table, closing the distance between us. To my horror, he looked close to tears. "This isn't a book. This is real life. Whatever puzzle you've been trying to work out, well, I'm telling you, there ain't nothing there."

Angered and frustrated, I could only sit slouched in my chair, my arms folded protectively over my chest, one leg bouncing spasmodically on the floor. Once more I was that punk kid, pouting in the principal's office.

Adam chewed on his lower lip. It was something he had always done in his youth when he found himself in a difficult spot. "I was putting off saying this to you," he said eventually, "because I wasn't sure how to say it. But I'm just gonna say it anyway. Because you're not getting any better."

"You make me sound like a heroin addict."

"You're acting like one."

"Go to hell," I said, kicking my chair back and rising.

"No," he said calmly. "Sit down. You want to pull the tough-guy routine, fine, but do it after we're done here. This is important."

"I'm sick of you telling me what to do."

Adam took a deliberate breath and said, "Sit down for Jodie's sake, then."

Fuming, I sat back down.

"Jodie's upset. I'm talking really upset. She's worried you're falling into another depressive state, just like after Mom died—"

"Jodie's got her nose in too many psychology textbooks," I growled.

"—and just like how you were after Kyle's death."

"Jodie didn't know me then."

"But I did. I saw how it decimated you."

There was a burning in my face. My eyes itched.

Adam sighed. "You're making up something because you so desperately need to be the hero."

Curling my toes in my boots, I turned away from him . . . and found myself staring at a framed photo of us from his wedding sitting on a shelf. I couldn't wrench my gaze from it. It ridiculed me.

"You're chasing this thing, hoping that if you fix it, you'll absolve yourself of your guilt over Kyle."

I felt my whole body flinch.

"You can't undo what happened to our brother,"

Adam said flatly. "No matter how many imaginary murders you solve, no matter how many books you write about it, you're still powerless to change what happened to him." He paused. "And now you're letting your marriage fall apart in order to fix your own mistakes of the past. You're caught in a cycle here. Can't you see that?"

I couldn't answer.

"Travis?" he said, and his voice was impossibly distant now. He was talking from the moon.

I turned away from the picture, a noxious soup broiling in my stomach.

Adam stood, stacking the photos into a neat pile. Then he glanced at the wall clock, biting his lip again. "Go home. Think about what I've said. If any of it makes sense after you sober up, maybe you should give Jodie a call in the morning. All right?"

Numbly, I nodded. I stood and collected the photos from the table. As I followed Adam to the front door, my boots squelching muddy tracks in the hallway, I curled the photos into a tube. My palms were sweating.

"Go," he said, opening the door. "Get some sleep."

I stepped into the dark, my shadow stretching before me in the panel of soft rectangular light that spilled out from the open doorway, and hoofed down the icy driveway. The sound of Adam's door closing echoed across the cul-de-sac.

I was shaking.

It was a mistake to move here. We should have stayed in North London. My relationship with Adam has always been better by telephone.

Crossing the cul-de-sac, I pulled my coat tighter about my body and strode with my head down against the biting wind. Off to my right, someone flashed a pair of headlights, temporarily paralyzing me in the middle of the street like a deer. I could make out the bracketed shape of an old two-tone pickup idling silently against the curb. I could smell the fetid exhaust pumping from the tailpipe as I approached the driver's side of the vehicle.

The driver rolled the window down.

Sitting behind the wheel was David Dentman.

CHAPTER TWENTY-SIX

"Get in the truck," Dentman muttered off-handedly. The only light inside the cab was from the burning ember of a cigarette.

"What are you doing here?" There was an icy finger tracing the contours of my spine.

"Looking for you." He leaned across the passenger seat and opened the passenger door. The interior dome light came on, sending inky pools of shadow running down his face.

"No. We can talk out here."

"Christ, Glasgow, don't be such a pussy. I'm not gonna hurt you. Get in the truck." He sounded disgusted with the whole ordeal.

It was a stupid damn thing—one of those stupid damn things that cause audiences in movie theaters to shout less than flattering names at the ignorant but well-meaning protagonist—but I had my reasons. So I walked around the front of David's pickup, feeling the heat of the headlamps wash over me as I passed, and got into the passenger seat. All too aware of the photographs I was carrying, I held my breath; rolled into a cone, they couldn't have been more conspicuous if they'd been adorned with Christmas lights.

The vehicle's interior smelled of turpentine and tobacco and whiskey and sweat. This close, I could smell Dentman, too, and it was a strong, masculine, canine smell—almost feral.

Dentman dropped the truck into gear. The engine roared and caused the entire chassis to shudder. It sounded like there was an army tank under the hood.

"I thought you just wanted to talk," I said.

The pickup's headlights cleaved into the darkness as we pulled out into the street and headed for the intersection. Watching as the speedometer climbed well past fifty, fifty-five, sixty, I reached for the seat belt but found none. *Yeah, this is smart.*

Dentman slouched in the driver's seat, huge and filling it completely, both his big, meaty paws gripping the steering wheel, his head tilted slightly down while watching the blackened, narrow roadway from beneath the cliff of his Neanderthal brow.

"This is a residential neighborhood," I reminded him.

His profile affected the faintest smirk.

Wind whipped in through the open driver's side window, freezing the air and emitting an aboriginal hum as it funneled through the tube of photographs I held. I tried to will the photos away into nonexistence by mere thought. *Please, please, please.*

Dentman cast an empty stare at the photos and, presumably annoyed by the sound, rolled up his window. "You stink like a distillery," he commented after a moment, actually sniffing the air like a bloodhound.

The pickup bucked along the road, the engine furious under the hood. I counted the seconds until the doors came loose on their hinges.

"What do you want?" I said.

"Open the glove compartment."

"No, thanks. I'm fine."

"Open it."

Hesitantly, I opened the glove compartment. The door dropped like a mouth, and a little orange light spilled out onto my lap. There was only one item inside, and I had to blink several times to convince myself that it was actually what I knew it to be. "I take it you don't want an autograph," I said, staring at the paperback copy of *The Ocean Serene.*

"I highlighted my favorite paragraphs," Dentman said.

"Is that right?" Heavy with sarcasm.

I opened the book and flipped through the pages.

What moonlight there was allowed me to see the highlighted portions of the text. I stopped on one of the pages and read it. Then I closed the book, pushing it back inside the open glove compartment, and stared at Dentman's sharp profile, outlined in phosphorescent moonlight. "I'm flattered you're such an avid fan, but where the hell are we going?"

"Tell me something," Dentman said, his tone almost conversational as we barreled through the streets. "Whose life is that book about?"

"Huh?"

"That's what you do, isn't it? Steal people's lives? Cheapen their tragedies for the sake of entertainment? For the sake of your bank account?"

"I don't know what the hell you're talking about."

"What is it you think about me? What is it you think about my family?"

"You've lost your mind," I told him.

"Reach under your seat."

"No. Enough bullshit. What's this all about?"

"You tell me."

"Look, I don't know what you're getting at. If this is about the box I brought by your house, I thought we'd already—"

"Reach under your seat," Dentman repeated with more than just a hint of irritation in his voice.

Reluctantly, I leaned forward and slid one hand

beneath my seat. My breath was rattling in my throat. I patted around the stiff carpeting, not knowing what to expect, what I was searching for . . . and then the tips of my fingers touched something. I took it out and put it in my lap, blessedly covering the photographs with it. Looking at it, I felt something thick and wet roll over in the pit of my stomach, and I thought I would throw up. My hands were shaking, and I couldn't keep my teeth from vibrating in my head. In my throat, my breath temporarily seized up. I prayed for unconsciousness.

On my lap was my missing writing notebook.

There were a million questions—a trillion questions—shooting through my brain, but my mouth, that traitorous cretin, would not formulate the words.

Dentman maneuvered the shuddering pickup straight down Main Street and past the depressed little shops of rural Westlake, now dark and closed. Only the shimmering pink neon lights of Tequila Mockingbird were visible, radiating with a dull sodium throb in the darkness. Ahead, through the windshield, the night was a tangible thing—a black velvet cloak draped over the valley.

"W-where did you get this?" I stammered, finding my voice at last. My mind reeling, I felt the cold cloak of fear settle over me the moment I realized that I had never changed the locks on the doors upon moving into the house on Waterview Court. *My God*, I thought, unable to move, unable to breathe. I couldn't pull my gaze from the notebook—the camouflaged black-and-white cover, the string-bound spine, the frayed edges.

We bumped along the roadway, leaving Westlake behind us like a distant memory; all that existed of the town was the spatter of fading lights in the pickup's rearview mirror.

"You son of a bitch," I muttered, lifting the notebook. It weighed two hundred pounds. "You broke into my house."

"I did no such thing." He gunned the truck to seventy miles an hour. I could feel the tires spinning over black ice. "Actually, you left it at my house. In that box you brought over."

The world struggled to remain in focus.

"You been asking around town about me," Dentman said. "Don't think I haven't noticed."

"I can explain."

"You can explain why you've got my family's name written in that notebook of yours?"

"It's going to sound strange, but yes, I can explain all of it."

"I don't like it." His attention was fixated on the darkness ahead. There were no houses here—no lights and certainly no signs of civilization—only the black-on-black wash of heavy trees on either side of the truck. "I don't like you sniffing around in my private life, my private business." He paused, perhaps for dramatic effect. "I don't like what you did to my sister even more."

I choked down a hard lump of spit. "I didn't do anything to her."

"You got her all stirred up." Denton faced me. His eyes were hollow pits in the darkness. I could smell cigarette smoke coming through his pores. "She loved that boy. It broke her heart what happened to him. What kind of sick fuck follows her to a new town to revisit such a tragedy?"

"That wasn't my intention."

"Oh," he countered, "I know your intention. I seen your books and how you like to exploit people's tragedies."

"They're just books. They're not real." I gripped the dashboard with one hand. "Please watch the road."

He shook his head like he was disappointed in me. "She told me about you. Said you talked about the boy. Told her she could have all that stuff back if she came out to the house."

"No. I never said that. I never told her to come out to the house."

"So you're saying my little sister's lying to me?"

"The road," I groaned. "Watch it."

Ahead, the road forked. Dentman took a right

without signaling. We were nearly riding on two wheels. "The hell's the matter with you? You sick or something?"

"It was all a misunderstanding."

"What about the stuff in your notebook there? That all a misunderstanding, too?"

"Just let me explain—"

"Oh yeah," David said. "I can see how that could happen. A misunderstanding. Sure."

"Where are we going?"

"What's the matter?" He motioned toward the open glove compartment. The paperback vibrated against the hanging mouth of it as the pickup gathered speed. "You write this scary stuff, but I guess you're just a shitless little weasel in real life."

"Stop the truck."

"That makes you a coward in my book."

"David—"

"Not facing a situation, not confronting it—that makes you a coward."

"Stop the truck. I want to get out."

"Get out? Now? I thought you wanted to learn all about my family. For your book."

"I'm not writing a book. This is just—this was—it's my private business—"

"Which involves *my* private business," Dentman said, his voice rising. "Which involves my *family's* private business."

"Just tell me where we're going."

"I'm taking you to meet someone."

"I don't want to meet anyone. Let me out of the goddamn truck."

Ahead, I noticed the glimmer of lights through the trees. Fresh hope welled up inside me. I wasn't familiar with where we were, but at least there were other people around.

If Adam wanted proof that David Dentman was a homicidal maniac, he'd certainly have it when they found my body torn to bits on the side of this wooded highway tomorrow morning . . .

"I'll say," he went on, the accelerator flat on the floor now, "you've got me made out pretty colorful in that notebook of yours. Call me a murderer and everything."

"It's not you."

"No? Used my name."

"If you're too fucking stupid to understand what I'm trying to tell you—"

The pickup squealed as Dentman slammed on the brakes, causing the rear of the truck to fishtail. Forward momentum drove me into the dashboard. The Fourth of July was going on somewhere at the back of my brain. Dentman corrected the fishtailing until we leveled out. He muttered something to himself about nearly missing a turn as he rotated the steering wheel.

"You're a fucking psychopath," I said, pulling

myself back into my seat.

To my astonishment, Dentman laughed. The sound was like a thousand barking dogs. "You know what I think?" He tapped his temple. "I think you're blind and I think you're ignorant. I think you're a selfish son of a bitch. If you keep on nosing in other people's business, you'll eventually get what's coming to you."

"Go to hell."

"You have no idea how you upset her. You have no idea what it was like trying to get her through that. You stupid motherfucker, she loved that boy."

"What about you? How'd you feel about him?"

"I don't feel like answering any of your goddamn questions," he snarled. "Wind up in one of your shitty books."

"Tell me what you did to him."

Again, Dentman stopped the truck—this time with more care. The pickup idled in the middle of the road, the engine ticking down around us, our mingling respiration fogging up the windshield. The residential lights I'd spotted, which I'd hoped would prove my salvation, were still too far away. Here, alone with a child killer, I was surrounded by trees, by shadows and darkness and night.

"Get out," Dentman breathed. His eyes were small and a bit far apart but like two burning embers affixed to the carved stone face of an idol. His teeth were little and evenly spaced. He had thin lips that curled when he was angry.

"Was it an accident or did you do it on purpose?" I said. It was like listening to someone else using my voice. I couldn't stop myself. "Maybe it was an accident. Maybe you panicked."

"Yes," he said. "Just like you wrote in your little notebook. Now get out of my truck."

Not needing a third invitation, I popped the door handle and dumped myself out onto the ice-slicked blacktop. Held tightly to my chest were the crime scene photos and the notebook. The night was cold and damp, but my heart was racing, and I was sweating so profusely that I hardly noticed.

Dentman shut the truck down, then turned off the headlights. As he got out of the cab and came around the front of the vehicle, I was certain he was going to pull a handgun from his waistband and blow me away right here on the side of the road. I could easily imagine my blood staining the snow a deep crimson hue, the liberated crime scene photographs fluttering like tumbleweeds down the empty single-lane blacktop all the way into the next town.

He came up to me and grabbed my elbow. "Come on." He tried to jerk me toward the shoulder of the road.

"Where are we going?"

"This is what it's all about, isn't it? The climax of

your fucking story? This is what the readers have been waiting for, right?"

I couldn't stop my feet: they moved of their own will. Beside me, Dentman was huge, and it was like being ushered by a giant stone bell tower. He was breathing strenuously, and I could feel his heartbeat through the tightened grip of his palm around my elbow.

"He was autistic," I said.

David grunted.

"Your nephew. He was autistic, wasn't he?"

"You're out of your mind."

"Is that why you killed him? Because he was different and you didn't understand him? Maybe he frightened you a little, too."

"You don't know what you're talking about."

"You may have fooled the police but you didn't—"

Dentman yanked my arm back, nearly dislocating it at the shoulder.

I stumbled and almost spilled the notebook and photos to the ground.

Still gripping my elbow, he swung me around until I was staring directly at him. "You . . . shut . . . up," he breathed.

My mind rattled with things to say, none of them strong enough for the moment.

We crested a snowy embankment and slipped beneath a canopy of trees. The moon was blotted out almost altogether. I paused only once, more than certain of my own impending doom, but Dentman jerked me forward, and I clumsily continued to follow. We crossed through a shallow grove of trees that emptied into a vast clearing covered by sinister ground fog. I was surprised (and relieved) to see more lights ahead. In front of us stood what must have been a ten-foot-tall wrought iron fence. Beyond the fence, the dorsal fin crescents of tombstones rose from the rolling black lawn.

A cemetery.

"Come on," Dentman urged, letting go of my arm and moving along the length of the fence.

I watched him lead for some time, his enormous head slumping like a broken puppet's, before following. We came to a small gravel driveway that wound through an opening in the cemetery gate. Without waiting for me, Dentman passed through the entrance and continued to advance up the slight incline of the cemetery grounds, passing granite botonées like mile markers.

I pursued the hulking behemoth, suddenly less apprehensive of my own safety. Curiosity drove me now. Curiosity and finality. I walked across the cemetery lawns, the frigidity of the air finally driving its point home. My breath was sour and raspy. I could sense my pulse throbbing beneath the palms of my hands. We passed a large mausoleum and beyond that several grave markers fashioned to look like stars and stone angels. Now trying to keep up, I hurried down a gradual slope and saw him stop beneath a great oak tree at the far end of the cemetery grounds. He stood looking down, half leaning against the wrought iron gate. For all I knew, he could have forgotten all about me.

Solemn was my approach. Strong wind rattled the bare branches of the oak. What sat before us were two headstones with two different names on them. The first:

BERNARD DENTMAN

The second:

ELIJAH DENTMAN
BELOVED SON AND NEPHEW

Along with their respective dates.

"I'm not a smart man, Glasgow. I don't write books, and I don't wear a suit and tie to work. But I'm not an imbecile, either. I know you. You're the type of person thinks they can get away with any damn thing they want. Any damn thing in the world. You think this whole fucking universe would just crumble to pieces if you didn't exist to keep it all together."

"I don't."

"That's bullshit. See, you been asking about me. But I been asking about you." He sprung at me, causing a moan to escape my lips. Again, he spun me around, and looked at the fresh granite tombstone, still too new to be overgrown with vines and weeds. *Beloved Son and Nephew.*

I felt a fist strike the small of my back. Wincing, I dropped my notebook and the crime scene photos. The wind was quick to gather up the photos and bully them across the cemetery grounds.

"You're kneeling on my nephew's grave. I'm trying to instill a little humility in you, a little reverence. You ever have to bury an empty coffin?"

"Get . . . off me . . ."

"All your writings about ghosts and murders and dead children," he said at my back, his voice trailing in the wind. He could have been shouting ten stories above me for all the difference it made. "Go on. Ask the grave whatever ghostly questions you got, you motherfucker. Ask it."

Twisting in his grasp, I told him again to get the fuck off me.

He didn't. "I can't have you sniffing around in my family's business. My sister ain't strong enough, and I won't let you torment her anymore." His head just over my shoulder, I could feel his hot breath crawling down the nape of my neck. "See," he practically whispered, his mouth nearly brushing my ear now, "my father was a rotten, miserable son of a bitch who caused more harm than anyone should ever have to endure. I took my sister away from him and raised her. Until I die, she will be my sole responsibility. *Until I die.* Ain't no one gonna hurt her. Especially you. She's my sister and I love her, no matter what."

I managed to turn and look at him. His eyes were the eyes of a wolf—hungry, desperate, wild. "I've already told the cops about you. My brother's a cop. He knows what I've been up to. You kill me, they'll catch you this time."

Dentman grasped my right wrist. His face was nearly on top of my own, his breath reeking. There was a complete absence of expression on his face— no smile, no bared teeth. Just a set face, set mouth, clenched jaw.

In a futile attempt to wrench my wrist free, I lost my balance and cracked the side of my head smartly against Elijah's gravestone. Instantly, capering swirls exploded in front of my eyes, and I felt the world tilt to one side. I thought of fireworks and a filmstrip slipping in the grooves of a projector. Blindly, I began clawing at the front of Dentman's shirt.

With seemingly little effort, Dentman pinned my right hand to the ground while stepping on my wrist with his booted foot. "You stupid bastard. If I wanted to kill you, I would have done it already."

He brought down his fist on my face. Eye-watering pain blossomed from my nose and spread out across my face, rattling like a rusty shopping cart with crippled casters through my head. I hardly cared about struggling free at that moment. I just prayed my death would be swift and painless. All I could do was cringe in anticipation of the next punch.

But it did not come. Instead, Dentman grabbed my hands and dragged my body about two feet to the left of the gravestone and allowed me to roll over on my side.

I inhaled a deep swallow of air. It hurt my lungs, my chest. I still couldn't open my eyes, still couldn't bring myself to do it until I caught my breath. I was aware of Dentman's hulking shape above me, and I imagined him withdrawing that same imaginary handgun I'd dreamt up from before and plugging me once, assassin style, in the head.

Finally, I opened my eyes and rolled over on my back. Coughing. Sputtering. My vision was still blurred, but I managed to turn my head and seek out my attacker.

His face stoic and unreadable, Dentman moved away from me like an out-of-breath hunter admiring his catch.

"What the hell are you going to do to me?" We say such pitiful things in our final moments of desperation.

Dentman sneered. "Jesus fuck, boy. You're pathetic. Look at you."

"You can't kill me."

"Piece of shit." Kneeling down beside me, he gripped my wrists again.

Peripherally, I caught a glint of moonlight on metal, then heard a sound like pocket change being jangled. When I looked up, I saw he'd handcuffed me to the fucking iron fence. "You can't leave me out here. I'll freeze to death."

David's enormous shoulders heaved with every breath. I could see vapor trails rising like steam from each nostril like a bull. He spat on me, turned, and sauntered away.

I listened to his heavy boots crunch through the snow. With my head still spinning, I sat up and watched him leave. Once he passed through the trees and into the darkness, disappearing from sight, I nearly forgot what he looked like.

I think I'm going to pass out, I thought. *I think I'm going to pass out. I think I'm going to—*

Darkness.

CHAPTER TWENTY-SEVEN

A slight and indistinct form crept beside me without making a sound. Weightless, it climbed onto my chest. Hot breath fell across my forehead. I felt its tongue lap up the tears that were searing hot ruts down the sides of my face.

—Kyle, I said.

No answer.

When I finally came to, the sun was just beginning to crest through the cemetery trees. It hit my eyes in that perfect way only the sun knows how to do, and I winced and turned my head, suddenly unsure of my surroundings. Sunlight caused the trees to bleed and the snow-covered hills to radiate like a thousand Octobers. I could make out a distant church, its spire like the twist of a conch shell against the pale sky.

Struggling to sit up, a nauseating wave of dizziness filtered into my brain. I tried to bring my right arm up but couldn't—I was still handcuffed to the fence. Tenderly, I touched the side of my head with my free hand. Winced again. The bump there felt like a softball pushing its way through the side of my skull.

The events of last night rushed back to me in a suffocating whirlwind. I glanced at my left hand and found it was sticky with blood. A sizeable gash bisected my palm. Somehow, in the jumble of events, I'd sliced it open pretty nicely. The fingertips were blue.

Then I realized how badly I was shaking. I couldn't calm myself, couldn't get warm, and figured I must have been out here lying in the snow for at least five or six hours.

My head was woozy, and I probably had a slight concussion. The blood from my injured hand had dried in the night, running in bright red parade streamers from my wrist down the length of my arm to the crease of my elbow and into the snow. I looked like I'd just gutted a pig.

"Fuck . . ."

The sound of my own voice sent shards of broken glass into the soft gray matter of my brain.

Voices: I heard voices then, coming from afar. I caught movement through the trees and watched three people advancing toward me. As they drew nearer, I realized two of them were police officers in uniform. The third person I assumed to be the cemetery groundskeeper.

The three men paused a few feet in front of me. I spied my notebook in the snow next to one of their shiny black shoes.

"Hey," said the taller officer. "What the hell happened to you?"

"I'm fucking freezing," I chattered.

The groundskeeper pointed in my direction. He was a fat little shrew with atrocious teeth, a character in a Dickens novel. "See that? See his hand? I said he was chained up, didn't I?"

"My n-n-name's T-T-Trav—"

"I know who you are." The taller cop, it turned out, was Douglas Cordova, my brother's partner whom I'd met at the Christmas party. In his unblemished uniform and with his square jaw and jade-green eyes, he could have marched straight out of a recruiting poster. To the other officer, Cordova said, "Unhook him."

The second officer dropped to one knee in the snow while fumbling around on his belt for his handcuff key. Less intimidating than Cordova, this guy had a slack, sleepy-dog face, and his chin was minimal and abbreviated, giving his profile an overall unfinished look. His nameplate said *Freers*.

"You need an ambulance or anything?" Freers

said too close to my face. His breath smelled of onions.

"No."

"You're bleeding, you know."

I glanced at my lacerated palm.

"I meant your face," said Freers, standing.

On shaky knees, I climbed to my feet and steadied myself against the large oak tree. My jeans cracked audibly, frozen stiff to my legs. Had I not been wearing my coat, I surely wouldn't have made it through the night.

"Who did this to you?" Cordova said. He had one hand on the groundskeeper's shoulder, and they looked like mismatched football players about to form a huddle to discuss the next play.

"David D-D-Dentman," I said.

Cordova did not alter his expression. "Okay," he said, turning to his partner, "let's get him in the car before he turns into a Popsicle."

Freers took me by the forearm and led me around the tombstones.

"Wait." I paused to pick up my notebook from the ground. Glancing around, I tried to see if I could spot any of Earl's crime scene photos, but they were gone.

"That there's littering," barked the groundskeeper. Pointing at the notebook in my hand, he said, "There's a fine to pay for littering."

"No one's littering," Cordova assured him, his

hand still on the smaller man's shoulder.

"There's a fine," he repeated, though his tone was much less stern.

"Come on," Cordova said, saddling up beside me and placing a couple of fingers at the base of my spine.

"I think I can manage, thanks," I said.

"This is trespassing, too," said the groundskeeper as we trailed out of the cemetery and down the gravel drive toward the road. The police car sat there waiting. "Trespassing!"

"Don't mind him," Cordova said close to my ear.

"Watch the skull bone," murmured Freers as he unlocked the back door of the cruiser and helped me inside. Across the roof of the car he called out to Cordova, "Pump the heat up for this guy, will ya?"

Doors slammed. Cordova negotiated his big bulk behind the steering wheel while Freers reclined in the passenger seat. Cordova cranked the heat, and despite my frozen state, I began to sweat into my shoes.

"You okay back there, Travis?" Cordova asked. "Feel the heat?"

Not trusting my lips to form words, I simply nodded repeatedly at his reflection in the rearview mirror.

My head pounding like a calypso drum, I watched the landscape of Westlake shuttle by the windows. The string of shops, the collection of little white-washed two-story homes, the parade of vehicles filing through the streets. We went by Waterview Court.

"You missed my street," I said through the holes in the Plexiglas partition.

"We're not taking you home," said Cordova.

"Where are we going?"

Freers leaned over to Cordova, peering at me from the corner of one eye. "Maybe we should take him to the hospital first. He's shaking like a tambourine."

"We can take him after," Cordova said.

"I asked where you were taking me."

Cordova's eyes blazed in the rearview mirror. "Down to the station. Strohman wants to talk to you."

"Am I under arrest?"

"Should you be?" said Freers, turning around and grinning at me like an imbecile.

Decidedly, I did not like Officer Freers.

Paul Strohman's office was a square cell of cinder blocks painted the color of bad beer. There were no photographs or awards on the walls, and aside from an oversized coffee mug and a telephone, the top of Strohman's slouching wooden desk was bare as well. A single inlaid window, roughly the dimensions of a collegiate dictionary, was seated in the wall above the desk, the pane reinforced with wire. Had it not been for the stenciling on the pebbled glass of the office door—Paul J. Strohman, Chief—I would have thought this was one of the interrogation rooms.

Strohman was handsomer in person. Tall and solid, with good hair and well-defined features, the chief of police exuded an indistinct celebrity quality. He wore a white dress shirt with no tie, the sleeves cuffed nearly to his elbows, and charcoal slacks with pleats. He was leaning back in a rickety wooden chair, the telephone to one ear, when Cordova nudged me through the door.

Beforehand, Cordova had suggested I wash up in the men's room at the end of the hall. He handed me a grubby-looking towel and a sliver of soap flecked with pebbly granules, which told me it needed a good washing of its own. As I washed the dried blood from my palm and my arm, along with the streamer of red ribbon that had trailed from my left nostril and down over my lips and chin, I heard Cordova and Freers murmuring in the hallway outside the door. Their communication was brusque. I made out only bits and pieces, though I was certain I heard Adam's name mentioned. Leaning closer to the streaked and spotted mirror, I daubed at the shiny new bruise on the edge of my forehead.

Now, as Strohman's door closed behind me, I wasn't necessarily a new man, though at least I felt less like some vagrant who'd been picked up for loitering.

"Okay," Strohman said into the receiver. He motioned toward the only other chair in the office, which faced his desk. "Thanks, Rich . . . Yeah, no problem. Sure . . . Say hello to Maureen for me . . . Right. You, too."

I sat in the chair as Strohman hung up the phone. Still clutching the notebook to my chest, both my feet placed firmly on the floor, I had a sudden flashback of my interrogation with Detective Wren twenty years ago—how I'd sat shivering on a bench along the river, a towel draped over my scrawny shoulders as I sobbed and explained as best I was able what had happened. Summer crickets popped in the tall grass like popcorn, and clouds of gnats covered my ears. Detective Wren had leaned in close to me, put a hand on my shoulder, and talked very low and very lethargic. I could tell that it was difficult for him to speak quietly, even with ample training in the art, so I was sure it was a taxing exercise for him.

"Travis," said Strohman, "I'm Paul. I'm the chief down here. I work with your brother."

"I know who you are."

He seemed unfazed. "Nice shiner you got there."

"You should see the other guy."

"Right." I felt him take in not only the discolored bit of fruit swelling from my forehead but also the mud-streaked condition of my clothes, the knotted tangles of my hair. Scooping up the telephone, he punched three digits on the keypad. "Hey, Mae, bring us some coffee in here, will ya? Thanks." Then he hung up. "Looks like you could use some."

"Why'd you want me brought here? How do you know who I am?"

"Because I spent yesterday morning talking David Dentman out of filing harassment charges against you," Strohman said evenly.

My laugh sounded like the caw of some strange bird. "You've got to be kidding. Me?" Although it hurt to do so, I tapped the shiny knob at my forehead with two fingers. "He hit me so hard I think he left his DNA in my skull."

Still leaning back in his chair, Strohman looked infernally bored. "He came in all fire and brimstone, saying you went to his house in West Cumberland and taunted his sister with her dead son's things. Said you wrote her some horrible story in a notebook making them out to be a couple of loons."

He didn't ask me if it was true or not, but I felt the need to refute it nonetheless. "This has all been a series of misunderstandings. I wasn't tormenting that woman. My wife and I moved into their house, and they'd left some stuff behind. I was just taking it back to them."

Strohman sighed and fingered the dark cleft in his chin. "I really don't care."

"Then why am I here?"

"Because I like your brother," Strohman said. "He's a good man. I'm trying not to embarrass his family."

"I don't follow."

"You're causing quite a stir around town. Allegations of murder and police cover-ups—"

"I never said anything about police cover-ups."

"Whatever." He prodded the air absently with an index finger to signal just how banal he found this whole conversation. "Westlake's a small family community. It's my job to make sure everyone stays happy. You've been asking a lot of questions about stuff that doesn't concern you, bothering people in the process. I figured I'd give you the opportunity to ask them directly to me."

"I want to know why the investigation into Elijah Dentman's supposed drowning was quashed."

Strohman grinned. He was roguishly handsome. "You sound like Columbo."

"Humor me. How come David Dentman was let off the hook so easily?"

"Why shouldn't he be?"

"He's got a criminal record, a history of violence. His statement on the record says he'd been watching Elijah from the house that afternoon, but your officers missed something. I missed it too at first." I explained about the trees from the crime scene photographs, although I neglected to tell him from whom I'd gotten them. Probably in a town Westlake's size, there was only one crime scene photographer, and Strohman didn't need to ask.

"Where are these photos?"

I groaned inwardly. "Probably somewhere over Pennsylvania by now."

Strohman frowned.

"I had them with me at the cemetery. They blew away after Dentman punched me in the face, then handcuffed me to the fence." Now it was my turn to frown. "How come you haven't asked me what I was doing out there, anyway?"

"I already know."

"How?"

"Dentman phoned it in this morning."

"Son of a bitch. He admitted to it?"

"Phoned it in anonymously," Strohman said. "From a pay phone in West Cumberland. But I know it was him."

"Well, shit."

"I'm going to share something with you." Strohman got up from behind his desk and went to the door, opened it.

A round little woman with silver hair stood on the other side, two Styrofoam cups of coffee in her hands. I hadn't even heard her knock. Strohman took the cups and thanked the woman, then closed the door with his shoe. After he handed me one of the cups, he sat in front of me on the edge of his desk. I heard the wood creak in protest.

"This is what you wanted to share with me?" I said, savoring the warmth radiating through the cup. "Coffee?"

Again, Strohman grinned. My mind summoned an image of a young Kirk Douglas. "In situations like the one that happened to the Dentmans, the families are always the prime suspects. We always address the parents first. In this case, I spoke personally with both the boy's mother as well as his uncle. The mother"— he waved a hand to indicate her mental instability— "she was of limited capacity, let's say. Of course," he added, leering at me from over the rim of his cup, "you've met her, so you know."

He slurped his coffee. "I questioned David Dentman extensively. His story never changed."

"That doesn't mean he's innocent."

"We had no body and no evidence that a homicide had taken place. What I'm saying is there was no probable cause to even make an arrest."

A glimmer of hope ignited within me. I leaned forward in the chair. "So you believe he killed the boy?"

Strohman set his coffee on his desk, then folded his hands in his lap. "I did seven years in Los Angeles as a uniformed officer and another two in homicide. I love this little town—it's pretty and peaceful, and

I got a wife and a litter of youngsters who're much better off here than back in L.A.—but I'm aware of its shortcomings. I've been here four years, and we've only worked two wrongful death cases in all that time. And only one of those was an honest to God homicide. A squabble down at the 'Bird, fists flying, some guy pulls a knife. That's hot news around here. Most of my officers have never seen blood let alone worked a homicide investigation."

That tabloid celebrity smile returned. He had perfect teeth. "But I've worked some pretty gruesome cases. I could tell you stuff that would make you spend the rest of your nights sitting up in bed, listening for every little creak in your house. When it comes to doing those sorts of things, well, that's my bread and butter. And just because I moved my family out here for a better life doesn't mean I've surrendered all my training and instincts. You don't leave those things at the airport security checkpoint, so to speak. You catch me?"

"What about the fact that the kid's body was never found?"

"My guess is it'll show up sometime in the spring when the lake thaws. Point I'm trying to make is I'm not sitting around here with my thumb up my ass. I know how to run an investigation. I don't need you sniffing around in my shit. *Comprende*?"

Rising off the desk, Strohman returned to his

seat. The chair's casters squealed. "So tell me what I have to do to put your mind at ease."

"Aside from reopening the investigation, I assume?"

"This is a good town. The people are better served forgetting about an accidental drowning than to be the center of a homicide investigation that would never go anywhere."

"That's bullshit."

"I'm patient with you because your brother's a good cop and a good man. Anyone else and I would have let Dentman file those charges. Think about that." He checked his wristwatch. "Officer Cordova will drive you home now."

CHAPTER TWENTY-EIGHT

When we turned into the cul-de-sac and Cordova spun the cruiser around in a tight semicircle, Freers made some offhand comment about the Dentman house. Apparently he hadn't known I lived here now.

Cordova got out of the cruiser and opened the rear door for me.

I got out, stretching my legs. My head still pounded. "You interviewed Nancy Stein the day the Dentman boy drowned in the lake, didn't you?" I asked him.

"Huh?" It was probably the last thing he expected me to say.

I shook my head. "Never mind." Glancing at my house, I spotted Adam standing in the front doorway. "Christ."

"Yeah, well, you just take it easy," Cordova said,

climbing inside the car. "And you should probably go get your head checked out."

For one insane moment, I forgot about the bump on my head and assumed Cordova was recommending I consult with a psychotherapist.

As I walked up the gravel path to the house, my brother's formidable presence in the doorway like impending doom, I could hear the police car heading toward Main Street. Despite the cold, I was sweating. My shirt stuck to my chest, and I felt rivulets of perspiration running down the sides of my ribs from my armpits. I clutched my notebook, my fingernails cutting crescents into the cardboard cover. Reality wavered. *There is clarity here.* I felt like I was about to blink out of existence.

Adam stood in the doorway like a sentry. He was in jeans and a white sweatshirt with a star-shaped emblem at the breast, his muscular arms folded over his chest. On his face was the indignant countenance of a frustrated parent.

Hopeless, I paused at the bottom of the porch steps and laughed. There was nothing funny about any of this, not by a long stretch, but I had lost all control of myself. This sick, humorless chortle was all I had in me.

"Get in the house," Adam said, turning away and preceding me through the threshold.

Beth and Jodie sat on the couch in the living

room. As I entered, Beth stood. She looked more than just distraught—she looked ill, cancerous, bulimic. Jodie watched me with gaunt, dark eyes. Once again, I felt the urge to break into laughter. This time I was able to arrest the outburst before it made the situation even worse.

"Travis," Beth said, "what the hell happened to you?"

"Long story. I'm okay. I just need to talk to Adam."

"Goddamn right," my brother said from behind me. There was a cancerous quality to his voice as well. He gave me a shove, which set me in motion toward my wife.

"You all right, babe?" I said.

"Your head," Jodie said simply. On the coffee table in front of her, the wooden blocks were stacked into a pyramid, a staircase.

"It's fine. Just a bump." I could sense Adam and Beth communicating to each other without words.

Beth rubbed one of my shoulders, then took Jodie's hands. "We're going to put on some coffee and make sandwiches," she said, leading my wife off the couch and out of the room.

I remained where I was, not too eager to face Adam.

In the belly of the house, the furnace kicked on.

"So far," Adam said from behind me, "all I know is that you never came home last night and that Doug found you beat to shit in a cemetery outside of town this morning. You want to elaborate?"

"Good to see you're so concerned about my well-being. I'm okay, in case you wanted to know."

"Yes. I see that. Turn the hell around, will you?"

I faced him.

"I thought I got through to you last night," he said.

"No. You didn't listen. I tried to explain." I was exhausted; there was no fight left in me. The tone of my voice was like the droning over a high school intercom.

"You came to me with nonsense, with fairy-tale bullshit. I told you what to do, but you just wouldn't listen."

"I did," I said. "I listened. David Dentman was waiting for me in his truck when I left your place."

"And I guess that's who turned your face into pulp, right?"

"More or less."

"No wonder. I told you to leave those people alone."

"But who can really predict the actions of a homicidal lunatic?"

Adam's nostrils flared. He uncrossed his arms and placed his hands on his hips. His cheeks were flushed red, and I could see cords standing out in his neck. I could tell he wanted to hit me. "This," he said, "is *your* fault. No one else's. You couldn't leave well enough alone. I warned you."

"You just don't see it. How can it be that I'm the only one who sees it? It's like the fucking *Twilight Zone*."

"There's nothing to see."

"There's everything to see."

"No. You're making this up. It's all in your head. You've convinced yourself of this goddamn make-believe story. The boy drowned. It was an accident. Get it through your head."

A white rage quaked through me. I saw Detective Wren's face looming like a full moon in front of my own, one hand on my shoulder, asking me to go over once again what happened to my brother.

"You're wrong and you're blind," I growled at Adam.

"Goddamn it. You've lost your mind. You can't tell the difference between fiction and reality."

"The reality," I said levelly, "is that David Dentman murdered that boy and no one is willing to hear it."

"Then prove it." Adam slapped his hands against his thighs. "You're so goddamn certain. I want you to give me some actual goddamn proof."

"The proof is in the character. The proof is in the lousy goddamn notebook." I threw it into the air. "The proof is in this house. It's in the sum of all the stories. It's—" My gaze settled on the coffee table and the little wooden blocks from my childhood, though they were now Elijah's blocks, still constructed to suggest a tiny, colorful staircase. A strangled laugh erupted from my throat. "The proof is in these blocks. See? The proof is in the staircase!"

Around me, the world seemed to freeze. Something akin to a doorway unlatched in the center of my brain, flooding my skull with brilliant white light. I hardly noticed when Beth and Jodie appeared in the hallway.

"The perfect place," I muttered, turning to them.

"Travis," Adam said.

"So simple. It's the perfect place because it's been staring at me since the first day."

"He's lost his mind," said Adam.

"Oh," Jodie moaned, starting to cry. "Oh, God . . ."

"You want your body?" I cried at him. "You want your proof?"

Like a locomotive, I stormed past Adam and flung open the front door. I heard Jodie shriek my name but I didn't stop. I never even paused. I wasn't here—I was floating somewhere above, watching myself in a dream. I was a boulder gathering speed as it rolls down a hillside. I was a 747, engines burned to dust, hurling toward the Earth at a million miles an hour. Frantic, I hustled around the side of the house, breaking into a sprint by the time I reached the rear. Before me stood tree trunks like fence posts, a barrier separating me from the lake.

"Travis!" Adam shouted from behind me.

Charging through the snow, I continued down the gradual slope toward the trees and the lake. I made a beeline for the axe whose head was wedged into a tree stump chopping block, grasped the wooden handle with both hands, and gave the axe an almighty yank upward. The bladed head wrenched free of the chopping block, the release nearly toppling me backward.

From the corner of my eye, I saw Adam barreling toward me and Beth trailing behind him. Only Jodie—my Jodie, my girl—remained at the side of the house, watching as the events unfolded.

Axe in hand, I pushed through the trees, swatting branches out of my way, chopping at them when I could. Somewhere very close a flock of blackbirds took flight, startled by my presence. I was no longer running, and I could hear Adam crunching through fallen branches, closing the distance. He was still calling my name.

Consumed, driven, I broke through the last of the winter-brittle trees, my chest heaving with each breath. Before me: the lake. Directly before me: the floating staircase. Unlike the first time, there was no ice on which to walk. I hardly paused to consider this. Instead, I look another step right into the water. The ground was muddy and congested with reeds. My foot sank quickly in the mud. The water was an ice bath; I felt the chill race up through my body and explode like a rocket at the base of my skull. Possessed, I would not be thwarted.

"Travis," Adam yelled. The crunch of dead twigs

grew louder, nearer . . .

I waded out to my knees, my hips. My whole body shook, rattling apart the way I thought David Dentman's truck might when he gunned it past sixty. From nowhere, the weight of the axe increased by about fifty pounds, and I needed two hands to hold it. The water level rose to my chest, and I slung the axe over one shoulder. My teeth chattered a mile a minute. I was no longer taking steps but rather sliding along the silt at the bottom of the lake. How deep did it go? I had no idea. And I didn't care—I could walk across the bottom of the ocean floor right now.

Back on land, Adam finally cleared the trees and staggered to the lake. He shouted my name over and over again. I could hear Beth now, too.

I did not turn to see if either of them was pursuing me into the water, but I didn't think they were. Anyway, it didn't matter. The floating staircase, that prehistoric beast, crested out of the placid surface of the lake only a few yards ahead of me.

Splashing behind me: I turned and saw Adam stomping through the water.

There were stairs under the water. I climbed, the axe still slung over one shoulder. The wooden planks were weathered and beaten and ugly, brittle like diseased bone. I rose with them out of the freezing murk. The wind was unrelenting. The water had kept me preserved; now, the flesh exposed to the air was rendered immediately numb. Still, I mounted the steps, bullying straight to the top.

Something thumped against the framework of the staircase from beneath it. Under the water. Submerged. *Trapped*, I thought. *Trapped.* All feeling gone from my body, I approached the uppermost step, standing on the one just below it. The plank covering the top step was splintered and not completely nailed down. It had been pried up in the past.

I lifted the axe over my head. Somewhere—anywhere, everywhere—Adam shouted my name. I was distantly aware of my bladder giving out . . . and of warmth that spread from my crotch down my inner thighs.

I brought the axe down. The plank suffered a fatal gash. The dulled blade crashed through the sun-bleached plank, splintering it down the middle. The two halves remained nailed to their respective sides of the frame, a ragged eyelet chasm hollowed in the center. I dropped to my knees and, with my one free hand, pried both halves of the plank from the foundation. I couldn't feel my fingers, and it was difficult to instruct them what to do. My palm was bleeding again, too. There was blood on everything, everything.

"Travis!"

Rending both sections of plank free from the platform, I tossed them over the side of the staircase and into the water—*plink, plink!*—and peered into the abyss I'd created. Below, my reflection stared back at me, framed within a rectangle of black water.

Find an anchor.

Gripping the axe handle in both hands, I leaned over the opening and rammed the head of the axe below the surface of the water. I would break this whole god-damn staircase apart if I had to, shred it with my bare hands, my frozen fingers, my bloody palm, anything to save him, anything to save my—

The axe blade struck something and knocked it loose of something else.

Whatever it was, I could feel it thumping along the handle of the axe as it floated and bobbed to the surface of the water. Squinting at the brackish murk of the water, I waited for it to surface. Waited.

And then it did, coming right to the top, right up through the staircase's hollow frame, and floated near the surface of the black water, framed in that rectangular chasm.

Floating.

My grip on the axe failed, and I let it sink beneath the water. I could not take my eyes from the thing in the water. Numb, frozen, a ruined man lost finally in the doldrums of his own paranoia, I stared at it, and no one could take it away from me by denying what it was . . .

A rib cage.

PART FOUR:

INTO THE DEEP/THE HUMAN ABSTRACT

CHAPTER TWENTY-NINE

There are filaments of me that twinkle like sapphire. Calmly, I watch as my dozen-fingered hand smears trails through the ether. I am in a place somewhere far beyond conscious thought. Sitting at the kitchen table of my childhood home, I watch my mother prepare a chicken dish, dressing it with green peas and garlic, humming softly. She does not know I am there—I am a ghost, a shade, a shadow. I have gone willingly to the other side, have exchanged myself for another, have claimed a place at a table of the eternally absent, the eternally damned.

A scatter of feet on the floorboards. Whispers fall like cobwebs. *What's the most horrible thing you've ever done?*

I am shuffling along a desert highway. Steam rises in visible waves off the roasting blacktop. With each step, tar pulls like taffy and sticks to the soles of my shoes. I wince as I gaze at the horizon. Tufts of unruly weeds sprout in patches down the center of the black-top. As I approach, I see they are not weeds at all but clumps of hair. There are people below, submerged in the hot tar of the highway, with only their scalps rising like the bulges of humpback whales. It is possible to grip the hair, hot and brittle as it is from the sun, and pull. There is a sense of withdrawal, of surrender, as the sticky pavement yields and the buried corpses, amidst a gurgle of bubbling tar and an acrid methane stench, are liberated from their underground prison.

But they are only ragged scalps, decapitated from just above the eyes, and as each one comes loose, I fall backward at the ease of their surrender and slam down hard on the pavement.

I think, *Somewhere there is a great and mysterious sea where people struggle to stay afloat while the magic of the water gradually makes them insane.*

I am wandering the desert highway, collecting scalps like gypsy treasure.

My fever broke by the end of the week.

Jodie was in the kitchen cleaning the stove. She seemed surprised to find me standing in the archway. "I was just going to make you soup."

I went to her and hugged her, kissed the side of her face. Soon my neck was damp from her silent tears.

On a Tuesday, two men in navy-blue coveralls arrived in a truck that said Allegheny Pickup & Removal on its side in bright orange foot-tall letters.

"What's this?" said the fatter of the two men. "Some sort of secret passageway?"

I watched as they cleared out all of Elijah Dentman's things—his bookcase, his writing desk, his trunk of toys, his tiny bed. I helped them carry the boxes out and load them into the truck, my personal relief seeming to grow as the room in the basement cleared out.

"Your kid lives down here?" asked the fat man's partner. When I didn't answer him, he must have suspected the worst, and both men worked the rest of the hour in deferential silence.

After they'd gone, I spent some time gazing at the hollowed-out room. It felt like I was looking into my own coffin. Jodie briefly appeared beside me. I wondered if she felt like she was staring into her coffin as well. Or maybe she was looking into mine, just as I was. Rubbing my back with one hand, she handed me some hot tea, then felt my forehead to make sure my temperature wasn't coming back. It wasn't.

She wanted the room sealed up, but I decided on a better solution: I tore down the walls, those blind panels of Sheetrock. Particularly the one with the sage-green handprint on it. It was backbreaking work, and when I finally finished I was covered in white powder. Jodie laughed and said I looked like a mime.

We did not talk about what happened that day after the cops dropped me off at the house—a day now two weeks gone. While I'm sure the image of her husband straddling the floating staircase, smashing it to pieces with an axe, would be burned in my wife's memory for a long, long time, she was good about putting it all aside and loving me again. It had been a frightening thing, but I suppose it was also a necessary one; the revelation that day had shaken reality back into me, which was just what I'd needed. I'd needed to know if I had been right or if I had been wrong.

I had been wrong.

After I cleaned the basement, I took my writing notebooks—the ones in which the initial stirrings of Elijah Dentman's make-believe story still lingered, unfinished—and tucked them away in one of my trunks. *I tried, kid*, I thought. *I was trying so hard that I was searching for something that wasn't even there.* And at that moment I wasn't sure if, in my soul, I was talking to Elijah Dentman or to my dead brother, Kyle.

Yes, it had been a rib cage. And I had stared at it, fascinated and dumbstruck by my own premonition, because *I was right; I was right; I was right*, and my work was done, and the writing was done, and the boy was saved. I had saved him. I had championed him, vindicated him.

Adam had clambered out of the lake and up the staircase, nearly losing his balance twice. When he reached me, he threw his arms around me and held me tight against him. I could feel his heavy breathing as he held me, could feel his hot breath against my freezing neck.

"Look," I'd said, not even bothering to point.

Adam had peered down and did not say a word. He did not say a word for a very, very long time. Finally, he said, "It . . . it looks like . . . is that . . . ?"

"Yes," I said.

Quieter—in my ear: "How did you know?"

"I don't know," I admitted. "It just occurred to me. Just now."

"But how?"

I turned my head in his direction. Our faces were close. "A ghost. I think a ghost told me."

Adam appeared confused and scared . . . but somewhat relieved, too.

"I'm not crazy," I'd told him then.

Adam glanced down the shaft of the hollow staircase. "Look."

Confused, I saw a second object float to the surface—more bone. But not just bone—another rib cage.

"Adam . . ." My voice was thick, my throat too tight to articulate properly.

We both stood there and watched as countless bones drifted to the surface of the water and bobbed there, carnival prizes in a barrel, eventually crowding the hollow shaft. Among them were skulls. Tiny skulls.

Thinking about all this, I closed the trunk and climbed the stairs where a nice lunch was waiting for me.

Animals. Animal bones. There were even the remnants of a dog collar affixed to one of the larger skeletons, the band black with slime, the little brass nameplate dull in the overcast light. Still, I thought I could make out one word on it—*Chamberlain*.

"Wait," Adam said. "What are we looking at?"

"The mass grave for Elijah Dentman's pets," I said. Then I collapsed onto the stairs, extremely weak and unable to maintain equilibrium.

With one hand, Adam gripped my shoulder and kept me from toppling into the cold, black waters.

That night Jodie came home. I promised her I was done and was putting it all behind me. Something broke inside her, and she cried in my arms. At first I was terrified, but then, in holding her and in feeling her hitch and sob against my chest, I knew she was okay. She needed to cry and I let her. In that moment, it occurred to me that I hadn't held my wife in some time.

(Two nights after the incident, a violent thunderstorm accosted the town and thoroughly demolished the weakened structure of the floating staircase. In the morning, all that remained were the bone-colored planks of wood that had washed up along the frost-stiffened reeds in the night.)

I took off several days from writing altogether—partially because I was still out of sorts from the hideous flu I'd caught slashing around in the lake in near-freezing weather, but mostly because I owed that time to Jodie. We made love several nights in a row. We went to the movies together like a couple of high school sweethearts, and I helped her edit a rough draft of her dissertation. Valentine's Day arrived, and I bought her flowers and chocolate, and she made my favorite meal—baked macaroni—and we watched old Woody Allen movies until the early hours of the morning. In the weeks after my nervous breakdown on the floating staircase, everything was as perfect as pie.

Then Earl telephoned me one rainy afternoon and said, "Boy, you're a goddamn genius," and it started all over again.

CHAPTER THIRTY

By the time I arrived at Tooey's bar, the drizzle had increased to a steady rain, driving craters in the hummocks of graying snow along the shoulders of Main Street.

The day before, Earl had met me at the front door of his trailer where, with near childish jubilance, he handed over a cheese-yellow envelope sealed with packaging tape. Inside the double-wide, I could hear dogs barking.

"I can't believe it worked," I said, hefting the weight of the envelope. It had been a long shot; I hadn't expected it to actually amount to anything.

"I told them I was with the union, that we needed the paperwork for an impending audit. Just like you said to." The old man grinned like someone who'd just figured out a secret. Had he been just a bit younger,

I had no doubt he would have been bouncing on the balls of his feet. "They bought it."

"Hook, line, and sinker," I said. "Listen, I know you're a reporter. Without insulting you, is there any possible way I can—"

He cut me off. "I won't print a word of this before I hear back from you."

"Thank you." I was looking very hard at the envelope he'd given me.

"You know what this means," Earl said evenly.

"Of course," I said. We both knew what it meant. "Of course."

Now I crossed the sawdust floor of Tequila Mockingbird and sat at an empty table toward the rear of the room. My chair faced the door. The jukebox was rolling through a sad country number, visibly making the shoulders of the few assorted patrons at the bar slump. Rain hammered the tin roof and sluiced down the windowpanes. The whole place felt hollowed and bleak, like a grave site that had been violated by vandals. I checked my watch.

Wiping a glass with a dishrag, Tooey Jones approached the table. "One of the few lost souls who dare to brave the rain," he commented. "What'll it be?"

I ordered a glass of water, which I gulped down the moment it arrived, as well as a gin and tonic (so that I wouldn't arouse suspicion), which remained untouched on the table beside the envelope I'd gotten from Earl. On the juke, the sad country song segued into some old but upbeat Charlie Rich tune. Across the room, the framed panels from Blake's *Songs of Innocence and Experience* were like startling and irrational anomalies that somehow made their way into an otherwise mundane dream. My gaze lingered on the reproductions of "The Little Boy Lost" and "The Little Boy Found."

When Adam arrived, his hair was matted to his head with rainwater, and he was blowing into his hands for warmth. He ordered a beer at the bar, then came over and sat opposite me at the table. He was in plain-clothes—khaki slacks, an outdated American Eagle sweater, canvas peacoat with corduroy cuffs and collar—and he looked exhausted from a long day.

Smiling at him, I tried my best to look casual.

Under the pretense of brotherly companionship, I'd phoned Adam this morning and asked him to meet me for a few beers down at the 'Bird when he got off work. I had said nothing about Earl's envelope (which was now tucked beneath the table in my lap) or the contents therein. I would sit here and engage my brother in idle small talk and wait to see if the rest of my plan fell into place.

Just as Jodie and I had overcome my little episode—the "incident," as I thought of it—following my breakdown on the floating staircase, my brother and I had seemingly bridged our differences as well. Whether it was genuine or only the illusion of authenticity, we became brothers again. (Suffice it to say, I knew my intentions on this evening—as well as the envelope in my lap—risked destroying all that we had rebuilt, although I hoped it wouldn't. Had I possessed any doubt about the contents of the envelope, I would have set it afire in the hearth back at the house and never brought up the Dentmans to my brother again.)

"You're looking better," Adam said over the rim of his pint glass. "How're you feeling?"

The flu had passed for both of us—following me out onto the floating staircase that afternoon, Adam had gotten sick, too—and I'd shaved and had my hair cut.

"Better," I told him. "Stronger." For a second, I wondered if he could sense the nervousness just below the surface of my voice.

Five minutes later—right on time—the pub's door banged open. David Dentman's broad-shouldered outline was framed against the stormy, gunmetal sky. Dripping rainwater on the floor, Dentman pushed through the doorway, his considerable bulk exaggerated by the heavy corduroy coat he wore. Behind him, the pub's door slammed shut on its frame. Aside from my brother and me, no one looked at him.

Adam did not say anything at first. He didn't

even glance at me. Not that I was prepared to look at him; my stare was locked on Dentman.

When Dentman noticed me from across the room, it was like being spotted in the beam of a prison yard's searchlight. His expression was the same one he'd had that day when he came home and found me in his house with his sister—like a pot graduating to a slow boil on the stove.

"Travis," Adam said, his voice small. He was still looking over his shoulder.

"He's going to want to hit me," I said quickly as Dentman approached our table.

The big man stood before the last empty chair at the table. If he recognized my brother, and I was pretty sure that he did, he didn't acknowledge him. Glaring at me, Dentman squeezed a folded slip of paper in one fist.

I didn't need to examine it to know it was the letter I'd printed on my word processor and stuffed into a plain white business envelope. I'd driven to the Dentmans' house in West Cumberland yesterday evening and fed the letter through the mail slot in the door. Then I'd knocked and quickly climbed back into my car and pulled backward down the drive. Until now, I'd had strong doubts that Dentman would even show up. Despite what I'd written on that letter . . .

"What is this?" Dentman's voice seemed to come

from deep down in his chest. I could tell his sentiment echoed my brother's, who remained silent.

"Sit down," I told Dentman.

"Travis." Adam had found his voice, weak as it was.

Dentman pulled out the empty chair and slowly lowered himself into it. Both his hands were in his lap and beneath the table, and a swimmy, unsettling thought crossed my mind—maybe he'd brought a gun. I was pretty certain Adam had his gun on him— even off duty, he typically carried it—but would he be able to pull it in time if Dentman decided to plant a bullet in my brain?

"What's going on here, Travis?" Adam continued.

Dentman took Adam in. He must have assumed my brother was in on this, that we'd both come together to gang up on him.

"This is it," I told them both, setting the cheese-yellow envelope on the tabletop. "This is what I found." I turned to Adam. "You can do with it what you want, but I'm done after tonight." Thinking of my marriage, I added, "I have to be."

"I can see I made a mistake not filing those charges against you," Dentman said. He was red faced and fuming.

Pushing the envelope in front of Adam, I tried to sound calm. "It was something you told me last month. You said murderers have motives, innocent people have alibis, and you can't lock people up just because the pieces don't fit."

"Travis . . ." There was a stomach-weakening distress evident in Adam's tone. With the sober perception of a clairvoyant, I knew I was breaking his heart.

"Open it," I told him.

He picked up the envelope but didn't open it right away.

Dentman adjusted himself in his seat, and I thought he was going to stand up and march right out of the bar. But he remained seated, and I could almost see the anger radiating off his scalp like steam from hot coals.

"Do it," I urged Adam. "Go on."

Adam slipped his thumb beneath the tape and ripped open the envelope. What slid out onto the tabletop was a stack of papers bound together by a metal clip. He fingered the first page, lifted it to see the printout underneath. "What am I looking at?"

"It's the time and attendance records of the construction company where you work," I said, speaking directly to Dentman. "You'll notice the date on the top sheet is the same day Elijah supposedly drowned." I leaned over and absently tapped the column I'd highlighted. "Those are Dentman's hours."

"Where'd you get this?" Adam said.

"Doesn't matter. It's all there."

"I don't have to sit here listening to this," Dentman said, but he didn't get up.

"You couldn't have been at the house the day Elijah disappeared," I went on, "because you were at work. You clocked out at a quarter after six. The job site was just over thirty miles away, so the earliest you could have gotten home was six thirty, and that's if you were speeding. More like quarter to seven is my guess. Which would account for the delay in calling the police."

"This is bullshit," Dentman muttered, his teeth clenched.

"What's bullshit is your statement to the police." From my pocket I took the articles I'd torn from the library newspapers and unfolded them and set them on the table. "According to Nancy Stein's statement, that scream she believed she heard happened around five thirty."

"The sound of the boy falling off the staircase," Adam said, studying the paperwork.

"Only it wasn't," I said. "I think the wail Nancy heard was actually Veronica Dentman down by the water."

Dentman stood. "You son of a bitch."

"You told me yourself that night in the cemetery that your sister was your sole responsibility and you wouldn't let anything happen to her. That's why you lied to the police. You were covering for her."

Dentman's chest was expanding, retracting, expanding, retracting. From across the table I could feel his hot breath in my face. "You don't know nothing."

I turned to my brother. "It's all there in the paperwork."

Very slowly, Adam set the printout down on the table. His face was white. He said nothing.

"I'm getting the fuck out of here," Dentman said, turning to leave.

"Stop," Adam called after him.

Amazingly, Dentman froze in midstride. His hands were trembling, and his profile resembled something that might have been on the bow of a pirate ship.

"Is this true?" Adam asked him.

"Fuck you. I didn't have to come out here."

"Will you sit down, please?"

"I don't have to answer your goddamn questions."

Adam stood. "I need you to come to the station with me, Mr. Dentman."

"I don't have time for this."

"I'm not asking. We're going to the station."

"I want him in jail," Dentman said, glaring at me. His eyes were slits cut into the ruddy fabric of his face. "I want the son of a bitch arrested for harassment."

Gathering up the paperwork from the table, I stood and said, "Fine. Let's all go downtown."

"You shit!" Dentman lunged at me, knocking the

table onto its side with a crack.

I jumped backward as one of Dentman's massive fists swung at me like a wrecking ball; the wind from the blow blew the hair off my forehead. I braced myself for a second strike—Dentman already had his arm cocked and ready—but Adam was on him in a heartbeat, pinning one wrist behind his back and throwing his weight against the larger man. Dentman's second punch went wild as he fell forward on his knees.

Adam shouted something unintelligible at him and pressed down on Dentman's shoulder as if he feared the larger man might fly away. "Stay down. Don't resist."

Handcuffs appeared. Their serrated teeth ratcheted at the small of Dentman's back.

Tooey charged out from behind the bar. "What the hell's going on?" He paused when he saw the handcuffs.

"Get up," Adam said to the side of Dentman's face.

At first, Dentman did not move. With his yellow eyes locked on mine in a death stare and his flushed cheeks visibly quivering, I thought we would all remain frozen where we were until Armageddon turned us into smoldering piles of ash. Then Dentman got one foot on the floor and, with Adam's assistance, pulled himself up.

The next one to move was Tooey—he rushed over and righted the overturned table.

Adam pivoted and shoved Dentman toward the door. "Let's go, Travis," he said without facing me. "Let's go."

Bending down, I picked up the copied records from the construction company and crammed them back into the envelope. As Tooey went on setting the chairs back around the table, I noticed something else, too: the letter I had slipped through the Dentmans' mail slot, the one he'd had clenched in one fist when he first arrived. I picked that up, too.

It said:

David—

Meet me at Tequila Mockingbird in Westlake tomorrow at 5 p.m. sharp, or Veronica goes to jail.

There had been no need to sign it.

Stuffing the letter into the rear pocket of my jeans, I followed Adam and Dentman out into the rain.

CHAPTER THIRTY-ONE

As it turned out, Strohman's office *did* function as an interrogation room, albeit only when the main interrogation room was occupied. On this night, David Dentman, escorted by two uniformed officers, was led into Strohman's uninspired little office where he awaited a meeting with Paul Strohman himself.

The ride from the 'Bird to the police station had taken only four or five minutes, though it had seemed like half an hour. Adam had shoved Dentman into the backseat, then barked at me to get in the passenger seat. Behind the wheel, Adam cranked the engine and flipped on the flashers and siren. No one spoke until we pulled into the bay at the station when Adam muttered to me under his breath, "Get out."

As I sat in the hallway just outside Strohman's office, I heard one of the officers inside issuing

Dentman his rights. Each time Adam went by me in the hall, I made a half-assed effort to stand up and not look so incongruous. Each time, he told me to remain seated. So I sat.

When one of the two uniformed officers exited Strohman's office, he seemed perplexed to see me—it was just that obvious I didn't belong here—that his eyes bugged out comically. Someone else came by and wordlessly gave me a cup of coffee.

Two more uniformed officers appeared at the end of the hall, standing on either side of the walking skeleton that was Veronica Dentman. In a tattered cotton nightgown of faded pink and nothing but a pair of dirty socks on her feet, they led her down the hallway like nurses ushering a patient through a psych ward. Her scraggly hair hung in tangled ropes over her gaunt face, and her eyes were sunken pits in the center of her skull. As they passed, her socks made whooshing sounds on the fire retardant carpet. I caught the acrid scent of unwashed skin.

Nearly spilling my coffee, I shot up like a bolt out of my chair. In their passing wake, I felt a whole other presence brush by me—almost tangible, almost visible. Frigid as the basement of 111 Waterview Court. I thought of dead autumn leaves and creaking hinges on the doors of haunted houses.

Strohman's office door opened. I caught a glimpse

of a number of people inside—David Dentman among them—before Strohman quickly closed the door behind him. He held the time and attendance records in one hand, bound down the margin with brass pins. When he saw me standing there, he did a double take, the rubber soles of his shoes skidding on the linoleum. "I thought I told you to keep your fingers out of my soup," he said, proffering the bound galley of paper out before him like a gift.

Before I could think of a retort, he pivoted on his heels and clomped down the hallway. As he turned into another room, I heard him bark at someone to get him coffee.

When Adam returned, he was with another officer who was wearing a ski cap and a Redskins jacket over his uniform. "This is Officer McMullen," my brother said. "He's going to ask you a few questions."

"I think your chief wants to punch me in the throat," I told him.

"Call me Rob," said McMullen, ignoring my comment. He was lantern jawed, with eyes like chips of gray ice. He looked young enough to still reek of the womb. "You need more coffee? No? So, uh, let's go chat by the vending machines, yeah?"

There was a circular Formica table with immovable chairs affixed to steel poles in the floor at the other end of the hall. The table sat in front of a wall of vending machines that looked like they hadn't been serviced since the Vietnam War.

We sat and McMullen fumbled a small spiral notepad from the breast pocket of his shirt. He seemed to put too much thought in every question he asked me, which dealt primarily with how I'd gotten a hold of the time and attendance records from the construction company. I answered the questions as truthfully as possible, though I refused to give Earl Parsons's name. McMullen did not seem interested in Earl's name, however, and appeared mostly concerned with the rapidly dulling point of his pencil.

"You write books, don't you?" was his final question.

"What's that got to do with any of this?"

McMullen shrugged and looked bored. "Just what I heard is all. Never met a writer up close and in person before." Examining his notes, he added, "Except for one time I went into Philadelphia to one of Pamela Anderson's book signings. She's amazing in person. You ever run into her at writing conventions or whatever it is you guys go to?"

I told him I had not.

"Yeah. Too bad. She's hot shit in person. Really something. I mean, sometimes, you know, in person, well . . ." He seesawed one hand to illustrate his disappointment in meeting other celebrities in the past. "Huge fuckin' tits."

"Are the Dentmans under arrest?"

"They're being questioned."

"But they're not under arrest?"

"You ever see an interrogation?"

"No," I said.

With a grin like the front grille of a tractor trailer, McMullen said, "Come with me."

Winding through a maze of sawdust-colored corridors, we eventually stopped outside a closed metal door with a glass porthole of smoked glass in it. It looked like a door on a submarine. Humming what sounded like the theme song to *The Muppet Show*, Officer McMullen punched a code into the cipher lock, then opened the door. Without offering any direction, he stood there with the door partially open and examining his cuticles until I stepped inside. McMullen followed me in, shutting the door and continuing to hum.

We were the only two people in a room as small and as lightless as a photographer's darkroom. Folding chairs sat facing a one-way mirror. On the other side of the glass, in a windowless room only slightly bigger than Strohman's office, Veronica sat at the head of a gouged and splintering wooden table. I recognized the officer scribbling in a notebook at the other end of the table as Officer Freers.

"Go on," McMullen said, nodding at the folding

chairs. "Take a seat."

"Can they hear us?"

"Naw," McMullen said, sounding like he had chew in his lip.

Freers's questions were of the baseline variety—Veronica's full name, date of birth, social security number (which she didn't know), address, telephone number (which she didn't have), and current occupation (ditto phone number).

"Is there any way to listen in on David Dentman's interrogation?" I asked McMullen after a while.

"He's in the chief's office," McMullen said, which I assumed to mean no one was permitted to view anything that happened in the chief's office.

Freers got up and left the interrogation room, returning less than a minute later with a Dixie cup of water. He set the cup in front of Veronica. Turning her head toward the cup, her scraggly hair hung down in her face, some clumps of which dipped into the cup like tea bags.

The cipher lock popped and the metal door eased open, cracking the darkness of the viewing room with a sliver of fluorescent light from the hallway. Two or three bodies shambled inside, breathing heavily. The room suddenly smelled of bad breath and day-old perspiration. Two big shapes scuttled like crabs in the seats behind me while the third remained standing beside McMullen. The two behind me muttered in tones just above a whisper. I thought I heard one of them blow a fart against the metal seat of the folding chair.

"We're gonna ask you about the day your son drowned," Freers said to Veronica.

Veronica said nothing.

"Anything you want to start with?" Freers asked.

Veronica said nothing.

"We're gonna need a statement from—"

"I was asleep," she said automatically. Her voice was very quiet through the speakers mounted at either side of the two-way mirror.

"Can we begin with the last thing you remember about that day? Before you went to sleep?" Freers tried.

"I had a headache," she said. "I was asleep."

"Fuckin' creepy," said one of the shapes behind me. "Like she's a robot or something."

"Possessed," suggested his partner. "Like that movie about the devil takin' over the girl."

"*The Exorcist*?"

"I meant that new one."

"Been brainwashed is what I think."

Leaning forward in my seat, I attempted to drown out their voices with my own concentration. Behind the glass, Freers was attempting with zero results to approach his questioning from a different angle.

The third officer who stood over with McMullen

made his way to the two-way. He stood close enough to leave breath-blossoms on the glass. "Come on, Freers," he mumbled under his breath. "Give it up already."

One of the baboons behind me started humming the theme to the *Twilight Zone*.

As if he'd received messages through the glass from osmosis, Freers eventually set down his pen. He sighed and leaned back in his chair; a series of dry cracks that could have been the chair or his back channeled over the intercom. Freers said one last thing to Veronica, the details of which were muffled by his fat thumb rubbing his lower lip. Then he stood, grabbed his pen and notebook, and left the room.

Alone, Veronica looked like a wax impression of herself in the colorless lights of the interrogation room.

"Strohman's gonna want a shot," one of the men said behind me. The resentment in his voice was as subtle as a cannon blast.

"Won't matter," said someone else. "Look at her. You'll sooner get a confession out of a telephone pole."

"I'll bet even she don't know what happened." This was McMullen, still standing by the door and edged into conspiracy by his comrades.

After a few more minutes, they all grew bored. There was some rumor about coffee cake in the lounge, which seemed to light a fire under their asses. I watched their dark shapes get up and lumber out into the hall. Before me, Veronica sat motionless and alone at the wooden table in the interrogation room.

"What will happen to her?" I asked McMullen, who was the last to head for the door.

"Don't know," he said. "Come on. Follow me."

Out in the hallway, it was like New Year's Eve. This was probably the most action the department had seen in a very long time. Possibly the most action they'd ever seen. In the milieu, I thumped a shoulder with Adam as he passed me in the hallway.

"I called Beth and told her to call Jodie," he said over his shoulder, continuing to walk by me with two other policemen. "Told her you were over at the station helping me with something. Said you'd give her a call." He mimed holding a phone to one ear before disappearing into another room.

"Is there a telephone I can use?" I asked McMullen before he followed his coworkers into the lounge.

"Christ." He paused with his hands on his hips, lapping the sweat off his upper lip with his tongue like a dog. He looked maybe eighteen years old. "All the offices are occupied." Then his eyes lit up. "Let's take you to Mae."

Mae was the stout little woman who'd brought Strohman and me our coffee the day I was picked up in the cemetery. She sat at a computer in what served as a combination dispatch and secretarial office. A bank of telephones sat on an overturned bench, a numeral painted in Liquid Paper on each handset.

McMullen waved a hand over the phones, suggested any of them would be more than happy to oblige. "Dial nine to get out," he said before he vanished.

"Hey," I said as Jodie picked up at the house. "It's getting late. I wanted to give you a call. You spoke to Beth?"

"She said you're down at the station with Adam. She said they've made an arrest in a murder investigation?"

"I don't know. They're questioning some people."

"What are you helping him with?"

"I guess I'm sort of a witness."

"Is this about the drowned boy?"

I closed my eyes and said, "Yes."

There was a lengthy hesitation on her end. I couldn't imagine her expression. Was she fearful I was falling back into it again?

"Are you okay?" she said finally.

"Yes. Are you?"

"I'm okay if you're okay."

"I'm okay."

"When will you be home?"

"I don't know. I rode here with Adam. The car's still down at the 'Bird. I guess I'll be home whenever Adam gets off."

"You want Beth and me to come get you?"

"No," I said. "Sit tight. I can't imagine I'll be too late."

"Okay," she said. "I love you."

"Love you, too." And I hung up.

"So nice," Mae said, beaming at me. She had lipstick on her teeth, and her silvery hair was pulled back into a bun. "Your wife?"

"Yes. Is there a place where I can smoke around here?"

"Outside on the front steps."

Freezing and wet, I chain-smoked cigarettes on the front steps of the Westlake Police Department like someone about to be executed. When the wind blew, it caused a whirring in the nearby trees that sounded like the ocean. The sky was a black web speckled with stars.

It was closing on eleven o'clock when Adam pushed through the front door and stood behind me. His shadow fell over me as I sat on the concrete steps, shivering in my coat and working down to the bottom of my cigarette pack. The parking lot's lights cast an unnatural orange glow along the flagstone sidewalk that ran the length of the building.

"Can I bum one of those?"

"You don't smoke menthols," I said, handing him my last cigarette anyway.

He lit it and coughed as he inhaled. Leaning against the railing, he said, "I've been thinking a lot about that summer."

There was no need for him to explain what he meant.

"Maybe it's you coming to live out here or maybe

it's everything that's been going on lately. I don't know."

I watched him suck hard on his smoke. His head was enveloped in an aura of cold orange light.

"Christ," Adam uttered, crushing the half-smoked cigarette beneath his boot. "Let's get out of here."

On the car ride to Waterview Court, I asked him what was going to happen next.

"We're gonna hold them both overnight. The DA will want statements before he takes a step."

"How's that looking?"

"The statements?" There was a disheartening resignation in my brother's voice. "David won't say a word, and Veronica's completely out of it. Even if she admitted to anything, it won't hold water unless her brother gives a statement that's pretty much on the same level. Also, we'll need to subpoena those time and attendance records from the construction company. That'll take a while."

"I already gave you the records."

"I know. But we need to go through the appropriate legal channels."

"Will it screw anything up that I've already given you the records?"

"It shouldn't, although a good defense attorney will certainly try to make an issue of it. But you weren't operating under the direction of law enforcement. No one bullied or persuaded you into getting those records and handing them over. Truth is, they're fair game. The subpoena's just to make sure we've got no holes in the case."

"Do you think this thing will really go to trial?"

"I have no idea. I've never been a part of anything this big before."

Like the static-laden call over a CB radio, I could hear Paul Strohman inside my head saying, *Most of my officers have never seen blood let alone worked a homicide investigation.* And on the heels of that, as poignant as a warning: *I could tell you stuff that would make you spend the rest of your nights sitting up in bed, listening for every little creak in your house.*

As Adam weaved through the dark streets, I watched the shapes of the trees whip by on the shoulder of the road.

"So let's say Dentman did cover up for his sister," I said to the passenger window. "Let's say she killed her son and he knew nothing about it, had nothing to do with it. What sort of charges is he looking at?"

"Obstruction, false statements, conspiracy, aiding and abetting. Christ, I don't know."

"Jesus," I mused.

"Don't tell me you're having some change of heart. Not after all this."

"No," I said. "I'm just trying to digest the whole thing."

Adam choked on a laugh. "Are you kidding me? You're the only one who had any clue. Imagine how Paul fucking Strohman feels right now."

"But I was wrong. It was Veronica, not David." I thought about this, my mind racing. "What did you mean, David won't say a word?"

"He refuses to talk. He won't give a statement. No one's heard him open his mouth since we brought him in."

We, I thought. *Since we brought him in. This is fucking surreal.*

"Would Strohman consider dropping the charges against David in exchange for a statement?"

Adam's face was a ghastly green in the glow of the dashboard. "That would be up to the DA, not Strohman. Besides, what makes you think Dentman would agree to that? He lied for his sister the first time around. I doubt he'll be willing to toss her in the fire for some reduction in charges."

"That's not what I'm thinking," I said. "Not exactly."

He glanced at me. "What is it?"

"It's just . . . I'm just thinking. Any chance you can get Strohman to feel out the DA?"

"About dropping Dentman's charges in exchange for some incriminating confession against his sister?"

"Not a confession," I corrected. "A statement. I don't think Dentman's got anything to confess."

"Well," he said, not without some brotherly condescension. "That's certainly a change in your tune." He turned the wheel, and the cruiser crawled onto Main Street. Ours were the only headlights on the street. "Anyway, if we're talking first degree murder, the DA's going to want someone to do jail time."

"And it won't be Veronica, will it?" I said.

"You've seen her, talked to her," said Adam. "There's not a jury on the planet who'll put that woman in prison, no matter how gruesome the crime. Not that we even have a body," he added sternly, as if this were somehow my fault. "Given her background, even a court-appointed defense lawyer will push for insanity and will probably get it. The only bars that woman will see will be on the windows of a sanitarium."

I let this sink in.

"Do you think we'll ever find out exactly what happened to Elijah?" I said as we pulled onto Waterview Court.

Adam seemed to chew on this for a second or two. "I can't say. But we're one step closer, aren't we?"

The headlights pierced the darkness of our street. The streetlamps were out, and it was like driving along the floor of the deepest ocean.

"You scared the shit out of me that day on the lake," Adam said out of nowhere. "When I saw you pick up that axe . . ."

"I scared myself," I admitted, surprised by my own candor. "I just had to know."

"How did you know?"

In my head, Althea Coulter spoke up: *Nature does not know extinction. It knows that when life is snuffed out and the soul vacates the body, it must, by definition, go somewhere. And if you don't believe in God or a god or in heaven and hell, then where do souls go?*

"Ghosts," I said as we came to a slow stop in the cul-de-sac. "Do you believe in them?"

CHAPTER THIRTY-TWO

Jodie was propped up in bed, reading a Louis L'Amour paperback illuminated by a reading lamp over the headboard.

Kicking off my shoes and crawling into bed on top of her, I kissed up her neck and chin to her lips.

"Quit keeping me in suspense," she said. "What's it all about?"

"I don't know how much I'm actually supposed to say."

"Just tell me."

"I think they arrested David and Veronica Dentman," I said.

"Did they find out what happened to the little boy?"

"No." My head on her chest, I was talking to her breasts.

"What did they need your help with?"

"Information." I couldn't go into it all now, not now. Out of nowhere, exhaustion had clunked me smartly over the head. "Details. Stuff I'd uncovered in my research."

"My smart writer." She kissed the top of my head. "Wow. My stinky writer, too."

"I'll shower."

In the bathroom, I peeled off my clothes and stood beneath the hot spray until it turned cold. Back in the bedroom, the reading lamp had been extinguished, and Jodie's light snores could be heard over the ticking of the clock in the hallway.

The figure of a small boy stood in the doorway of our bedroom. It was too dark to make out any details, but I knew it was Elijah.

"What is it?" I whispered. "What else do you want?"

The shape drifted soundlessly out of the doorway.

I went out into the hall, the staircase to the first floor empty except for the puddles of moonlight coming in through the far windows. Standing at the top of the stairs, I peered down into the well of shadows that made up the foyer. The hallway clock ticked louder, louder.

Elijah moved through the depths of the foyer, a black shape against a background of black shapes.

I descended the stairs, the floorboards cold under my bare feet. I was wearing only a pair of sweatpants, my body still wet from the shower, and my chest broke out in goose bumps.

"Elijah!" It was a shouted whisper through clenched teeth—the way a stern parent might reprimand a child in church. "Where are you?"

The boy had vanished among the sofa and end table, the lamps and television and armchairs. Upstairs, the hallway clock still ticked, the only sound available to mingle with my hesitant respiration.

But no . . . not the clock . . .

It was the sound of the wooden blocks being stacked on the coffee table. It was too dark to see them but I could hear them, less than five feet in front of me—*clack, clack, clack.* Slow and precise.

Crouching down so that I was able to frame the coffee table against the curtained glow of the front windows, my breath caught in my throat. The blocks formed a pyramid, its silhouette solid and black against the windows, and as I looked on, I could make out one of the blocks settling down on top of the others, as if having floated there from the ceiling.

I was unafraid. Instead, a liquid calm filtered through me, causing my joints to tingle and my legs to go wobbly. I sat down hard on the floor. Beside me, one of the heating vents whirred to life: the sound of a foghorn out at sea.

The definitive shape of a child moved across the

front windows: there and then gone.

My heartbeat caught in my throat. Althea yammered on in my head—*One afternoon I was out playing in the palmetto grove when I saw a little girl*—and the memory of her words caused me to spring to my feet.

I could hear him now, moving behind the sofa, the highboy, the swooshing of his bare little feet on the shag carpet. He was moving fast.

I called his name in rapid fire, my breath rasping through clenched teeth. Blind, I lurched forward in the dark toward the sounds, but each time I reached the spot where I'd heard him, he made a noise in another part of the room. He flitted like a tormented bird that had gotten trapped in the room, desperate and panicked to find a way to the outside world.

There's no outside world, I thought. *We're all underwater.*

Suddenly paralyzed by uncertainty, I remained with my back against one wall as I listened to the shuffling across the room. A moment later, I was accosted by what felt like a twinge of electricity sparking to life in my right shoulder, then tracing down my arm until, like strands of gossamer, the electrical current radiated from my fingertips and dispersed into the blackness of the room.

He just touched me, I thought and shivered.

Then there were the footsteps at the other end

of the hall. Still frozen in a combination of fear and perplexity, I listened. The basement door opened with such force, I expected to hear the hinges wrenching out of the frame. This was followed by the distinctive sounds of human footfalls descending the basement steps: I heard each step creak under imaginary weight, my heartbeat echoing the sentiment. And when the sounds vanished from the other end of the hall, the heating vent in the floor by my feet picked them up: the rattling and commotion of someone moving around down there. A deep, resonant clanging began emanating through the vent, probably coming from the belly of the furnace.

All went quiet. It happened so quickly it was like someone had stuffed cotton in my ears, like stepping off a battlefield into a silent bunker.

I stood there for a very long time before I was able to regain control of my muscles. Once I had, I went down into the basement, my bare feet padding on the freezing concrete floor. I turned on the ceiling light and shielded my eyes with one arm as I pressed on toward the furnace. With magnanimous certainty, I approached the furnace and undid the brackets that held the metal facing in place. Beneath, a black cauldron of steel faced me. An iron lid hung down on a hinge. I lifted the lid and peered into the dark maw. It was like looking into the belly of an ancient robot.

If the body were burned in this furnace, I thought, *it would have to have been chopped up into smaller pieces to fit through the hole. If the body were burned in this furnace, there's probably nothing left inside.*

Or was there?

By the time the early stirrings of sunlight had crept into the sky, I had shoveled out what amounted to several handfuls of gummy soot from the unit. It sat on a mat of newspapers, reeking like oil and resembling the evacuated matter of a fevered horse. Once I started scooping the gunk out of the furnace, a part of me had hoped to find bits of bone or something in the drippy, fetid mass. But once I'd laid everything out on the sections of newspaper, I knew all the movies I'd seen and books I'd read had been wrong: there was nothing left except carbon detritus and wet ash.

Exhausted and dejected, I went upstairs where the bedroom alarm clock read 6:09 a.m. Crawling into bed, I curled up beside Jodie and hoped that the sound of her breathing would carry me back to sleep.

It didn't.

CHAPTER THIRTY-THREE

At noon the telephone rang.

"We need your help," Adam said, nearly breathless.

"What is it?"

"Dentman said he'd give us a statement on one condition." He paused, possibly for dramatic effect. "He said he wants to talk to you first."

"I'll be there in ten," I said and hung up the phone.

"This," exclaimed Paul Strohman, "is complete bullshit."

We were in his cramped little office, Strohman behind his desk, Adam seated beside me in one of the two chairs facing the chief of police. Strohman's big feet were propped on the desk, creating a slight but obvious bend in the desktop.

"There's no harm in it," Adam said.

"Other than this entire department looking like a

school bus full of stooges."

"He requested Travis by name. After that, he promised to give us a statement."

"Oh, I guess if he promised." Had Strohman not sighed and run his hands through his hair at that moment, his sarcasm might have struck me a bit harder. Addressing me, he said, "Before you go in there, I need to lay down the ground rules. For starters, we've made no promises to him. If he talks, it's of his own accord. I don't want to give this fool immunity only to have him confess to chopping the kid into kindling and burying him out in the woods."

"Then don't," I said. "Only promise him immunity for the charges he's currently facing—conspiracy, obstruction, whatever."

"I hate the idea of giving him a reduction while we go balls-to-the-wall with his retarded fucking sister."

"Do you want his statement or not?" I said. "And besides, she's not retarded."

Strohman thumbed the dimple in his chin. "If I sound callous, it's because this whole thing's one steaming pile of shit, and I got it all over my shoes. It doesn't help that you've got your nose in everything."

"I'm not planning to tell anyone."

"Yeah, well, you're just a swell guy, I guess." Strohman stood up, all six and a half feet of him. "You go in there and listen to what he has to say. You make him no promises. You tell him nothing he doesn't already confess to knowing."

"Check," I said, also standing. "Where is he?"

"In one of the holding cells."

Slump-shouldered and withdrawn, David Dentman looked like an overgrown child in the single holding cell. As I approached, Adam shutting the door behind me, he didn't even bother to look up. Wan midday light spilled in from a number of recessed windows high in the wall. The whole place smelled of camphor and gym socks.

I sat down in the folding chair in front of the cell and did not speak.

Sitting on the edge of his cot, Dentman seemed content to stare at his big feet. The shoelaces had been removed from his boots, and his hands, clasped between his legs, looked about the size of hubcaps. With his head bowed, I noticed the whirl of hair that faded to baldness at the topmost portion of his scalp. When he finally looked at me, his face was hard as stone and almost expressionless. This surprised me; I had thought he'd been crying.

"What else do you know?" he said, his voice just barely above a whisper.

I spread my hands out on my knees, palms up. "Nothing."

"Don't lie to me. It's over now."

"What makes you think I know something more?"

"You've figured everything else out, haven't you?"

"I don't know anything else. This is where we are."

"Goddamn you."

"Tell me what happened."

He hung his head again.

"They need a statement from you."

"Why? So they can put my sister in prison?"

"Veronica won't go to prison. But if you cooperate, you might be able to avoid going yourself."

"What good does that do me?"

"Maybe it doesn't matter to you," I said. "But maybe it matters to Veronica. Maybe if you cooperate and get your sentence reduced—if you tell them all you know about what actually happened that day— then you'll still be free to help her. If she goes away to a hospital someplace, she's going to need you to check in on her and take care of her. You can't do that from prison."

David lifted his head and stared at me. Despite the distance between us, I could count the fine blond hairs that made up his eyebrows. "I don't trust the police," he said. "I won't say nothing to them unless I know they don't got nothing else up under their sleeve."

"There's nothing else. Just the evidence that you lied for your sister."

"Where is she?"

"They're holding her here, too."

"What has she told them?"

We were treading dangerously close to the territory Strohman warned me to stay away from. "She hasn't said anything yet," I told him anyway. *Fuck Paul Strohman*, I thought.

"And she won't," Dentman said. Astoundingly, I thought I saw the stirrings of a smile. It never materialized, however, and I was somewhat grateful for that, for I feared that smile would have haunted my dreams for decades.

"Tell me what you know," I said again, leaning closer to the bars of his cell.

He said nothing for a long time. As he rubbed his face, I once again expected to see his eyes grow muddy with tears, but that didn't happen. When he looked at me, I felt a twinge in my spine, as if he'd speared me with an iron lance. "Tell the chief I'm ready to talk to him," Dentman said and turned away.

"Come with me," said Adam.

I followed him down the hall to the same darkened viewing room McMullen had taken me to yesterday. This time, all the folding chairs facing the two-way mirror were occupied, and the room was warm and smelled strongly of bad breath. I clung to the wall beside Adam as the lights in the interrogation room fizzed on.

Through the intercom system, the sound of the door opening was like something from a 1930s radio show about haunted houses. Escorted by two uniformed policemen, David Dentman entered the interrogation room. His hands cuffed in front of him, his enormous size dwarfing the two officers at his sides, he was ushered over to the seat his sister had occupied yesterday.

Strohman came in next and shut the door behind him. He was wearing the same unbuttoned shirt and slacks from our previous meeting, only now he'd thrown a suit jacket over his shirt. He looked like someone recently roused from a fitful sleep. "Okay, David," Strohman said, sitting in a chair at the opposite end of the table. He placed a large folder on the table in front of him as the two uniformed officers faded against the far wall.

I had been anticipating a certain formality to the interrogation, something direct and witty and straight out of an Elmore Leonard novel, but instead I found myself quickly disappointed with Strohman's unceremonious approach.

Sleepy-eyed and looking terminally bored, Strohman sat half-slouched in his chair like someone at an AA meeting. Casually, he flipped open the folder and asked Dentman if he understood his rights.

"Yeah," Dentman muttered. Even in low tones, his voice vibrated the intercom speakers.

Someone from the audience got up and adjusted a volume control knob on the wall.

"Are you ready to give your statement?" Strohman asked.

"Not yet."

Strohman looked nonplussed. The expression was out of place on his face. "Oh yeah?"

"I want to make something clear first," said Dentman.

"What's that?"

"My sister. She isn't well. She hasn't been well in a long time. I think you already know that"—his gaze shifted almost imperceptibly toward the two-way mirror, as if he knew we were all behind it, watching him—"but I want it stated for the record anyway."

"Okay."

"I love my sister. Now that Elijah's dead, she's all the family I got."

"Understood. Are you ready now?"

Dentman nodded.

Strohman patted his shirt pockets. An arm emerged from the shadows as one of the officers handed him a pen. "Tell us what happened the day your nephew disappeared," Strohman said.

"I was at work all day. I'm not exactly sure what time I got home, but the sun was starting to go down. I remember that. Veronica was home alone with the boy, just like she was every other day. She was a good mother. She tried to be, even when she was having one of her moments."

"What do you mean? What moments?"

"Sometimes she draws a blank. Sometimes she just stares and doesn't answer, and some part of her mind retreats far back inside her, I think. It's important you understand that part, too."

"They're already gunning for insanity," one of the officers in the viewer's room commented.

There were a few assenting murmurs.

"All right," Strohman told Dentman. "Go on."

"When I came in the door, Veronica was sitting on the stairs, staring straight ahead at the wall. I thought she was, you know, having a spell again. I called her name a couple times, but she didn't answer. So I went over to her and sort of lifted her up by the shoulders." Dentman mimed the motion, awkward with his hands chained together. "That seemed to wake her out of it. She blinked and her eyes came back to normal again. That's when I noticed she was covered in mud and that her housedress was wet."

Strohman raised one eyebrow. "Wet?"

"Real wet. From top to bottom. There was water and mud on the step where she'd been sitting, too." Lowering his voice, he added, "There was blood on her. That's what scared me right away."

"Okay."

"I asked her what happened and she said, 'He disappeared.' Just over and over again, that's all she would say. 'He disappeared; he disappeared.' I mean, I knew she was talking about Elijah—there was no one else in the house—so I started going around the house calling the boy's name. He didn't answer, but that wasn't unusual for Elijah—he was special, like his mom—so I did a real thorough search of the whole house before I again started asking Veronica what had happened.

"But she just kept saying the same thing—that he disappeared. Finally, I sat her down at the kitchen table and told her calmly to tell me what happened. She said Elijah was swimming in the lake that afternoon. She was out in the garden, keeping an eye on him. The boy liked to swim, but it was important to watch him. She said he started to climb on that staircase thingy in the water there, and she yelled at him to come down off it. It was dangerous for a boy like Elijah to be climbing it."

Again, Strohman's eyebrow arched. "A boy like Elijah?"

"He was special, just like I said," Dentman reiterated, a bit of irritation in his voice. "He wasn't like other kids."

"All right. Keep going."

"She said at one point she saw him standing at the topmost part of the staircase. She got scared and shouted to him. That was when he fell."

"The blood on the step," mumbled someone in the back row of the viewing room.

Strohman leaned back in his chair and whapped the pen against his chin. He seemed content to sit in the increasing silence without prompting Dentman to continue.

"Veronica said he hit his head hard on one of the stairs," Dentman went on eventually, "and then fell backward into the water. She ran down to him and out into the lake. That's how her clothes got messy, with the mud and water and all. Anyway, my sister's pretty small, but she somehow managed to pull Elijah onto land. She said she carried him all the way to the house while he bled from one whole side of his head. She was afraid to look at the wound because it was bleeding so much. That's how she, you know, how the blood got on her dress."

"Then what happened after Veronica got Elijah to the house?"

"She brought him inside. He started to moan and his eyelids fluttered. She said she laid him on the floor against the wall at the foot of the stairs and ran into the kitchen. She wanted to get something to clean up the blood, to stop the bleeding."

"Why didn't she call an ambulance?"

"Because Veronica doesn't think that way. All her life she's only looked toward one person to make things better."

"That person was you," Strohman said. He wasn't asking it, was simply stating it as fact.

"You'd understand if you grew up in our house."

"Because your father had been mean. Abusive." He said it in such an offhandeded way, I thought Dentman was going to spring out of his chair and throttle him, handcuffs and all.

"He'd been something, all right," Dentman said from the corner of his mouth. He shifted in his seat, and his gaze once again ran the length of the two-way mirror.

I felt a chill ripple through my body.

"Okay," Strohman said, glancing at his notebook. That pen was still tap-tap-tapping away, this time on the corner of the table. It was a wonder he hadn't driven the entire viewing room mad. "So she didn't call an ambulance. Then what? Is that when you came home?"

"No. She said she went around looking for bandages and antiseptic. She finally found some under the kitchen sink."

"Naturally," said Strohman.

"When she came back to where she'd left Elijah, he was gone."

Strohman's pen tapping ceased just long enough for him to jot down a few notes in his notebook. Then he looked at Dentman. "Gone?"

"He disappeared," Dentman said.

No, I thought, shivering against the wall while watching all this unfold on the other side of the glass like someone watching a stage play. *No, that's not right. People don't just disappear. Nature does not know extinction.*

Exhaling with great exaggeration, Strohman said, "Disappeared."

"She came back, and all that was left of him was a wet spot on the carpet. Lake water. And blood."

"This is what she told you?"

"Yes."

"What did she say she did next?"

The officer in the folding chair closest to me cursed as his cell phone began chirping with a tune that sounded incriminatingly like Britney Spears. Bolting from his chair and rushing out into the hallway, he caused enough of a ruckus for me to miss the beginning of what Dentman said.

"—his name and then started looking around the house. She said she thought he might have gone down to lie on the sofa, but when she looked, he wasn't there. So then she checked upstairs, the bedrooms and the bathroom, but he wasn't there, either."

"He wasn't in his room?"

"Elijah's room was in the basement. He would

have gone past the kitchen and down the hall to get there. If he'd done that, Veronica would have seen him."

"But did she check the basement?"

"She looked there last. He wasn't there."

Strohman checked his notes. "His bedroom was in the basement, you said?"

"It was a room my father built a long time ago. Elijah liked it. He could hide in it, and it was dark and quiet. Veronica hated that he liked it, but she couldn't get him to come out. Eventually we just moved his bed and the rest of his stuff down there."

Strohman rubbed his forehead and looked like he was ready for a nap.

In the shadows toward the back of the interrogation room, the two uniformed policemen shifted soundlessly.

"Okay, David. So Veronica looks and she can't find him. What did she do next? Did she just sit down on the stairs and wait for you to come home? Because that's how you found her, correct?"

"No. I mean, yes, that's how I found her. But that's not . . . it didn't happen like that."

"Tell me how it happened."

"She said she couldn't remember it all. It went black for a while."

Strohman asked him what that meant.

"One of her spells," Dentman said. "She must have

worked herself up real good and had one of her spells."

"A blackout," said Strohman. "Like, uh . . ." He snapped his fingers in rapid succession. "Like, hey, nobody's home. Right?"

Strohman's glibness about the whole situation stirred something inside David Dentman. Even from my vantage, I could see it simmering and kicking off white sparks just beneath the surface of his eyes.

He may not have killed Elijah, but those are the eyes of a cold-blooded killer, all right.

"Veronica didn't know how long she'd been out," Dentman went on, "but when she came to, Elijah was still gone. That's when she sat down on the stairs and waited for me."

"All right. So you come home. Then what?"

"Just like I said—just like she said. She told me what I've told you now."

"And did you believe her? That the boy had just vanished into thin air?"

Dentman didn't respond.

"Are you going to answer the question?"

"My sister, she's very delicate."

"I understand. We've been over that already. Are you going to answer my question?"

"What do you want me to say?"

"Then what do you think happened?"

"I don't know. But whatever it was, it was

an accident."

"I think I know."

Dentman grinned. "Yeah?"

"These blackouts—"

"I know what you're getting at. She didn't do anything to deliberately hurt that child."

"Okay. But accidentally, maybe—"

"Stop it. You're putting words into my mouth. I didn't say that."

"Then tell me how we've got to this place. Tell me how we're hearing this story from you now when back in the summer we heard a completely different one—that you'd been home watching the boy and that Veronica had been in bed with a headache. It's obvious you concocted that to protect her at the time—you didn't want her answering any direct questions, sure—but look where it's gotten the both of you."

Quick as a jackrabbit, Dentman stood. His chair went skidding backward on the floor, causing the two uniformed officers to fumble into one another in an attempt to catch it. His chained hands planted firmly on the tabletop, David looked about ready to spit fire.

At the opposite end of the table, Strohman could have been watching an old black-and-white movie on AMC.

"Down!" instructed one of the uniformed officers, clamping a hand around one of Dentman's massive shoulders.

The second officer quickly shoved the chair against the backs of Dentman's knees. "Sit down!"

Like a ship sinking into the ocean, Dentman slowly lowered himself down on the chair.

"Your temper calls into question everything you're telling me," Strohman said. "I'm beginning to think we're all wasting our time here."

"You wanted a fucking statement. I gave you one."

"What happened after you got home and your sister told you Elijah had disappeared? After you searched the house and couldn't find him?"

"You want me to say it, don't you? You're going to make me say it."

"Yes," Strohman said, "I am."

Dentman leaned closer to Strohman over the table and said, "I thought she might have hurt him real bad and that she hadn't realized it."

"Hurt him?"

"Killed him," Dentman said. It was like an absolution.

At that moment, I realized I was holding my breath.

"I kept asking Veronica what she did, but she said she couldn't remember, that she had blacked out while looking around for him. I asked her if it was possible something happened to him by the water. She just cried and said he'd hit his head. She said this over and over again, too. So I went down to the water. I called

Elijah's name. I searched the surrounding woods and then waded into the lake. I couldn't find him . . . but I saw the blood on the step."

"How long did you search for him?"

"A long time. Maybe thirty minutes. I couldn't imagine where he'd gone. If he'd . . . if he'd gone under and gotten stuck somewhere, I had no way of knowing and no way of finding him, of pulling him out."

"Then what?"

"I went back to the house. I told Veronica to go upstairs and change into fresh clothes. She did. I took her wet and bloody housedress and tossed it in the basement furnace."

My heart leapt. The blood pumping through my veins sounded like a freight train in my ears.

"Then I told her we needed to call the cops because if Elijah was under the water, I couldn't get to him. We needed the cops to get to him. She was fading in and out fast, and I thought she was going to have another attack. I had her sit down on the couch as I called the police. When I hung up the phone, I went over to her and let her curl up in my lap. I rubbed her head and told her exactly what to say to the police when they arrived—that she'd been asleep the whole time, up in bed with a migraine, and that I had been downstairs looking after the boy. 'Let me take care of it,' I told her. I promised her."

Dentman had been talking too fast for Strohman's pen to keep up; the chief of police had simply set it aside midway through Dentman's statement and merely listened, his hands in his lap, one leg over the other. After a moment, Strohman had Dentman repeat the story, which he did verbatim, before suggesting they bring in Veronica to corroborate it.

"You'll have to wait in holding while we talk to her, of course," said Strohman, closing his notebook.

"Then she won't talk to you."

"Why's that?"

"Because the last thing I said to her was to say she'd been sleeping. Until I sit with her and tell her otherwise, that's all you'll ever hear from her."

A small chuckle began to rumble up through the chief of police. A similar rumbling could be heard from his men throughout the viewing room.

"That's a neat trick," Strohman said after his chuckling had subsided. "You know we can't have you two—"

"Bring her in here now. With me. With all of us. I'll sit right here and tell her to tell the truth."

Strohman sucked on the inside of his left cheek. Then he clapped, startling everyone except Dentman, and said, "All right. Let's do it. But I need to take a piss first."

Outside on the front steps, a group of us burned

through cigarettes and shuddered against the cold.

"Coldest fucking winter in a decade," McMullen said, digging around in the seat of his pants. "Miserable godforsaken place."

Five minutes later, we were all gathered in the viewing room as Veronica was brought in, unshackled, and placed in a chair midway between her brother and Chief Strohman.

Flipping to a clean sheet of notebook paper, that goddamn pen beginning to jitterbug in one hand, Strohman started asking Veronica questions.

Her responses, never changing, started out almost comical . . . then turned sad and somewhat frightening. "I was asleep."

"Veronica, your brother just told me you—"

"I was asleep."

"You need to understand—"

Pulling her hair and shouting like a child: "I was asleep! I was asleep! I was asleep!" She slammed her hands down on the table, her nails digging audibly into the wood.

A good number of us cringed.

"Fuck's sake," Strohman uttered.

"Wait," said Dentman. With surprising tenderness, he clasped one of his sister's skeletal hands in both of his. The sound of his thumbs rubbing along the back of her hand was like the crinkling of carbon paper. "Darling," he said quietly, "it's time to tell the truth now."

Trembling like a day-old fawn, Veronica drank her brother in, scrutinized him, as if he were a stranger she was supposed to know. A second before the tears came, I could sense their arrival. They began streaming down her sallow, colorless cheeks, her lipless mouth quivering. The tendons in her neck stood out like telephone cables. "He . . . hit his head . . . on the stairs . . . on the lake . . . blood . . . on me, on him . . . carried him back to the . . . the house . . . blood everywhere . . . went to . . . went . . . turned my back . . . when I came back . . . gone . . ."

No one said a word. All eyes were locked on the fragile woman who was breaking apart right in front of us. Her words suddenly didn't matter. Her brother's words, either. It was on her face, all of it. I prayed for someone to say something—anything—and only hoped that until they did the silence wouldn't crush the life out of me.

In the interrogation room, Strohman closed his notebook.

CHAPTER THIRTY-FOUR

Adam dropped me off that evening. Weakened, spiritually fatigued, I entered the house with no greater designs other than to crawl beneath the stream of a warm shower and wash the tiredness from my marrow.

Jodie was standing at the foot of the stairs, half-cloaked in shadow.

The look on her face immediately froze my blood. "What?"

"I think . . ." She looked around—a blind child suddenly given the gift of sight. "I think . . . someone was in the house."

"What are you talking about? Were you asleep?"

"Yes. But noises woke me. Thumping noises. Like an animal in the attic or trapped behind the wall. I got out of bed to see what it was. I thought maybe you'd come home and I hadn't heard the front door. So I called your name." I watched as a chill zigzagged through her. "Oh, Jesus."

"What? Jodie . . ."

"I called your name, and then I heard someone run across the living room and slam the front door."

"Babe." I went to her, embraced her. "You were dreaming."

"No. I was awake."

"There's no one here. I just unlocked the door now. It was locked."

"Are you sure?"

"I swear it."

"Jesus." She laughed nervously against my collarbone. "Oh, Jesus."

In the morning, Adam showed up with a document for me to sign. It looked very official and said Consent to Search at the top. "Strohman wants your permission for us to dig up your lawn once the ground thaws a bit."

"He thinks Elijah's buried in the yard?"

"He thinks if David Dentman could brainwash his sister so easily to lie to the police the first time, what's to say any of what was said last night was the truth."

"Are you serious?"

He handed me the consent form and a pen. It was serious, all right.

"They've both been charged."

"With lying to the cops?"

"With murder," Adam said. "David's still at the station. He's being charged as an accessory. Veronica's being shipped to a hospital over in Cumberland this afternoon. She's been practically catatonic all night."

"Jesus Christ."

"What is it? You look sick."

Truth was, I *felt* sick. "It feels wrong."

Taking the signed form from me, Adam folded it in halves, then slipped it into the back pocket of his chinos. "Vindication's a little harsher than you'd hoped, huh?" He went to the door.

"Hey, you really think they're going to find the body buried in the yard?"

"I don't know what to think," Adam said and left.

I called Earl and told him everything I knew. He would be the first to break the story.

"What do you do now?" he asked me after I'd given him all I had.

"Nothing," I told him. "My part in this is over."

CHAPTER THIRTY-FIVE

February was angry and eager and shook us to our souls. Once again, the whole world seemed to freeze. But by early March, the snow had receded, and the gray slope of our lawn rose as if out of ash. The blustery winds grew tame and warmed up. We celebrated Jacob's eleventh birthday, and he dazzled us with card tricks. Jodie finished her dissertation and looked forward to receiving her PhD in May. She had verbally accepted the full-time teaching position at the university, and although it wouldn't start until the fall, she went out one afternoon with Beth to shop for a whole new wardrobe.

Sales for *Water View* continued to climb. The whole Dentman ordeal nearly a month behind me now, I began to feel the writing bug edge closer and closer again. That was good; like the parent of a child gone away to summer camp, I had been eagerly awaiting its safe return.

Jodie surrendered the upstairs office to me. I stocked it full of my writing implements, fresh heaps of notebooks, word processor, and lucky ceramic mug. I wrote there in the mornings before Jodie woke up, downing cup after cup of overpowering Sumatra coffee. Sometimes when I knew Jodie was still sound asleep, I would open the single window and smoke a cigarette, my head poking halfway out into the chilly morning air.

Having aborted the story of the Dentmans and the floating staircase, I resumed the partially finished manuscript of which I'd already sent sample chapters to Holly Dreher in New York. It was coming smooth and good and honest. As with every other book, it was important to write it honestly.

(Once, at a writers' conference in Seattle, I'd had a few drinks with a best-selling novelist. Like teenagers confused about their sexuality, this author's novels traversed that blurry and often fatal line between genres, and he drank expensive scotch and listened to jazz records in his hotel room because he thought those things made him more writerly. We must have talked for hours that evening at the hotel bar, but the only thing I took away with me was his comment that all good books were honest books and that all the rest could suck a fat one. I took half of that sentiment and filed it deep down in the writing center of my brain and have used it ever since. All good books *are* honest books.)

So I wrote, and it was strong and good and honest.

One afternoon, I heard the bumping sound. It was the same sound Jodie had heard that night when I'd come home from the police station—I was certain of it. The first time I heard it, I was alone in the house and standing in my underwear in the kitchen about to pour a fresh cup of coffee. It sounded like it was coming from upstairs. But when I reached the top of the stairs, the sound stopped.

The next time I heard it, I was lying in bed at night. Beside me, Jodie was sleeping the sleep of the blissfully innocent. I could hear it across the hall, and for one insane moment, I imagined a dozen tiny elves walking on the keyboard of my word processor, finishing my book for me. I got out of bed and crossed the hall, flipping the light on in the office. The sound had stopped. I stood there holding my breath, listening for a very long time, but it didn't start up again.

The third and final time, it happened on the day a big yellow bulldozer appeared in my backyard to dig up patchy sections of my lawn. A few officers milled about, and even Strohman made an appearance. Tugging on some clothes, I met Strohman outside, and we both smoked cigarettes without talking to each other. The smell of the bulldozer's diesel exhaust was cloying.

Back in the house, I started making lunch. Jodie was at the movies with Beth and the kids, and despite the racket in the yard, I knew that I could finish the first draft of the new book today. The thought made me happy. Alone, I ate lunch on the front porch until the clouds of bulldozer exhaust crept over the roof and settled down around me like nuclear winter.

I showered, shaved, and dressed in clean clothes. I sat in the office and fired up the word processor, smelling its electric body, feeling the keys as they hummed lightly beneath the pads of my fingers.

Then the thumping started again. It was right behind the desk against the wall.

Dropping to my hands and knees, I slid the desk away from the wall with little difficulty. Instantly, I felt foolish. The culprit, of course, was the cubbyhole door. It had come ajar, and as the wind rattled the eaves, the door had been thumping against the back of the desk.

I pushed the cubbyhole door shut but didn't stand up right away. Outside, I heard the bulldozer's gears grinding and someone shouting.

There was a gooseneck lamp on the desk. I yanked it down and switched it on. The light was dull but it would serve its purpose. With one hand, I pushed the cubbyhole door, and it popped open on its hinges. Cold air breathed out.

I thought of Elijah telling Althea Coulter that he had gone away.

I thought of Veronica in the interrogation room saying, *When I came back . . . gone . . .*

Bending over, I shoved the lamp into the cubbyhole and peeked inside.

It was just a tiny square box, a space for storage, with wooden struts and pink insulation for walls. The frayed baseball was still inside. So were the Matchbox cars and the Scrooge McDuck comic book. A child's secret hiding place. I thought about the time Adam and I treaded water beneath the double dock, hiding from the rifle-toting lunatic marching on the boards above us. *Hiding*, I thought. *Children hide.*

When I came back . . . gone . . .

But of course, there was nothing here. The cubbyhole was empty. I'd known that—I'd known it since that first day I'd opened the door and found the shoe box full of dead birds. Just what had I expected to find?

And then I smelled it.

Sickeningly sweet, like day-old chamomile tea. Borne on the cold air, it grew more and more pungent with each inhalation. I craned the neck of the lamp farther into the cubbyhole and squeezed my head and shoulders inside. By no means am I a big man, but the opening was too tight for me to slip in past my chest. I recalled my nightmares from so many weeks ago—being squeezed to death in a constricting wall. Sweat suddenly sprung out along my brow.

Sometimes we go in; sometimes we go out.

In, I thought. *He went in.*

I reached out and fingered a curled bit of insulation paper. The Pink Panther's face smiled slyly at me. Slowly, I peeled the curl of paper away from the wooden struts. I expected to find Sheetrock behind there, the back of the office closet. But what the light from the gooseneck lamp brought into view was a narrow cavern between the eaves and the back of the closet, a slender vertical cut behind the wall. This wasn't just a cubbyhole; this was a crawl space.

Bringing the lamp closer to the narrow sliver of darkness, I held my breath and felt the sweat run down my face.

Sometimes we go in, I thought.

Holding my breath.

I saw him.

CHAPTER THIRTY-SIX

Unseasonably cold weather had practically preserved it, keeping the body from stinking up the whole house. This was the medical examiner's inference, anyway. It was also the opinion of the police officers who for several hours occupied the rooms and hallways (and walls) of 111 Waterview Court.

I stood on the front lawn as they removed Elijah Dentman from the house. It required only two officers to carry the body to the ambulance, although I estimated one could have done it without breaking a sweat. They carried him on a flat wooden board with handles on either side. A white sheet covered his emaciated frame. His profile looked like a distant mountain range. Some neighborhood dogs came sniffing around, and it took another officer to chase them away.

By this time, a crowd had formed in the cul-de-sac, and the more brazen onlookers stepped on the front lawn and even pooled around the side of the house. They all watched in horror as the body was exhumed and taken away in the ambulance. When the ambulance departed, it did so with its lights and siren off.

Upstairs, I stood in the doorway to the study. I was instructed not to touch anything in the room. My impression of crime scenes (admittedly acquired from too much television) was that they were always sterile, sober environments, and the officers were always stern and emotionless and wearing ties tucked into their buttoned dress shirts.

Here, though, everyone kept the atmosphere as casual as possible, even at its most somber moment when the body was extricated from the crawl space via a fresh opening cut into the hallway wall. There was no yellow police tape anywhere. The cops wore uniforms. They did not look like they had everything under control nor all the answers, though nothing ever got out of hand. They looked so young and seemed to be learning as they went along, much as I was. These officers were not all-knowing, all-powerful beings; they were regular guys doing their job and they wore their emotions on their sleeves. It was as real as it could get.

All these years, I thought, *I've been writing crime scenes wrong.*

Adam appeared beside me. "You look green," he said.
"Yeah? So do you."

"I feel it." He surveyed the room.

Two officers took photographs of the carpet and the enlarged opening the cops had cut into the wall in order to access the crawl space.

A third officer's black boots poked out of the mouth of the cubbyhole as he backed out. "It's a tight fit in there," he said, sweat causing him to glisten like an eel. "Goes all the way through the wall and behind the stairs. There's a bunch of junk, too. Kid must have used it as a clubhouse or something."

No, I thought. *Not a clubhouse. That's where he hid when he was afraid. Or when he was hurt.*

Adam put a hand on my shoulder. "You were right, you know."

"Maybe," I said. "About some things."

"No," Adam insisted. "You were right all along. You said it yourself—that the proof was in the staircase. Well, this crawl space goes behind the wall, behind the staircase in the hallway. That day on the lake, you just had the wrong staircase."

Driven by some imprecise loyalty, I telephoned Earl and told him to bring his camera and best writing pad. When he arrived at the scene, he snapped photos of the spot where police busted through the upstairs wall and even took snapshots of the passage between the interior walls and the outer shell of the house, where Elijah's body had been hidden.

Before Earl left, he hugged me with a surprising amount of emotion behind it, then held me at arm's length while he grinned. "You'll be leaving after this," he said.

"We can't stay."

"Thank you for giving this to me."

"You helped make it happen," I told him.

It looked like Earl wanted to say something heartfelt and poignant. Maybe if we'd had more time to get to know each other, he would have. But as it was, we were pretty much strangers, and in the end he settled for shaking my hand firmly and nodded. "You keep hold of my phone number," he told me. "Stay in touch, now."

I promised that I would. "Take care," I said, watching him trudge through the thinning snow to his Oldsmobile.

(His news story would get picked up by papers throughout the state, landing him his first and only syndication. And I did keep in touch with him . . . until a massive stroke took him in the night some eighteen months later.)

When he left, I felt empty.

Adam arrived home sometime around midnight. The rest of the house was asleep, including Jodie on the pullout couch in the living room. I was propped up in a chair in Adam's kitchen, the lights off, the small television set flickering in the darkness, the volume low.

"Hey. You weren't waiting up, were you?"

"Are you kidding?"

"Jodie?"

"On the couch. She's all right."

"How about you?"

I held up one hand to show him how badly it shook. "Ready to perform surgery."

Adam flipped on the light above the kitchen sink and turned on the water. He scrubbed his hands with dishwashing detergent.

"You hungry?" I asked. "I'll throw together some sandwiches."

"Yeah. That sounds good. Thanks."

I went to the refrigerator and produced some sliced turkey, mayonnaise, half a head of lettuce, and two cans of Diet Pepsi. There was a loaf of French bread on the counter. I sawed off two sizeable pieces, then cut them both down the middle. I asked Adam if he was a lot hungry or a little hungry.

"A lot," he said, drying his hands on a dish towel.

"I can't remember the last meal I ate."

I loaded the bread with mounds of sliced turkey and shook some pepper on it. I rinsed the lettuce in the sink and laid several leaves on top of the turkey. Then I lathered mayonnaise on the underside of the bread. Setting the plates down at the table, I watched my brother stare out the window over the sink and at the pinpoints of light across the cul-de-sac and through the woods. The cops had left the porch lights on across the street.

"It's not a pretty thing," Adam said, still looking out the window.

"I want to know."

"Cause of death was due to severe head trauma. Heavy fracture at the back of the head, consistent with the fall Elijah would have taken off the staircase on the lake. We'll have more specifics once the autopsy comes back, of course, but it's pretty evident what happened."

He turned around and sat at the table. Together we ate.

Several minutes passed before Adam spoke again. "There's no way a grown human being could fit in that crawl space. Not even Veronica and especially not David."

"I know." I wasn't surprised. I'd known all afternoon, it seemed. "He must have crawled in there after Veronica took him to the house. When she turned her back on him, he went up the stairs and hid in his special place." I was talking but I wasn't listening to myself. Instead, I was remembering the story Althea Coulter had told me that day at the hospital—about how she'd come to the house two days in a row and never saw the boy. How David had answered the door, an oddity in itself. How, on the third day, Elijah had simply admitted to Althea that he had just gone away.

"The DA dropped the charges against David and Veronica," said Adam. There was mayonnaise at one corner of his mouth. "David still could have been prosecuted for lying to the police, but both the DA and Strohman figured this thing was already such a fuckup they just wanted to sweep it under the rug and be done with it."

"So what's going to happen to them?"

"I don't know. I guess they go back to their lives. At least they know the truth now."

The idea of that child crawling through the darkness of the crawl space to die, like a wounded animal, was too much for me to comprehend. For some reason, the idea that he had been murdered was easier to swallow.

"Listen," Adam said, rising from the chair and tugging up his pants. "Why don't you go inside and get some sleep?"

"I will. Not just yet."

"That's my kid brother. Always thinking." Rubbing his forehead, he suddenly looked so old it nearly brought tears to my eyes. He smiled wearily at me and headed into the hallway. Then he turned around, his face cloaked in darkness. "Does this finally put him to rest for you?"

I knew he wasn't talking about Elijah. After a moment, I said, "I don't know."

"I'm sorry," Adam said.

"For what?"

He shrugged. "I'm not quite sure."

"Well, thanks."

"I love you, Bro."

"Yeah," I said. "I love you, too."

Five minutes later, in my underwear and socks, I slipped beneath the fresh sheets on my brother's pull-out couch. I was careful not to wake Jodie, but as I eased my head onto the pillow and listened for the sound of her breathing, I could tell she was awake.

"Hey, you," I said.

"You know we can't stay," she whispered, her back in my direction.

"I know."

"You're going to miss him."

For one insane moment, I thought she was talking about Elijah Dentman, my obsession with him.

As if reading my mind and finding the need to clarify for me, she added, "Adam."

I closed my eyes. "Yes."

"It's too bad. You both had the chance to be close again."

To my own surprise, I had to fight back tears. "Jodie?" I said. Distant.

"What is it?"

"I need to tell you something." Like a fading star, my voice wavered. "It's about Kyle. About what really happened."

She pulled closer to me. I could feel her warmth. "Good," she said. "I've been waiting a long time."

CHAPTER THIRTY-SEVEN

Perhaps the only event of any significance during our last remaining days in Westlake, Maryland, occurred two nights before Jodie and I were scheduled to drive out to California where we had a nice little apartment waiting for us just outside San Diego's Gaslamp Quarter. I'd spent the last month packing our belongings and stowing much of them at a personal storage facility in town. Since the day Elijah's body had been extricated from the wall, Jodie had refused to return to the house, not even for a minute. I couldn't blame her. So we sustained at Adam and Beth's house for the remainder of that month while I scrambled to secure a new life for Jodie and me somewhere far, far away from Westlake, the house on the lake, and the tragic memory of the Dentmans.

Utilizing my remaining college contacts, I got in touch with an old acquaintance. He was a screenwriter in Los Angeles and, for the better part of our phone conversation, confessed to me that he was jealous to the point of clinical depression of his pseudonym's success. Nevertheless, the conversation proved profitable: he knew of an apartment that had recently gone up for rent, and the owner of the complex owed a friend of a friend of a friend. The prospect of leaving the cold winters behind for the West Coast pleased Jodie, which meant it pleased me, too.

Two days before our scheduled cross-country drive, I sat at the bar at Tequila Mockingbird for the final time while I waited for Adam to meet me after his shift. I had a map spread out before me, and I was tracing possible routes with different color markers. The plan wasn't to rush things. It was to use that time to strengthen what had weakened between Jodie and me over the past couple of months.

"Here," Tooey said, setting a fresh pint in front of me. "On the house."

"This actually looks good," I commented, picking up the glass and examining it in the light. "I think you may have mastered the recipe." I took a sip. "Wow. It's great."

"Thanks. It's Sam Adams." Leaning over the bar, he peered down at the map. "California, huh?"

"I can hardly believe it myself. I've never even seen the Pacific Ocean."

"Fell in love with a woman from California once."

"Yeah?"

"Name was Charlie. Funny name for a chick— Charlie."

"What happened?"

"She lost her mind."

"Is that right?"

"Yeah. She was convinced time was changing."

"Times *are* changing," I informed him. "Didn't Bob Dylan tell you?"

"Not *times*, Travis. *Time*."

"I don't follow."

"She became convinced that each day was getting shorter by thirty seconds. That in two days, it would be a minute earlier than it was two days before at the exact same time. If you can wrap your head around *that*."

I whistled.

"She seemed very concerned about it," Tooey said. Then he leaned closer to me, like a conspirator. He was staring at something over my shoulder. "Have you noticed our friend there at the back of the room?"

I started to turn my head.

"Don't make it obvious," he warned, then slipped farther down the bar.

Taking a long swallow of my beer, I casually rotated

around on the barstool.

David Dentman sat alone at one corner of the barroom, perched buzzard-like over a pitcher of beer. He wore a red and black flannel shirt, the sleeves cuffed to the elbows. The skin of his face seemed to be dripping off his skull and into his beer, and there was a bristling sheen of beard at his jaw. Sensing my eyes on him, he glanced up and stared me down.

Discomfited, I turned away.

My mind returned to that evening in the cemetery—the way he'd looked standing over his nephew's grave. Now, despite all that had been revealed, I found that my impression of the man remained unchanged. Something about him was innately wrong.

"Glasgow." Dentman's baritone voice punctured me like an icy quill. "Travis Glasgow. Glasgow the writer."

I swiveled around on the stool. "David," I said, nodding. We could have been old acquaintances. And in a way, I guess we were.

"Come here," he said. "Sit down. Have a beer with me."

"I'm waiting for someone, thanks."

"Be a sport, Hemingway." His gaze was shackled to mine. I couldn't turn away. Haunted, he was a shape without substance: a hollowed husk.

Also, he was grinning at me.

It took a fair amount of willpower to get off my

stool and cross over to his table. It was the perilous trek around the ridge of a great mountain. A few lumberjacks shooting pool paused to watch me while on the jukebox someone was attesting to the fact that his gal was red hot.

As if by design, a single chair stood empty across from him at the opposite end of the table. Without a word, I pulled the chair out and dumped myself into it.

"That's the spirit," he said humorlessly.

"I'm buying this round."

Dentman eyeballed me like I was a Thanksgiving turkey. "Your face healed up okay."

"No worse than it was before." When I realized I was rubbing my cheek, I quickly dropped my hand. "Anyway, I'll consider it a going away present."

"Shots," Dentman said. "Bourbon."

I motioned Tooey over to the table. He'd been watching me since I sat down. "Bring us a bottle of your nastiest, angriest bourbon."

In under a minute, Tooey returned with two shot glasses and a dark carafe shrouded in dust. He unscrewed the cap, then set the bottle and the glasses on the table. "I brought glasses. Unless you two want to drink this shit out of an ashtray?"

"Thanks," I said. "We're good."

When he walked away, he did so with the uneasy gait of someone who feared he might get shot in the back.

Dentman squeezed the bottle. I expected it to shatter. He filled both shot glasses, spilling much, then picked up his glass, scrutinized it. "Here's to world peace."

Together we downed the shots. It tasted like piss spiked with lighter fluid. I felt my insides tremble.

"I'm sorry for what happened," I said once the sinister aftertaste had faded.

"Ain't for you to be sorry about."

"You didn't let me finish," I said. "I'm sorry for what happened to your family. But I still don't trust you."

"That's good," Dentman said, "because there's still a part of me that wants to smack your face around to the back of your head."

"Well, shit," I said. "We should have toasted to friendship."

To my astonishment, Dentman laughed. It was a low, drilling, lawn mower sound, much like the engine of his pickup, but it was a laugh just the same. After the laughter died, he said, "I suppose I owe you a bit of gratitude."

"How's that?"

He made a clicking sound at the back of his throat. "My sister, she needs me. She needs me to look after her. She isn't well."

I wondered if he had any idea I'd been watching his testimony through the two-way mirror.

"Our mother died when we were very young," Dentman said. "Car accident. I guess I don't remember her much." Very sober, he looked straight at me—through me, I would have bet. "My father was a bad man." Slowly, he shook his massive head, as if trying to shake the memories loose. "What was your father like?"

My father had been warm and understanding, given to periodic bouts of capriciousness and whimsy when the spirit struck. Before Kyle died, he had been a good father—so I suddenly hated myself for my inability to summon any memory of him other than the day when he beat me black and blue with his belt.

"Just a regular guy," I said.

"Our father," he said, and it was as if he were about to recite a prayer, "was crazy before he ever went crazy. This crazy man would tie his children to trees out in the yard when they were little. If you broke a dish, you would have to kneel on the pieces. You leave the stovetop dirty, you felt just what those hot burners could do. Hold your hand. Hold it. Keep it there until you learn your lesson." He thrust his chin at me. "You ever learn your lesson when you were a kid?"

"No. Not like that."

"He made me do things that no grown person—especially no father—should ever make a child do. He did worse things to Veronica. Things he couldn't do to me."

This summoned images so brutal and horrific in

my head, I could feel a physical illness breaking out in my stomach and spilling like poison through the conduits of my veins. The horrible things Veronica suffered in that house . . .

"See," Dentman went on, unflustered, "I left him once I was old enough. But then I came back for Veronica. I couldn't let him . . . let him at her like that anymore. I had to go back. That room in the basement? The one hidden behind the wall? He built that room for her. She was terrified of it, but he'd lock her down there every night."

"Jesus."

"And sometimes he would be down there with her," he added. "In the dark."

"Stop," I heard myself say distantly and ineffectually, like the yowl of a lost cat somewhere in the woods.

"One day I came back for her and we both left. Together. Fuck, she was a mess." Dentman sounded instantly disgusted with the whole thing yet strangely rehearsed at the same time. "She hit some roadblocks and spent time in the hospital. Then, of course, she fell in with people who didn't know how delicate she was. That's how she got Elijah." There was a curious combination of offhandedness and affection in his voice. It took me a moment to understand that maybe in a confused and intricate way he had loved the boy.

Dentman poured two more shots. He knocked his back before I even picked up my glass.

"When she heard he was sick, she said we needed to go back. She said it was her duty as a daughter to take care of him in his final days." His eyes glittered like jewels. I watched him with more intensity than I had ever watched anything in my life. "Can you believe that? After all he'd done to her?"

"Why are you telling me this?"

He glanced at my shot glass. I had my fingers on it but hadn't moved it from its spot on the table. "Drink it," he told me.

"I don't want it."

"Drink it or I'll push that shot glass through your forehead."

It burned like acid going down my throat. I felt it trigger my gag reflex, and I thought I was going to vomit.

"Look at you," Dentman growled, pleased with himself.

My eyes blurry with tears, I slammed the shot glass on the table.

"I hate you but I need to thank you, too." He stared at his hands. Palms up, fingers only slightly curled, they looked like a pair of undiscovered sea creatures tossed on the deck of a ship. "I hate you because she's going to go away for a little while. Doctors want to make sure she's stable, that she's okay. You stirred up a lot of emotion in her. You did some damage to my little sister."

On a gale of laughter, the pub's door swung open.

I cocked my head to see if Adam had arrived. I recognized the men who entered—they were two of Tooey's regulars—but my brother was not among them. When I turned back around, Dentman had poured a couple more shots. "Jesus, I can't . . ."

"Drink it. We're doing this thing, aren't we?"

"Doing what?"

"Drink," he said.

My hand shaking, I downed the shot. Dentman doubled, trebled, grew fuzzy around the edges. I watched in detachment as one of his reddened hands curled into an enormous fist. A man was at his most dangerous when he had nothing left to lose.

"David," I managed after too much uncomfortable silence.

"You're a pretty fucking good writer," he said in a calm, steady voice. He slipped two fingers into the breast pocket of his flannel shirt and pinched out a folded sheet of paper. I thought it might have been torn from a newspaper, but when he unfolded it and laid it on the table, I could tell it was a single page torn from a book. "It's my favorite passage," he said.

He'd highlighted the text in the middle of the page. Just one line. Nothing more.

Because he is my brother, I will suffer a thousand deaths to vindicate his.

Wordlessly, I pushed the torn sheet of paper across the table to him.

Dentman picked it up, folded it neatly into squares, and pushed it back into his shirt pocket. "I spent many nights wondering just what had happened." His eyes distant, he was midway between reality and some outlying recollection. "Did Veronica remember what she did to Elijah, or had her mind wiped the memory clean? Had all those horrible things our father had done to her finally caused her to snap? I'm not stupid. They say that kind of abuse is hereditary, that it's passed down the way alcoholism is passed down. I went to sleep every night believing my sister had done something horrible to her boy."

Returning to the present, he looked directly at me. "She's my sister. So thank you for showing me my sister's not a monster, that our father hadn't completely ruined her. Thank you for clearing that much up for me."

"There's something you're not telling me. Something you're leaving out."

I thought I saw the hint of a smile play at the corner of his lips. "See, you're a good writer. But you're not a great writer. To be a great writer, you got to upend every little stone and look underneath each one, almost like a detective would. You got to examine all the possibilities. No matter how much you want to force characters to behave one way, you got to let them do what comes natural."

"That's pretty fucking astute."

"You remember the cemetery? You called me a murderer. And I told you I didn't kill my nephew." He picked up the bottle of bourbon and poured two more shots. "What I'm saying, Glasgow, is maybe we're both right."

We stared at each other for a long, long time. At first I didn't understand what he meant . . . and when it finally dawned on me, it didn't strike me all at once like an epiphany but rather it gradually trickled in, filling all the recesses and crevices and gouges of my brain like black water into a pair of drowning lungs.

David Dentman eased back in his seat. Sweat dampened his brow. He lifted his shot glass and examined it as if it might be the last drink he'd ever take.

"To fathers," he toasted.

When Adam arrived at the bar, I was still at Dentman's table, although Dentman had left some time ago. Adam came up behind me, dropping a hand on my shoulder.

Startled, I jumped out of my seat, nearly knocking

the half-empty bottle of cruddy bourbon to the floor, where presumably it would have eaten through the floorboards.

"Who walked on your grave?" Adam said.

"Forget it."

"Everything okay?"

"Everything's fine," I said, summoning a smile. "Sit down. Have a drink with your little brother before he leaves you for sunny California."

Adam sat, picking up the bottle and pulling a face. "What is this stuff?"

I pushed an empty shot glass in his direction. On the jukebox, a Springsteen song came on, harmonica wailing. "Just drink."

We spent the night in approximate silence, thinking so much but never needing to speak a word of it.

Like brothers.

EPILOGUE/PROLOGUE:

WE WERE A SPECK ON THE LANDSCAPE OF THE WORLD

We were a speck on the landscape of the world. Can you see us? A glittering scuttle across this charted topography, reflecting great bursts of silvery sunlight and emitting exhaust, trundling the curves and slaloms and straightaways as if we were the only significant thing for miles and miles. And perhaps we were. Our little Honda trekked along, burdened with the weight of our escape, low enough to the ground to scrape the undercarriage on certain passes.

Look closer and you would see us—me behind the wheel, sunglasses on, my hair freshly cropped, my face newly shaved. I was Tom Cruise, Tom Sawyer. Beside me, Jodie played Tom Petty and Sheryl Crow and Better Than Ezra on the radio, sunglasses also on, her body looking smooth and taut and untouched, smelling clean and of soap. The days were long and sunny, marred not by a single passing cloud. Nights were cool and pleasant. The land hugging us was fresh and new, all of it, and it made us feel fresh and new as well. Everything—*everything*—was fresh and new.

Occasionally, I would glance at the rearview mirror, my memory still holding strong to the last image of my brother's family watching as we pulled out of the cul-de-sac and out of Westlake forever, waving good-bye, heartfelt and heartbroken yet hopeful of the prospects of all that awaited us. We'd embraced. *Be good, little brother.* Now we drove in some remote county of some remote state with the little rural town of Westlake nothing more than a fleeting, dreamlike memory, and once I thought I could actually still see them framed in the rectangle of reflective glass, waving.

We stopped at roadside diners in forgotten locales and imaginary realms. We ate greasy hamburgers as thick as Bibles and sucked down milk shakes with the zeal of lifelong competitors.

We spent the first night in a small motel off the main highway. A million stars lit up the sky, and we stood for a while in the parking lot just gazing heavenward. We showered together in a mildew-smelling shower, then made love in a strange bed, and after Jodie had fallen asleep, I drifted outside to gaze at the sky some more.

If you're content in the notion that you know where things stand—or at least think you know—and you are happy about those things, then close your eyes. Go on. Keep them closed.

A different night, in an isolated part of the country, I awoke with a scream caught in my throat.

"What is it, baby?"

"Nightmare," I breathed.

"Tell me."

"I dreamt we were in one of my books," I said.

"You're sweating so much. Come here."

Jodie held me tight to prove her existence, but I could not help but think, *None of this is real. Don't be fooled by it. Nothing ends this perfectly.* It was the therapist's voice from my childhood. *You lost your mind that day on the floating staircase, and Jodie couldn't take anymore. She left you, Travis, and you never found the boy, and you fell apart. The clues are all there; they've been there all along. That's the truth behind the fiction. That's the clarity here. Everything that happened after that day is merely the imagination of a wistful, regretful writer who should have done things differently and is making up for his mistakes the only way he knows how: by rewriting them. So don't be fooled.*

Don't be fooled.

We drove for days, relieving ennui by singing along with the select few radio stations we were able to harness from the air. Somewhere west of Mesa Verde, having just crossed old Route 666, there was a dull report, like a gunshot. The whole car shuddered. Continuing down the highway, I could feel the frame of the vehicle bucking against the road. Jodie grew nervous.

"A flat," I told her.

"Out *here*?"

There were mountains and forest all around us. We hadn't passed another vehicle for half an hour.

I said, "There's a spare in the trunk."

Pulling off to the side of the road, I popped the trunk and spent the next twenty minutes unloading our belongings so I could lift the panel and retrieve the spare. (The clothing we'd crammed in there had been so tightly packed that they retained their cubed forms even as I set them on the side of the road.)

Jodie walked the length of the highway while I jacked the Honda and replaced the tire. The Midwestern heat was fierce, even at this elevation, and by the time I'd finished, my shirt clung to my torso by a sticky wallpapering of perspiration.

Finished, I waved to Jodie's silhouette along the highway. Her image was distorted behind the curtain of heat waves rising off the pavement. For a second, she disappeared altogether.

We decided to stop for the night at the first motor lodge we saw.

"I'll make some phone calls and find a new tire in the morning," I promised.

There was a family-run restaurant, The Apple Dumpling Diner, across the highway from the motor lodge. It sat before a backdrop of fir-studded mountains. We ate there that evening. I ordered their best bottle of wine, which turned out to be a nine-dollar bottle of Cartlidge & Browne pinot noir. The food was home-style, and everything on the table was fried. For dessert, we shared a bowl of pecan ice cream and a carafe of coffee.

"You're thinking of something," Jodie said halfway through dessert. "What is it?"

"Let's not talk about it."

"Travis, what is it?"

"I just want to look at you."

"That's sweet." She lifted my hand off the table, cradled it in hers. "But what is it?"

I looked past her and through the wall of windows on the highway side of the diner. Dusk having fallen all around the countryside, our little motor lodge was just a dark smear highlighted by pinpoints of sodium light across the highway.

"There was something in that house," I said. "I think maybe you felt it, too. That's what started this whole thing."

"You're talking about ghosts," Jodie said.

"It sounds ridiculous."

"No." She rubbed my hand. "No."

"Then . . ." My voice trailed off. I was thinking of how Dentman had thanked me that night at the 'Bird. But it was really Elijah—or some part of Elijah that had been left behind—that had set everything in motion.

"Honey, tell me."

I almost told her what was bothering me. But in the end I just summoned a smile and said, "This is crazy. I can't believe we're talking about ghosts."

"Forget about ghosts. It's all in the past now."

"Yes," I said. Because I couldn't possibly explain the empty hole that Elijah's ghost had unwittingly opened up in me. How one ghost could come back while another remained elusive, adamant that I should forever suffer . . .

"Are you okay?"

It was all I could do not to cave in on myself. "How could I possibly be any better?"

I slept soundly for the first part of that evening. In the middle of the night, though, I awoke to a dream where I was drowning in the center of the ocean, struggling to keep afloat. Each time my head broke through the surface of the stormy, gray sea, I could make out a floating wooden dock just barely out of my reach. So I swam to it, swallowing and choking on water, my body growing numb. But when I came back up for air and to reassess my location, the floating dock appeared farther and farther away.

Unable to sleep, I snuck out into the night and smoked cigarettes until my head groaned from the nicotine.

Early the next morning, even before Jodie was out of bed, I drove to the nearest town to have the tire repaired. I waited in a small, shoe box–shaped room, where country music was piped in through plastic wall-mounted speakers. There was a little television set with rabbit ears resting on a folding chair, the volume turned all the way down, the vertical hold in desperate need of adjustment. A box of stale donuts stood open atop a magazine rack. I sat by myself in the room for forty minutes until my name was called, and I paid for my new tire at the register.

Driving back, the sun directly in my eyes, I detoured through a twist of wooded roadway. In a good mood, I attempted to locate an alternative rock station on the radio, but after several minutes fooling with the dial, I abandoned my quest. Up ahead, the road narrowed to a single paved lane. I slowed the car. Like something staged, two female deer strode out into the middle of the road. I eased to a stop and sat, both hands gripping the steering wheel, watching. They seemed to acknowledge me with their wet, ink-black eyes, then bounded off into the veil of gray stone firs on the other side of the highway.

I was just about to take my foot off the brake when I caught more movement in my peripheral vision. I turned and winced through the heavy foliage. It was like trying to discriminate between the shadows.

I pulled the car onto the shoulder of the road and got out. The air was perfumed by the earthly scent of the wilderness that surrounded me. My boots becoming entangled in spools of vines, I walked along the reedy shoulder to the suggestion of a part in the trees. I peered through the part and saw what looked like a trampled path of weeds and underbrush.

I crossed through the trees and walked the path.

Soon I was standing on the crest of an enormous precipice overlooking a blanket of green fields, Technicolor in its greenness, and they appeared to go on forever. There was a stream that wound through the valley passing directly below me, bisecting the field into perfect halves. The banks of this stream were well manicured and flanked by great bursts of colorful flowers. Some were colors I'd never seen before, and my brain had some difficulty processing them at first.

Carefully, I scaled down the side of the precipice and into the valley. The stream wove through the flowers just inches from my feet. The surface was as smooth as glass; the flowers crowding its banks were reflected as if in a mirror. Something made me touch the water. A single extended index finger barely touching the surface sent a widening ripple of rings across the surface. The flowers' reflections trembled and fell apart.

I stood and followed the stream through the valley. It wasn't until I'd traveled halfway across the field that I realized I was not alone. The sensation was over-whelming and undeniable, yet I felt oddly at peace. Giddy, almost. And as I continued across the field, the morning sun at my back, I thought I glimpsed on a few occasions more than my own shadow in the grass in front of me.

Before I knew it I was standing at the other end of the field, an intimidating wall of pine trees block-ing my passage. The stream continued on, winding through the forest, those colorful plumes of flowers like lights on an airport runway in the shade beneath the trees. Hunching down, I entered the woods, creeping under the low-hanging branches. The sun was imme-diately blotted from the sky. I could feel the forest breathe me in.

The woods were dense, but I noticed sunlight through the branches up ahead: another clearing. As I advanced in that direction, I also could see the reflection of the sky on the ground, and I realized that I was looking at a lake. For whatever reason, this caused me to hasten my pace. I hurried along and finally broke out into fresh daylight on the other side. Before me, spread out like a smear of smoked black glass, was an immense body of water, so magnificent that I could barely make out the trees across the way on the other side of the reach.

I stood there by the edge of the water for some time, letting the sun warm my back and shoulders. Cream-colored water lilies drifted across the surface of the lake, cartwheeling lazily over the reflection of my own face.

Kyle was here. The realization was like a car crash, an explosion. Kyle was *here*. I could taste his memory in the air, could catch the fleeting scent of him on the passing breeze. Dropping to my knees, I leaned over the rocky edge of the lake and brushed the lilies off my reflection. The water was so cold I could feel my bowels clench. My image rippled and glittered and after a moment reassembled itself again. It was me—only me—staring back at myself. Still, I did not move. I held my breath, not wanting to exhale and disturb the water. I wanted to see him so badly. But it was me, only me. I recognized my eyes, my freshly cut hair, the structure of my facial bones beneath my tanned skin. I recognized the slightly crooked bend to my nose and the faint dimple on my chin.

Only me.

Crestfallen, I crawled away from the water on my hands and knees. I couldn't bring myself to stand, not just yet. Then I laughed. It tumbled out of me, uncontrolled. And with it came tears that dropped straight from my eyes into the bright green grass. Laughing and crying, laughing and crying.

I'm sorry, Kyle. I love you, Bro.

But I didn't have a dimple on my chin.

I was you.

I sprang forward and nearly dumped myself into the lake. Staring over the side, I once again faced my reflection and scanned the face, recognizing everything I'd always known about me . . . yet catching, in flickering flashbulb images, details that were completely foreign to me . . . emotions that did not exist in my catalogue, expressions that I did not possess in my reserve . . .

"Kyle," I whispered.

I was you.

And who's to say he wouldn't have been? Who's to say he wouldn't have been me?

I was you.

"Yes," I said, seeing him, *seeing him*, the laughter unavoidable now, my tears spilling into the water and dispersing the reflection, "yes, yes you are, yes, yes you are, yes, yes—"

Something like three months later, in a bright little studio apartment in San Diego, I was accosted by an urge. Without thinking, without reservation, I stood and went into the bedroom. I knelt on the floor and felt around inside the clapboard trunk at the foot of the bed. When I found the notebook I was looking for, I carried it, along with a ballpoint pen, out onto the porch that overlooked the Gaslamp Quarter where, in the promise of a fading summer, I began to write.

MEDALLION

P R E S S

Be in the know on the latest
Medallion Press news by becoming a
Medallion Press Insider!

<u>As an Insider you'll receive:</u>

· Our FREE expanded monthly newsletter, giving you more insight
into Medallion Press

· Advanced press releases and breaking news

· Greater access to all your favorite Medallion authors

Joining is easy. Just visit our website at
<u>www.medallionpress.com</u> and click on the Medallion Press
Insider tab.

medallionpress.com

MEDALLION
P R E S S

Want to know what's going on with
your favorite author or what new releases
are coming from Medallion Press?

Now you can receive breaking news,
updates, and more from Medallion Press
straight to your cell phone, e-mail, instant messenger, or Facebook!

Sign up now at www.twitter.com/MedallionPress to stay on top of all
the happenings in and
around Medallion Press.

For more information
about other great titles from
Medallion Press, visit

m e d a l l i o n p r e s s . c o m